BLACK
CLASHING COLORS #1

Copyright © 2016
By Elin Peer
All rights reserved.
No part of this book may be reproduced in any form without written permission from the author, excepting brief quotations embodied in articles and reviews.
ISBN-10: 1537281402
ISBN-13: 978-1537281407
Clashing Colors #1 - Black
First Edition
The characters and events portrayed in this book are fictitious. Any similarity to real persons or organizations is coincidental and not intended by the author. Recommended for mature readers due to adult content.
Cover Art by Damonza
Editing: www.martinohearn.com

Books in the Clashing Colors series

For the best reading experience and to avoid spoilers, below is the recommended order of the five Clashing Colors books.

BLACK - Clashing Colors #1
VIOLET - Clashing Colors #2
GREEN - Clashing Colors #3
BLUE - Clashing Colors #4
YELLOW - Clashing Colors #5

For a full overview of my books and to be alerted for new book releases, discounts, and give-aways, please sign up to my list at
www.elinpeer.com

PLEASE NOTE

This book is intended for mature readers only, as it contains a few graphic scenes and some inappropriate language.

All characters are fictional and any likeness to a living person or organization is coincidental.

DEDICATION

This one is for you, Mom.
As I was writing this story I was reminded how blessed I am to have grown up with loving and supportive parents.
Thank you!

Elin

"It's impossible," said pride
"It's risky," said experience
"It's pointless," said reason
"Let's try it anyway," whispered the heart

CHAPTER 1
Black

When I was seven, someone broke into our house. Thinking back, it must have been some really desperate thieves, because it was a shitty neighborhood and none of us had anything worth stealing, even on a good day.

Nevertheless, that break-in stayed with me for a long time and made me afraid of going to bed at night.

I used to hug my Hello Kitty teddy bear and tell her we would be all right. It would have been nice if my mom had offered me a goodnight kiss or a lullaby to make me feel better, but hey, I didn't have that kind of mom.

My mom, Tina, was seventeen when she had me.

My dad is the asshole who took her virginity behind the bleachers after a high school dance, and handed her a hundred dollars to "take care of the problem" when she told him she was pregnant.

Needless to say, I grew up with my mom, and of all the childhood memories – that for the most part aren't very good – the one about thieves breaking into our home has played a major part in my career as a criminal.

This might surprise you, but criminals have morals and values too. Some criminals even say they have honor. I don't know about the last part, but I, at least, have a set of rules.

I don't commit any violent crimes, and I don't steal from private homes – because it's a violation of people's privacy and can be traumatizing to kids.

Neither do I steal from small mom-and-pop shops with hard-working people who are just trying to make a living.

I also don't hustle or steal from the following categories: old people, sick people, mentally or physically handicapped people, and of course children.

So who do I steal from? Mostly companies with big fat insurance policies who will get compensated for the shoplifting I do.

Now before you have a moral hissy fit about me, don't! You're wasting your energy and my time. I might as well tell you straight up, I'm a lost cause.

People see me walking on the street and look the other way. I dress as I feel, and that's why my friends call me Black. My hair is black, my nail polish is black, my clothes are black, and most of the time I'm wearing heavy, dark make-up too.

Most likely you've seen people like me. And most likely you've looked away too.

I get it. And I don't care.

Caring is a luxury I can't afford. My life isn't about caring. It's about surviving, and it's been that way ever since I ran away from home seven years ago.

Today is my twenty-first birthday, which means I can officially drink alcohol. The thought alone is laughable. The first time I drank I was ten. The second time I was eleven and got drunk with my mom. That night I puked so hard I thought I was going to die, and as a result I haven't touched a drop of alcohol ever since.

If watching my mom's alcoholism taught me anything it was that happiness isn't found in bottles.

For me, happiness comes in the shape of little white pills with the letters OP on top. In my opinion it should say UP, which would be a good allusion to the high I get from taking them. My friend Daniel gave me my first rush for my nineteenth birthday, and I can honestly say that I'd never experienced anything like it. Never felt so good inside.

Clashing Colors #1 BLACK

My head is usually full of bad memories and fear of the future, but that night – oh man, it was freaking surreal to feel completely free of worries, pressure, and pain. I was on a euphoric high, and it only took that one time to make me want more. I guess you could say that the first pill got me hooked and now, two years later, I'm in a lot of shit because of it.

The first problem is that those Oxy pills are damn expensive. Depending on the supply on the street, it's between fifty and a hundred dollars for just one pill, and when you're a street artist like me, you don't make a lot of cash.

That's why I have to shoplift, which leads me to my second problem. My looks.

Mostly I do my "shopping" after the stores are closed, because I'm easy to spot with my black Goth looks; shop detectives get automatically suspicious when they see me. I'm good at what I do, and only take what I need to survive.

Unfortunately, today I got impatient and went to Bartell Drugs to help myself to a few Oxy pills.

I would have never done it, if my after-dark field trip to Costco last night hadn't failed. There was no way I could have known that the night guard at Costco got a new badass Rottweiler. He used to have an old German shepherd that slept most of the time and was practically half deaf, but this new dog – shit, I'm a fast runner, but that black devil chased me down like a rabbit on the run, and I only barely escaped.

Sneaking out a few bottles of pills isn't rocket science, so I'm a bit ashamed that I got caught red-handed today.

It's a damn shame too, because I had already stuffed my backpack with several bottles of Oxy pills. I could have made a fortune on the streets with that many and kept a good portion for myself.

I'm sure I would have made it out, if not for my stupid walk through the store to get a bottle of whiskey.

I wanted to surprise Daniel with one for his birthday next week, but that won't happen now, since my little walk landed me in police custody. That's what I get for being a good friend.

There's a pay phone on the wall in my holding cell, but I have no one to call. If my mom is even alive, I still would rather stab my eye out than call her for help.

My dad... well, I've only seen him once. The night I ran away from my mom when I was fourteen, I went to his house thinking he would take me in once I told him about the horrible things that were happening at my mom's place, but I never got that far. He wouldn't even let me into his fancy house or listen to me.

He had a new family with a wife and three small children, and the only thing I got from him that night was two hundred dollars and the message that he had been right to give Tina money for an abortion; he had known she wasn't mom material and he felt sorry for me, for being born.

Sure, he had been right about her, but she had been right about him too; Brent was a cold bastard without a heart.

Still, it's not like I'd have anything to lose by giving him a call. He has money, lives in a fancy house, and if anyone could afford to bail me out of this hole, it would be him.

I hadn't spoken to Brent in seven years, but that only meant there was a slim possibility that he had found Jesus or grown a conscience since I last saw him, so I reckoned I might as well try it.

I had his number on a scrap of paper in my hand. The police officer had been nice enough to look it up for me, and it turned out that Brent still lived in the same place.

As I was listening to the sound of the phone ringing, part of me was hoping that he wouldn't pick up. I didn't want his help. I didn't want to owe him anything.

"Hello." His voice was slightly nasal, like someone with a cold.

"Hey, this is Black... I mean Darcia, your daughter."

Silence.

"I need your help... Dad."

"How did you get this number? I told you to leave me alone."

I sighed. "I know, but I was arrested."

"You were arrested?"

"Yes."

"What did you do?"

"I stole a few things."

"Where are you?"

"Downtown at the police station. They told me I'll see a judge within a few hours. I think it's basically just to charge me and set the bail."

I waited for him to say something, but there was only silence.

"Could you come down here and help me get out? The bail shouldn't be more than a few hundred dollars."

He was still quiet, so I swallowed my pride and added a soft "Please..."

"I don't think so," he said in a low voice. "You caught me in the middle of an important family celebration and I can't just leave. I'm sorry, but you know what they say: don't do the crime if you can't do the time."

That arrogant bastard! I squeezed the phone hard enough to make my knuckles white. "So you're just going to let your own daughter rot here, while you celebrate with your *real* family?"

"You know I don't think of you as my daughter," he said in a cold voice.

What an absolutely redundant thing to say. The man hadn't been in my life for twenty-one years. The fact that I was his dirty secret and biggest regret didn't come as a shock and, yes, I know I should have just hung up and cut my losses, but I give as good as I get, so of course I had to have the last word.

"You know," I said sardonically, "talking about crime and time… you shouldn't have made a child if you aren't prepared to be a father."

"That's not the same thing," he said.

I kept my cool. "No, in your book, stealing a bit of medicine is a much bigger crime than leaving your baby to an alcoholic and abusive teen mother, and later sentencing that same child to a life on the streets."

I didn't give the shithead a chance to say more after that. I hung up, plunked myself down on the steel bedstead that held the thinnest mattress in history, curled my legs up to hug myself, and, yeah, you guessed it – I felt fucking sorry for myself.

My dad comes from a large and rich family. The kind that sends their kids to summer camps, goes on vacations, celebrates Christmas, and gets into colleges. They are my family too, even though I've only seen them from afar. I know I have two younger half-brothers and a half-sister, grandparents, aunts, and uncles, and apparently they were having a family celebration, right now.

With a pout I rested my chin on my knees, and imagined them all laughing and sharing jokes, while I sat here, alone and unwanted. The outsider no one cared about. And it fucking hurt!

CHAPTER 2
Uncle Gabriel

I don't like formalities. I never did.

Sure, I can dress up in my fine black uniform, keep an excellent posture, and do a perfect salute like any good soldier, but that whole ceremonial thing that comes with receiving a medal of honor is not my favorite thing.

My family, however, is going overboard with their pride, and every one of them wants pictures with me in my uniform, now nicely decorated with the Silver Star medal. My mom has even arranged for family and friends to come and celebrate – even though I told her not to.

I don't think she'll ever understand how unworthy I feel to receive recognition for my actions and valor in war, when so many of my friends and colleagues didn't even make it home alive. They gave their lives, and in comparison my sacrifices seem insignificant.

Thinking about it suffocates me with sadness, so I try not to dwell on it. I have to move on – it's the way of a combat engineer.

My job is to pave the road for others by building bridges, blowing up things, and coming up with creative solutions in the field. I love my job, and I know I've made a difference and saved lives during my three deployments in Afghanistan. And ultimately, *that* is why I became a soldier. To make a difference!

It would be an understatement to say that I'm excited to be home, and this time – I'm staying!

Not that I'll be in Seattle for long, but at least my next job won't be in a war zone. It'll be in Missouri, as an instructor on the Sapper Leader Course.

But first, I'm going to chill and enjoy four months of doing as little as possible – except, of course, catch up with family and friends, which is exactly what I was doing when Brent, my stepbrother, got a call that made me pay attention.

I wasn't supposed to overhear Brent's phone conversation but it's hard to turn off the alert sensors after being constantly on edge for years, and something about his facial expression when he took that call made me instantly alert. That's why, when Brent pulled away from the crowd and went inside the house, I discreetly followed him. If my stepbrother is in some sort of trouble, I'm not just going to look the other way. Not that we're close but we are family, and family stick together.

The way he hissed "How did you get this number? I told you to leave me alone," confirmed that whoever was on the line was no friend of his.

Brent's next sentence – "You were arrested?" – told me the person was bad news. And hearing him mutter "Don't do the crime if you can't do the time" revealed that he was harshly refusing to help the person calling for help.

But it was his next sentence that blew my mind: "You know I don't think of you as my daughter."

Thirty seconds later my stepbrother put down the phone and took a deep breath while I took a step forward asking the obvious: "You have a daughter?"

Brent stiffened and shot me a dirty look. "You weren't supposed to hear that."

"How old is she?" I asked in astonishment. How the hell had he managed to keep this hidden from me?

He banged his phone rhythmically against his palm. "I'm not sure… nineteen or twenty, perhaps."

"Why didn't you ever tell me?"

Brent's eyes were zigzagging between me and the glass door leading out to the patio and the pool area. Our entire family was barbecuing, and he raised a hand and waved to Janice, his wife, before he made a subtle signal for me to follow him.

We ended up in the mud room behind the kitchen, with him leaning against the dryer, looking just as annoyed as the time I found his collection of porn magazines and threatened to tell Mom if he didn't let me borrow his Nintendo for a week.

"Listen, G," he said. "It was a stupid mistake. I was just a big high school kid when I accidently knocked up a girl."

"Who?"

"Some white trash chick, you don't know her and it doesn't matter."

"But you had a daughter with this woman?"

"Yes."

"And your daughter got arrested?"

"Yes."

"What for?"

Brent looked at his nails. "Theft... some medicine, I think."

"And she called you to get your help?"

"Uh-huh."

"Do you know her?"

"Of course I don't know her. I already told you she was just a stupid mistake from my past, and I don't want Janice or the kids to find out about it."

"Why not?"

"Listen, I appreciate your concern, but the kid had it coming," he said. "I mean she literally admitted to being guilty."

I used to look up to Brent. He's ten years older than me, and when my mom married his dad he was already seventeen and practically a grown man in my eyes. Right now, I wanted to strangle him for being such an ass.

"You have to help her, Brent. She's your daughter; you can't just turn your back on her."

He laughed. "That ship sailed a long time ago. The minute Tina told me she was pregnant I let her know that I didn't want a kid."

"That's not the girl's fault. How can you be so cold to your own child?"

Brent stopped laughing. "Well, sorry to disappoint you, but I don't want anything to do with her and that's that!"

He tried to push past me, but I'm a head taller and have forty pounds more muscle than him. If I don't want to move, I ain't moving.

"Move, G," he said with a scowl.

"Not until you tell me that you're helping her."

He rolled his eyes. "If you want so badly to help the kid, then why don't you go down to the police station and get her out? You're the hero in the family, aren't you?"

When I spoke it came out through gritted teeth. "What's her name?"

"Darcia Nilsson."

"You have to tell the others about her," I said.

"No." His answer was quick and firm. "And don't you dare reveal my secret, either! I've kept her away for all these years and protected our family from the shame. I can't stop you from going there to help her, but I refuse to let you bring her back here."

I moved enough for him to open the door and leave the small room – mostly because I was afraid I might actually hurt my brother if he said one more selfish thing.

He left me no choice.

If he wasn't going to do the right thing, I would have to do it for him.

$\{\infty\}$

When I walked into the police station I was still wearing my black uniform with my Silver Star.

I don't know if I thought I would be able to just sneak away from the party for a short while and return without anyone noticing, but I had left the minute Brent and I were done talking, and on the twenty-minute drive to downtown Seattle I had gone over the few details he had told me and arrived at one clear conclusion: I had a niece, or at least a stepniece, and she was in trouble. If I could, I would help her, like any uncle would.

"I'm here for Darcia Nilsson," I told the officer at the counter.

He informed me that until she had been in front of the judge and the bond had been settled, she couldn't leave.

"She's already been taken to the holding cell behind the courtroom, but you can speak to her lawyer."

"She has a lawyer?" I asked and he gave a sharp nod.

"Yes, she asked to have a defense lawyer appointed for her."

"All right, sure, I'll talk to the lawyer then," I said and was taken to meet a young man who looked like he was straight out of law school.

"Michael Young," he said and shook my hand.

I tried not to smile at the irony of his looks and his last name. This was no laughing matter.

"Ehhh..." I cleared my throat. "I'm Darcia's uncle, or rather stepuncle, but I only just found out about her today."

"Oh." Michael wrinkled his forehead. "That explains why she didn't mention you when I spoke to her a few minutes ago. According to her, she doesn't have any family at all."

"What about her mother?" I asked.

"She doesn't have any contact with her mother."

"As I said, I only heard about her today, but I'm here to help."

Michael looked through a few papers. "That's good; according to her this isn't her first time being arrested. There was another incident three years ago when she was eighteen."

"Did you say eighteen? How old is she now?"

Michael let his finger slide to her info. "Her birthday is May fourth and she's twenty-one."

"May fourth. That's today."

Michael arched a brow. "Not the best way to celebrate a twenty-first birthday... but anyhow, she was arrested for civil disobedience at a demonstration in the Queen Ann district, three years ago, but luckily she got off with a warning."

"Does it say what they were protesting against?" I asked.

Michael read the papers and nodded. "Yes, it was in relation to some budget cuts that resulted in the closure of a homeless shelter."

"Do you know why she was arrested today?"

"She's been charged with theft in the third degree. Also called shoplifting."

I crossed my arms. "Is she going to jail?" I had been in my share of gloomy places as a soldier, but the atmosphere of this place wasn't nice and the protective side of me wanted to take her far away from here.

"It's too early to say... it really depends on the judge. It's what we call a gross misdemeanor, and that can mean up to 364 days in jail and up to a five-thousand-dollar fine.

I whistled. "All right, so what do you want me to do?"

"The best thing you can do is let me do all the talking and be present in case the judge has questions for you."

Thirty-five minutes later I sat in the courtroom, ready to watch my first arraignment.

The judge entered and asked everyone to take a seat and for Miss Darcia Nilsson to be brought in.

I was curious to see how much my niece looked like Brent, but it was impossible to say from the way her head was bowed, making her long raven-dark hair cover her face completely. She looked small compared to the two armed police officers behind her, and she was wearing handcuffs and an orange prison uniform.

"Miss Nilsson, I'm going to have you stand up there next to your attorney," Judge Kent said and pointed.

Darcia walked over and now had her back to me.

"Please state your name and address for the court record," the judge said.

Darcia lifted her head up and listed an address in Kirkland.

"Miss Nilsson, I want to advise you that you are charged with theft in the third degree. That is a gross demeanor punishable by imprisonment for up to 364 days and a fine of up to five thousand dollars. Do you understand the nature of the charge?"

Darcia looked at Michael Young, who nodded.

"Yes," she said.

"You have the right to be represented by an attorney and in the event you can't afford one, and you economically qualify, the court will appoint an attorney for you to act on your behalf."

The judge kept on educating Darcia about her constitutional rights in a speedy, monotone manner before he said, "Mr. Young, how does Miss Nilsson plead?"

"She is pleading not guilty, Your Honor," Michael said.

A date was set for the first court hearing and Judge Kent set bail at three hundred dollars.

"A last piece of advice, Miss Nilsson," the judge said. "Since the alleged crime involved theft of drugs, no sentence will be imposed in the state of Washington until a chemical dependency evaluation has been made. I would strongly advise that you start and complete any needed treatment, as it can help you avoid being placed on active probation by the court."

It all went extremely fast, and then Darcia was taken out again.

I stood there a bit confused about my next move, until Michael signaled for me to meet him outside.

"She doesn't have money to pay the bail. Do you?" he asked.

I nodded.

Michael turned out to be a really nice guy; he was twenty-nine like me and had an older brother in the military who had been in both Iraq and Afghanistan.

I don't think it was really his job, but Michael stayed until Darcia was released and made our first meeting a bit less awkward.

"Darcia, this is your uncle, Gabriel Thomas."

She looked at me with a puzzled expression.

"Nobody calls me Darcia except when I'm in trouble," she said. "People call me Black."

"Hello, Black." I offered her my hand and she hesitated for a few seconds before she shook it. "Nobody calls me Gabriel except my mom; feel free to call me G or Thomas."

"Nice uniform, G," she said dryly.

I didn't comment on that.

"Do any of you have any last questions for me?" Michael asked.

Darcia, who reminded me of a Goth chick I used to know in high school, put her hands in the pockets of her black military pants. "What did the judge mean when he talked about the chemical evaluation thingy?" she asked.

"Oh, yes, I should have mentioned it myself, but he's absolutely right. Since you were caught with drugs and alcohol in your backpack, the judge is going to want a chemical dependency evaluation. No matter what category you'll be placed in, it's a good idea to do the counseling now."

Darcia gave Michael a dirty look. "Counseling? Nah, I don't think so."

"I'm afraid that's not really up to you, since it will undoubtedly be part of your sentence. Either you get it done now, before the first court hearing in a month, or you wait and get placed on active probation by the court."

"Why would I do it now?" she asked.

"Because showing the judge that you take this seriously and want to change your ways could potentially keep you out of jail."

Darcia seemed to be thinking hard.

"And it can save you a pile of money in probation fees," Michael added.

Darcia was focusing only on Michael when she spoke. "So you want me to go to AA meetings, is that it?"

"A support group is good, but you need counseling or therapy to impress the judge. Let me give you the number to a phenomenal place that has turned people around in a matter of weeks. Their methods are supposedly a bit unorthodox, but one of the judges referred a client of mine to this place six months ago, and he became a whole new person."

"You're serious?" she asked skeptically and took the business card he had found in his bag.

"Yes, I definitely think you should go," Michael said and then he shook our hands for goodbyes. "Good luck with it."

When he walked away, we stood for a moment in awkward silence.

"Do you have time for a cup of coffee?" I asked.

She shrugged. "Sure, but you're buying because I'm broke."

Her comment hit me hard. I had just left my childhood home in Medina, one of the poshest places around Seattle. My parents, Darcia's grandparents, regularly dined and golfed with neighbors that included Bill Gates and others like him. There was no reason why anyone in our family should be unable to buy a cup of coffee.

I took her to the nearest Starbucks and even though she only ordered a cup of hot cocoa, I made sure to buy a selection of cake and fruit in case she was hungry.

We found a table in the corner and I noticed how she meticulously wiped the table clean with napkins before she sat down.

For a moment we sat and looked at each other. She had a lot of piercings in her ears, a large nose ring, and one more in her lower lip. Her long hair was pitch-black but I could see blond roots and figured she was naturally dark blond like her father. She might be a pretty girl, if not for the exaggerated use of black eyeliner, mascara, and purple lipstick. The only thing that looked remotely natural were her green irises and the little beauty mark above her upper lip, and even that had me wondering if it was real or painted on like Madonna's used to be.

"Are you just going to sit there and stare at me all night, or do you have something to say?" she asked in a bitchy manner.

I took a sip of my coffee. "You're not being very nice considering I just paid three hundred dollars to bust your ass out of jail."

She gave an uninterested shrug. "I'll pay you back."

"How?... You said you're broke."

I received a look of annoyance from her. "Yeah, well, it may take me a while, but I always pay my debts."

"Tell me about yourself," I said and leaned back in my chair.

"Why?"

"Because I just found out I have a niece and I want to get to know you."

"So I reckon Brent is your brother, then?" she asked.

"Stepbrother," I corrected.

Her eyes narrowed. "That explains why you look nothing like him." She glanced me over, speculatively. "I bet you played football in high school and was popular with all the girls." It didn't come out as a compliment, but sounded more like an accusation.

"You say it like it's a bad thing…" I laughed, but she didn't laugh back, so I tried again from a different angle.

"What makes you say that?"

With an arched brow she picked up a blueberry muffin. "Because you have that wholesome boy kind of look. You've even got a dimple when you smile."

"I'm twenty-nine. I hope you don't think I look like a boy."

She didn't look at me but picked off a large chunk of muffin and put it in her mouth. "Nahh… I can see you're not a boy; I'm just saying that I bet you were dreamy in high school."

"Dreamy?"

She lifted her shoulder in another shrug and chewed her cake.

"I don't think I've ever been called dreamy before."

"Maybe not to your face."

"I don't know if I should be amused or offended," I said. "I see myself as a badass soldier, not a dreamy high school kid."

She gave me a bored expression. "Again, I'm referring to the past."

"Oh, I see, so I'm not dreamy anymore?" I teased, but she didn't take the bait.

"I'll tell you about me if you tell me about you," I suggested.

"Okay." She pinned me with her green eyes. "Here's something about me. I've been living on my own for seven years, I don't have any family, I'm good at drawing, and I like lime pie."

Has she seriously lived on her own since she was fourteen?

I cleared my throat. "Okaaay, I just came back from Afghanistan. I've been there three times as a sapper."

"What's a sapper?" she asked.

"A combat engineer, which means I'm good at building things, blowing up shit, and repairing things that are broken.

"So have you seen a lot of action?"

"What do you mean?" I tried to hide my emotions. "Are you asking if I've ever been in combat?"

"Yeah."

"I have."

Her eyes widened. "Did you ever kill someone."

I nodded.

Maybe she sensed my resistance to talk about it because she moved on. "How old are you?"

"Twenty-nine."

"I'm twenty-one," she said.

"I know."

"Right." She looked away. "So, are you home for good, or just on a break before you go back?"

"No, I'm home for good."

Her next question came out with a sarcastic undertone. "And was your family happy to see you?"

I nodded. "Yes. My mom threw a party today to celebrate that I received a Silver Star."

Her eyes fell to the medal on my chest. "So *you* were the reason for the family celebration Brent talked about."

"Yes."

"And you left all of them to come and help me?" For the first time her voice was soft. She looked puzzled.

"I would have found you earlier, if I had known I had a niece."

"Stepniece," she corrected me.

"Listen, Darcia, family is important to me and I'm ashamed on my brother's behalf for having failed you."

"I told you not to call me Darcia."

"I'm sorry."

"It's okay. It's not your fault that my mom had a thing for stupid romance books."

"She named you after a romance book?"

"Yeah, ever heard of Darcy from *Pride and Prejudice*?"

I nodded. "That's Jane Austen, right?" I said it without admitting that I had actually seen the TV show once.

"Oh, yes. Good old Jane was my mom's obsession all through her pregnancy with me. She used to tell me that I was named Darcia Emma Nilsson after her two favorite characters, but I'm not sure it's true because I once overheard her say that my middle name Emma was short for dilemma."

"So you don't like either of those names?"

"No. I've been Black since I was fifteen."

"Well, I can't blame you – I think Gabriel is kind of pompous too."

She looked up at me. "Yeah, I suppose being named after an archangel does put you under pressure," she said.

I don't know why I was surprised that she knew about the origin of my name. Maybe because she looked more like a Satanist than a Christian, but it made me ask, "Are you religious?"

She picked up the banana on the table and peeled it. "No, I'm not religious, I just like to read. Besides, when your home is a dump and your mom is an alcoholic, a library offers a warm place to hang out. I once read the Bible out of curiosity."

"You read the whole Bible?"

"Yes, and other religious books. I like to read."

"But if you're not religious, why would you do that?"

"Maybe I was looking for answers. I don't know."

I still couldn't get over the mental image of this hardcore Goth chick reading the bible. "Did you find any?"

"Some, but dude, don't you need to get back to your party or something?"

She was right, it was getting late and I too could hear the cell phone buzzing in my inner pocket.

"Maybe I should. Can I give you a lift somewhere?" I asked.

She lifted her palms up. "It's okay, I can walk."

"I don't want you to walk. Come on, let me take you home," I said.

She wrapped the two last pieces of cake in some napkins and carefully placed them in her backpack.

"Thank you for bailing me out and for this." She lifted her white cup of cocoa and gave a small smile. It was the first time I had seen anything close to a smile on her face.

"Where do you live?" I asked.

"Don't worry about it," she said dismissively. "But give me your number so I can pay you back."

I pulled out my phone, opened up a new contact, and handed it to her. "Just give me your contact info and then I'll send you a text with my number."

"I can't." She pushed up from her chair. "I lost my phone – can't you just scribble your number on a napkin?"

I did, and handed it to her. "Come on, let me take you home."

"No." Black lifted the napkin. "I'll see you around, Uncle G." She was just about to walk away when I got up from my chair and stopped her.

"I'm taking you home," I repeated and for a silent second she narrowed her eyes and gave me a defiant stare down.

"If you think that killer glance is going to make me back off, you're wrong," I said. "I want to make sure you get home safely."

"I think you're forgetting one thing, soldier. Unlike you, I don't take orders from anyone!"

"I don't mean to order you around, I'm just doing what I would do to any of my female friends and family."

"But I'm not like them," she said calmly. "I'm a rebel; I go my own way."

Unimpressed I folded my arms across my chest. "And look where that got you," I said dryly.

"I don't need you to come in and rescue me, I do just fine on my own," she said with an attitude and walked out of Starbucks without looking back. For a moment I watched her cross the parking lot and flip a finger to a driver who almost ran her over.

She might think she was better off without me, but I wasn't just some random guy she had met in a coffee shop. I was family, and it was my duty to make sure she was safe. No way could I go home without knowing she was going to be all right… so I followed her.

CHAPTER 3
Home
Darcia

I didn't know what time it was but I was tired and grumpy from this hellish day. I didn't sleep last night because of my failed after-dark field trip to Costco, where I barely escaped that damn dog, and I was in no mood to go to work.

Work, to me, means painting portraits and doing street art, but it requires a bit more energy than I had when I left Starbucks. Not even the heavy intake of calories from the hot cocoa, the muffin, and the banana helped. I just wanted to sleep.

The only good thing was that I had my bus card. With that I took the bus back to Kirkland and walked to The Inn, a motel in Kirkland that has been my sanctuary for the last seven years. Years ago, on my fifth night as one of the homeless, the owner, Lee, who is a Chinese immigrant, found me curled up in the supply room where I had sneaked in to avoid the heavy rain. I begged him not to call the cops, and that night we came to an agreement. I would help clean the motel rooms after school, and in return he would allow me to stay overnight.

For a homeless person it's actually not a bad deal; I have access to a shower and a meal a day.

When the motel is fully booked I sleep on the floor in the supply room. It's not very comfortable, but it's much safer and cleaner than being out on the streets.

"Where you been?" Lee asked when I walked into the reception.

"I slept at a friend's house," I lied.

"You no clean rooms. Lee not happy," the old man said in his funny Chinese accent, using third person to talk about himself, which never ceased to amuse me.

"I'm sorry... did you get Mona to do it?"

He nodded.

"I'm really tired, Lee, where can I crash?"

"All rooms full." He lifted a hand and pointed his thumb over his shoulder. What can I say? Lee doesn't use a lot of words, but I understood him perfectly well and trudged down the hall to the small room full of toilet paper, cleaning products, and clean towels. The room isn't big enough for a mattress. In fact, I can't even stretch my legs out, but at least I had a pillow, a blanket, and privacy.

Unfortunately, those things didn't do it for me tonight and I was tossing and turning, trying to fall asleep.

Judge Kent's words from earlier weighed me down; three hundred and sixty-four days is a long time to spend in jail for a failed crime. I was bummed that I didn't even get as much as a single pill and wondered how I was going to cope without them. It's not that I was a hardcore addict, but now that I had more to worry about, I could really use a pill to escape the craziness in my life and find a minute of peace.

But instead of pills, all I had was a court date and lame advice from the judge and the lawyer to get some counseling. As if my life wasn't complicated enough.

I was lying on my back with my legs bent, trying to think of a plan to contact the therapy place and offer them some sort of barter. Maybe I could make some art for them, or clean... or something. If they asked me to pay cash, I couldn't

When I heard loud voices from the foyer, I craned my neck, and listened in the darkness. Lee was shouting, which isn't a rare thing as he's a temperamental old man and often shouts at the Weather Channel when they promise more rain. Yet, this time, someone was yelling back and it made me raise myself up on my elbows wondering if I should go and see if old Lee was okay. Before I got a chance to, the door was flung open.

It was dark in the supply room, and the bright light from the hallway blinded me like a beam putting me in the spotlight.

"What the fuck," a deep voice said.

I blinked a few times to focus and saw Gabriel stare at me with anger on his face.

"Get up," he barked as if I was one of his goddamn soldiers to command.

"I try stop him, he not listen," Lee apologized to me while I got up from the floor and faced Gabriel, who was looking down on me with intense determination.

"What's wrong?" I asked. But he was too angry to answer so I asked him my next question: "What are you doing here?"

"Just get your things and come with me."

I didn't want to make a scene, especially not in front of Lee, who hates drama and has kicked guests out of the motel without blinking.

"It's okay, Lee, this man is my uncle. I'll just go talk to him for a second," I explained and pushed past the mountain of a soldier in front of me.

Gabriel let me pass before he bowed down to pick up my backpack. "Take your things with you," he said. "We're going to my place."

And so we did.

Of course I tried to object at first, but even I could tell he meant business and a small part of me wasn't sorry at all. Even though I'm kind of a loner and I prefer to do things my own way, I can't always afford to let pride rule me. Beggars can't be choosers and all.

Gabriel was quiet and thoughtful on the drive from Kirkland to his place in Seattle, but that was okay. The people I hang with all have quirky personalities, so I dealt just fine with silence and brooding.

His apartment was small but offered a great view of Union Lake.

"I've rented the place for the summer," he said as we entered. "It's not much but it was either this or staying with my parents," he added and threw his keys on the kitchen table.

"Make yourself comfortable, Black, there are sodas in the fridge and I'll be right back."

"You know that rhymed, right?" I said dryly and kicked off my black boots.

He disappeared into his bedroom while I took a seat on the large couch, which was comfortable and soft. Sleeping here would be much nicer than on the floor in the supply room at The Inn.

Gabriel was only gone for a few minutes and when he returned he looked very different in jeans and a t-shirt.

I knew he was eight years older than me, but I felt like we could be the same age... maybe it's because I feel much older than my years, which isn't so odd, since my childhood stopped when I was fourteen, and I've been the only responsible adult in my life since then. The kind of shit I've seen makes you grow up real fast.

Gabriel sat down next to me. "We need to talk."

I didn't like his intense glance as he turned toward me, tugging his right leg up under him and leaning his elbow on the back of the couch.

"How long have you been sleeping in a closet?" he asked.

"It's not a closet, it's a supply room."

"How long?"

"Years."

"How many years?"

"More than you've been abroad."

He sighed. "Black, I need you to be honest with me and tell me what the hell happened to you."

"Shitty parents is what happened to me," I said with a mild snort.

"Why didn't you come to us for help?" he asked. "We're your family."

I gave a bigger snort. "I did. When I ran away from my mom's house, I went to see Brent, but he told me he was sorry I had been born and paid me two hundred dollars to stay away from him and his family."

"Christ." Gabriel rubbed his forehead with frustration. "Well, just so we're clear, whether or not Brent likes it, *you are* part of our family too," he said with resolve.

"Not according to Brent, I'm not."

"Well, he's a jerk. Now tell me, why did you run away from your mom's house in the first place?"

I didn't like to think about it. Even less did I like to talk about it, so I set my boundaries like I do best and told my new Uncle G, "That's none of your business."

He didn't blink but fired off his next question.

"Did you go to high school?"

"Uh-huh, four."

"Four years?" he asked.

"Yes, and four different schools."

"Black, can't you just talk to me? I feel like I'm interrogating you. What's with these short answers?"

I took a long deep breath. "There's not much to tell. My mom is an alcoholic; I ran away as soon as I could, hoping my dad would take me in, which he didn't… After that, I've managed on my own. End of story."

Gabriel looked thoughtful for a few seconds. "But why didn't you go to child services? Didn't your mom have the police search for you?"

"I don't think so… she was probably just grateful to have one less problem."

"But what about school?"

"I moved schools a lot."

"Why?"

"Because when they started to ask too many questions or asked to see my parents, I would just move."

"But this makes no sense... we have a safety net that prevents kids from living on the street," Gabriel said.

"Right!" I crossed my arms. "You obviously haven't been to downtown Seattle lately. I see lost teenagers all the time."

"But surely if you had spoken up to a teacher you could have been put in a foster family."

I snorted. "Ha! Do you have any idea what goes on in foster families? Let me ask you this: did you know any foster kids growing up, G?"

"No."

"No, of course you didn't, because you probably went to a private school, didn't you?"

"Yeah, so?"

"So rich families don't take foster kids. But unlike you, I knew enough foster kids to know that it wasn't for me."

"Why not?"

"Because I wasn't going to allow anyone to abuse me ever again."

Gabriel's hand closed in a fist, but he kept his eyes on me. "Are you saying that your mom abused you? Is that why you ran away?"

God, enough with all his questions.

"I asked you a question," he said stubbornly.

"And I told you that's none of your business," I shot back.

He gave me a grim look but didn't press any further. "You're staying here until we figure this out."

"Figure what out?"

"You and your legal problems. We need to get you a place to stay and a job so you can pay the fine," he listed quickly. "And tomorrow you're contacting the counseling service that your lawyer referred you to."

"Hey, back off, Uncle G, I'm not some broken thing for you to fix, you know."

Gabriel lifted both hands and spoke in a soft tone. "I'm just trying to help."

"Okay," I said and softened my tone. "If I can crash on your couch that would be a help. I haven't slept for almost forty hours and I'm exhausted."

"You would probably be more comfortable in the bed," he pondered out loud.

"Don't worry about that, this couch is pure luxury to me."

"Okay." His eyes flashed to the TV, and I understood his dilemma. It was too early for him to go to sleep and he didn't have a TV in his bedroom.

"Feel free to stay and watch TV; it won't bother me; I'm used to noise when I sleep."

"Are you sure?"

I yawned and curled up in the corner. "Yup, I'm sure."

"I could give you one of my t-shirts to sleep in," he offered.

"No thanks, I always sleep in my clothes."

"Why? I thought only soldiers did that."

"Nope," I said and closed my eyes. "Women living in motels with thin doors do too, at least I do."

"You have nothing to fear from me, you know that, right?" he said quietly.

I shrugged, because the truth was that I didn't know. I had just met him today, so how could I?

"Here." He put a thin blanket over me and it felt awkward to have someone pamper me like that.

"Are you sure you don't mind if I watch some TV?"

I opened an eye and shook my head. "Hey, it's your house, just forget I'm here and if I snore, kick me."

"All right." He smiled.

⟨ ∞ ⟩

The next day I woke up to the smell of coffee. I stretched and opened my eyes to see Gabriel tiptoeing around in his kitchen. I'm not used to people showing such consideration, so for a minute I lay completely still and just watched him.

There was a trace of something either Asian or Inuit in him, with his dark almond-shaped eyes and robust nose.

"How tall are you?" I asked and sat up.

He gave me a charming smile. "Good morning to you too."

"Good morning."

"I'm six-two, and you?"

"Five foot six."

"Why do you ask how tall I am?" he wanted to know.

"No reason, I was just wondering. What's with your heritage? You're definitely not a pure Caucasian like my dad – Is your mom Asian or something?"

"No." He found his wallet and pulled out an old photograph and came over to show it to me.

"My dad was from Hawaii." The photograph showed a happy young couple. It was easy to see the resemblance between Gabriel and his father, who stood in full uniform in the picture.

"Your dad was a soldier too?"

"Yes, he was a marine." Pride shone from him.

"What happened to him?"

"He died in Kuwait during the Gulf War. I had just turned five."

"I'm sorry," I said. "Is that why you became a soldier?"

"Maybe... who knows, but it's probably one of the reasons." He walked back into the kitchen. "It's almost nine thirty. I think you should call that counselor and get an appointment set up."

I moaned. The thought of some hippie therapist telling me to think positive thoughts and be grateful for what I have made my hackles rise.

"You might as well get it over with," he pressured. "Coffee?"

"I don't like coffee."

Gabriel knitted his brows together. "How can you live in Seattle and not like coffee?" he asked.

"I like the smell, but not the taste," I explained.

"Here... use my phone and make the call." He handed me his cell phone, and I found the business card Michael Young had given me in my pocket.

To my delight, I only got voice mail.

"Hey, I got your number from my lawyer... who says I need some counseling to avoid jail, so if you could call me back on this number, I would like... ehhm... appreciate that."

Blahh... I hate to talk to voice mail, I always sound like a complete idiot.

"What do you want for breakfast?" Gabriel asked and moved around the small kitchen as if he was looking for something. "I have cornflakes and bagels."

"Don't worry about it. I still have the cinnamon bun from yesterday," I said. "But would you mind if I take a quick shower?"

"No, of course not. If you want, you can wash your clothes too. There's a washer and dryer in the bathroom."

"It's okay... I just need a quick shower," I said and retreated to the bathroom.

I didn't find a comb in Gabriel's bathroom but luckily I don't have any curls, so my hair was fairly easy to finger comb after the shower and when I got out of the bathroom, Gabriel was waiting for me in the living room, looking excited.

"The therapist called back," he said. "I spoke to him."

"And what did he say?"

"That they are willing to take you right away."

"All right," I said, drawn out.

"But he wants to do a screening of you first."

I sat down on a high chair in the kitchen. "What does that mean?"

"Well, he wants to speak to you and determine if you're the right fit for his camp."

"His wha – what? Did you say camp?"

"Yes, they have a place down in the Quinault Rain Forest about three hours from here and offer some intensive therapy programs."

I closed my eyes. An hour in an office I could survive, but a fucking camp in a forest with twenty-four/seven structure... it sounded horrible.

"Hang on, I'll call him up on Facetime and then you can talk to him; he seemed really nice."

Gabriel was already pushing buttons on his phone, and I heard a ringing sound.

"This is Bruce," a male voice answered.

"Hey, Bruce, Gabriel Thomas here – Black is out of the shower and ready to talk to you."

No, I wasn't! But I didn't have much choice when Gabriel pushed the phone at me.

"Hey," I said and looked at the screen, where a guy around fifty, with large square glasses, was looking back at me.

"Hello, Black, nice to meet you. My name is Bruce Connelly and I'm the founder of the Regression Therapy Center."

"Nice to meet you too." Yeah, I can be polite when I want to.

"I understand from your uncle that you've gotten yourself in a bit of a pickle and need to impress the judge before your first court hearing."

"That's right."

"When is that hearing?"

"May twenty-eighth."

"Good, then we have time. I would suggest you come down and follow our two-week treatment plan. You'll be happy to hear we can squeeze you in right away."

"What? You mean, like... today?"

"Yes. Can you come today?"

I looked up at Gabriel, who nodded his head and mimed "I can drive you."

I wanted to say no, but the unpleasant memory of facing the judge yesterday made me say, "Okay, I suppose I could."

"Good, but before you start packing your bags, I need to make sure you're the right fit for our program.

"Okay."

"Now tell me, are you addicted to drugs? And before you answer, let me warn you that we will have you give urine and blood samples when you arrive to see if you have anything in your system."

"No, I'm not a drug addict," I said.

"And yet I understand from your uncle that you were caught with oxycodone by the police."

"That's right, but I was going to sell them to make a profit, not take them all myself."

"You say not take them *all* yourself... how many were for you?"

I sighed. "Sometimes I take a pill to make me relax and feel better."

"And how often is sometimes?"

I hesitated. "That depends... daily if I have the money, but sometimes I go a week without a pill."

"When did you take your last pill?"

This guy was relentless with his questions, but I answered. "Maybe four days ago."

"Okay." He seemed to be thinking for a moment before he continued. "You say you're not a drug addict, but for someone to commit theft to get their drugs doesn't sound like recreational use to me."

I shrugged in response.

"Let me ask you again, are you addicted to oxycodone?"

"Maybe to a small degree," I admitted.

"All right, so I'll add drug addict to your papers then."

"No, I told you I'm not a drug addict," I protested.

He pushed his glasses up on his nose. "Yet, you just admitted to being addicted to oxycodone."

"Yeah, but I'm not like shooting myself with needles or prostituting myself to get high or anything," I pointed out.

"That's good to know. I'll note that down too," he said and scribbled some more. "When and why did you take your first pill?"

"About two years ago. It was a present from a friend."

"And what do you like about taking the pills?"

"The amazing feeling I get in my whole body."

"Would you say it's an escape from your problems or is it because you're bored?"

"An escape."

"What do you need to escape from?"

Ahh, come on... I felt compelled to press the red button and end the call. I *hate* when people start probing around in my misery, but Gabriel was standing next to me and his presence was a reminder that I didn't have much of a choice, so I huffed out air in annoyance. "Where do you want me to start?"

Bruce waited patiently.

"I'm homeless, I'm unemployed, I don't have any money or family, and I'm fucking tired of swimming upstream, when everyone else seems to be floating downstream on an air mattress with a drink in their hand," I said with an attitude.

"Okay. Now, if you could change one thing in your life what would it be?"

Loved.... I would like to be loved. It was the first thing that came to mind, but I couldn't say that and there were enough other things to pick from, so I said. "I would like to have money."

"Why?"

I arched a brow. "Seriously?"

"Yes, tell me why you would like to have money."

"So I could have a place to stay, so I could eat every day, so I didn't need to steal... do you need more reasons than that?"

"So if we accept you into our program and you leave here in two weeks, what would you like to have changed?"

I leaned my head back and glanced up in the ceiling for a few seconds before I looked at him. "I know you want me to say that I want to be free of my addiction to the pills, but unless you can help me figure out all the things that aren't working in my life, then I honestly don't want to give up on the pills. They are my only escape."

"I see," he said thoughtfully. "I appreciate your honesty, but tell me: How many days of your freedom is each pill worth to you?"

"I don't know."

"From what your uncle told me on the phone, you're potentially facing a year in prison. How many pills are worth a year in your life?"

How do you answer that? I didn't. I just scowled at him. He had made a point.

"Listen, Black, I can understand that you're using the pills to numb your pain. It's a classic situation. When we can't figure out how to solve the problems in our lives, we do the next best thing. We numb ourselves. Some use porn, others food, power shopping, gambling, alcohol, or in your case drugs. But it's a very destructive type of behavior because it never solves anything."

"So what do you suggest?" I asked feeling defensive.

"We need to get to the root and discover what went wrong, and fix it, so that you can make better decisions for yourself and get back on the right track. Are you ready to do that?"

I gave a hollow laugh. "I don't see how you can change what has already happened."

"We can't. But we can change your perspective of what happened and give it a new meaning. One that will empower you."

I must have looked very skeptical, because Gabriel spoke up on my behalf. "That sounds good!"

"Then let me tell you a few practical things," Bruce said.

"All right." I studied the man on the screen. His square glasses gave him that look of an intellectual, and if he thought his little blond mustache made him look good, I'm sorry to say it didn't. His eyes were very intense; I felt like he was looking straight inside my brain, which was unnerving as hell.

"The kind of therapy that we offer is a bit unorthodox, but to simplify it I want you to think of a computer."

"Okay."

"When a computer doesn't function we reboot it, yes?"

"I guess."

"Yes, and in case of a really destructive virus, we have to reinstall the software."

"Right."

"We believe it's a bit of the same with people. Often we need a simple reboot to make things right again. In other words, we'll restore your past to make your present better."

Gabriel raised both brows but didn't say anything.

"Your uncle already told me you had a rough childhood, so I think you'll benefit enormously from our program, but for it to have the best impact, you need to bring your parents."

"My parents?"

"Yes."

"That's not happening," I scoffed.

"Are they dead?"

"I have no clue where my mom is and I prefer it that way, and my dad won't have anything to do with me."

"Are you sure? Because it would make a huge difference if you could bring at least one of them."

"Yes, I'm sure," I said firmly.

"Can your uncle come with you and step in for your parents? Worst case, we can have one of our therapists act as your parent during the exercises, but we always encourage having a real parent or at least a family member."

"No," I said at the same time as Gabriel said, "Yes."

I gave him a hard stare and mimed *no*... he just tilted his head and mimed *yeah*.

"Did I hear you correctly there, Gabriel? Would you be willing to help your niece through the program?"

"Yes," Gabriel said loud and clear.

"That's good, it's a very admirable thing to do; but I need to warn you that therapy of this kind can get intense at times and you might see sides of your niece you haven't seen before."

Gabriel and I exchanged a glance and there was a smile in the corner of his mouth. He didn't know me – of course he would see new sides of me.

"There are many more practicalities but I think we can deal with those when you get here. You'll find driving instructions and a list of things to pack on our website, and the price of the course is a fixed rate of three thousand five hundred dollars for the two weeks."

"What?" I spit out. "I can't pay that."

"Do you take credit cards?" Gabriel said loud enough for Bruce to hear.

"Of course, and you can just pay when you get here. I'll see you in a few hours, and I look forward to meeting you both."

"We'll see you soon." Gabriel took the phone from me and gave me a bright smile.

"Ferfucksake?" I exclaimed with frustration. "I already owe you three hundred dollars, and now you want to put me in more debt without asking me first."

"You can consider it a birthday gift for all the years I didn't give you a present."

I placed my hands on my hips. "Are you serious?"

"Yes."

"You want me to believe that you're just going to give me three thousand five hundred dollars and not ask me for something in return?"

He looked a bit perplexed. "Ask you for what? What do you mean?"

"You know... like sexual favors or things like that... because I'm not a hooker, you know." Okay, so I'm not the most articulate person when I'm under pressure and, yes, I was freaked out by this new uncle popping into my life and starting to make decisions on my behalf. If there's one thing I've found to be true in life, it's that when something looks too good to be true, it usually is. Nobody just gives almost four thousand dollars to someone they just met – that doesn't happen in real life. I knew there had to be a catch. A major one.

"You're my niece, Black," he said with a frown.

"So…? We both know we're not blood related, and I'm not stupid."

"I didn't say you were stupid."

"Everyone knows men fantasize about sex with their nieces and daughters, all the time."

The look of disgust on his face was almost comical. "What the fuck are you talking about? What kind of sickos do you associate with?"

"Ohh, come on, like you've never watched porn and seen scenes of incest."

For a moment there I worried he was going to throw a complete hissy fit on me, but despite his face being almost tomato red and his hands forming into fists, he managed to keep his calm, although his voice was strained.

"I can assure you that my interest in you is not sexual. I just hate how my brother failed you and I feel that our family owes you for letting you down. Since he's not stepping up, I am."

I blinked a few times. "So you're not going to ask me to spread my legs for you?"

"No."

"All right, good, just had to check."

"And just so we're clear," he huffed out. "I don't have to pay for sex and to be honest, I prefer my girls a bit less Goth." He took a deep breath. "I'm sorry… I shouldn't have said that."

I felt stupid. He was right to be offended. I'm not exactly the hot cheerleader kind of girl, and this dude is gorgeous. To accuse him of wanting to have sex with me seemed a little ridiculous, as I have never been with anyone remotely that hot. But then again, I haven't really been with anyone. Seeing my mom practically prostitute herself made me commit to being different, and guys generally find me cold and reserved.

"I'll just pack my bag and then we're leaving. It's a long drive," Gabriel said and went into his bedroom.

I turned my head toward the entry door. I could run, right now. Maybe the police and Gabriel wouldn't find me. I could go to a new city, maybe hitchhike to New York. Anything was better than two weeks in the hands of some brain twister who would reboot me like a computer and cure me of whatever virus he thought I had going on. *What a bunch of crap.*

My shoulders sank when what-if thoughts filled my head. Hitchhikers end up raped and killed all the time. New York might be fun in the summer, but they have cold winters and where would I sleep?

So yeah, I was still standing in the same spot when Gabriel returned with a military backpack tossed over his shoulder.

"Are you ready to go?" he asked.

"Sure," I lied and started walking toward hell.

CHAPTER 4
The Regression Center

Gabriel

You would think a three-hour-long drive should give you plenty of time to talk, but Black wasn't very talkative, and at some point I grew tired of asking her questions that she avoided answering.

From Tacoma all the way to Olympia she didn't say a single word but just looked passively out the window. That's why it startled me when she finally spoke up.

"So what's your family like?"

I had been waiting for that question and had an answer ready. "You mean *our* family."

She didn't comment on that so I continued talking. "They are crazy on bad days and amazing on good days, like most other families, I think."

"Tell me about the good days," she said in a low voice and fidgeted with her pants.

"Do you remember I told you how my dad died when I was five?"

"Yeah."

"When I was seven my mom married Steve, your grandfather, and we moved into his large house in Medina with him and his three children."

"Brent, Brittany, and Melody," she said to my surprise.

"Yes, how do you know their names?" I asked.

"My mom told me."

"Oh, okay. Anyway, Brent was already seventeen, Brittany was fourteen, and Melody was ten, so a lot older than me, but I was like a fun younger brother to them, and they were good to me."

"And your stepdad?"

"Let's just say that Steve is not my favorite person."

"So there's nothing amazing about him then?"

I tilted my head from side to side as if to weigh evidence. "He's a brilliant businessman and he's been a good provider for my mom and all us kids."

"But you don't like his personality."

"God no, the man is a tyrant."

"And your mom?"

"My mom is sweet and considerate, but too much of a people pleaser. She always tries to make everyone happy. From what I heard, your biological grandmother lives somewhere on the east coast. She left Steve and the kids when Brent was around ten, I think. But don't worry, I'm sure you'll like my mom a lot."

That last comment made Black turn her head away from me. Once more silence fell upon us and lasted until we drove into the camp area inside the Rain Forest, ninety minutes later.

I got out of my car and stretched my limbs, taking in the beauty and the lushness of this amazing place. Going to the rain forest had actually been on my list of things to do while in Seattle for the summer, and I was looking forward to some long hikes while I was here.

Black on the other hand looked completely out of place with her Goth looks against all the green around us. Somehow the contrast made her dark appearance seem even more dramatic.

"Hello." I recognized Bruce when he came toward us from the biggest of the cabins. There was one large main house and ten small cabins placed in a large circle. In the middle there were stones placed in circles for campfires, and to the side a playground with a set of swings, a sandbox, a slide, and some monkey bars. It all looked very family friendly but I saw no people around.

"Welcome," Bruce said and reached out to shake our hands. "Good to see you made it here so fast."

"The traffic was good," I told him and got my bag from the trunk.

"Follow me." Bruce led the way into the main house and walked us through a large common area with a cozy fireplace and toys, books, and board games laid out. "Come in to my office," he said.

Once we were seated around a table in his office Bruce started talking to Black.

"As I told you on the phone, we follow a program that has proven successful. Our methods are somewhat unorthodox but our results speak for themselves and that's why people come here."

"Okay," Black said with mild interest.

"We've already determined what you want to achieve from your stay. You said money, but we boiled it down to your need for a place to stay and money for food. Which really translates into your understandable need for safety and certainty."

She nodded.

"In a minute my colleague Therese will come and take you to our neutralizing zone, while I will go over the payment and the sleeping arrangements with your uncle."

"What's a neutralizing zone?" I asked, a bit worried.

"It's just a room where Black will change her clothes and get rid of her jewelry and things. Regression, as the word implies, means going back in time to a younger version of oneself, and obviously Black didn't have nose piercings or colored hair when she was a small child."

Her hand flew up to a piercing. "I'm not taking out my piercings or changing my hair."

The expression on Bruce's face was stern. "Yes, you will. When you leave in two weeks you can dress in black as much as you want to, but while you're here there will be no façade of make-up or black clothes to hide behind; we want to see the real you – which reminds me, what is your real name?"

Black crossed her arms and pouted, so I answered for her. "Darcia Emma Nilsson."

"And do you prefer Darcia or Emma?"

"Neither," she said.

"Well, pick one," Bruce told her, unimpressed with her attitude.

"I told you I don't li–" she started but I interrupted her and said, "How about Cia?"

She closed her mouth and after a few seconds she gave a slight nod.

"Cia it is," Bruce said.

She was still pouting when Therese came in to escort her out of the room.

Therese, in contrast, was a happy kitten in her mid-twenties with long auburn-colored hair to her waist. She had cute dimples and when she shook my hand she placed her other hand on top and gave me a warm smile.

Maybe these two weeks wouldn't be so bad after all... Nature, hiking, and some fun with Therese might turn out to be a good kind of vacation.

When we were alone in the room, Bruce took my credit card information and gave me more instructions.

"It's important that you understand what is expected of you. Cia doesn't really want to be here and most likely doesn't think she needs our help. Our methods can seem strange at first, especially since it's a combination of traditional therapy sessions and practical assignments."

"Okay."

"We use role-play to re-enact childhood situations – the purpose of course is to repair some of the emotional damage that is currently causing problems. Once we start taking Cia back to her childhood I must prepare you to expect strong reactions from her. There will most likely be triggers, so if you know of anything in her childhood we should be aware of, then I would like to know about it."

I squirmed a bit in my seat. "I've only know Black – ehh, I mean Cia – since yesterday, so I can't really tell you much about her childhood except for what she told me."

He held his pen over his paper and looked at me expectantly.

"Go ahead."

"All right, ehhm…" I held up my hand and counted on my fingers. "Her mother was an alcoholic. She ran away when she was fourteen; her father Brent, who is my stepbrother, rejected her and basically told her he wished she hadn't been born."

Bruce didn't flinch or show any sign of emotion, but just took notes.

"She has survived by working in a motel where the owner allowed her to sleep at night. That's all I know."

"Good."

He was still writing when I remembered another detail. "Oh and she got through high school and didn't want to be in a foster family because she said she didn't want anyone to abuse her. She wouldn't tell me, but I got the feeling that her mom abused her in some way."

"Thank you." He took a few moments to finish his notes before he looked up. "Now, Gabriel, your role will be the parent and since you're male you'll take the role of Cia's father. Do you have any children?" he asked.

"No."

"Did you have a good father yourself?"

"For the first five years I did."

"Elaborate, please."

"My biological father was awesome and fun. But he got killed in battle and then my mom married my stepdad, who isn't a very nice man."

Bruce tapped his chin. "What do you mean by that?"

I scoffed. "Well, to be frank, my stepdad is extremely self-centered and mentally tortured his children."

"Including you?"

"No, mostly his own three kids. My mom always protected me, so I never got the worst of it like they did."

"Did he hit them or abuse them sexually?"

"No, nothing like that. It was more about verbally demeaning them a lot. I mean, the guy is old school and believes in shame, blame, and punishment."

"Physical punishment?"

"Yeah, but nothing extreme… just a quick spanking or a slap on the face. It's mostly the hateful words that he masters."

"All right. Now, with Cia, you should expect her to challenge you. Especially as we move her up in her years."

"Years?"

"We'll start her out as a baby and you'll care for her."

My brows shot up to my hairline and then I broke into a laugh. "Come again?"

Bruce didn't even smile. "You will be assigned a cabin and it's your job to offer Cia the care of a father."

"But what does that mean exactly?" I asked, feeling perplexed.

"It varies depending on her age of course, but today you'll start out by nurturing her as you would an infant."

"I've never cared for an infant."

"Well, it's not complicated. Basically you make sure she gets fed, you put her to bed, sing her a good-night song, and take care of her needs."

I scratched my neck and searched for something to say, but I couldn't stop smiling, wondering if this was a prank of some kind.

"You understand that I met my niece yesterday, right? We don't have a close relationship and even if we had, what you're asking is bizarre."

"As I said," Bruce said dryly. "Our methods are hands-on and somewhat unorthodox, but the good news is that I'll be following Cia's progress closely and I'll be here to support you. The more she cooperates and shows healthy behavior, the quicker she can progress to the next level."

"And what is the next level?"

He pointed up to a board on the wall behind me. "Those are the age group definitions that we work with.

"Infant is from birth to twelve months.

"Toddler is from one to four years.

"Child is from five to ten; and preteen is from ten to thirteen, where we reach the teenage years.

"Of course after that comes young adult, adult, and elder adult, but with Cia those are irrelevant. Her problems seem to derive from her childhood and that's what we'll focus on."

"I see..." I took a deep breath. "So the next two weeks you want her to go through role-plays of being a baby, a toddler, a child, and a teenager."

"Yes, and a preteen too," he added and pushed up from his chair.

"And you want me to act as her father?"

"Yes, she will call you Daddy or Father and you'll refer to her as Cia, honey, or whatever endearment you find works for you and her."

He held out his hand to signal he wanted me to get up from the chair and walk with him.

"Do all your clients go through this program?"

"More or less," he said.

"I don't think Cia is going to like it," I said slowly and followed him out the door. The thought of the Goth girl I had come to know was incompatible with what he wanted her to do. The image of her walking out of Starbuck yesterday and flipping a finger at a guy in a car came to mind. There was nothing childish about her. Cia was hard, edgy, and angry, and she certainly didn't take orders well.

We walked from the main house to one of the small cabins, and Bruce entered and spread his arms. "This is it. Your room for the next two weeks, I trust that you and Cia will be comfortable here."

I looked around and bit my inner cheek. It wasn't that it was bad or anything... but it was just one room with a queen-size bed, a closet, two nightstands, and a chair.

Bruce opened the door to the bathroom. "All our cabins have a bathtub, and you'll need it to give Cia a bath before bedtime."

"Wow, hold on. You can't be serious?"

Again, the man looked very serious.

"A bath before bedtime, and don't try to get out of it, because all cabins are video monitored."

"But surely you don't expect me to physically touch my niece while she's naked?"

Bruce closed the door to the bathroom. "There's nothing sexual in this. I want you to think of her as an infant, and give her the paternal love and care that she didn't receive as a child. She might resist it, but it's critical that you do it. You will bathe her, wash her hair and body, and dry her afterwards. When that's done, you will dress her in her baby jumpsuit and put her to bed with a lullaby. If you can't do it, I will have one of the therapists take your place, but I can't stress enough how much better it will be when a family member does it."

Fuck! To say I didn't like this would be an understatement, but somehow the logic in rebooting

Cia's shitty childhood made sense to me. So as the good soldier I am, I would follow orders.

"But about that video surveillance – who sees those tapes?"

"I do. I'll be Cia's therapist during her stay, and I will be looking closely at her reactions to the exercises as well as the dynamic between you two."

"I don't like that you can see us even in the bathroom," I said.

He arched a brow. "You would be surprised how uninteresting it is to see people groom themselves, and I can assure you that I don't get a kick out of it. What I'm looking for is mental breakdowns and breakthroughs. Cia is a minefield, and we are about to go map those damn bombs placed throughout her childhood and blow them up once and for all."

I grinned. "Now you're talking... I'm a sapper; blowing up things is my specialty."

"A soldier, huh?" He smacked me on my shoulder. "Then this is going to be just another mission."

"To be honest," I said, "I would much rather go face-to-face with an ISIS warrior in Afghanistan than tell Cia what you just told me. I think she's going to go bat-shit crazy on me when I tell her about the baby thing."

"Are you afraid she will physically attack you?" he said in all seriousness.

"Hardly," I replied, trying to mimic his earnestness. "I hope she doesn't, but I can pacify her if it comes to that."

"Good, and that reminds me, I'll have them bring a pacifier too... it goes with the baby equipment. If you need me there's a phone on the wall that connects to my cellphone."

"Thanks, but – ehhh – it's only two p.m. – what do we do until bedtime?"

He stepped outside and I followed him. "In my experience that black hair color will take a while to wash out, and our last Goth client ended up with yellow hair afterwards, so Therese had to color it to something as close to his natural color as possible. Luckily Therese is a trained hairdresser, so she'll make sure Cia looks nice before she leaves her. There's a collection of books in the great room, so go find one to kill the waiting time. You'll also need it when she takes a nap tomorrow because you'll need to stay with her at all times until she becomes a preteen."

"Anything else I should know?" I asked.

"We eat dinner at six p.m. in the dining room; that's where you'll meet the others."

I did as he had suggested and went to find a book to read while I was waiting. I got through five long chapters before I heard footsteps outside the cabin and looked up to see the door open... and oh my fucking God... did I gape.

CHAPTER 5
Baby
Cia

I was happy to be out of the neutralizer room but felt completely naked without my armor of black.

Therese walked me over to cabin number five, as if she was afraid I would run away... not that I wasn't tempted, but where the hell would I go? I was beginning to understand why this place was so isolated.

"Just go right in," Therese instructed. "Your daddy is inside."

I arched a brow, not understanding what she was talking about but feeling confident I wouldn't find Brent inside the cabin. I was right.

I found Gabriel lying on a bed, reading.

"Hey," I said and if I hadn't felt stupid and naked already, I certainly did after the way he stared at me as if I had grown an extra head.

"Wow, you look so... different," he said and sat up.

I had seen myself in a mirror and knew I looked like a bloody sixteen-year-old with my girl-next-door look.

"At least we're in the forest so no one will see me like this," I said grumpily.

"You're blond now," he pointed out and took me in from head to toe in my sweatpants and t-shirt with a printed logo that said Camp TRC – which I had been told by Therese was short for "The Regression Center."

"So the beauty mark *is* real," Gabriel said and pointed to my mouth.

"Yes, it's real, why wouldn't it be?"

"I thought that maybe it was a tribute to Madonna... you know, the singer... she used to paint on a beauty mark and she..."

"Yes, I know who Madonna is," I cut him off and pointed to the pile on the bed. "What is that?" For some reason it made me nervous.

Gabriel put his book down and got up from the bed. "I think you better sit down for a minute," he said.

"Why?"

"Bruce gave us the first assignment and left it to me to explain it to you. Come sit down."

I got on the bed, leaned my head against the headboard, and tugged my feet up under me. "I'm ready, so what is it?"

Gabriel was rubbing his forehead and giving me a troubled look.

"How bad can it be? Just spit it out," I demanded.

Five minutes later when he was done explaining, I was pacing the room, ready to kill someone.

"If you think that I'm going to allow anyone to dress me up in a baby jumpsuit and sing me lullabies, then you must be out of your mind. I can call you Daddy if I have to but that's as far as I'll go."

He swallowed hard. "Well, actually, that's not the worst part."

I narrowed my eyes and clenched my jaw. "Then what is?"

"That as your father I have to give you a bath and feed you."

"*No!* Absolutely not!" I shrieked.

Gabriel shrugged. "I'm only doing it to help you and I promise there will be nothing sexual about it."

"You're damn right there will be nothing sexual about it, because *it's not happening,*" I said in a raised voice.

"Those were our instructions," Gabriel said.

"I don't care. I'm not doing it. I told you... I don't take orders from anyone." My voice was loud and high-pitched and inside me my heart was hammering so fast. What he was asking me to do was terrifying. Fuck the baby costume, I could pretend it was Halloween and make a joke of it, but the part that brought out a full-fledged anxiety attack was the realization that Bruce wanted me to relinquish all control and let Gabriel take care of me.

"Calm down," Gabriel said with a frown.

"No, I won't calm down," I hissed back. "I'm not taking orders from you... and certainly not that crazy Dr. Jekyll who thinks he can play twisted games with me, and call it therapy. Fuck him!"

"You can use that phone and call Bruce directly." Gabriel pointed to a phone on the wall. "But wouldn't it be easier to just play along?"

"Oh, I'm calling Bruce right now, because this is crazy."

Gabriel took a seat on the bed while I called up Bruce, who remained completely calm no matter how much I screamed profanities at him. It was like banging my head against the wall.

"You can spend your two weeks here being a baby if you refuse to work with us, or you can comply and move up to become a toddler tomorrow. It's up to you, Cia. If you cooperate, you could be a teenager by the end of the week."

When I hung up the phone, I slid down the wall and pulled my legs up to my chest, hugging myself. I couldn't even look at Gabriel or face the humiliating things before me.

I couldn't see him with my head hidden against my knees but I felt him sitting down next to me.

"Hey, it's not so bad," he said in a soft voice. "We'll get through this together, and what if it actually helps? Won't it be worth two weeks of craziness if you end up feeling a lot better?"

I raised my head and looked at him, not caring that he would see the moisture in my eyes. "I don't want to do it."

"I know," he said and stroked my back. It made me jerk and I shot him an angry glance, not feeling comfortable with his touches. "But I don't think you have much choice."

"Of course I have a choice," I said, got up, and left the cabin, slamming the door after me.

Some people might have been brave enough to just start walking home. I know I wanted to, and maybe I would have succeeded if the sign at the end of the road hadn't been there. "Beware," it said and showed pictures of bears, cougars, and wolves. That sign made me stop and ponder for a minute. It would take me hours to hike to a road large enough to hope for a ride, and it would be dark before I got there. I had nothing with me. No flashlight, no water, no map. Chances were I would get lost or end up as dinner for some wild animal.

This therapy was ridiculous and disgusting, but was it worse than dying or going to jail?

My feet dragged when, thirty minutes later, I turned around and headed back to the cabin, to find Gabriel sitting outside on the porch.

"Let's get this over with," I hissed as I passed him, hoping he didn't see me dry away an angry tear.

He got up and followed me inside, closing the door.

"So how do you want to do this?" he asked and moved forward to grab the pile on the bed. "We have to get you into the baby costume and since you're a baby, I have to dress you."

I reached for the pile, and when I lifted the black and yellow jumpsuit my eyes widened. Underneath were a diaper, a pacifier, and a baby bottle. *Hell no!* I had been ready to do this, but the diaper was a deal breaker.

Gabriel swallowed a laugh, and I snapped my head up and gave him my most evil look.

"If you think this is funny, then why don't I dress you in a diaper?"

"I'm sorry, but it's so grotesque that it's funny," he said, still trying to suppress his laughter.

I stuck a finger up his face. "If you want to get out of this cabin alive, you will not even attempt to put me in a diaper. Do you understand?"

He was nodding when the phone on the wall rang.

"What?" I asked angrily, squeezing the phone in my hand.

"The diaper will have to go on. It's an important part of the role-play," Bruce said on the phone.

My eyes flew around the cabin and stopped when I saw the camera. "Are you fucking spying on us?" I hissed.

"It's all for the purpose of helping you, Cia. The diaper has to come on."

"What kind of pervert are you to spy on people and then have them strip naked?"

Bruce's voice remained calm. "I assure you I feel no more excitement about seeing your naked body than your doctor does when you get an examination."

"I won't do it," I sneered. "This is a gross violation of my personal boundaries."

"That's your choice, but unless you do it, I can't give you the papers you need for the judge. I'm not saying this is easy or fun, but the sooner you allow your father to care for you like his little baby girl, the sooner it will be over."

"Then at least give Gabriel back his money, because we're leaving right now." I gave Gabriel a sharp look but only received a frown in return.

"I'm afraid I can't do that," Bruce said. "You are free to go if you think jail is a better option, but we don't do refunds."

I smacked the phone back on the wall and flipped a finger at the camera in the corner of the ceiling.

Gabriel sat quietly beside me for a few minutes.

"I know you just met me, but if I had known you as a baby I would have been happy to bathe you and change your diaper – I like kids."

I didn't look at him, afraid I was going to take my anger and frustration out on him, I kept my head down and tried to focus on my breathing. A few minutes later I was calm enough to say; "You would have been eight years old when I was a baby. Don't you think you would have been too busy riding your bike to care for an infant?"

Gabriel got up from the floor and sat on the bed, facing me. "Maybe," he said; "but I always wanted a younger brother or sister."

"I'm not your sister."

"I know." He said quietly. "Can't you just pretend you're playing a part... like an actor doing a show or something?"

I still didn't budge but sat for an eternity thinking about my options. Leaving would be impossible without Gabriel driving me somewhere, and there wasn't much chance of convincing him to leave when he had just spent a fortune on me. I could refuse to wear the baby costume, but that would get me nowhere. I needed Bruce to give me the papers for the court. If not, I wouldn't be wearing a baby jumpsuit but an orange prison jumpsuit.

No matter how I searched for an alternative I was pressed into a corner and my only way out was to suck it up and get it over with.

I lifted my head and looked at Gabriel, who was lying on the bed reading. "I'm hungry," I said grumpily.

He gave me a faint smile. "Me too… There's dinner in the main house."

His words gave me the last piece of motivation.

"Okay," I said.

Gabriel pushed off from the bed and looked at me expectantly. "Are you ready to do it?" he asked.

I nodded with my jaws clenched too tightly to speak.

He slapped the bed, signaling for me to get on it, and as soon as I did, he started to take off my clothes with great concentration. I closed my eyes and placed my arm across my face to avoid being part of this humiliating role-play.

Gabriel removed my pants and panties, and I heard the plastic sound from the diaper and died a little.

"How does this thing work?" he asked and I was forced to move my arms and open my eyes to see him study the diaper and turn it in the air. "How do I know which way is front and back?"

"Give it to me," I hissed and reached for the diaper, which was like a big white pair of underwear. After turning it a few times I handed it back. "It probably doesn't matter, just put the damn thing on."

"Okay, okay." He tugged the diaper up to my thighs before he asked me to lift my butt.

I took a deep breath and lifted my ass so he could get the diaper underneath me, and tried not to think too much about how exposed my private parts were.

Luckily Gabriel seemed completely uninterested in that part of me and solely focused on getting me into the diaper and jumpsuit while touching me as little as possible. He didn't remove my top until he had covered me up to my waistline and even then he was careful not to touch my breasts.

In the end, Gabriel zipped up the jumpsuit and looked pleased with himself. "See, that wasn't so bad," he said and tried to put the pacifier in my mouth.

I turned my head and refused to take it.

"Cia," he said in a persuasive tone.

"Don't even think about it. I didn't use a pacifier as a baby and I won't do it now."

He gave a questioning glance to the camera in the corner while I got up from the bed and took a look down at myself. "Who the hell decided on black and yellow?" I said dryly. "I look like a freaking bee."

Gabriel grinned. "You look cute."

Cute was one word no one had ever called me.

"Now what?" I asked and threw my hands in the air.

"Let's get something to eat." For a moment Gabriel looked uncertain and then he simply picked me up.

"Put me down," I demanded.

"Stop wriggling – you're a baby, you can't walk yet."

Having him carry me in his arms forced me to be close to him, and I was stiff as a board.

"Relax, Cia, I won't drop you, I promise."

I remained stiff in his arms and growled into his ear, "If you ever tell anyone about this, I will personally find you and castrate you."

"Your secret is safe with me," he muttered back.

CHAPTER 6
Dinner and Bath

Cia

Dinner with the circus freaks.

Really, that's how it felt.

I was the only one in a baby jumper but five others were clearly patients or clients... or inmates, whatever the right term was in this horrible place.

Bruce banged his glass and silenced the group.

"I would like to welcome baby Cia and her daddy Gabriel to our group," Bruce said. "I trust that you'll all welcome them and introduce yourselves over the next few days."

A total of fourteen people were around the table and most of them smiled.

"Now let us eat," Bruce said and picked up a napkin from his plate.

Platters with food were spread around the table and I reached for a bowl of salad but it was quickly snatched out of my hands by Therese. "Babies don't eat salad," she said with a tsk-tsk sound. "This is for you, dear." She reached for a small bowl of porridge and handed it to Gabriel with a baby spoon.

"For your baby girl," she said and gave him a bright smile.

Gabriel was busy putting food on his own plate but stopped to take the bowl and sat it down in front of me.

"Here you go," he said when Bruce cleared his voice and discreetly pointed to a mother feeding her son a meatball.

Gabriel got the message and offered me a spoonful of the porridge.

I turned my head away.

"Sometimes it helps using endearments," Therese suggested.

Gabriel cleared his voice. "Here you go, sweetheart," he said and gave me a strained smile.

I crossed my arms, two seconds away from telling them all to go fuck themselves.

And then Gabriel did the most ridiculous thing ever... he started playing the airplane game, pretending that the spoon was flying through the air and towards my mouth. And the worst part was that by making a complete fool of himself, the big guy actually managed to make me crack a small smile. The whole scenario was too comical and absurd not to. When I rewarded his effort by opening my mouth and taking a small spoonful of the porridge, Gabriel broke into a grin.

"Good girl," he said but quickly closed his mouth when I shot him a don't-push-me glance.

"While we eat I want to take the opportunity to congratulate Martin, who will be going home tomorrow and who has done an excellent job these past weeks," Bruce said.

A man around forty nodded his head to Bruce. "Thank you, it's been an amazing journey of self-discovery," he said. "I can't thank you enough."

Bruce raised his wine glass. "Let's drink to Martin and his future," he said, and everyone raised their glasses too. Except me, of course; I had to let Gabriel offer me a sip of water like I was handicapped.

When we got to dessert, everyone had chocolate cake but me. Therese brought in a ripe banana for Gabriel to feed me. I looked enviously at his chocolate cake but ate half of the banana.

When dinner was done everyone made their way into the large room where board games, toys, and books were scattered. I looked over to see a pool table and a foosball table when Bruce approached us and spoke to Gabriel.

"It's seven-thirty, and I think now would be a good time for you to give Cia a bath and put her to bed."

Gabriel had carried me in here and not yet put me down, so he just nodded and walked out the door, towards the cabin.

I didn't fight him this time and helped a bit by placing my arms around his neck. "Am I too heavy," I asked?

"Hardly," he scoffed. "I've had to carry backpacks heavier than you for twenty mile hikes."

"Still..." I said.

"Don't worry about it, you're light as a bee." He started laughing. "Get it? You're dressed like a bee and light as a bee."

"Ha ha," I said sarcastically and made a grimace.

When we got into the cabin it quickly became awkward. We both knew what was about to happen and he put me down on the bed and went to run a bath.

I bit my lip and counted to a hundred, trying to calm myself down. I don't remember my mother giving me a bath, but I suppose she must have.

When Gabriel came back he looked crimson red in his face and he obviously found this as difficult as me.

"This is really weird," he said.

"You think?"

He was tripping from foot to foot assessing me before he clapped his hands and exclaimed. "Right, I'm just going to do it."

"You sound like a Nike commercial," I replied dryly but otherwise kept still while he got me out of the bee costume and the diaper. I tried to think of a thousand things to distract me from the situation but I still registered him picking me up when I was naked and carrying me the seven steps to the bathroom, where he gently put me down in the bathtub.

At least the water was nice and warm.

Gabriel was a bit out of breath and I wondered if his heart was racing like mine. He spun around in the bathroom and finally grabbed a bottle of shampoo and kneeled down next to me.

"I have to wash your hair."

"Uh-huh."

"I've never washed another person's hair and I have no clue how to wash your long hair."

"You don't need to wash it; Therese already did that," I told him, referring to the hours of treatment my poor hair had gone through to get the black color out of it.

"Okay, then at least let me make it wet."

Placing a hand under my neck, he signaled for me to lower myself down in the tub and then he used his big hands to scoop up water and make my hair wet. Once that was done, he found a washcloth and started gently washing my body.

Seeing how nervous he was made me feel almost sorry for him. He didn't say a word but kept his eyes on the cloth and gently washed my hands, shoulders, arms, neck, and face. He even washed behind my ears and then he moved down to wash my feet and legs.

"I know you don't like being naked, but imagine you're a baby. Then you wouldn't be the least bit shy. You wouldn't even be aware that certain parts of your body were private," he said.

"But I'm not a baby."

"I know, but try to pretend that you are... or pretend that you're German."

"German – why would that help?"

"Someone told me Germans are pretty much nudists as a people; men and women go naked to the spa and don't think anything of it."

"I think that's a gross generalization," I told him. "I'm sure there are shy Germans."

"Okay... but then try to think of how absurd it really is to be shy about certain parts of your body and not others. I mean, we're only shy because someone told us those areas are private, but what if instead of telling us breasts and genitals are private they had told us our noses were the most private part of our body."

I frowned, but he just smiled and carried on. "Then right now you would be covering your nose and feeling super shy about showing it to me, but at the same time not caring a rat's ass about me seeing the rest of your body."

I didn't laugh, because nothing about being this exposed was funny, but I did have a mental image of people walking around wearing fashionable pieces of textile to cover their noses, and at least that thought kept me a bit distracted, as he kept washing me.

"Do you like it, sweetie?" Gabriel asked softly.

He was washing my shins gently and moved up to my knees. I instantly pressed my thighs together to make sure he didn't go higher.

He got the hint and moved his hand with the washcloth to my belly instead but stayed in safe distance from my chest.

"I think I'm clean now," I said a bit harder than I intended.

Gabriel actually took all this craziness seriously, and I guess he should have a medal for his patience with me.

After letting out the water, he dried me off without ever really touching me anywhere inappropriately. Ten minutes later I was back in the baby costume with a baby bottle full of water.

"I think I better brush your hair," Gabriel said and sat down behind me. His hands were clumsy and maybe that's why he overcompensated by being extremely careful when brushing my hair.

"It's not a wig... my hair won't fall off if you brush a bit harder," I bitched.

"I just don't want to hurt you."

"That's nice, but at this pace it will take you an hour to comb my hair."

He sped up and brushed it harder. As soon as he was done I lay down and pulled the cover over me.

"Bruce asked me to sing you a lullaby but I can't sing and I don't know any lullabies," he said with obvious frustration.

"That's fine with me."

"Yeah, but I don't want him to keep you a baby for another day just because I failed to sing to you. I think I might know a few of the words to a song my mother used to sing."

"Okay, or just hum something," I suggested and tried not to bat his hands away when he tucked me in and brushed my hair behind my ears.

"Hush little baby, don't you cry, daddy's gonna buy you a diamond ring, and if that ring something something, then he'll buy you something else," Gabriel sang in a voice much softer than his normal deep voice.

Somewhere inside of me laughter bubbled. Even I knew that he was screwing up the song lyrics, and it was funny to see him so out of his element.

I closed my eyes to avoid offending him with my laughter and felt him caress my hair while he kept humming and singing.

"And if that mockingbird won't sing, daddy's going to buy you a bull and if that bull won't pull a cart da da da, you're still going to be the sweetest baby in town."

He was off-key, singing the wrong lyrics, and messing up the simple melody, but he was here. For the first time in years I wasn't alone.

I lay completely still, feeling the heat from his body and his big calloused hands that clumsily caressed my hair. And all the while, I kept my eyes firmly shut and close to the pillow. If I hadn't, he might have seen my tears.

CHAPTER 7
Toddler

Gabriel

That night I woke up several times because of sounds coming from Cia. Her nightmares made her whine, and I wasn't sure whether to wake her up or let her dream through it.

I blame her nightmares for the fact that we woke up completely entangled with my body enclosing hers. I must have been trying to calm her in my sleep, and I explained that to her when she shoved me off her.

Breakfast was much like dinner. I had to feed her some oatmeal, and I almost considered smuggling out one of the large muffins she sent long glances after.

Bruce wanted a session with us at ten and I carried her into his office. To my delight, she was no longer fighting me but actively helping when I picked her up, by holding on to me.

"How did it feel to be in your father's care yesterday?" Bruce asked.

Cia gave me a quick glance. "It felt strange,"

"Did something pop up that you would like to discuss... maybe memories from your childhood?"

"Not really... I was just aware of how naked I was."

"And you didn't like that?"

"No, I didn't like that."

"Why is that? Were you afraid your daddy would touch you inappropriately?"

Cia moved annoyed in her chair. "No, it's just hard to take seriously and I don't think of G as my father." She gave me a side glance. "No offense."

I was going to tell her that I didn't see her as my daughter either, but Bruce continued.

"The fact that no traumas came to the surface is a good sign, and I'm very proud of you both for completing the task. I suggest that you go back to the cabin and change into the next outfit, as you are ready to be a toddler.

"Great, can I have real food then?"

"Yes. You still need help from you father when you eat, but you can play with toys and eat the same as the rest of us."

"Wonderful," Cia said dryly. "Can I bathe myself too?"

"No, I'm afraid not – and in fact I noticed that you still keep some boundaries between you. I would like you to trust your father more today and let him wash you all over like a real father would. Again, let me remind you both that there is nothing sexual in this. Fathers and mothers wash their children daily to clean them." He looked directly at me. "I'm not asking you to dwell between her legs or on her breasts, but it's all a natural part of her body and should be washed too."

No doubt my face was crimson. "I can't do that," I said and squirmed in my seat.

"Of course you can, and if you use a washcloth you won't even be in direct contact."

"But surely we're allowed a few personal boundaries," I protested.

"No, you're not. Parents and babies bathe and sleep together. It has been that way for thousands of years and helps the child develop the ability to bond and trust."

He turned his attention to Cia. "I think you'll agree with me the bonding and trusting doesn't come easy to you, which indicates that this crucial part of your development is lacking.

"In the light of your drug addiction this is particularly crucial since new research tells us that the root cause of addiction is really a lack of connection."

Cia and I both took deep breaths and exchanged looks of discomfort.

"I know you feel like I'm pushing you, but I'm really not." Bruce returned his gaze to me. "Ideally I would ask you to shave all Cia's pubic hair since that isn't part of childhood either, but I'm leaving that up to you both."

It was the first time I felt a reaction to his words that was far from appropriate. I always found it arousing to shave a woman's pubic hair and it stirred something in me. "That's not happening," I said quickly. I didn't have to look at Cia to know she agreed.

Bruce raised both palms. "As I said, I'll leave that up to you. My agenda is to build intimacy between the two of you and get Cia to relax and take in the tenderness from a parent. Ultimately we want her to develop her ability to trust and bond with others."

"I'm right here," Cia said and pushed her jaw out. "Talking about me in third person when I'm sitting right in front of you is just rude."

"I apologize," Bruce said with a smile. "If you don't have any more questions I suggest you go and change in the cabin, and Cia..."

"Yes," she said with her brows knitted.

"The diaper stays on until you advance to being a child."

She arched a brow but didn't answer him.

"There are clean diapers under the sink in the bathroom," he said to me.

The eerie way Cia turned her head in slow motion and raised herself up in her seat spoke volumes. "Please tell me you don't actually expect me to do my business in the diaper."

He nodded his head. "I already know you used the toilet this morning and I take full blame for not explaining myself clearly enough. As long as you use a diaper, you'll not be able to use the toilet.

"There is no way in hell I'm doing number one or two in a diaper," Cia growled.

"Thank God," I muttered, feeling a bit pale myself.

"Then we better hope you advance to being a child soon," Bruce said calmly.

Cia was so mad she was actually sputtering when she spoke. "I don't think this kind of thing is legal... there must be some kind of rules or ethics... or something."

Bruce didn't even lift a brow; he just looked at her and waited for her to get it all out.

When she had told him how disgusting, perverted, and crazy he was at least three times, he spoke in a placating tone. "What part of it upsets you the most? That you'll get dirty by peeing in a diaper or that your father has to clean you up?"

"Both," she yelled at him.

"But if you had to pick one, which one would you say bothers you the most."

"I don't like to be touched when I'm clean, so why the hell do you think I would tolerate him touching me when I'm dirty?"

"Would it be okay if he was to clean your foot? Is it because it's your vagina that he has to clean?"

God, it felt like a sauna in here. I pulled the neckline of my t-shirt out and blew down to cool myself off. I felt sorry for Cia and could completely sympathize. I would hate to be in her shoes.

"Of course it would be different, you insensitive prick," she sneered.

He looked at me for help. "Maybe it would help Cia if you told her that you don't mind changing a wet diaper for her."

"I don't mind…" I started to say, but she cut me off by snapping her head around and pinning me with her burning eyes.

"Of course you mind, and so do I."

She was fuming, but Bruce was unwavering and simply continued on as if nothing was wrong. "Any other questions before you go?"

"Actually I have a question," I said and moved forward in my chair. "When Cia has nightmares, what should I do? Wake her up or let her sleep?"

Bruce looked at Cia and tilted his head like a bloodhound onto a trace of something. "How often do you have nightmares?"

She was scowling at him but to my surprise, she answered. "I don't know… pretty often I guess."

"Do you remember your dreams?"

"Sometimes."

"Is it the same recurrent dream?"

"No."

He looked thoughtful. "How violent was her nightmare would you say?" he asked me.

"Not bad, she just whined and babbled on about something I couldn't understand."

"In that case, don't wake her. Offer her your comfort but don't actively wake her up. If, however, you see her throwing herself violently around, then wake her."

"All right. I got it."

"Good – nightmares are a normal way to process things from our lives, it's not necessarily a bad thing, but if you remember anything about your nightmares, Cia, then please write it down and bring it to me. It might be helpful for us to find out what traumas you have from your past."

We got up and went to the cabin, where a new pile of clothes had been placed on the bed.

I gently sat Cia down on the bed. She moved away and curled into a ball, closing me out.

"Do you need a minute?" I asked.

She didn't answer, so I got on the bed next to her and picked up my book and started reading. I could be patient.

Half an hour later Cia sat up and picked up the new clothes on the bed. It was all pink and girlish and made her wrinkle her nose up.

"Jeez," she muttered. "Did they run out of black and yellow?"

I was in awe of her. I think honestly if it had been me, I would have been hiking through the woods by now... on my way back to Seattle. I had witnessed her rage and seen her revulsion with this program and yet, only half an hour later, she was trying to make a joke.

"At least in this role-playing universe, no one will mistake you for a boy with that outfit," I said in an attempt to keep the irony going.

"I'm going to look like walking candy floss," she said.

"Then don't be mad if I lick you," I answered quickly and saw her eyes widen.

"No, I didn't mean it like that... it was just a joke."

She didn't get angry but just shrugged. "Yeah, this whole thing is a cruel joke. Good thing I have a sense of humor or I would go crazy, real quick."

"You and me both," I agreed.

"Really... you think you're having it tough?" she asked.

"No, but... I don't know, I mean, it's not easy for me either," I babbled.

"How do you think you would feel about me undressing you and bathing you and putting you in a diaper?"

I looked into her green eyes and found them much more attractive without all the black make-up. She had long lashes, and when the time was right, I would tell her that her chance of getting a boyfriend was much bigger without all the depressive blackness. I didn't know how she would react if I told her she was pretty, because she didn't seem to appreciate that kind of attention, but uncle or not, I'm still a guy and I can tell when a girl has natural beauty, and I think she should know.

"I would hate it if our roles were reversed, and the thought of you bathing me makes the hair on my arms stand up."

A ghost of sadness flew over her face.

"For all it's worth though, I think it's much worse for you to get the diaper on, than it is for me to do it," I said.

Her eyes were blazing. "Of course it is. So I have a suggestion."

"What?" I asked.

"Why don't you let me put you in a diaper... you know, just for the balance of things."

I narrowed my eyes, waiting for her to say "Just kidding," but she didn't.

This was a fucking dilemma... I wanted to help her and to support her, but the thought of being subjected to that sort of humiliation made my heart race triple time.

"Sweetie, I don't think I can do that," I said hoping that my endearment would soften her up.

"So you're willing to strip me naked and touch my body and humiliate me with the whole diaper thing, but you wouldn't allow me to do the same to you?"

My head was spinning, trying to find a solution.

"I suppose I could let you see me naked if that would help."

"You've seen me naked, *and* touched me."

I frowned. "Are you asking if you can touch me while I'm naked?"

"No!" She rubbed her face with both hands. "This is all so messed up. I don't want to see you naked, or touch you, and I certainly don't want to put you in a diaper, but I just feel so fucking powerless and I *hate* it."

"So you think that we would be more balanced if the humiliation went both ways."

"Yes."

"I understand."

"No, you don't understand."

"I'm okay with stripping out of my clothes, Cia. Being in the military will make you used to being naked in front of others. We shared open showers and stuff. I mean, if it makes you feel better."

"It won't make me feel better and I don't want you naked and close to me. I just wanted to see if you were willing to do it."

"All right, then what *do* you want?"

"I want these two weeks to be over and get out of here."

"I understand," I said again.

She was compliant when I dressed her in the pink set of soft clothes, which had a picture of a kitty on her belly. She even allowed me to put the hairband with a bow in her hair.

"You look cute," I said, but that only made her roll her eyes.

"Do you want to go and play a board game or something?" I asked.

"Can a toddler play pool?" she asked and reached her hands up to me. As the most natural thing in the world, I picked her up and held her close.

"I think I'm going to call you my little candy floss while you're a toddler," I joked as we walked up to the main house.

Cia held on to me and sighed. "I can't wait to be Black again."

I didn't say it, but a part of me hoped that she would never go back to that awful look. She was so much softer and sweeter without all that darkness.

Cia

Therese was in the common room when we walked in, and it was impossible not to notice how she lit up when she saw Gabriel.

"How cute you two look together," she said and placed her hand on his arm.

"You can put your daughter down now, she's a toddler and can walk by herself. Actually we've never seen anyone carry their little ones before, but we didn't want to stop it since the intimacy was good for you."

"Oh." He lowered me to the floor and took a step back. "Go play then," he said and turned to talk with Therese.

I found a jigsaw puzzle and tried to block out the flirtatious conversation between Gabriel and Therese.

I couldn't.

Although I would have never asked him directly, I was curious about him and had wondered many of the same things that she asked him. It turned out that he was born in Bellevue, just east of Seattle. He had always known he wanted to be in the military like his father, and no, he did not have a girlfriend.

Therese spoke more than he did and from her many questions, I could tell she was interested in him. I don't know why that bothered me, except that his full attention was a new and strangely exciting thing for me.

Gabriel was the first family member that I liked and who treated me with kindness. Maybe I'm selfish, but I didn't want to share him with Therese.

"G, do you want to help me with the puzzle?" I asked him and had to repeat myself to get his attention.

"No, that's okay," he said dismissively and turned his attention back to Therese, who had the nerve to give me a sweet smile and remind me to address Gabriel as Dad or Daddy.

I bit my inner lip and thought for a minute. Then I picked up a toy phone and went to him. I pressed the ringing sound and handed it to him, but to my annoyance he gave me a distracted glance and ignored the phone in my hand.

"Hey," I said, "No matter how old or badass you think you are, when a toddler hands you their ringing toy phone, you answer it."

Gabriel crossed his arms and I interpreted the look in his eyes as: "Are you kidding me – you're interrupting me and Therese – go away."

I went back to my jigsaw puzzle and thought about a way to get him to see me instead of her.

The solution was obvious.

For the first and hopefully last time in my adult life, I peed myself. It felt warm, funny, and forbidden.

"Daddy," I called, but of course he didn't react to that name, so I walked over and pulled on his arm. "Daddy," I repeated.

Gabriel looked down at me with a question mark on his face.

"I think I need a clean diaper," I whispered.

His jaw dropped. "What?"

I looked down, pretending to be ashamed, which I was... sort of.

"Will you excuse me?" Gabriel muttered to Therese and took my hand.

"How the hell did that happen?" he asked when we got outside. "Why would you do it in there and not in the cabin?"

"I didn't know there were rules for when and where to pee," I said.

In our cabin he got a clean diaper from the bathroom and some baby wipes. "So what now? Do I give you a bath or how does this work?"

"I don't know," I said. "I would like to just shower. Can't a toddler shower?"

"If you can walk, you can stand, and if you can stand, you can shower," he said, breaking it down. "Let's just get you into the bath and then I'll hose you down."

"Hose me down?"

"Maybe you can do it yourself?" He walked to the phone on the wall and called Bruce.

"Hey, Bruce, can a toddler shower by themselves?" he asked.

"Okay, but if I'm standing next to her, she can wash herself right?

"What? No, I'm not getting in the shower with her.

"I don't care if I get wet... why can't she do it herself?

"But a two-year old can walk and talk and do stuff, right?

"Okay, yes, I understand."

He hung up and looked frustrated. "Bruce says it's normal for parents to take small children with them in the shower and I can do that, but that would mean for me to get naked in the shower with you and that's *not* happening. So I'm afraid we are back to the bath."

I don't know what possessed me to say it. Maybe it was his hurtful comment from earlier about not being into Goth girls or his comment from earlier today about the hair on his arms standing up at the thought of me giving him a bath. "What are you afraid of?" I asked provocatively.

He arched a brow. "What am *I* afraid of?"

"Yes. You said you were used to showering with people, so why not me?"

"Because you're a girl."

"So?"

He swallowed hard. "That would be awkward, not to mention wrong."

"Wrong how?"

"You're my niece, Cia."

"Right now I'm your daughter and you're my father and I'm two years old," I pointed out, intentionally putting him under pressure.

He shifted his balance from one foot to the other. "I'm sorry, but I can't do that."

"But you already offered to let me see you naked."

"I know, but that was different."

"Why?"

"Because you wouldn't be naked at the same time."

"And what's the difference?"

He gave me an "are-you-serious?" laugh and said, "Only a girl would ask such a question."

"I'm sorry for being so stupid, but explain it to me."

"I'm a dude and being in a shower with a naked girl could potentially make my body… react."

"But you don't think of me that way. You already told me."

"Of course not, but I'm only human and I just returned from a year in Afghanistan."

"Meaning what? You haven't had sex in a year?"

He puffed out air and nodded.

"But if you had just banged Therese, you could do it?" I asked and felt that little knife-twist in my heart.

"Why would you drag her into this?"

"You like her." It came out as an accusation.

Gabriel looked back as if he could see through the cabin wall and all the way inside the main house where we had left her. "Therese is a nice woman."

"Wow, so she's a woman and I'm a girl?"

He grinned. "That's a funny question, coming from someone dressed as pink cotton candy."

I plumbed down on the bed but quickly jumped up when I felt the wetness of my diaper. The warm feeling was gone, now it was just gross.

"Whatever," I muttered grumpily. "Just get me out of this dirty diaper already."

He nudged me into the bathroom and turned the water faucets on. "I feel like all I do here is dress you and undress you," he said.

I didn't say anything.

As humiliating, annoying, and embarrassing as this might be, at least he was with me and not her. There were a ton of things I would have much rather been doing with him like playing cards, pool, or even foosball, but this was still better than being ignored.

"You know what Bruce said." Gabriel was pulling my shirt over my head and left me topless. In a reflex I covered my breasts.

"You'll have to let me wash you everywhere this time."

"I know," I murmured low and lifted my leg when he pulled my leggings off. I didn't look when he took the diaper off but it felt cool on my skin where it had been.

"Come on, get in the tub," he said and took my hand to support me.

I sat down and pulled my legs up in front of me to cover my chest.

"You know that I've already seen your body, right?" he asked in a no-nonsense voice. "I think it's better if you just relax and let me wash you. Lean back and close your eyes if you're shy."

"I'm not shy," I lied.

"Good, because as Bruce has said many times, this is not a sexual thing. Why don't you try to play along and pretend that you're really just a little girl and that I'm your father."

I sighed and closed my eyes. "I'll try."

"Do you want me to hum that song from yesterday?" he asked.

"Sure, why not."

The water was warm and his hands were washing me in a firm yet gentle manner while he hummed a little and then he started chuckling low. "Once when I was a Boy Scout I went on a week-long camping trip. I don't remember what I did to deserve it, but I ended up scrubbing ten pounds of Russell potatoes."

I opened one eye. "Are you saying washing me reminds you of scrubbing potatoes."

"Apparently so, since the memory just popped up."

"Gee, thanks – you really know just how to flatter a girl."

"Sorry, close your eyes and think of something else while I wash your private parts."

I closed my eyes, but every nerve ending was alert when he gently and quickly washed my breasts. If I had been brave, I would have asked him what he thought of them, since he was the first guy to see me topless. But I wasn't, so I kept quiet and tried to keep my heart from galloping out of my chest when he gently pushed my legs aside and washed me between them. The cloth brushed my most sensitive spot and I involuntarily jerked.

"I'm sorry, did I hurt you?" he asked

I opened my eyes and looked into his concerned brown gaze. "No, I'm just not used to anyone touching me down there. It's very sensitive."

"I'll be more careful."

"Okay, try again."

Very gently he wiped me clean and washed my inner thighs and all the way between my cheeks.

I couldn't look at him but leaned my head back and closed my eyes.

"I think that should do it," he said softly. "Are you cold?"

"No, the water is nice and hot," I answered before I realized what he might be hinting at. I opened my eyes and saw him quickly look away. Yep, my nipples were hard and pointy.

He got up from the floor to get a towel. I should have just said something like "Hey, remember what you said about showering with a naked woman and potentially getting an unwanted reaction? Well, it's the same thing for women – just because my body reacts doesn't mean I want you." The old me would have said something like that, but Black wasn't here and as Cia, I didn't have the same armor or toughness.

I missed being Black.

CHAPTER 8
The Ugly Duckling

Cia

The rest of that day went by quickly. It turns out toddlers can't play pool, but we played with some of the things in the common area, and at one point we even wrestled in the mattress area where pillow fights were allowed.

I could have told you that everything was horrible and bad, but it would be a lie. I had fun with Gabriel and we laughed together like I haven't laughed since forever.

The guy is strong and threw me around like I weighed nothing, but I got him back and smacked him right in his face with a pillow. That had him check his nose to see if it was bleeding, and in his minute of distraction I wrestled him to the floor and shouted in triumph.

He didn't have to carry me anymore but he took my hand whenever we went from one place to the other, and a little part of me liked it.

Dinner was a huge improvement as I could have solid food. Gabriel still had to feed me but that was okay; I even teased him by annoying the hell out of him like a little baby bird constantly interrupting papa bird's own meal. Every time he tried to take a bite from his plate I would elbow him and point to my own mouth with a sad face saying feed me please.

He knew I was messing with him and elbowed me back a few times.

Bruce shot us a few hard looks and I figured we were a minute or two from being chastised, but we made it through dinner without any confrontations with the mad scientist.

As a toddler, my bedtime was a little later than a baby's, which meant I got to stay up until eight o'clock. Bruce recommended to Gabriel which book to read me for my bedtime ritual, and agreed that since I had already had a bath today we could skip that part tonight.

Halle-freaking-lujah.

The others around us were playing and talking, and I noticed one of the men in the group kept looking at me.

He was the father of another girl who was a bit older than me and I figured that just like Gabriel and me, they weren't really father and daughter.

While I was busy drawing with crayons, the man came over to speak to Gabriel.

"Hello, I'm Mark," he introduced himself.

Gabriel shook the man's hand. "Nice to meet you, I'm G."

"That's my daughter Anna over there." He pointed to the woman, who had to be in her mid-twenties. "You have a cute daughter, what's her name?" he asked Gabriel and gave me a smile.

"Her name is Cia," Gabriel said and lowered his voice. "And she's really my niece."

"Ohh, your niece. That's nice."

"Are you related to your daughter?" Gabriel asked.

The man, who looked to be in his late thirties, shook his head. "We're good friends and enjoy coming here."

I was glad that Gabriel asked the same question I was thinking. "You've been here more than once?"

"Yes, I come here a few times a year."

Bruce came over and gave Gabriel a discreet nod in my direction. "I think it's bedtime for the little one," he said.

"All right," Gabriel got up and took my hand. "Time to go, Candy," he teased and waved at Mark. "Nice to meet you."

"Same to you; maybe we could let the girls have a play date tomorrow," he called after us.

"Uh-huh," Gabriel answered on the way out and squeezed my hand. "Wanna have a play date?" he whispered.

I didn't answer until we were outside. "I've never had a play date in my life."

Gabriel grinned. "Well, this whole place is a first, so why don't we just take a day at a time? Right now it'll be my first time reading a goodnight story."

He brushed my teeth, and dressed me in pink Barbie pajamas before he tucked me in and lay down next to me, propped up on his elbow.

"Are you ready for your goodnight story, Candy?" he asked and brushed a bit of my hair away from my face.

I rested my head on the pillow and smiled. This was a new one for me too. My mother never took time to read to me, at least not that I can remember.

"This is the story of 'The Ugly Duckling' by Hans Christian Andersen," Gabriel started and continued reading aloud for a long time.

It was calming to listen to him and he even made funny voices when he imitated some of the characters.

"So the duckling was allowed to remain on trial for three weeks, but there were no eggs. Now the tomcat was the master of the house, and the hen was mistress, and they always said, 'We and the world,' for they believed themselves to be half the world, and the better half too. The duckling thought that others might hold a different opinion on the subject, but the hen would not listen to such doubts.

"'Can you lay eggs?' she asked.

"'No.'

"'Then have the goodness to hold your tongue.'

"'Can you raise your back, or purr, or throw out sparks?' said the tomcat.

"'No.'

"'Then you have no right to express an opinion when sensible people are speaking.

"So the duckling sat in a corner, feeling very low-spirited, till the sunshine and the fresh air came into the room through the open door," Gabriel read on.

I had never actually heard the whole story and found it touching and sad. When he closed the book he leaned in and kissed my forehead and whispered, "Sleep well, Candy."

"Sleep well, Daddy G," I whispered back and smiled with my eyes closed.

⟨ ∞ ⟩

Gabriel

For a while I lay awake listening to her soft breathing next to me. I had read "The Ugly Duckling" to her and was contemplating picking up my other book for entertainment, as it was too early to sleep. I wondered how Cia did it. Yesterday she fell asleep early too, but then again, she had complained she was sleep-deprived when I first met her.

It was amazing to see the transformation in her since we had arrived yesterday. The physical change was obvious, as she looked innocent and young compared to the hardcore exterior she had arrived in, but that was only half of it.

I turned my head to look at her again because a sudden thought appeared to me. I'm sure she had lip, nose, and ear piercings when I met her, but after she removed them I hadn't seen any holes in her skin, had I?

I was studying her closely in the dampened light when she opened her eyes.

"Will you stop breathing on me?" she asked.

"Why don't you have any holes from your piercings?" I asked her and turned her face to get a better look.

"Good night, G," she said and closed her eyes again.

"Hey, answer me," I demanded and used my thumb to force her eye open.

She batted my hand away and turned to face me.

"I don't have any holes because all my piercings, except two, were fake."

I touched her earlobe and felt the hole with my fingers. "You only have holes in your ears?"

"Yes."

"But how did the others stick?"

"It's just small rings that you squeeze tight around your nose, lips, or ears. I've been doing it for years."

"But why not get the real thing done?"

She was close to me and rubbed her nose. "I don't like pain much and I didn't have the money to get real piercings."

"So if you had the money, you would do it?"

"If I had money I would get a tattoo," she said.

"What kind of tattoo?"

"I would want a real nice compass between my shoulder blades." She pointed with her hand.

"Because you like to travel?" I guessed.

"I wouldn't know. I've never been outside of Washington State," she admitted.

"Then why a compass?"

"Because I've been lost for so long. It would be a symbol of hope to me… that I'll one day find my way."

Fuck – that hit me right in the solar plexus.

"Do you want to see my tattoos?" I asked her.

Her eyes lit up. "You have tattoos?"

"Uh-huh, seven." I removed my t-shirt and turned to show her the tattoo on my shoulder blade; it was the sapper army logo saying *Combat Engineer*.

Her fingers trailed over the tattoo taking in all the details, and then she got up on her knees to look at my other tattoos with eyes full of fascination.

"The other six are all Hawaiian tribal tattoos." I lifted my arm for her to see the side of my ribs.

"They are beautiful," she said and touched them gently with her hands. I was grateful that I didn't have any tattoos on the lower part of my body or I might have been in trouble with the way she looked at me and touched me.

I ended the show by pulling my t-shirt back on and got up from the bed to go brush my teeth.

"I like the idea about a compass, it's cute," I said.

When I came back in, she was once again lying on her side with her eyes closed.

I was grateful for that, because today had been a bit more challenging than yesterday. First of all, I was starting to really like her. Cia was the strangest combination of vulnerability and strength. One minute she would be verbally tearing Bruce to pieces or challenging me in a fight. And then the next minute she would be playing with crayons or making a joke. Her humor was starting to show more often and on several occasions today, I had managed to make her laugh, which always cracked me up because she made the funniest little grunts like a pig and the more she did it, the harder I laughed.

I had volunteered for this whole therapy thing out of a sense of family obligation and because I felt sorry for her. But now, I was starting to care for her; she was such a fighter and smart as hell. You would think I would be excited to discover that my niece was actually a cool kid underneath the hideous black make-up, but I was freaked out over what happened when I bathed her earlier. I didn't mean to, but when I saw her reaction to my touches, I got a hard-on from the sight of her hard nipples.

Normally, I wouldn't consider myself a pervert who would be turned on by his niece, so I blamed it on the fact that I hadn't been with a woman in almost thirteen months and reminded myself that Cia wasn't even that hot… I mean she was cute in an innocent way, but nothing like the women I'm usually attracted to. Heidi, my last girlfriend, was a gorgeous dancer and model. Cia was pretty at best.

I wasn't worried though. Therese had slipped me her number today and I was planning on making her help me break my unwanted celibacy real soon. She seemed eager enough to do it, and as soon as Cia got out of this baby/toddler phase and could be on her own, I planned to spend some quality time with Therese.

Despite my attempts to read, the book didn't catch my interest tonight and instead I found myself studying Cia again as she was lying with her back to me. I love the idea of her tattoo and even more do I like the idea of being her compass. I know I can help her and that I want to see her succeed.

CHAPTER 9
Nightmares

Gabriel

It was her crying that woke me up hours later – small sniffing sounds and muttering that made no sense.

It wasn't violent, so I didn't wake her up but tugged her into my arms and kissed her on the top of her head, hoping that my care for her would somehow reach her in her dreams.

When morning came she stirred and stretched and turned into me so that her face was against my collarbone. I registered it but was still too sleepy to move.

"Good morning," I mumbled and tried to open my eyes.

I got a muffled response and then we kind of drifted off to sleep a little. It wasn't on purpose that I farted; I was just relaxed and one, I'm a guy and two, I've been in the military for nine years. You get pretty desensitized to that sort of thing. It wasn't a small fart either, and for a moment I stiffened, waiting for her to get upset like Heidi, my last girlfriend, would have been. But to my surprise Cia just laughed.

"I'm sorry." I said. "What's so funny?"

Her grin was infectious, and her puffy eyes and morning hair made her look cute in an approachable way. Who knew that inside that black armor she wore the first time I met her, there was this sweet innocent soul?

I propped myself up on my elbow.

"Hey, you know what?" I said.

"What?" She mirrored me and propped herself up to.

"I like you a lot better like this."

"Like what?"

"You know, without all the piercings and the dark clothes."

"Yes, ugly morning face and stinky breath is much more me," she joked.

"No, I'm serious." I assured her.

"Why?"

"Because you're more relaxed and fun. What do you say that when you get to be a teenager and we can maybe leave here, I'll take you shopping in the nearest town? I would hate for you to have to wear the black clothes when we leave here."

She bit her lip and knitted her brows. "I don't know."

"If you ever want a boyfriend, you should lose the Goth look."

"What makes you think I want a boyfriend and how do you even know I don't have one already?"

I arched a brow. "Do you have a boyfriend?"

"No," she said. "Nor do I want one."

"Why not?"

"Because you just confirmed that guys only care about looks… and the ones I'm attracted to would never be interested in me anyway."

I could have said she was wrong, but I was guilty as charged. I wouldn't be interested in her either, especially not in her hideous Goth outfit.

"I sometimes wonder," she said; "if our eyes saw souls instead of bodies, how different our ideal of beauty would be."

"True… It would have saved me a few heartbreaks," I said dryly.

Her eyes were asking me to elaborate.

"I've been attracted to beauty that turned out to be only skin deep a few times. It's disappointing," I explained.

"I bet your girlfriends were all very beautiful," she pondered out loud.

"Uh-huh." I nodded. "But not always very nice."

She looked into my eyes. "There are some people who are both beautiful on the inside and the outside."

I shrugged. "If so, I would like to meet them."

She took a second before she answered and I got the feeling she was weighing her words. "If you want to meet someone that fits the description, look yourself in the mirror."

Before I really understood the depth of her compliment she had moved away and was sitting on the side of the bed.

"Thanks," I said to her back, but she didn't react.

Instead she changed the subject. "I'm hungry – what time is breakfast?"

I looked at my watch. "Eight-fifteen; breakfast is in fifteen minutes."

"Okay, good."

"Can I take a quick shower before I help you get ready?"

"Sure."

Ten minutes later I had showered and dressed. Cia was sitting on the bed reading "The Ugly Duckling" when I came back from the bathroom with her toothbrush.

"Okay, open up your mouth, princess," I said and brushed her teeth. When I was done she went to rinse and spit in the bathroom.

"I think they want you to put on the same toddler clothes as yesterday," I said, since I didn't see any other clothes she could wear.

"That's okay, I'm no sissy..." she said and this time she didn't even cover her breasts when I undressed her. I was pleased to see that she was getting used to my closeness and trusted me.

Breakfast was interesting. We were told a new client would arrive around three that day and asked to stay out of sight if possible.

That explained why we hadn't seen anyone when we first arrived and in a way it made sense, since arriving at a camp where people dressed like babies and toddlers would make any sane person run away as fast as possible.

We had another session with Bruce after breakfast and I noticed that Cia was sitting with her legs crossed really tight.

"Do you have to use the bathroom?" I whispered as we waited for him to join us.

"Yes," she whispered back.

I knew she hadn't done number two for at least twenty-four hours, and I could understand if she was pressured with the amount of food she ate for dinner last night and breakfast this morning.

"If you've got to go, we could go to the cabin." Not that I looked forward to changing her diaper again, but I would do it if I had to.

"No, I'm hoping he'll let me get out of the diaper after this session," she whispered.

Bruce entered and took his seat at the table. "How are we doing?" he asked and smiled at us both.

"I think Cia really needs to go to the bathroom, but she won't do it until you let her out of the diaper."

"But you already wet your diaper yesterday without problems," he said to her.

"Been there, done it, don't want to do it again," she argued.

"All right, but then let's just focus on our session today. Anything you want to talk about?"

"No," Cia said shortly.

Clashing Colors #1 BLACK

"And you?" He looked at me.

"I just want to say that I'm super proud of Cia and I think she's doing amazing."

"Good."

He turned to her. "Any nightmares or memories from your past that are popping up, Cia?"

"Nope," she said and uncrossed and crossed her legs again. She was beginning to get very red in the face and looked to be in pain.

Bruce frowned. "There are many things I would like to discuss with you, but I don't think now is the best time. Why don't you two go to the cabin and change into your child costume?"

A heavy sigh of relief came from Cia.

"You are now five years old and can use the toilet by yourself, although you still need help to dress, bathe, and brush your teeth," he instructed.

Cia was already up from her chair and out the door.

I gave Bruce a quick "Talk to you later."

We almost ran to the cabin, where she started to undress herself. I wanted to help but she hissed at me, "I got this," and disappeared into the bathroom and slammed the door with her foot.

We had certainly hit the age of independence, alright.

I waited outside the cabin and the look on her face, when she came out, was pure bliss.

"Feel better?" I asked.

"A trillion times better," she said with a soft smile and sat down. In her hands she held a mint-green skirt and a purple t-shirt with a printed-on pony.

"Who do you think picks out these clothes," she asked.

"I don't know; Therese maybe?" I suggested.

"Hmm... whomever it is, the person sure has a love for colors."

She sat for a minute and fidgeted with the print on the shirt. "I used to have one of these."

"You had a pony?"

"Not a real pony, but I had one of these toys. They're called My Little Pony."

"Oh, nice," I said distractedly because I had just spotted Therese outside the main house and she was looking good in her summer dress, with her long hair blowing slightly in the breeze.

"I think I might have stolen it actually."

That made me turn my head and look at Cia, whose eyes were glazed over.

"What did you say?"

"I stole the pony from a neighbor girl who forgot it on her lawn. I hid it in my room so no one would take it away from me."

"Why did you steal it?" I asked slowly.

"Because I was jealous and didn't have any toys myself."

"You didn't have *any* toys?"

She shook her head. "Except for Kitty."

"Who is Kitty?"

"My Hello Kitty was a stuffed animal that I took everywhere. I couldn't sleep without her.

"You still have her?"

"No, my mom burned her."

"What? No mother would do something that cruel. Are you sure she burned your teddy bear?"

Cia was biting the inside of her cheek. "My mom was a mean drunk, and it happened on one of those nights when she blamed me for ruining her life."

"Why did she think you ruined her life?"

She snorted. "Classic story. Sixteen-year-old virgin infatuated with rich pretty boy who says all the right things. She wants to make him happy and gives him what he wants. She ends up pregnant and alone and rejected by him, with her friends fleeing like rats, and her parents angry at her. And who gets the blame? The stupid baby who ruined her life."

"You're not stupid, Cia," I said and stroked her hair. She jerked away.

"I think you need to help me change into this Pony costume."

We didn't speak while I helped her change her clothes. What she had revealed made me grateful for the mom I have who has always given me support and love. Unlike Cia, I have never lacked any toys or comfort, and I wished I could somehow share it with Cia.

I couldn't. No one could. It was too late and the damage was already done. Or was it?

Later that day when Cia was drawing with crayons, which she could do for hours in her own little bubble, I spoke to Therese, who helped me find a multicolored My Little Pony in one of the toy boxes in the play area and wrap it in gift paper. I wished I could have gotten Cia a new one, but at least this one would be hers and not stolen.

"Sugar," I said and went to sit next to her. I wasn't prepared for what I saw.

Using only crayons she had drawn a spot-on portrait of me and in the lower corner she had managed to draw the sapper logo I have tattooed on my back.

"Wow, did you make this?" I asked, although it was a rhetorical question since she had been alone the whole time. "This is incredible."

"If you like it, you can have it," she said and handed it to me.

"I love it. Thank you."

She gave me a genuine smile. "It's nothing. I make portraits for a living, I'm a street artist," she said.

"But you're insanely talented, you know that, right?"

She shrugged. "I just like to draw."

Then I remembered and handed her the gift I had been holding behind my back. "This is for you, my dear."

"For me?" Her eyes widened in surprise.

"Yes, for you."

She opened the gift and held up the little plastic toy, which was the size of her hand, and then she turned it over in the air. "This is Rainbow Dash, she was one of my favorites in the movies."

"There were movies?"

"Yes... cartoons."

"That's nice."

We were interrupted by Bruce, who cleared his throat behind us. "Feeling better, Cia?" he asked.

"Yes. Thank you." She looked up at him and for the first time I didn't read hostility on her face.

"That's a nice drawing," he said and pointed to my portrait.

"Cia made it," I said, not hiding the pride in my voice.

He sat down on a chair beside us and asked to see it.

"How long have you been an artist?" he asked.

"I don't remember, but I started making portraits for money when I was seventeen."

"You forgot to sign it," he said and handed it back to her.

She picked up a black crayon and put it to the lower right side of the paper, but there was a moment of hesitation before she wrote "To G from Cia."

"Interesting," Bruce commented, and he had the look of a sly fox. "What name do you normally sign your portraits with?"

"I just write a B, nothing else."

"B for Black?"

"Yes."

"And yet you chose to sign this one as Cia – why is that?"

"I don't know, it just felt right."

"I'm wondering if you would be interested in helping me out with an art project while you're here."

"What do you mean?"

"I've been planning on decorating the dining room for a while, but I'm wondering if maybe you would like to have fun with it..."

"Like make pictures for the walls?"

"Yes... why not?"

"Sure, what kind of pictures would you like?"

"Whatever you feel inspired to make," he replied. "Just tell me what you need. We already have some art supplies here and if you need more I can get them for you."

Cia looked intrigued. "I just need large pieces of good-quality paper and quality pencils,"

"But what if I wanted some pictures in colors, could you do that?"

"I don't know, I've only ever worked with pencils"

Bruce smiled. "Then this will be a challenge for you."

Cia was quiet for a few seconds before she spoke. "I think I could do it."

"Wonderful. Therese can show you where we keep our art supplies," he said and got up from the chair. "Also, since you are now five years old, it might be fun for you to take a hike with your father. Nature here is breathtaking."

"What about boots?" I asked since Cia only had sneakers on.

"I'm sure her black boots will do fine for a hike; I'll have them brought to your cabin," Bruce said and got up to leave. "Enjoy your day; I'll see you at dinner."

"I've been dying to hike ever since we got here," I said and was pleased when Cia seemed as eager about the idea as I did.

Ten minutes later we set off with a water bottle each and big smiles. I was holding Cia's hand and she didn't object. It was crazy to think how much she had moved mentally in the last forty-eight hours.

"I think I already have an idea for a painting," Cia said and whistled happily.

"Wanna tell me about it?"

"Nope, I'm just starting to see it in my head... you'll have to wait for the finished painting."

We walked for about an hour and spoke mostly about nature and my memories of being a recruit and doing survival drills in the forest.

"They really had you walk through ice-cold water?"

"Yes. Carrying our bags above the water. One of my pals lost his balance and got ducked under with his backpack."

"Oh no."

I grinned. "He had no dry clothes for days."

"How is that funny? Didn't he get sick?"

"It's not funny, but shit like that happens in the army and you learn how to deal with it."

"Yeah, I can relate to the dealing with shit part," she said. "I spent my first four days as a homeless person on a park bench and it rained every night."

"And you were only a child."

"I was fourteen and scared shitless."

"Was there something specific that made you run away?"

I knew the answer instinctively from the look on her face. *Yes*, there had been something specific, but she closed down on me and wouldn't answer.

"I don't want to talk about it," she said.

When she tried to walk away, I grabbed her wrist and pulled her into my arms. "Hey, I'm sorry, but whatever happened, it's over now... no one is going to hurt you anymore. I promise"

If I had done this yesterday, I know she would have pushed me away, but today she didn't. Instead she stood passively and allowed me to hold her tight.

"Do you want to go back?" I asked her after a minute. There was no reason to push my luck, and I understood that she was already far out of her comfort zone.

When we walked back I said, "I almost forgot, that guy Mark came over to talk to me while you were drawing. We agreed that you two girls can have a play date after dinner tonight."

"Did you now?" she said dryly.

"Yes, I wanted to ask you but he said that a father doesn't ask a five-year-old for her opinion and that it would be fun for both of you."

"Huh."

"You wanna hear something funny?"

"What?"

"He literally asked me if you play nice." I laughed. "As if you were some sort of danger to his daughter or a dog that might bite his precious poodle."

Cia rolled her eyes. "That guy takes this role-playing thing way too seriously."

"I know, but now that we are getting used to it, though, it's not so bad." I pulled her under my arm and used my knuckles to rub the top of her head. "Although you'll never feel like a daughter to me... more like a fun little sister."

She gave me a playful elbow to my ribs. "First of all, you big dork, I'm not fun, and I'm not your little sister. I'm not even your real niece."

"I know, but you let me call you Candy, and Sugar, and Sweetie and stuff, and I like that."

"I would never let you call me any of that in real life, you know that, right?"

I grinned. "Yeah, I figured that much."

"Good, just wanted to make that clear."

"Pull my finger," I said with an earnest expression.

"Why?" she asked with confusion on her face.

"Just pull it," I said and leaned forward.

She did it and I don't know what was bigger, my grin or my fart, but I was clapping my hands, amused at how naïve she was.

Cia placed her hands on her hips but smiled. "Very funny."

"Ohh, come on, every dad does that joke with his kid – you can't go through a simulated childhood without being fooled at least once. I can't tell you how many times I pulled my dad's finger."

"Why would you do it more than once if you knew what was going to happen?" she asked.

"Because it was fun and it was our thing... you know. Didn't anyone ever pull that trick on you?"

She shook her head. "No, my mom never did that."

"Didn't your mom have any boyfriends?"

Her smile vanished and a dark cloud fell on her face. "Yes, she had boyfriends."

I knew I had stumbled on a bomb in that minefield Bruce had described as her childhood. And I wasn't so sure I had the right safety equipment to detonate it, so I carefully withdrew to a safe topic and asked her how old she would guess the trees in this part of the forest to be.

CHAPTER 10
The Play Date

Cia

"Hey, I'm Anna, I'm seven," the woman said and gave me a good long looking-over.

"I'm Cia and I'm supposed to be five, I think."

"Do you want to play with Barbies?" she asked.

"No, not really – how about a board game?" I suggested and couldn't believe Anna actually broke into a pout.

"Daddy," she cried out, "Cia doesn't want to play with Barbies."

What the hell?

Mark, who was sitting close by and talking with Gabriel looked over. "Sweetie, try to find a compromise, maybe you can play ten minutes of Barbie and then do what Cia wants to do."

"No, Daddy, I don't want to compromise," she pouted.

"Baby, I want you to be a good girl. You know what happens to naughty girls."

Anna lowered her eyes. "Yes, Daddy," she said in a tiny voice.

I was still temporarily in shock that she was so invested in the role-play but agreed to compromise and picked up a male doll that she handed me.

"You can be Ken and I'll be Barbie," she said.

"Okay, what do you want me to do?"

"Well I don't know, you're the man, you're in charge."

"Excuse me?"

"Hi, Ken, how was your day, would you like something to drink or maybe a massage before dinner?" she said in an annoyingly high-pitched voice.

Okay, here's my two cents. The brilliant thing about playing with a person who is a cuckoo is that you can have fun with it. I made my best imitation of a deep male voice and said; "Hey, Barbie, honey bunny, you look good. I don't want anything, my dear, except maybe to rub your feet and make sure you feel good... would you like me to cook dinner tonight?"

Anna shot me a displeased gaze but continued in that horrible voice.

"Oh no, Ken darling, you know my greatest joy is to please you, my dear. I made your favorite meal and I was thinking I could run you a hot bath."

"Only if you come with me, ha ha," I laughed in my deepest voice, trying not to crack up over the stupidity of two grown women playing with dolls.

"Sure, I'll come with you and do that thing you like so much," Anna purred.

"Oh, you mean wash my hair," I said a wiggled the doll from side to side.

"No, that other thing," Anna said amorously.

Eww! I threw Ken down. "I don't want to play this game. It's stupid."

"No, it's not," Anna said and tried to make me pick Ken up again.

"If you want to play, we can find a board game or something," I said and felt damn proud for setting my personal boundaries. I don't know in which disturbed reality Anna lives, but I'm not stupid and I have no interest in playing a porn version of Barbie and Ken for her amusement.

She pouted but agreed to play Candy Land.

"Daddy," she called out to Mark. "We need more players – can you and Cia's daddy come and play with us?"

"What do you say, sweetie?" Mark said in a very strict parental voice.

"Please, Daddy."

I swear the look of male pride that Mark shot at Gabriel made me want to vomit. I don't know what kind of problems Anna had, but I doubted they could be fixed in two weeks. That woman had to learn how to stand up for herself, because it creeped me out how Mark acted like her goddamn owner or something.

"Good girl. Yes, we'll play with you," Mark said and joined us at the small table where I had already spread out the game.

"Your Daddy told me you went to the woods today," Mark said to me with a smile.

"Uh-huh," I answered, picked my first card, and moved three steps forward.

"And as I explained to him, we like the woods too," he lowered his voice. "There are no cameras."

I honestly didn't know the hidden meaning of his words but I gave him a strained smile.

"Your Daddy mentioned he is looking forward to a bit of private time, and I offered to babysit you if needed."

Gabriel at least had the decency to try and dismiss that comment, but I knew it was true. Gabriel and Therese had been flirting since we arrived and he wanted to be alone with her. Most likely because he wanted to have sex with her.

I clenched my jaw and played the board game, but I didn't talk except short answers to direct questions.

I was happy when it was time to go to bed but more than ever I wished I could be alone. For someone like me, who is used to being alone eighty percent of the time, being with others constantly drains me.

I wished I could pause this stupid program and take a time-out to catch up to all the emotions inside me. Especially my jealousy toward Therese.

I had no right to feel possessive about Gabriel – it was lame – but try to explain that to the knot in your belly.

"Do you want a bath?" Gabriel asked me when we were back in the cabin.

"No," I said and curled up under the blanket still fully dressed. I didn't even want him to undress me or brush my teeth. I just wanted to be left alone.

"What's wrong?" he asked and sat down next to me.

"Nothing, I'm just tired."

"Hey, if I said something wrong, tell me."

I shrugged his hand off me and pulled the blanket over my head, trying desperately to stop my tears.

But I couldn't.

From deep inside my wounded soul, heartbreaking sounds of sorrow broke through and I had a complete meltdown, sobbing in a fetal position.

At first Gabriel tried to comfort me and when that didn't work, I heard him call Bruce, asking what to do, but even that didn't stop me.

I cried like... a five-year-old.

Gabriel

I had been warned about this, and knew it was to be expected. Still, to see it actually happen was worse than I could have ever imagined.

Cia was falling apart and I couldn't reach her. She was sobbing her eyes out, and after being with her for days it was impossible not to be deeply affected by her pain.

I didn't know what else to do but call Bruce.

He told me to let her cry and meet him outside the cabin.

When I closed the door behind me and took a seat on the small porch, I felt like the biggest piece of shit.

Two minutes later Bruce came walking calmly toward me and sat down with a satisfied smile.

"How can you look so happy when Cia is lying in there crying?" I asked. I really didn't like the guy at that moment.

"I'm happy for her, because we're finally at the point in her regression where some of the pain is stored. This is what we've been looking for."

"What do you mean? Are you saying that you've been waiting for her to break down? What are you, a sadist?"

He chuckled. "No I'm not a sadist. But you need to understand that before every breakthrough there is a breakdown."

"Why?"

"That's not important. It's just how it is. When Cia was a small girl she faced situations she couldn't cope or deal with, things that were painful or frightening."

"Didn't we all?" I asked.

"Yes. I want you to think of a child finding something so frightening that they store it in an inner closet and slam the door shut. For years the child doesn't dare to open that closet, and in time they forget what is actually in there and only remember that's it's something terrifying."

"All right." I had followed him this far.

"Now, our job is to empower Cia to open those rattling closets and confront whatever she has stored in there."

"How?"

"That depends on what is in there. But I can tell you that for the most part it's not half as frightening as people fear. You see, when we go back as adults and take a look at the frightening memory we have a different perspective and a new cognitive understanding. Let's say that the sound of dogs barking always makes you uncomfortable and you don't know why, since you like dogs in general. When we dive down you realize that as a child you were told something traumatic, such as your parents announcing their divorce or telling you that someone has died, and at the same time the neighbor's dog barked like crazy… years later you are left with that uncomfortable feeling every time you hear a barking dog even though you don't remember why."

"Okay, that make sense, I guess, but then what do I do about it?"

"As an adult you're able to cognitively separate the two and once you understand the reason, you can remind yourself that it's just a dog barking and it means nothing to you."

"But how do we find out why Cia is crying?" I said with a dampened soundtrack of her sobbing from inside the cabin.

Bruce smiled. "We ask her, of course."

"But what if she doesn't know?"

He arched a brow. "She might not know, but her body remembers and it will tell her if she listens."

"So what do I do now?"

"You wait."

"For what?"

"For her to be ready to talk."

"And when is that?"

"When she is calm and has digested all the sadness and fear that is running through her right now. She can't talk at the moment, and you should never seek to have a rational conversation with someone who is upset – they're not open to dialogue. My guess is that right now she just wants to be alone."

"So no bath tonight?"

"No, not unless she calms down and accepts your closeness. You don't want to overstep her boundaries."

"Is that a joke? I've been overstepping her boundaries ever since we got here," I said.

"Yes, well, sometimes it serves a purpose, but now we're on the right track and we need to give her time."

It sounded like the sobbing had slowed down.

Bruce patted my shoulder. "She'll feel better tomorrow, you'll see."

A bird landed on the ground in front of us and distracted us for a few seconds before it took off again.

"I think something happened with her mom's boyfriend," I said. "She got jumpy today when I asked about it."

Bruce tilted his head. "Interesting; good to know."

"Yeah, but I don't know what happened."

"It's good that you're watching for clues. Remember we're looking for hidden bombs, and something happened tonight to set off one from her early childhood. This could be important."

Bruce left and I went back inside the cabin. At that time Cia was no longer sobbing but quietly sniffling.

I didn't speak but brushed my teeth and climbed into bed without a word. For a few minutes I lay there wondering what to do; my instinct told me to offer my support, so I tested the waters by placing a hand on her back. She didn't jerk or shrug it off so I stroked her gently and then I moved a bit closer.

When I tried to pull at her shoulder she stiffened. She didn't want to turn around and face me, and I could respect that.

Instead I just brushed her arm gently, up and down, while humming that lullaby from the other night.

It didn't take more than five minutes before I could tell from her breathing that she had fallen asleep.

I had a ton of questions in my head and wasn't so sure I agreed with Bruce that tomorrow would make for an interesting day. I felt pretty shitty and afraid that something I had done or said had caused this reaction.

CHAPTER 11
Emotions

Cia

My favorite part of the camp was the food. Back at The Inn, Lee offered me a meal a day, but most days that just meant chicken and noodles, not that I was complaining or anything. But here, the variation and the quality were amazing. The others weren't as impressed as I was, but I couldn't get enough of breakfast muffins, fruit, and as many bagels as I could eat. I've been hungry most of my life, so I would go through this mental torture for the food alone.

My least favorite part of the camp was the mandatory therapy sessions with the mad scientist. Bruce was sharp and nothing escaped him. I've had counselors at school that were easy to distract or fool with lies, but this guy was like a freaking mind reader, and I didn't like it.

"You had a breakdown yesterday – do you want to tell me about it?" he asked when we sat in his office again.

"Not really," I said and crossed my arms.

"That's a shame. I would think that it served to show you something. Something you need to know and accept about yourself to move on and get better."

"And if I don't?" I asked.

"The closet is opened and you can look inside. It's a rare opportunity to clean it out, but if you slam the door shut again, it will just be a matter of time before the skeleton in it starts to rattle and cause trouble in your life.

"Can you speak English instead of that metaphorical BS?" I asked with a bit of Black's attitude.

"You know what I mean," he said.

"Yeah, I do. You want to know what I was thinking and feeling while I cried and felt sorry for myself."

"Yes."

"Well, I wish I could tell you but I don't know."

"But if you did know, what would you say?"

The answer popped into my head as clear as a neon sign.

"I was sad because I don't have a father."

He waited for me to elaborate.

"We were talking to Mark and Anna yesterday and Mark mentioned G wants some time for himself and offered to babysit me. I think it just made me feel unwanted."

"Excellent!" Bruce said with eagerness, "Do you see how that could correlate with your five-year-old-self?"

"Not really... I didn't lose my dad around that time, he was just never there."

"Ahh... but when did you become conscious of it? When did you start to compare yourself with other children and wonder why you didn't have a father?"

I bit my lower lip. "I don't remember. There's no specific time that comes to mind, but probably around that time."

"And here you are, finally having a great dad who gives you love and attention," Bruce said enthusiastically and pointed to Gabriel, "and then it turns out he doesn't want you either."

"I never said that," Gabriel protested.

"That's not important. What matters is that it brought out a feeling of what?" He looked at me.

"Of loneliness."

"Of loneliness," he repeated and left it hanging in the air for a few seconds. "Do you still feel lonely?"

I shot a side glance at Gabriel and thought about how he had been there for me last night and helped me fall asleep. "No," I answered.

"Good. That's good. Now let's talk about your father. Would you like to have him in your life?"

I took a long deep breath. "No, not anymore. I used to when I was a kid and dreamed that he would show up and take me to his house. Of course back then I imagined he couldn't find me, and that was the reason he hadn't come already."

"But now you know better?"

"Yeah, I know he's an ass."

"For letting you down."

"Yes."

"Do you hate your father?"

"Sometimes."

We continued on about my father for another twenty minutes and went over my only two disappointing interactions with the man, before I got so upset that I closed the session down and told Bruce I was done talking about my stupid dad.

Bruce pulled out a stack of cards and spread them out on the table.

"Do you see what these are?" he asked.

I read off their inscriptions. "Anger, rage, sadness, joy, euphoria, happiness, and many more."

"These are all emotions. Yes?" he said and I nodded.

"You have thirty seconds to categorize them in good and bad emotions. Starting now."

It was an easy task; it only took me ten seconds to separate the twenty cards into two piles.

"Which pile is good and which is bad?" he asked.

I pointed to the stack with anger and hatred. "Those are bad emotions."

"Why?"

"They just are. Everyone knows that. They make you feel bad inside."

"All right." He took the stack. "And I assume the ones in the other stack are the good emotions."

"Yes."

He provocatively started to shuffle the cards. "Wrong answer."

I leaned backed in my chair. "How can happiness be a bad emotion? Explain that to me," I said skeptically.

"There are no bad emotions, Cia. Emotions are just emotions. They all serve a purpose."

"A purpose?" I laughed, "You really shouldn't eat funny mushrooms before our sessions. It makes you say crazy shit, you know."

Bruce ignored my comment. "You said the emotions are bad because they hurt, right?"

"Yeah."

"But pain is a useful feeling that motivates us into action. Anger for instance is a very powerful fuel against injustice, wouldn't you agree?"

I shrugged. "I don't know."

"I think you do. Remember when you told me that you were once arrested for protesting against the closure of a homeless shelter?"

I nodded.

"That's an example of using anger as a fuel."

"But that anger got me arrested." I scoffed.

"I would say that it was your actions that got you arrested. The organizers of that rally should have made sure they had a permit to protest."

I looked out the window and wished I could be out there instead of stuck inside this office. Bruce's eyes followed mine and he got up to open a window.

"Let me try to break this down for you, Cia: emotions serve us as a compass. Without emotions it would be hard to navigate what is right for us and what isn't. But we must apply a filter between our emotions and our behavior.

Gabriel and I exchanged a quick glance.

Bruce patiently explained. "I'll give you an example. Let's say you see Therese and Gabriel flirting."

"Excuse me." Gabriel cleared his throat and squirmed in his seat.

"Don't worry, it's just an example," Bruce explained while I narrowed my eyes and wondered what the fucker was up to.

"Let's pretend that you felt jealous because of the attention your daddy was giving this other woman. It would be very normal for any child to feel threatened by someone else who could potentially steal their dad away. Especially for a child who isn't sure about her daddy's love – wouldn't you agree?"

"Theoretically," I said.

"Good, so for the sake of the example we're assuming that you're jealous of Therese for stealing your father's attention. What do you think your body is trying to tell you with the jealousy emotion?"

"I don't know."

"Of course you do. How does it feel to be jealous?"

I could answer that right off the bat, as it was a feeling I was very familiar with. "It feels horrible."

"Yes, and we already established that the pain's job is to hurt enough to get our attention. Maybe your body is letting you experience the pain of jealousy to remind you that what you have is important to you. Your daddy means a lot to you and you don't want to lose him. The emotion itself is true, pure, and justified. Does that make sense?"

I nodded, because it actually did make sense.

"Now, what you do with the emotion is up to you. If you're smart, you'll use your insight to strengthen your bond to him by telling him how much he means to you.

But often people aren't smart when it comes to jealousy and they'll blame and punish others for their own insecurities.

I leaned forward. "So what you're saying is that there are no bad emotions, just bad behavior?"

"Exactly." Bruce smiled. "You have a wonderful way of simplifying the complicated; I like that about you."

If he was fishing for me to say I liked him back, he could fish all day – it wasn't happening.

"So to sum it up," he continued, "your anger with your dad is a perfectly normal *emotion*, but if you're actively punishing him by making bad decisions in your life, then that is destructive behavior and the only person suffering would be yourself."

My head felt deep-fried when we walked out of the office and to my disappointment I still had to be a girl, although Bruce told me I was now six years old.

"What do you want to do?" Gabriel asked me and the answer was obvious.

"I want to paint."

It was a perfect escape and a place where I could quietly go over all the things Bruce had brought up.

The mad scientist might actually have a few good points. How he knew about my jealousy of Therese I would never know, but it just showed me that I was right. The guy had an eerie ability to look into my brain and read my thoughts.

It made sense that the meltdown I had yesterday would have been a natural response of a five-year-old who acknowledged that her daddy didn't want her, and if I remembered right, I probably never cried like that at home. My mom would have flipped out on me and beat me to make me stop.

I made a sketch of the image I had in my head and transferred it with pencil strokes to a big canvas while thoughts roamed around my head.

So I had a shitty dad, but lots of people were in that situation and still made the most of their lives. Why would I let his failure define me?

I wouldn't. Not any longer.

"What are you doing?"

The voice made me look back over my shoulder to see Anna watching me.

"I'm painting."

"Oh, cool, I want to paint too," she said.

It annoyed me, but I couldn't really say no, since it wasn't my private place or even my articles.

"Suit yourself." I focused on my own painting.

"What should I paint?" Anna asked in that annoying little-girl voice.

I didn't answer so she started calling out to her dad, loudly. Mark was talking to Gabriel at a nearby table. He made a few suggestions and Anna finally decided on a dog.

It was hard to focus with her constant chitchat.

"Daddy wants to know if you want him to babysit you... you can come with us to the forest, if you want," she said.

"No thanks."

"Why not? It's fun, and there are so many good games we can play there."

"Like what?" I said dismissively.

"You know... Daddy-daughter games."

No, I didn't know because I've never played any daddy-daughter games and had no clue what she was referring to, so I lowered my pencil to look at her. "What do you mean?"

She winked at me. "My favorite game is when I've been a naughty girl and Daddy disciplines me. We call it the P game." She lowered her name to a whisper. "You know, P for punishment."

"Your daddy hits you?" I asked with concern – surely that wasn't part of the program.

"Yes," she purred and it had me so confused. "But afterwards we play the... ehh..." – she looked thoughtful – "let's call it the snail game... and he gives me lots of kisses to make me happy again."

"The snail game. What is that?"

She rolled her eyes and stepped close enough to whisper in my ears. "You know, the snail between your legs, the one that tickles when your daddy kisses it."

I was stunned and didn't answer. Was this woman seriously calling her clitoris a snail and telling me that her "pretend" daddy licked her after spanking her. It's not that I'm a prude, but I honestly don't care for other people telling me about their sex life. Unfortunately, Anna misread my stunned silence and kept talking. "Have you ever seen your daddy's snake?"

She turned her head and looked over at Gabriel. "Your dad is gorgeous; he can babysit me anytime he likes."

That's it!

I slammed down the pencil and marched right out of there.

"Where are you going, honey?" Gabriel called out, but I was fuming with anger and didn't stop to answer. Instead I went straight to the common area where I found Bruce, who was with a young man around twenty and his mom. The guy was wearing the black and yellow baby jumpsuit and looked miserable sitting close to his mom on the couch.

"Bruce, can I talk to you for a second?" I said and tried my best to conceal to the newcomers how angry I was.

"Certainly, why don't we step outside?" he said and excused himself to the mom and son.

Gabriel caught up to us and we all went outside to the empty playground.

"You look upset, Cia," Bruce observed.

I shot him an angry glance. "You tell me right now, what kind of fucked-up place is this?"

He tilted his head with a speculative expression on his face. "Care to share what has gotten you so upset?"

"I'm on to you and your perverted little scheme," I shouted and pointed a finger accusingly at him. "You are trying to make G and me have sex."

Gabriel gasped and Bruce lifted an eyebrow, which was the closest thing to a full-blown hissy fit I had ever seen from this permanently calm man.

"Certainly not – in fact I would strongly recommend that you don't. Why would you think otherwise?"

I placed my hands on my hips. "Because I was just lectured about games to play with your daddy in the forest."

"What games?" Gabriel asked and looked completely baffled.

"Let me think. There is the snail game, the P game, and something about a snake too."

"The what?" Gabriel asked and looked to Bruce for help.

"Oh, and you know what, *daddy*?" I said sardonically. "In case you're interested, Anna says you can babysit her anytime and that she would love to play games with you in the woods."

Bruce stood rooted to the ground but folded his arms and observed us closely.

Gabriel on the other hand placed both hands on top of his head and looked perplexed. "I'm sorry, but I don't know what snail and P stands for, I can kind of guess that snake has something to do with the male physiology... oh wait, so snail is..." Gabriel trailed off and a smile lurked in the corner of his mouth. "Right, but the P... what is the P game?"

"P for punishment," I snorted.

"Kinky." Gabriel smirked and squeezed himself into the swing. "And Anna wants to do that with me?"

I wanted to throttle him for being so damn insensitive.

"Yes, apparently she does – anytime you want."

Gabriel opened his mouth to speak but Bruce held up a hand to silence him. "I'm going to stop you right there, before you say something that you can't take back," he said.

"I was just going to say that..."

"I know what you were going to say and I strongly suggest that you don't say it."

Gabriel knitted his brows. "You can't possibly know what I was going to say."

"Your body spoke it before your words did, and trust me, you don't want to say it. You already said enough."

Gabriel shut his mouth and muttered low under his breath.

"I can understand that you're upset, Cia, but let me explain," Bruce said and looked straight at me. "Anna and Mark do role-playing for a different reason than you two, and I'll have a word with them since they've broken quite a few of our basic rules."

"So they aren't clients of yours," I asked.

"In a way, but they don't follow the program like you do. Mark is a regular, he comes a few times a year and typically brings a daughter. Anna has been with him for a few years now."

"But why do they come if they don't have to?"

"They are into age play and enjoy the opportunity to live it out among others. We welcome it, as it helps our clients feel more comfortable when others are wearing regression clothes too.

"However, they are not allowed to use the forest for sexual escapades, and they know not to approach clients here with any talk about age play."

Gabriel spoke up. "What the hell is this age play thing? Are they pedophiles?" he asked with disgust.

"Hardly," Bruce said and sat down on a bench. "People who are into age play are not sexually interested in children; in fact sometimes they role-play as an elderly person, although that's rare. It's often the whole element of nurturing and bonding and sometimes disciplining that appeals to them. In many cases it doesn't even involve intercourse."

"Are you talking about grown men wanting to get a diaper on and other absurd stuff like that?" Gabriel asked.

"That would be infantilism and that can be part of age play too, but doesn't have to be. Some people stick to the rebellious teen years and wear naughty school uniforms, but that is not what we do in this camp." Bruce closed his eyes and squeezed the bridge of his nose for a few seconds before he continued talking.

"I'm very sorry Anna told you what she did, and I can't stress enough that you will not be having sex with anyone as part of this program. We only use regression as part of a therapy program, because it works.

I pointed at Gabriel. "You are not letting that pervert, Mark, babysit me, do you understand?"

"Of course not – I'm not letting him anywhere near you. I've seen how he looks at you and now I know why."

"And I would also suggest that you don't take Anna up on her offer," Bruce said calmly to Gabriel, who looked a bit disappointed.

"But if..."

"Again," Bruce said. "Please don't finish that sentence."

Gabriel, who was still sitting on the swing with his feet planted solidly on the ground, scrunched his face and challenged Bruce. "I'm sorry but I don't see the problem. Cia and I will never be romantically involved; so why can't I see other women?"

Not all things make sense. And to me it made no sense that Gabriel's words hurt so much when I completely agreed with him. We were never going to be romantically involved. Still, the thought of him hooking up with a freak like Anna bothered me enormously.

Bruce waved a hand in the air. "Every little girl wants to be her father's princess and have his full attention. I can't explain it more simply than that, and since you two don't seem to enjoy my long explanations we'll just leave it at that."

"Yeah, but I'm with Cia twenty-four/seven; how is half an hour going to hurt?"

"You really don't get it," Bruce said and sighed. "Maybe Cia can explain it so you understand." He turned to me. "Cia, how would you feel if Gabriel went and had sex with Therese or Anna?"

All the emotions from yesterday came back like a wave about to crush me.

"He can screw whomever he pleases," I sneered and left, knowing that if I spoke another word my voice would betray how hurt I felt.

I hurried off and went back to get my canvas, pencils, and my colors. Anna had already lost interest in her dog and had moved on, but I still didn't want to stay. I would paint my picture in the cabin where I could be alone... well, almost alone.

Gabriel

"See, she just said it, she doesn't care if I have sex with others."

Bruce closed his eyes for a moment.

"Please tell me that you're not that stupid, G. I know you saw the pain on her face."

I shrugged. "I believe she made it perfectly clear that for all she cares I can go screw any other woman."

"Evidently, you were only listening to her words, but you know that is only a small part of communication, right?"

"Right." I didn't tell him that my desire to be with Anna or Therese had little to do with them and everything to do with Cia. She was a woman, I was a man and we were sleeping in a small bed. I needed to direct my libido in another direction... soon.

"You have to remember that you're not Gabriel. You're her father. As her father, would you seek a sexual relationship when your little girl was in need of your full attention?"

I kicked a stone on the ground. "Maybe I could wait until she sleeps. She always sleeps early; that way she wouldn't have to know," I said and found my plan both considerate and clever.

Bruce shook his head. "I know we're asking a lot of you and you got thrown into this; but your niece has no trust in men due to your brother's neglect, and you honestly seem more interested in getting laid than anything else."

"Hey, you try being abroad for a year with no access to women," I said with annoyance.

"You're barking up the wrong tree if you're looking for sympathy. I've lived in this place for nine years and only go into town a few times a month for practical reasons. I can't have intimate relationships with my clients or staff, so you do the math and see who has it worse."

Gabriel gaped. "How do you do it, man?"

Bruce laughed. "That's not important. But Cia is, and when you flirt with other women or talk about them in front of her, you're hurting her. You have eleven days left to show her that she's worthy of a man's full attention. Do you think you can put your own needs aside and give her that gift?"

I nodded slowly and mentally cursed this situation.

"You better find your daughter before she gets in trouble," Bruce said. "She is only six, remember."

I puffed out air and got up from the swing to go find Cia.

When I found her, she was at our cabin, painting. It was too soon to tell what the painting would look like but since she was occupied I asked if she would mind my taking a shower.

"But you already took one a few hours ago," she said.

"Yeah, but I'm feeling tired and sometimes a shower helps me wake up," I lied. I couldn't tell her that I hadn't been able to jerk off for days and that I needed a little privacy. It's not that I can't go a day without it, I just prefer not to; and besides, I just read an article stating that frequent ejaculation reduces the risk of prostate cancer. I'm all about prevention.

So there I was, in the shower - thinking dirty thoughts about a scenario too close to incest for me to ever admit it – when I heard shouting voices.

I turned off the water, grabbed a towel, and flew out the door.

Anna was standing inside our room with the door open and Mark outside. Anna was shouting at Cia, who looked small in comparison to the angry woman.

I don't know what came over me; I would have sworn I would never attack a woman, but I pushed Anna back harshly and got in front of Cia. "What the hell is your

Clashing Colors #1 BLACK

problem? Don't come in here shouting at my girl," I said angrily.

Anna pointed at me. "I have a right to shout when your little missy got us kicked out."

"You got kicked out because you took your little freak show too far," I said and opened my arms wide to shield Cia.

"We're not the freaks. Unlike her, we're not here for mental help," Anna lashed out at Cia.

I turned into a roaring lion and pushed her again. "Get the fuck out of here and don't ever let me see you near my niece."

Mark stepped closer and called for Anna. He and I exchanged an arctic glance but he was wise enough not to challenge me. As I stood practically naked with only a hand holding a towel in front of me, he could see my ripped body, and tribal tattoos. Honestly, I wouldn't want to pick a fight with me either and especially not when I was in this mood.

The two of them left the cabin and with adrenaline still pumping through me I turned to Cia. "Are you all right?"

She lifted her gaze to look at me and opened her mouth to speak but nothing came out.

I took a step closer and used my free hand to cup her face. "Are you okay?"

She nodded slowly. "I don't know what impresses me the most," she muttered. "That you came to defend me or that you came naked."

"I have a towel," I said and looked down.

"But I was standing behind you and you were butt naked." There was a faint smile on her face.

"I'm sorry – do you want me to call Bruce for some emergency therapy in case the sight of my naked ass has caused you a severe trauma?" I joked.

"No, I'll just pretend that you really are my father and that it's perfectly natural to see your naked body."

"Good plan," I walked over and leaned on the doorframe watching Anna and Mark get in their car. "They're leaving," I said in a matter-of-fact tone of voice.

"Good, I didn't like them," Cia commented and moved to stand next to me. When their car backed out and drove off she looked up at me.

"Thank you."

The expression of deep gratitude in her green eyes made me feel like a champ and I inclined my head to her. "Anytime, precious. I'm here for you."

I let the words hang in the air and walked back into the shower to finish what I had started, and this time the image of large green eyes looking at me like I was a freaking hero made me come quickly.

CHAPTER 12
The Bonfire

Cia

Three days later I had progressed to being nine years old and was dressed in what a nine-year-old girl would probably consider a beautiful princess dress. It was puffy and hideous, with a big bow and the most horrid pale pink color that reminded me of piglets. Gabriel and I had already had a lot of fun on that account.

In the evening we had a bonfire, and I was terrified of getting too close to the fire considering the amount of synthetic material I was wrapped in. One spark and I would go up in flames like a fake Christmas tree.

I was so afraid that I didn't even want to make my own s'mores, something I had secretly dreamed of since I was a kid. As always, Gabriel came to my rescue and made me as many s'mores as I could eat.

I noticed the new guy was still in his baby jumper and felt sorry for him when his mom fed him. I had only been a baby for a day... he had been here six days and hadn't progressed. On the first day, he hadn't left his room; on the second I had seen him shortly and he'd looked like crap. I hadn't seen him talk to anyone except his mom and the staff, but with the angry scowl on his face he wasn't the easiest person to approach.

I sympathized with him, knowing that I would be angry too, if I was still a baby. I totally pitied him for the way he looked at the s'mores with longing, because I remembered eating a banana while everyone else had chocolate cake on my first night here.

I went to talk to him, hoping that maybe I could cheer him up a bit. "Hey, how are you holding up?" I asked in a friendly way.

His mom gave me a smile but he didn't seem too happy about my attention.

I tried a bit of humor. "I was dressed like a bee myself a week ago... if you're lucky you can progress to being pink cotton candy tomorrow."

"Gee thanks, that would be something to look forward to," he said and looked away.

"Here," I whispered and sneaked half a s'more into his hand. "Don't let the mad scientist see it, okay?"

He didn't talk or even acknowledge what was in his hand, and I moved back to sit with Gabriel, who patted his lap. "Come sit here," he said.

Considering that I was a walking fire hazard, and that I had already been carried around, bathed, and tucked into bed by this big guy, it actually felt rather natural and safe to cuddle up in his lap.

"Oink, oink," he grunted and smiled.

"Hey, be nice to your little piglet."

He pulled me closer and laughed. "Don't worry, Miss Piggy, I'll protect you from any mean frogs or big bad wolves."

"I'm not so sure, you aren't a big bad wolf yourself," I said and laughed.

"Don't be silly. If you're a piglet and I'm your dad, that would make me a big boar." The fire lit up his face and gave his eyes a mischievous sparkle. "A big *wild* boar, that is."

"Oh yeah, and what did you do with my mamma pig?"

Gabriel made a bad imitation of sadness. "I'm afraid my beloved sow ran off with another boar who was younger and more handsome."

I played along and gave a pout. "No one is more handsome than you, Daddy," I teased and ended with a grunt myself.

We broke into laughter and a feel good vibe spread through my body. As I sat, sandwiched in between Gabriel's warm body and the heat from the bonfire, I relaxed against him, resting my head on his shoulder, and when Therese started playing a guitar and others sang along I closed my eyes and allowed myself to feel happy for the first time in a long time. I knew it wouldn't be long before worried thoughts would come knocking again, but this short break felt as refreshing as a week's holiday.

When we were back in the cabin again, Gabriel brushed my teeth and tucked me in with a goodnight story. I was tired and fell asleep quickly, only partly sensing the kiss he planted on my forehead.

My dreams that night were vivid, and all centered upon fire. I saw my Hello Kitty burn again; I saw my mom's crazy eyes as she threatened to burn down the house and me in it. I saw myself burn up, and woke up screaming.

Gabriel wasn't there. The bed was empty and I called for him, hysterically.

Gabriel

I kissed Cia on her forehead and rubbed her back until I was sure she was sleeping. This girl was getting under my skin.

I lay awake trying to suppress how good it had felt to have her in my lap and feel her complete trust as she cuddled up against me.

For seven nights I had slept next to her and woken up with her in my arms. It was as certain as the sunrise that during the night we would find each other and when we woke we would be entangled.

I liked it... a bit too much.

We still had another week to go, and I was getting worried that I might do something stupid in my sleep.

Last night I had woken up spooning her, and unseemly thoughts had entered my mind and made me frustrated enough that I got up and went for a run to get control of myself.

I really wanted to give Cia the gift of a man's full attention like Bruce had asked of me, but I was seriously worried I might end up screwing the whole thing up by offering her the wrong type of attention.

Looking down at Cia sleeping peacefully, I wanted to kiss her, and that's when I knew I had to do something desperate.

I got up and sneaked out, taking a few minutes to wait just outside the room to make sure Cia was still sleeping, and not calling for me.

When I was sure Cia was fine, I went to the one person who could help me take off some of the pressure. Therese welcomed me into her cabin. We had been flirting for a week and she had invited me over several times.

"What took you so long?" she asked with a charming smile and tossed her long auburn hair back.

I didn't talk but took a few steps closer and kissed her like the hungry, desperate man I was.

Therese kissed me back. She was beautiful and old enough to understand what this was about.

"Are you on birth control?" I asked.

"No, but I have condoms," she whispered back.

"I can't offer you anything serious," I told her.

"I know," she said and winked. "I'm cool with that."

"Good." I picked her up and carried her the few steps to the bed, where we undressed each other and played around. Therese was fun and uncomplicated. I got what I needed, which was release from the pressure I had felt. I took her twice that night and even though I didn't intend to, I fell asleep in her bed and didn't wake until a sunbeam hit my face.

Cia! It was the first thought that hit me, and I scrambled out of Therese's bed and dressed in a hurry.

There wasn't more than a hundred feet between Therese's cabin and ours but I still ran, hoping to get there before Cia woke up. When I came close enough to see the porch, I knew I had failed.

Cia sat outside, wrapped in the large blanket from our bed, with eyes red from crying. The disappointment on her face when she saw me tore my heart out.

"Hey, sweetie, what are you doing out here?" I asked in a pretend happy tone.

She looked away.

I took the two steps up and kneeled down in front of her. "I woke early, so I decided on a morning walk," I lied.

She dried a tear away and still refused to talk to me.

"Are you mad at me?" I asked, knowing the answer full well. "Come on, it's only six a.m.; we can still catch a few more hours of sleep." I reached to caress her face and was shocked at how cold she felt. Why hadn't I noticed how blue her lips were and how she was shivering? My eyes narrowed. "How long have you been sitting out here?"

Her voice shook because her teeth chattered when she answered. "Long en-enough to know your mor-morning walk has lasted more than seven hours and that it en-ended up in Therese's bed," she said and tried to get up.

I wanted to help her but she batted my hands away. "Don't touch me," she hissed. "I have a pre-pretty good idea where your hands have been and I don-don't want you to touch me ever again."

I was angry with myself and knew I had screwed up. I should have been wise and mature enough to just admit it, but I was neither; I fell back on the old "offense is the best defense" and sneered back at her. "Don't act like a jealous girlfriend, Cia. I have needs you can't fulfill, and I don't fucking belong to you."

She stumbled to her feet, which was hard because of the large blanket from our bed that she was wrapped in. When she finally got up, she staggered down the steps and away from me. I could see her bare feet making imprints in the grass wet with morning dew.

"Where the fuck do you think you're going?" I called after her.

She was crying too hard to answer and looked more like a crazy person walking without direction.

I had no other choice than to run after her and toss her over my shoulder and carry her back into our cabin. I wasn't going to risk finding her dead from hypothermia in the forest or drowned in some creek later, because she stumbled in that stupid blanket and couldn't get up by herself.

"I'm not letting you wake up the whole damn camp just because of a stupid misunderstanding," I told her through gritted teeth and placed her on the bed. "Are you going to be quiet or do I have to muffle you up?"

When she shot me a blazing look of anger and tried to get away from me again, I did something that wasn't very nice. I immobilized her by sitting astride her and held a hand over her mouth.

"Now you'll listen to me, Cia, do you understand?"

Her eyes were wide and full of tears. "I need you to calm the fuck down. So I slept with Therese? Get over it – it's not like I cheated on you or did something criminal. Let's talk about this like normal people."

As soon as she quieted down I removed my hand.

"Why were you outside?" I asked with a frown.

She took three deep breaths and I made sure my weight didn't press down on her. "I had a nightmare and woke up screaming, but you weren't there. I called for you."

I rubbed my face. "Fuck, I'm sorry, sugar."

"I dr-dreamed I was burning up and I nee-needed you," she said with her teeth still chattering.

"I'm sorry," I repeated, and the pain in her teary eyes made me feel like the biggest shit in the world.

I had to do something to warm her up. Not only was her body shivering and her lips blue, but she was cold as ice. I made a resolute choice and started to undress her.

"Don't," she said. "I'm s-soo cold."

"I know, but I'm going to warm you up. I promise." I pulled my own shirt and pants off and cursed the fact that I hadn't had time to put my briefs on when I ran out of Therese's cabin. Still, my body heat would warm her and that was all that mattered. If I had believed she had hypothermia I would have called for an ambulance, but her breathing and her pulse were fine and I could tell that she was just really cold.

"Don't wa-want you close to m-me, you smell of her," she stammered.

The shower. I quickly went to turn the shower on before I returned and picked her up in my arms. She didn't fight me, so either she understood that I was just trying to help, or she didn't have the energy to fight.

I stepped into the bathtub and set her gently down on her feet while holding her under the lukewarm shower spray, which would feel warm to her. She just stood there shaking, so I ignored her complaints about my smelling of Therese and pressed her close to me, hoping that the combination of my body heat and the warm water would warm her up faster.

"I'm so sorry," I muttered and pulled her arms up and placed them around my neck. "Lean on me, sweetie, I got you."

"No, you do-don't," she murmured back. "No one has me."

Fuck, that stung. For a week I had been the perfect soldier, following all orders and seeing huge progress with her. Last night at the bonfire, she had trusted me and we had been happy. Now I had screwed up by breaking her trust in me, but even if she had been my real kid, I would have still needed a sex life, god damn it. No parent could be that self-sacrificing, could they?"

"Cia, I'm sorry I wasn't here when you needed me. But I'm here now."

She didn't respond but hung onto me with the warm water cascading down her neck and back.

I stroked her hair out of her face and pulled her chin up to look at her. Her lips were less blue and her teeth had stopped chattering. "Hey, how do you feel?"

She blinked a few times. "I'm angry with you."

"I know."

"I needed you."

"I know."

"You chose her."

"Noo..." I puffed out air. "I didn't chose Therese over you, but I couldn't sleep next to you for another night without..." Okay, so clearly this was one of the situations Bruce had warned me against. My mouth had spoken before my brain raised the alert. I couldn't tell her the reason I had slept with Therese; that would only freak her out. Especially since we were both naked and pressed against each other.

"Without what?" she asked, still looking up at me.

Unfortunately, my thoughts were already providing visual answers to her question, showing me what I had wanted to do to her before I went to Therese. And unfortunately, my dick didn't get the memo that sexual thoughts about a niece are non-kosher and shouldn't cause an erection.

Cia gasped and I knew she felt my storm trooper growing against her belly.

I considered moving away from her but that would just expose the problem even more. Instead I tightened my grasp around her and closed my eyes.

When I opened them I gazed directly into her forest-green eyes. "Remember when I told you that showering with you might cause my body to react?"

"Yes," she said, slightly out of breath.

"It doesn't mean anything," I lied.

She lowered her head, so I couldn't see her eyes. I wished she hadn't, because you can tell so much from looking into people's eyes and I was dying to know if she was disgusted with me.

She unwrapped her arms from my neck. "I feel a little better now," she said and reached for the shampoo bottle. For the past week I had washed and brushed her hair. She had even taught me how to braid it.

I reached for the shampoo. "Let me do it," I said.

"No, I got it," she muttered and turned the hot water up a bit.

"Please." I sighed. "Tomorrow you'll most likely be a pre-teen so this will be my last time washing your hair. I want to do it."

Her brows knitted together. "Why, Gabriel?" she asked and used my full name for the first time.

"Because, *Darcia*," I reciprocated, "I like to take care of you."

She gave me an incredulous stare and then handed the shampoo over. "All right. For the last time then."

"Turn around," I instructed and when she did I noticed how her nipples were hard and pointy despite the warm water. Was she still cold? Or was it a sign that I wasn't the only one affected by the situation?

"Lean your head back," I instructed.

She did and I gently applied the shampoo to her long golden hair. "How do you feel?"

I received a sound of satisfaction from her as I massaged her scalp, and I couldn't help it when my fingers wandered down to her neck and shoulders and continued massaging her there.

"Too hard," she complained

I softened my touch. "Is this better?"

"Uh-huh." She let her head fall to one side, giving me a glimpse of her closed eyes. I was tempted to kiss her exposed neck, but instead I took the showerhead and rinsed out the shampoo from her hair. As I stepped to stand beside her I saw her face look relaxed with eyes closed. I know I shouldn't but I still planted a kiss on her nose.

Green eyes popped open to look at me with great intensity. "I'm sorry I can't give you what you need," she said softly.

"Me too," I whispered because in that moment I wanted her so fucking bad. "I mean, no, that's okay. I'm sure you have needs that I can't fulfil either... you know, with me being your uncle and all," I babbled.

She took the showerhead out of my hand and turned it on me. "Can I wash your hair too?" she asked.

I nodded slowly.

"Would you mind kneeling down? I can't reach."

That turned out to be a very bad idea, as I now faced her sweet perky tits and my hands were going into cramps from my trying to hold back from touching them.

I tried lowering my eyes so I wouldn't see them but that only had me looking down at a part of her body that my hands were equally interested in. I had already touched that part of her body while bathing her but never skin to skin. I had always used a washcloth, and I was curious to know how she felt.

Her hands massaged my scalp and washed my hair. My hair is trimmed short so it shouldn't have taken long, but she took her time.

"Stand up," she finally said.

I rose to my feet.

"Do you want me to wash you, like you've washed me?" she asked and her eyes fell to my saluting soldier.

Yes! my body shouted, but I remembered there was a camera in the room and forced myself to shake my head.

"No thank you, I think I'll do that myself."

If she was relieved, she didn't show it. She just handed me the showerhead and stepped out of the tub.

Thank God!

Cia

Gabriel had been right, it had been his last time to wash my hair – because Bruce promoted me to a ten-year-old after our morning session, which meant I was finally a preteen and fully capable of grooming myself. Hallelujah.

Gabriel and I didn't mention anything about our dramatic morning. We knew Bruce had it on video, but hopefully he had been too busy with his other clients to watch it.

Instead we three spoke about my nightmare, about my mom burning Hello Kitty, and once again, I felt like I had just run an emotional marathon with nowhere to hide from the crazy doctor's annoying X-ray vision. "You're a big girl now," Bruce said when we were rounding up.

"So what is my role then?" Gabriel asked Bruce.

"You'll still spend most of your time with Cia, but now you two can go on longer hikes, play pool, and you can even have a bit of time for yourself while Cia paints or hangs out with others. So enjoy that you're off the hook a bit."

Gabriel surprised me when he said. "I don't know, I was just getting used to it and I kind of liked it."

Bruce made a note on his paper. "I find that interesting and I want to investigate that a bit more in another session, but I think Cia has had enough for one day."

I nodded.

"Just think about what I said, will you?" he asked. "I know you don't want to see your mom, but carrying around anger and resentment will make you sick. If you could come to a place of forgiveness it would benefit you more than you can imagine."

"Yeah, you already told me... anger and hatred causes anxiety, which makes me produce too much adrenaline and cortisum, which undermines the production of my cancer-killing cells and shit."

"Cortisol," Bruce corrected. "I'm glad to see that you understand it on an intellectual level; now all you need to do is let me invite your mom to come for a session."

I got up. "You know, Dr. Bruce, I don't mind admitting that it's been good talking through some of all the things from my past, but I promised myself I would never have to see that woman again, and no one can make me break that promise."

"I understand, Cia, but just remember that forgiving is not the same as condoning, and you don't forgive your mother for her sake, you do it for your own."

"Yadda yadda yadda... same answer. No!"

Bruce chuckled. "Very well, all I ask is that you think about it. If you want to walk out of this camp feeling light and free, I can help you. If you choose to walk out and still be weighed down by your past, then that's your choice too."

"That's right; my choice!"

Bruce and Gabriel got up too. "I think Cia has done some great work," Gabriel said to support me.

Bruce nodded but his brows were firmly knitted together in a thoughtful expression. "Yes, but it's going to be interesting to see what pops up in her pre-teen years."

A voice deep inside of me was whispering warnings but I didn't stop to listen.

"Can I take Cia to the city and go shopping for a few hours?" Gabriel asked.

Bruce walked to his door that had the same brown color as the wood panels in the room. He opened it for us before he answered. "I would prefer if you waited a few days. I certainly can't stop you if you decide to do it, but it's important that you stay in your roles, and that will be hard to do if you leave the camp."

Gabriel sighed. "I really want to see something else for a change."

Bruce lifted an eyebrow and gave Gabriel a hard look. "Give it a day or two, but remember, I expect you to treat Cia with the same care and devotion as you would your ten-year-old daughter."

"Of course." Gabriel nodded and took my hand. "The day after tomorrow then?"

I nodded. Even though a change of scenery was tempting, I actually didn't mind waiting a few days. I was physically drained from not getting much sleep last night and overwhelmed from the drama with Gabriel and the therapy session. There were about a million thoughts in my mind, and one of them was Gabriel's raw reminder from last night that he wasn't my boyfriend and I had no right to be jealous. Yet I was.

I was annoyed and on edge. Angry at Gabriel for making me confused. Angry at Bruce for making me think of my mom and even consider seeing her again.

When we got outside Gabriel grabbed my hand but I pulled it away. "I'm ten, you don't need to hold my hand," I said.

"But I like to hold your hand," he protested and tried to grab it again.

"Maybe later – right now I'm going to get out of this awful pink dress and take a nap, and later I'm going to paint. Why don't you go for that long hike you've been talking about?" I suggested, praying he would take the hint and give me space to breathe and get my head straight.

His face fell. "But I wanted us to do that hike together."

"Yeah, well, I'm a preteen now, I need some alone time."

"Okay, if you insist," he said and went to pack his backpack to bring with him.

I watched him gear up while I stepped out of the puffy dress and got under the blanket on our bed.

"Are you sure you don't want to come?" he asked a last time. "I'll tell you some really gory stories from the war on the way, if you come."

I gave him a tired smile. "Tell me later, okay?"

"Can a dad still hug and kiss his ten year-old?" he asked.

"I don't know."

He leaned forward and kissed the top of my hair. "Well, I'm doing it. Sweet dreams, darling, I'll see you in a few hours."

When he left, the room felt empty without him. Just like it had when I woke up from my nightmare last night.

I'm not stupid, I knew it was problematic that I had become addicted to his company; I suppressed the part of me that wanted to call him back and ask him to curl up with me and be my pillow of safety while I slept.

In a week I would be back on my own. Hell, after the trial I might even go to jail for a year. I needed to get a grip on myself, before I turned into a pathetic girl depending on a man to save me.

⟨ ∞ ⟩

Two days later we finally went on a drive to do a bit of shopping. Gabriel wanted to take me to Olympia, which would offer the biggest selection of shops, but being so close to the ocean I begged him to take me there instead. Seattle has a lot of water, but it's all lakes and Puget Sound, meaning that whenever you're by the water, there's a view with mountains in the background. I wanted to stand on a beach and see nothing but water, just like in the movies. No mountains in the distance, just blue ocean as far as my eyes could see.

We ended up in a place called Ocean Shores, which turned out to be a nice vacation spot.

Luckily, my clothes had been upgraded to something less girly, now that I had finally reached the age of twelve years old. I was wearing a simple denim skirt and a marine blue t-shirt with a cat wearing large purple glasses. Obviously not something I would have ever worn if I had a choice, but then again, I only wore black in the real world.

We had promised Bruce to stay in character and maybe for that reason, Gabriel asked me a lot of questions about my art project, which was almost finished and offered a safe topic.

It was the middle of May and one of those unusual warm days with almost eighty degrees, so the minute we arrived at Ocean Shores, Gabriel wanted an ice cream.

"What do you want, sweetie?" he asked and I looked around to see if anyone had heard him. It's one thing to be called Sweetie, Sugar, and Candy back in the camp, but here, where strangers didn't know that it was a role-play, I suddenly felt shy about it.

"You know people are going to assume that we're a couple if you keep saying things like that," I muttered low.

"I don't care what strangers think," he said and took my hand. "Come on, let me get my girl an ice cream."

I chose a big vanilla soft ice, and we walked down to the beach and found a bench to sit and enjoy the view.

"Can I taste yours?" he asked and offered me his cone with pistachio.

"It's good, right?" he said as I took a bite.

"It's better than mine… I'm keeping this one," I teased him and held it away from him when he wanted to swap back.

He laughed. "Hey, give me my ice cream back."

"Never," I said and took off running toward the sea, laughing out loud.

Gabriel was right behind me, balancing the soft ice while chasing me.

I didn't stop when I reached the water, but kicked off my flip-flops and continued until the waterline hit my knees. Still laughing and with my hair blowing in the sea breeze, I stopped and looked back at him. He wore long pants and would get wet if he went after me. I on the other hand had the denim skirt that was just above my knees.

"Uhm, your ice cream tastes amazing, it's like a little piece of heaven," I said and took another big bite.

Gabriel studied me for a moment. "I hope your little piece of heaven is worth the hell you're getting when you come over here, young lady."

I kicked at the water to make him wet and grinned. "Ohhh, is Daddy going to punish his little girl for being naughty?" I said, but the expression on his face almost made me drop the ice cone.

"What did you say?" he asked, but he wasn't laughing, and the way his Adam's apple jumped in his throat made me go over what I had just said in my head. "Oh shit, no, I didn't mean it like that." I tried to explain. "I don't want you to spank me or play the P game or anything."

We both knew I was referring to Anna and Mark's perverse games of age-playing. But we were nothing like them.

Gabriel stood there, staring at me with the soft ice dripping down his hand.

"Okay," he said and blinked a few times. "No, of course I won't spank you." But there was no conviction in his voice and the way he looked at me made my heart beat faster.

"Here, you can have your ice cream back," I said and hurried to him.

He looked down at the half-melted soft ice in his hand and then he threw it far into the ocean.

"Hey, that's littering," I accused him.

He squatted down to wash the soft ice off his hands. "No, it's not. I'm simply feeding the fish."

"I was going to give you back your pistachio, but now that you threw my ice cream away, I'm keeping it."

He got up and surprised me with his speed when he reached out and grabbed my wrist. "We'll share it," he said and brought my arm closer to his mouth. Keeping eye contact, he licked a large chunk of the ice cream, and I swear it did funny things to my stomach. Then he pushed my arm back toward my mouth and by default I spread my lips and tasted the sweet pistachio.

I didn't know what to do when he stepped closer and took another bite of the ice cream while it was still in my mouth. The way he leaned in while gazing into my eyes made me think of kissing, but of course our lips never met, as the ice cream was between us.

Yet with his closeness and the burning expression in his eyes it felt dangerous, and I was starting to freak out.

In reflex, I pushed the ice cream away from me and because he was so close, most of it ended up on his nose.

"I'm so sorry," I said while he was trying to get the ice cream off him. He used the ocean to wash his face and hands and got pretty wet in the process. It was a good thing that the weather was so warm and sunny.

"Let's do what we came here for," he said and started walking toward the main street again. "Let's find you some clothes."

I followed him and when he reached his hand back I even took it. We were, after all, still playing the roles of father and daughter.

Gabriel found a small shop with women's clothes. The selection wasn't big but he was excited when he found a colorful stack of t-shirts.

"How about this one?" he asked and held up a yellow t-shirt with a v-neck.

I wrinkled my nose at his suggestion and picked up a black one that I liked.

He arched a brow. "No black, Cia."

With a questioning look I picked up the same style in a charcoal gray.

He shook his head and pointed to the third color in that style. White.

I picked it up and held it out in front of me. I couldn't remember ever wearing anything white, but it was better than the rainbow colors I'd been wearing at the camp and the yellow color he had just suggested. I agreed to at least try the white shirt on.

"How about a pair of jeans?"

"Black jeans?" I asked hopeful.

"No, white jeans or blue."

I chose white since the blue ones reminded me of my mother who had always worn tight blue jeans.

"What about bras and panties?" he asked and went to the rack and picked out a white set with lace.

"I don't even know what size I am, I only ever wear sports bras," I told him.

He held out two sets to me. "I think one of these two will fit."

I took the jeans, the shirt, and the two sets of underwear and headed for the fitting room.

"Remember, as your dad, I need to see it on before we buy it," he said with a charming grin.

A woman turned her head and gave us a curious look.

"He's much older than he looks," I muttered as I passed her.

Gabriel followed me with a chuckle.

The jeans were a size too small, so he went back and got me the right size. The shirt looked nice – too nice, but he liked it. The underwear was sweet and yet seductive. I was flattered that he had chosen two in a C cup because even though it was ridiculous I was still happy that he estimated my breasts to be much bigger than they were.

"Why don't we try with a B cup? I think that's more realistic." I told him."

He frowned. "Not to sound cocky or anything, but I've seen my share of tits and yours are definitely a C cup," he said. "My ex, Heidi, was a lingerie model, and I know about these things."

Figures that Gabriel's ex was a lingerie model, and here I was trying on my first set of grown-up underwear with lace. To my surprise, the man was right. I was a small C cup. I took a minute to admire the design in the mirror.

"Wow, you look good," Gabriel said and I lifted my head to see him peeking in from behind the curtain.

"Hey, don't be a creep, I didn't say you could look."

His head disappeared quickly and I got into my pre-teen clothes and met him outside the fitting room.

He took the pile from me. "Anything else you want?" he asked.

I shook my head. "No, I already owe you too much money."

He paid for the clothes and handed me the shopping bag.

"Come on, sugar, I need a cup of coffee."

The woman in the store told Gabriel where to get the best coffee, and since the town was very small we reached the small coffee house quickly.

"There is something I wanted to discuss with you," Gabriel said when we sat at a table with our drinks in front of us. "You owe me three hundred dollars for the bail and I wanted to make you an offer on how to pay it back."

I tensed and sat down my glass of iced tea. This was it. I had known all along that he was too good to be true. I prepared myself for the disappointment over his proposal and wondered how many sexual favors he felt he should get for three hundred dollars.

"Can you cook?" he asked, and that made me raise my brows.

"No," I answered. "Not unless you call scrambled eggs and microwave noodles cooking."

"Can you clean?"

"I've cleaned the rooms at The Inn for the last seven years. Of course I can clean, why?"

"Because I was hoping you would help me out over the summer until I go to Missouri."

He had told me about his new job, training sappers, and I didn't like the thought of him going away. "When is that?" I asked.

"September. We still have almost four months, and I don't like cleaning and cooking, so I wondered if you would help me out and work off the money that way."

"What about the money I owe you for the therapy?" I asked.

"I told you that was a gift," he answered.

I looked down. "How often do you need me to come by your place and clean?"

"Daily."

"Daily?" My head whipped up. "How messy are you? I can't come daily."

"Why not?"

"I live in Kirkland. It will take me at least an hour a day on the commute alone, not to mention the cost of the bus fare to Seattle. You'll have to cover that."

"Nope."

I played with my glass. "Come on, G, it's at least five dollars for a round-trip ticket. That's thirty-five dollars a week; I can't pay that."

"Why take the bus when you can crash on my couch?"

I narrowed my eyes. "Are you serious?"

He took a sip of his coffee. "Yes. I'm very serious."

"I don't know. What happens when you leave in four months? Lee is probably already pissed at me for staying away these two weeks. If I disappear for months, he might not take me back and where would I be then?"

The way Gabriel slammed his coffee cup down on the table made me jump in my seat.

"You are never going back to sleeping in that closet," he said with fierce determination.

"All right. So let me get this straight. You are willing to let me sleep on your couch if I clean your house and cook for you."

"Yes."

"Can you cook?" I asked him.

"That's debatable, but I guess we'll just have to learn together."

"I make a mean bowl of cornflakes and milk," I joked.

He grinned at me. "Then at least we won't starve."

"Okay." I smiled at him.

"Okay," he repeated and smiled back. "Then that's settled."

When we drove back to Camp Crazy we were both quiet, and I for one was contemplating the generosity of his offer. We had already been roommates in a small cabin for ten days, but still, for him to share his apartment with me was something else completely.

I turned my head and studied him for a long minute.

He shot me a side glance. "Do I have something on my face?"

"Were you always such a kind and generous person?" I asked.

"Ha. If you ask some of my exes, they'll tell you I can be a real ass, and as I recall it, you weren't too impressed with me a few nights ago yourself."

"I know, but still, you didn't have to bail me out of jail, or take me home with you, but you did. You even went above and beyond when you came with me to Camp Crazy."

He kept his eyes on the road but a smile lurked on his lips.

"No one has ever done anything remotely as nice for me, and when you got between me and Anna, that was just…"

He turned his head and looked at me. "Just what?"

"It was amazing. No one has ever stood up for me before, and I've had to face bullies all my life. I can't tell you how cool it was to have you as a huge wall of human protection between me and that lunatic."

Gabriel scratched his stubble thoughtfully. "I could have sworn I would never push a woman, but seeing her go at you just made me furious."

"So you came to defend me."

"And protect you." After a minute he added, "When I was a kid and my mom married my stepdad I couldn't do anything when he talked down to my stepbrother and -sisters. I used to sit at the table and watch it happen and I knew deep inside my soul how wrong it was, but there was nothing I could do."

"Could you have spoken up?"

"I tried speaking up a few times, but I was only a small kid and he would just ignore me like I didn't even have a voice. I think seeing Anna attack you brought me back to that feeling, only this time I could actually do something."

"Is that why you became a soldier? To fight injustice?"

He nodded slowly. "Yeah, and to protect the weak."

"I'm not weak," I objected.

"Really?" he said and I sensed a challenge.

"Why would you think I'm weak...? I've survived on my own always."

"Yet you're not strong enough to face your demons."

I snapped my head toward him and clenched my jaw. "What is that supposed to mean?"

"Your mom. You're still scared of your mom."

"Ha!" I scoffed. "The only thing that scares me about her is that I might end up killing her if I ever see her again."

"I won't let that happen, I'll make sure she doesn't touch you and vice versa."

I didn't answer him but sat quietly and thought about it.

"As I see it, this is an ideal chance to confront her and find your peace. Bruce is on your side and will be there to mediate between you. I'll be there as your bodyguard, and I guarantee she won't touch a hair on your head."

"A bodyguard has to be willing to take a bullet for their clients, you know," I said in an attempt at humor.

"I know," he answered simply.

"So if I don't confront my mom, you think I'm weak?"

He lifted his shoulders. "Maybe not weak, but you would definitely earn some serious street credit in my book if you did it. That would make you a real badass."

"And who doesn't want to be a badass with street credit in your book?" I said sardonically.

Gabriel grinned and turned on the radio. "Whatever you decide, I'm on Team Cia."

"Even if I decide to confront my father."

"Especially if you decide to confront Brent. I would even make a huge banner, if it helps."

"If you promise to dress up in a cheerleader uniform and bring pompoms, I'll do it."

He laughed. "I don't think cheerleading uniforms come in my size – and besides," he said dryly, "if you're strong enough to confront your mom, Brent will be a walkover."

"So you really think I should do it?"

"Absolutely."

I took a deep breath and felt momentarily brave enough, so I held out a fist. "Okay… but you promise to be there and if she tries anything, you knock her out."

He bumped my fist with his own. "You got it, partner."

When we got back I found Bruce and told him I would do it. I knew if I didn't tell him right away, I would probably chicken out.

Bruce was pleased with me and promised to contact her to set up the session.

In the meanwhile I went to finish my art project, which was a series of six paintings that illustrated my mental journey. The first five were already done and taking up too much space in our small cabin, so Gabriel helped me carry them to the main building, where we placed them in the common room for Bruce to see.

"Wow," he said and took in each painting. "I would love to hear your thoughts on your work."

"This one represent my day as a baby," I said and pointed to the first painting. The background was a dark green meadow with eerie trees all around, and in the middle I sat in a black and yellow baby jumper. My legs were crossed, and my head bowed. The painting had a depressive darkness to it, and only a small circle of light fell upon me as I sat bent forward with my long black hair hiding most of my face. All that was visible was my nose and my mouth with a big pacifier in it to compliment the baby bottle in my hand. Above me hung a swarm of angry bees ready to attack and I was holding an arm up to shield against them.

Bruce was waiting for me to elaborate and when I didn't, he said, "Care to hear what I see in this painting?"

"Sure," I said.

"I see a person who is sad and defensive, feeling under attack and put in the spotlight."

"Me too," Gabriel seconded.

"And that one?" I asked and pointed to the next one.

Bruce tapped his finger on his upper lip. "Ah yes, how interesting."

It showed me as a little blond girl stumbling on roller skates in a pink tutu skirt with a humongous cotton candy in my hand. I was trying to find my balance with my little tongue sticking out in concentration while my long shadow went to the lower corner of the painting, where another version of me as a little girl sat crouched over, wearing nothing but black.

"I suppose it could mean several things – why don't you explain it?" Bruce suggested.

"I already expressed it through my art. You are the one who loves words; if you want to translate the meaning into words, be my guest."

"All right," Bruce leaned forward. "The Black girl is being left behind while the young child dangerously makes her way into the world of uncertainty."

"And the cotton candy?" I challenged.

He took off his glasses and rubbed his nose. "Is she finding something in this new world tempting and delicious?"

The thought hit me hard. *Gabriel is tempting and delicious.* Was that what I had portrayed without realizing it on a conscious level?

"I know what the cotton candy is about," Gabriel said and looked pleased with himself. "It was a joke between Cia and me because being dressed in all that pink made her look like cotton candy."

"Really," Bruce said and squinted his eyes. "I would have thought it held a more significant meaning with the prominent size and placement of it."

I inwardly cringed, knowing he was right.

"Personally this one is my favorite," Gabriel said and moved to the third painting. Bruce put his glasses back on.

"Ah, yes, the bathing. Such lovely colors."

It was a blue picture with me floating on water with my eyes closed. A man's hand came from underneath me and was splayed over my genitals and another arm was placed across my chest with the hand firmly placed on my right breast.

On the side of my face a yellow rubber duck broke the blue color of water.

"It's beautiful," Bruce said, "but I can't really determine if she's relaxed or sleeping."

"She's relaxed," Gabriel interjected. "And underneath her there's a man that helps her float."

"Are you sure he isn't trying to pull her down?" Bruce asked.

Gabriel pushed his chest out. "No, he's definitely helping her float."

"Is that so? And I suppose you assume that man is you."

Gabriel gave me a quick glance. "It's me, right?"

I smiled, but didn't answer, so we moved to the fourth painting.

"Oh wow, this one holds so much aggression," Bruce said and leaned closer to take in the details of the lion roaring at the viewer.

"It's not just an aggressive lion. Don't you see that it's protecting the child?" Gabriel pointed to a young girl who peeked her head out from behind the lion.

"But protecting her from what?" Bruce asked.

I laughed. It was entertaining to hear them try to analyze the meaning of my paintings.

"From the snake, of course. It's right there." Gabriel pointed to the tree, where a snake was almost completely hidden.

"You're right." Bruce turned to me and his eyes were sparkling. "Let me guess; Anna and Mark?"

I nodded.

"Excellent. You are truly talented Cia, this makes an old man's blood pump faster. So many colors and emotions."

"Then what do you think of this one?" I asked and went to stand in front of the fourth picture.

Bruce frowned. "It's very dramatic and sinister."

"Yes, it is." Gabriel looked away. I knew he didn't like that picture.

It showed the camp, and one of the cabins was on fire. A man stood on the porch of another cabin with his back to the burning house, busy talking to a woman. He didn't see the child running out of the burning cabin engulfed in flames and with an expression of misery.

Bruce cleared his throat. "This represents the nightmare you had?"

"Yes."

"And the man, is that your father failing you?"

I didn't answer that question. Bruce hadn't found out about the night Gabriel spent with Therese, and we both preferred it that way.

"I don't see the Hello Kitty that your mother burned, and I'm a little confused why it would be the cabin burning and not your childhood home."

After another minute of studying the picture Bruce added, "I'm surprised your mother isn't in the picture, but maybe she's the woman he's talking to?"

"Hello Kitty is right there." I pointed to a little white burning pile on the porch.

"Aha."

The last painting was all white with only a small and a big hand merging fingers.

"A father and daughter bonding?" Bruce analyzed. "I think this is my favorite."

"Why?" I asked.

"I like the simplicity. Holding hands and bonding holds such powerful healing; it's the essence of what we do here."

"Cia is planning to make six paintings in all."

"Wonderful. When will the last be done?" Bruce asked.

"Before I leave."

"Great; as I said, I would like to hang them in our dining room."

I nodded, but the truth was that I would have liked to take the paintings with me. They were more personal than anything I'd ever painted before. But a promise was a promise, and I would just have to suck it up and be a big girl about it.

CHAPTER 13
Dennis

Cia

It turned out that I'm not the only one with nightmares. The second night after we came back from Ocean Shores Gabriel had a major one, and I woke up when he almost punched me down off the bed in his frantic movements. He was sweaty and muttering about being trapped, and I could tell from his movements that he was trying to break free of something.

My friend Daniel is ex-military and has severe post-traumatic stress syndrome, so I knew better than to try and wake him up. Daniel once attacked a friend who tried to wake him up and although the guy didn't die, I wasn't taking any risks.

I got up from the bed and moved away, shouting at him, "G, wake up, you're dreaming."

It didn't help; he was still throwing himself from side to side and it sounded like he was crying in panic.

Then I picked up a shoe and banged it against the closet, hard and repeatedly. I didn't care if I woke up the whole damn entire camp; I needed to help Gabriel break free from whatever nightmare he was caught in.

I was contemplating throwing water at him when he finally sat up with a gasp.

"You had a nightmare," I said and moved to stand in front of the bed, still at a safe distance.

He blinked and looked around, pulling his hands through his hair.

"Are you okay?" I asked.

"Yeah, I think so. Why are you over there? I didn't hurt you, did I?" he asked with concern in his voice.

"No."

"Then why are you looking so wary of me?"

"I didn't want to risk you attacking me."

"Why would I attack you?"

"I don't know... soldiers come home all fucked up and attack their wives in their sleep, thinking they are the enemy and stuff."

He rubbed his eyes. "I don't have a wife... you're not my wife."

"Nor will I be anyone's wife if you strangle me by accident, before I'm even able to meet Mr. Right."

He shook his head. "Come here. I promise I won't hurt you."

"All right." I sighed and crawled back on the bed, where he pulled me into a tight hug.

"Eww... you're all sweaty," I complained.

"Deal with it. I need a hug," he said and so I did. With everything Gabriel had done for me, I could deal with a bit of manly sweat, which actually didn't smell bad at all.

I relaxed into him but when he squeezed me harder I pushed back. "Hey, big guy, you can hug and touch me all you want but I need to breathe, so hug me from behind, okay?"

I placed myself in the spooning position I knew he liked so much and he pulled me into his arms and rested his face in my hair.

"Sorry I woke you," he muttered.

"Don't be... I've woken you up plenty of times. Do you want to talk about your dream?"

"Uh-huh... but not now," he said in a drowsy voice and caressed my arm.

"Stop it, it tickles and I want to sleep," I muttered with my eyes already closed.

"Nuh-uh," he said in an exhalation of air, "You said I could touch you as much as I wanted."

"Whatever." I yawned and placed a hand under my ear, waiting for sleep to take me away.

Gabriel

I must have fallen asleep after my nightmare, because the next thing I remember is waking up with Cia fighting to get away from me. Even in the dark I could tell her eyes were wide with fear and my first thought was that I had somehow hurt her. "Don't touch me, Dennis," she whined.

"Dennis? Who is Dennis?"

"I don't want to. Leave me alone."

From the way Cia was looking at me, she had either gone mad or was somehow still sleeping. She kept calling me Dennis and accusing me of abusing her for at least two or three minutes until I finally had enough and went to shake her. That only made her scream, but at least it made her come to her senses.

"Stop shaking me, G."

I did.

"Who is Dennis?" I demanded.

"Who?" she said confusedly. "I only know one Dennis."

"And who is he?"

She hesitated.

"Cia," I said in a deep no-bullshit-voice. "Who is Dennis?"

She answered in a whisper, "My mother's boyfriend,"

My heart was already racing, but now bile rose in my throat too. "What did he do to you?"

"Nothing," she said and looked away.

My voice softened. "Don't lie to me, precious. You thought I was him and just begged me not to touch you. Did he..." I swallowed hard. "Did he molest you?"

Cia started crying but when I tried to touch her, she pulled away.

"Talk to me, sweetie, tell me what happened."

"I can't," she said in a broken voice that fucking tore my heart out.

"You can tell me anything, sweetie, you know I'm here for you, I'm not him, and I'll never judge or hurt you," I begged and avoided touching her.

She was still crying and curled herself up in a fetal position, facing away from me. If she didn't want me to touch her, I didn't have any other choice than to lie down behind her and whisper once again that I was here for her and that I would listen.

"My mom met Dennis in a bar," Cia started, in a voice so low that I had to listen carefully. "He was different from all of her other no-good boyfriends: younger than her and always dressed in nice clothes. The fact that I never saw him hit her was a big change too. My mom was so proud of him, because he worked in an office, had some money and a car. I remember being happy that my mom had met Dennis. She was nicer when he was around and he would occasionally buy me a slush ice or give me a lift to and from school. I was thirteen when they started dating and he was the first of her boyfriends to insist I called him Daddy." Cia stopped talking and I waited.

"At first I didn't want to call him Daddy, but my mom got furious and said I had to. She told me he loved kids and wanted to be the father I never had. It was lovely at first: his interest in me and how he always included me in everything they did... until..."

"Until what?" I swallowed hard.

"Until it started getting weird. He would ask me if I had gotten my period and if I needed a bra now that I was beginning to get breasts. There were times when he would accidentally touch me; and one time when my mom needed to go somewhere, he insisted on babysitting me, which was strange since I've been left home alone for as long as I can remember.

"The first time I remember being scared was that night when we were alone. He asked me if I had ever kissed a boy and suggested I could use him for practice."

"Did you?"

"No, but later he started coming to my bed when he thought I was sleeping. He didn't do anything except pull my blanket away and breathe funny. After months of doing that he started touching me and pulling my panties aside. I always pretended to sleep, but one day he tried to take my panties completely off me and I made sounds as if I was about to wake up and it made him leave. The next day I told my mom."

"Good for you," I said.

She scoffed. "My mom said I was lying and that I was just jealous of her man. But I think she must have confronted him because they had a loud fight that night and he threatened to leave her.

"I don't know why she wanted him to stay, but she begged him to, and after that they sometimes came to my bed together. There were noises that I didn't understand, slurping noises, and he would still sit on my bed and touch my legs, arms, breasts, and sometimes more. Now of course I know she was making him come, but I was so scared and would often cry when they finally left me."

It was hard to listen to Cia's memories, but I kept quiet and didn't touch her.

"Shortly before my fourteenth birthday it escalated and they would talk quietly and say dirty things about me. Sometimes he would cum on my belly and my mom would wash it off with a wet cloth afterwards"

"Did they never suspect you were awake?"

"I don't think so, but then the day before I turned fourteen I saw him give her a bottle of pills in the kitchen. It made me suspicious so I eavesdropped after they thought I had gone to sleep. I heard them plan everything."

I held my breath, not wanting to hear more, but I had to.

"Dennis asked my mom if she had managed to slip me the pill and she confirmed that I had emptied the glass of Coca-Cola she gave me. What she didn't know was that I had poured it out my window because I knew she was up to something. My mom had never brought me a glass of anything before that day.

"They talked about giving me another half hour before going in to my room, and Dennis promised her that I wouldn't wake when he took me."

I sucked in air. "Shit. So that's why you ran away from home. Because he was going to rape you that night."

"Yes, I even saw him kiss her and thank her for the gift – me – before I went back to my room, grabbed a few things, and slipped out the window."

"And that's when you went to Brent, who then rejected you," I said with a clenched jaw and felt even madder at my big brother for having failed his daughter.

Cia took a deep breath and steadied her voice. "Yes, and I've never seen my mom or Dennis since that night."

I couldn't see her face, but her voice told me she was crying and I could see that she used her hands to dry away her tears.

"Sweetie, can I touch you?" I asked, feeling a burning desire to comfort and protect her.

She nodded and I instantly pulled her into a hug from behind. "I don't even know what to say except to thank you for sharing it with me."

"You still think I should meet with my mom?"

"Yeah, although now we might face a different problem."

"What?" she turned her head and looked at me over her shoulder.

"Now I want to kill her for you."

Cia turned her body around and cupped my face. "Please don't, G, she's not worth it, and you're not a killer."

I actually was, but I didn't say that. My time in Afghanistan hadn't been a picnic, and there was a reason I had been awarded a silver cross for my bravery.

I brushed her tears away and kissed the tip of her nose. "I'm so sorry that it happened to you," I whispered.

"Me too."

"I wish I could have been there to protect you."

She lowered her eyes.

"Cia, look at me."

She did.

"Those assholes will never touch you again, and you should press charges against them for child abuse."

"I thought about it," she said. "But I didn't know where to begin, and I basically just wanted them to leave me alone."

I trailed her lips with my finger and looked deeply into her wet green eyes. "You're not alone anymore."

More tears sprung from her eyes.

And then I kissed her. On her lips.

She stiffened and I pulled back, holding my breath and waiting for her reaction.

Her eyes lowered to my mouth and she wet her lips as if she wanted to sample the taste of me.

"You kissed me," she said and it sounded neither accusatory nor disgusted, but rather like an observation. "Why did you kiss me?"

"I don't know." I didn't apologize or tell her it would never happen again, because at this point I honestly didn't know what was up and down anymore.

Instead I hugged her tight and told her everything was going to be all right. Of course that was before I met her mother.

CHAPTER 14
Facing Tina

Cia

It came as a shock when Bruce told me my mom was on her way. How he had managed to locate and contact her in less than a day, let alone convince her to come all this way to do a therapy session with me, was beyond my comprehension.

I threw a small tantrum out of fear, and Bruce took me on a walk and talk in the forest to help me calm down. Half an hour later, I had told him the same story I told Gabriel about the events that led me to run away.

Bruce didn't say much, but listened and stroked my shoulder when I cried too much to talk.

He suggested I use the waiting time until she arrived to channel my emotions into my art, and promised over and over that facing my mom was the right thing to do.

I painted a picture of a glass, two pills, and a Coca-Cola bottle and called my painting *Betrayal*.

At four o'clock that afternoon, Gabriel came into the cabin. "Your mom has arrived... She's here," he said and looked as serious as I was frightened. Luckily he didn't ask me if I was ready to face her, because my answer would surely have been a big fat "no." He just took my hand and led me into the main building toward Bruce's office.

Before we entered he pulled me close and whispered. "I'm here for you. You can do this, precious. Place the blame where it belongs."

I wanted to say something funny or sarcastic, but my brain was frozen in fear and I would much rather have

Clashing Colors #1 BLACK

entered a cave full of bats and spiders than walk into that office.

There was a last moment when we looked deep into each other's eyes and simultaneously took a long deep breath before Gabriel opened the door.

And there she was.

My mom, sitting in a chair looking straight at me.

I wanted to back away, but Gabriel gently nudged me forward and held out a chair for me.

I sat and kept my gaze fixed on the glass of water in front of me. I had to calm my pounding heart before I found the strength to look at her.

This woman was my mother but I felt no love for her. Only anger and contempt. She was still an attractive woman although she looked older than her thirty-nine years.

Bruce cleared his voice.

"Tina and Darcia, I'm very proud of you both for trusting in me to facilitate this meeting. I want to stress that the desired outcome for this session isn't to reunite you, although if you choose to do so that is entirely up to you. The goal is to help Cia confront you, Tina, and to find as much peace as she can with her past. You, Tina, have agreed to listen without judgment or interference and you, Cia, will get a chance to have honest answers to any question you might have."

Tina was looking at Gabriel, who sat beside me and held my hand. Bruce must have noticed it too, because he introduced them. "Tina, before we start I want to introduce you to Gabriel, who is the stepbrother of Cia's father and has supported Cia throughout her time here at the center."

Gabriel inclined his head to her, but his gaze was frigid. She nodded back.

"Tina, you asked if you could start by saying a few words to Cia." He turned to me. "Cia, when your mom talks in a minute I want you to write down her words on the paper in front of you. You don't need to say anything, just write down as much as you can."

I grabbed the pen in front of me and focused on the paper. In a way, it was nice that I didn't have to look at her, I just had to scribble down.

"Go ahead, Tina."

"Well... Ehhm," Tina cleared her throat a few times. "What I wanted to say was just that I'm really glad to see you again and that I've missed you like... a lot." She exhaled in a long deep sigh. "I was so happy when Dr. Bruce called me and asked me to help you, because if I can do anything to help you, I will."

I didn't look up.

"I know you probably don't like me very much," she continued. "But I want you to know that even though I'm not the best mother, I always loved you and I still do."

I wrote as fast as I could, putting her words down on paper.

"I want to apologize for all the things that happened in your childhood and especially for blaming you for everything that was wrong in my life. I'm in a much better place now and have stopped drinking... I'm doing a twelve-step program with AA and taking responsibility for my actions, and I would like to ask for your forgiveness and make amends if possible."

When her words registered I put the pen down and lifted my head to look at her. She looked at me full of hope.

"Is it my turn to talk now?" I asked Bruce through gritted teeth.

"Tina, while Cia talks, you will not interrupt but write down as much as you can. Okay?"

She nodded and picked up the pen in front of her.

My voice shook with anger when I spoke. "I can't believe you have the nerve to come and *ask* something from me. You say you want to help me, but in reality you're just here for you. You don't care one bit about me – you're just using me like you did when I was a child. And while we're at it, how is Dennis? Are you still molesting children together?"

Tina looked pale.

Bruce gave her the word and I picked up my pen.

"Dennis left me right after you ran away from home. I don't know what happened between you two, but if he did something to you, I'm sorry."

"You're sorry," I snorted and didn't wait for Bruce to give me permission to talk. "How dare you make it sound like you weren't part of the abuse? You gave him blow jobs while he groped me, thinking I was sleeping. You allowed him to cum over my body and didn't try to stop him." My voice broke and tears streamed down my face. "You egged him on and got off on seeing him molest me, you sick fuck." I spit out the last words.

Tina's lips started quivering. "No, no, honey, you don't understand."

"You're right, I'll never understand how a mom can betray her own daughter like that. You were going to let him take my virginity the night I ran away. Admit it... he was about to rape me."

Tina hid her face in her hands and cried, and we all waited for her to calm herself down. Bruce handed her a tissue.

"Tina, feel free to respond, when you're ready."

Tina dried her nose. "I was in a bad place and Dennis was so wonderful to me. I was blinded by him and deeply in love with him. That's why I wasn't thinking straight and he always knew exactly what to say... he promised you would never know about it and that it wouldn't hurt you in any way. I believed him and I only egged him on to help you."

"Bullshit," Gabriel sputtered but Bruce held out a hand to silence him.

"Go on, Tina, you were saying."

She blew her nose and reached for another tissue to dry her eyes. "He was completely out of my league and I wanted so bad for him to love me and felt lucky to have someone like him. I think that's why I ignored the little signs."

"What signs?" Bruce asked calmly.

Tina sniffled and looked at me. "It started out with small things. I noticed how he looked at you and then he would say your name when we had sex. I tried to tell him I wouldn't have it, but then, whenever he threatened to leave me, I would get desperate and he would add on a tiny thing that I could do for him. He went from calling me Darcia when we made love to having me call him Daddy and begging him to take his little girl." She sniffled again. "I hoped that would be enough, and to be honest, I've been with men that wanted much worse things than dirty talk, so I didn't think too much of it, but then he wanted more and in time we had to be in your room where he could see and touch you while I satisfied him. I was so afraid that you would wake up, so I wanted him to get off as fast as possible to leave you alone. That's why I talked dirty to him… I knew what to say in order to make him come faster, but I did it for you, I promise."

I looked away.

"Please believe me, darling, I just tried to protect you."

Gabriel formed a fist and I felt my nostrils flare in anger.

"Were you just trying to *protect me* when you slipped me sleeping pills so he could rape me?"

She gave me a pleading look. "I was desperate, you don't understand. I had no money, we were being put on the street, and he offered to pay if I would let him have you. It was only going to be that one time."

I rolled my eyes and angrily dried away a tear that slipped from my eye. "I can't believe how naïve you are."

"I was trying to keep a roof over your head."

"By selling my body."

Tina opened her mouth to speak, but then she closed it again and sunk lower in her chair.

"It wasn't like that," she finally muttered.

"It was *exactly* like that," I said with conviction.

My words hung in the air for a minute before Bruce spoke again. "Tina, now would be a good time to acknowledge the damage you did and apologize to Cia."

She couldn't look me in the eye for more than a split second at a time. "I'm so ashamed," she said low. "And I'm deeply sorry for what I did to you."

I figured that while we were at it, I might as well clear off the table. "You burned Hello Kitty," I said.

"Did I? I don't remember," she said quietly.

"That's because you were drunk. You were always drunk"

"I'm sorry," she said and kept her gaze down.

"You also didn't feed me or show me any love. You were a mean drunk."

"But I did love you and you have to understand how poor we were. I couldn't afford much."

"You could afford booze. I survived on school meals and hated the weekends because they meant being hungry and being alone, which was almost better than being with you."

"I'm so sorry. You didn't deserve that," Tina said and blew her nose again.

Bruce handed her the tissue box and took charge again. "Cia, when you look at your mom now, how do you feel?"

I thought about it. I had been so full of anger and fear when I entered the room, but somehow, over the last thirty minutes, that had changed. I wasn't afraid of this woman anymore.

"I don't like her," I said slowly. "If anything I pity her."

"Why do you pity her?"

"Maybe because it's my only alternative to being angry at her. She's weak and naïve, and she is the worst mom in history. She's just a pathetic person not worth my time."

Tina sniffled.

"Tina, do you think Cia's words are unfair?" Bruce asked her.

"No," she said softly. "I understand why she would feel that way."

"Is there anything else you wish to say to Cia?"

"I just hope that me being here has helped you heal a bit of the damage I've caused in your life."

"And Cia, do you have anything you wish to say to your mom before we end this session?"

"Yes. I want to thank you." My words surprised her, and even Gabriel turned his head and gave me an incredulous look.

"My friend Violet says that every person serves as either an inspiration or a warning. Because of you I don't touch alcohol. Because of you I haven't had sex or gotten pregnant by accident. Because of you I know what kind of mom *not* to be if I ever have children. Watching you has served as the clearest warning, and I'm confident that I'll *never* be like you."

Tina sat there and blinked like her eyelashes could somehow protect her from my words.

I felt an incredible surge of power and liberation as I spoke to the woman whom I had feared and now only pitied. "The best thing I can say about you is that you didn't get an abortion when you were pregnant with me, and for that I want to thank you too."

Tina gave me a stifled smile and looked to Bruce who cleared his throat.

"With Cia's thanks, I think we should close this session, and I want to thank you both for your great work.

Bruce gave a nod to Gabriel. "Will you please stay with Cia while I take Tina to her car?"

"Of course."

Tina got up and looked at me. Maybe she was hoping to shake my hand or give me a hug, but I gave her a short goodbye and looked away.

As soon as Tina and Bruce had left the room, my shoulders sank and I released a heavy sigh.

Gabriel took my hands and leaned close to me. "I'm so proud of you – you kicked ass."

My hands were shaking from the built-up adrenaline and I was suddenly a bit lightheaded.

"I did it." I looked at him. "It's over."

"How do you feel?" he asked.

"Good. Surprisingly good… what did you think about the things I said?"

We went over the things that have been said, and Gabriel told me what he had wanted to say and how hard it had been for him to sit still and keep quiet.

When Bruce returned ten minutes later, I was looking through my notes and still discussing my answers and questions with Gabriel.

"Why did you have me write notes?" I asked Bruce.

He took a seat at the table and started polishing his glasses on his shirt. "Because most people don't listen very well; they interrupt and are busy thinking about what to respond. Taking notes forces your brain to pay attention. I also know from experience that afterwards you won't be able to remember much. The notes will help you later if you want to return to the conversation you had with your mom."

"Okay."

"How was it?" he asked. "Better or worse than you feared?"

"Both. I felt physically sick when I saw her, but now, I feel so much lighter, almost like I'm high on Oxy pills or something."

Bruce smiled. "You're just high on endorphins and relief, and you should be – you did really well."

"Thank you."

"The next step for you is to forgive your mom. You don't need to tell her if you don't want to, but it's an important part of releasing the past."

"So you keep saying," I said dryly.

"At least think about it, Cia. Forgiveness won't change your past, but it'll change your future."

"Yeah, yeah, small steps, my friend." I got up and walked toward the door. When I looked back over my shoulder I saw Bruce smiling at me.

"You look as pleased as a cat who just filled its tummy with milk and found a spot in the sun to take a nap," I said.

"I am pleased," he said with a smile on his face. "You can't see it yet, but your life just took a monumental turn and I'm honored that I got to witness it. I'm truly proud of you, Cia.

It moved me deeply – this authoritarian figure expressing his pride for me. I'm sure my body was a grand mix of all sorts of hormones being pumped around, and that's part of why I felt so emotional.

"Thanks," I said and left before I did something lame, such as hugging the mad therapist.

CHAPTER 15
Money

Cia

On my last day at the camp I overheard Gabriel talking on the phone with his mom. He had kept in regular contact with her; I got the impression they were close.

"Sure, I can swing by in a few days. I'm heading home tomorrow morning."

He was sitting on the bed with his back to me, but turned his head to see me when I came out of the steaming bathroom after my shower.

"I know, but it was a spontaneous thing. I needed this time alone to decompress and a cabin in the forest was the perfect place." He winked at me as I stood with my towel around me.

He hadn't told her about me but repeatedly explained that he was by himself. I understood his motives and rationally knew a phone wasn't the best way to break the news of my existence, but on a deeper level it bothered me that Gabriel was treating me like a secret, just like my dad always had.

"Love you, Mom," he said, ended the call, and reached his hand out to me. "Come here."

I moved closer and he pulled me down on his right thigh and placed his arms around me.

"You're still my daughter for one more day," he said and leaned his head on my shoulder.

"I don't think teen daughters sit on their father's lap," I said dryly.

"I'm going to miss this," he said quietly.

"Me on your lap?"

"The closeness between us. It feels so natural to be around you and I've come to... really care for you over these two weeks."

I gave him a smile. "Well, I'm still going to be around, you know, crashing on your couch and all."

"I know..." he said, "But will you still allow me to touch you like this and call you sweetheart and precious?"

The answer was a loud all-engulfing *yes*, inside my head, but I played it cool. "Do you want to?"

He looked me deeply into my eyes. "Yeah, I want to."

"Right, because family is important to you and I'm your niece?" I asked to clarify.

His brows knitted together and he opened his mouth to speak when there was a knock on the door.

"You get the door," I said and disappeared into the bathroom with the small pile of clothes that was today's outfit.

I could hear Gabriel talking to Bruce while I dressed in a pair of black, ripped denim shorts, and a loose mint-green t-shirt with a neckline wide enough to fall casually over one shoulder. I took a minute to study the print on the shirt, a cartoon skater girl with her arms crossed and a text saying "Who said I need your freaking approval to feel good about myself?"

It figured that my last teen outfit was the first I actually liked. I wondered if they would let me keep the t-shirt as a souvenir.

"What did Bruce want?" I asked when I returned to our bedroom.

Gabriel stood topless and was searching the closet for a clean t-shirt. I would never get tired of seeing his ripped body but as soon as he turned to look at me, I dropped my gaze to my hands.

"He wanted to know if you had finished the last painting."

"Impatient much?" I muttered and went to pick it up. "Did you show it to him?"

"No, of course not. It's your painting. You should show him yourself."

All six paintings were done now, and this last one would be especially hard to part with.

Gabriel put on his t-shirt, hugged me from behind, and placed his head on top of mine. "I love that painting," he said.

"Me too."

We both stood for a while and just looked at it.

It was a portrait of me standing strong, with my blond hair blowing in the wind, and an expression of determination on my face. I was wearing my black pants and my military boots with my left hand victoriously in the air, clutching a wig of long black hair.

My other hand was tearing off a black button-down shirt, revealing that underneath I had a Superwoman costume on.

Ten minutes later when we brought it to Bruce he, of course, had his own interpretation of my painting.

"I see you have torn off your black façade and found your inner strength," he said and gave me a nod of approval.

"Yeah, pretty much, although I don't feel like a hero or anything," I emphasized.

"Cia, sit down for a moment." Bruce pointed to a chair. "I like your paintings."

"Thank you."

"I mean, I don't know much about art so my opinion isn't worth much, but I know someone who does know about art."

Gabriel sat down too. "Who?" he asked.

"Darren, a former client that I helped a few years ago. I remembered him when I saw your first portrait of G, because he always sends me invitations to his art gallery in Seattle, and I thought that I would ask for his guidance on how best to help you. I called him last week and we discussed ways for you to make money off your talent and came up with different ideas."

"Such as?" I asked.

"Well, to mention a few, you could illustrate children's books, or work at paid company events painting portraits. And of course there's the option of teaching art classes to children or others who want to learn. Anyway, he asked me to send him photos of your paintings, so he could spread them around in his network to see if someone has a job for you."

"And?" I asked and almost held my breath.

"And he called me today with good news."

I moved to the edge of my chair. "Someone has a job for me?"

"Not yet, but he was so impressed with your paintings that he wants to do an exhibition with your paintings in his gallery."

"What?" Gabriel cried out and broke into a huge grin. "That's amazing, sugar."

I could hardly breathe. "What does that mean?"

Bruce pushed his glasses up on his nose. "From what I understand, he'll exhibit the paintings and invite people who love art to come see them and buy them. He gets a cut and you get the rest."

"But I don't own the paintings, they belong here." I said. "I'll have to create new ones."

Bruce made a "tsk-tsk" sound and waved a hand dismissively. "Of course you own the paintings, Cia, I just wanted you to express your emotions as part of the therapy. If you want to donate one of the paintings to our facility we would be honored, but you're welcome to take them all with you when you leave."

I resolutely went to the row of pictures leaning against the wall. "I want you to have this one," I said and picked up the one with the two hands he had loved so much, and handed it to him.

"My favorite one," he said and smiled. "Thank you, Cia, I hope to see you make good money off your art and I will cherish this painting."

"So what happens now? Are we done now?" I asked and sat down again.

"No, today we will sum up what has happened these past two weeks, which means a lot of reflection. I'm happy that you'll move in with Gabriel when you leave tomorrow morning, and hopefully you'll have a job and a place to live before he moves to Missouri in a few months. We'll continue with weekly phone sessions, and I'll write a report for your court hearing."

"All right, sounds good."

Bruce leaned back in his chair. "So let me ask you this, Cia, did you achieve what you came for?"

I was trying to think back to my first day at the camp. The anger I had been consumed by. The anxiety that had filled my thoughts, and the defensive attitude I had portrayed to the world. It seemed like a complete shift had occurred, and even though I was still scared of the upcoming court hearing, I hadn't missed the oxycodone pills as much as I had thought I would.

"I don't even remember what I said I wanted to achieve," I said and looked at Gabriel. "Wasn't it something about money?"

Bruce answered before Gabriel. "Our primary goal was to get you off the oxycodone pills and you said that in order to not need them, you needed money, remember?"

"Yes, and you translated money as a place to stay and food and stuff,"

Bruce nodded. "Safety and security."

"Then I suppose I kind of got what I came for."

"Kind of?"

"Well, it's not like I'm leaving here with a job, but there's the potential of making money at the exhibition – and more importantly, I feel so much better inside than when I came. I'm well rested, I'm well fed, and…" I looked at Gabriel. "G has given me more hugs and kisses these past two weeks than in my twenty-one years combined.

Gabriel grinned. "What can I say, I like to cuddle."

"What do you think of our methods?" Bruce asked.

Gabriel and I exchanged a glance and then we broke into a loud snicker. "Oh, your methods are crazy. To be honest I don't even think they're legal, but hey… I feel better and stronger than I have ever felt before, so I can't really be angry with you."

"Which part was the hardest for you?" Bruce asked.

"The diaper, definitely the diaper."

Bruce frowned. "Interesting. I would have thought you would say the part about letting your daddy bathe you."

He turned to Gabriel. "What part was the most challenging for you?"

Gabriel looked thoughtful. "Seeing Cia upset and crying was the hardest part. It's been some emotionally intense weeks, for sure."

"Will you two keep in contact when you move to Missouri?" Bruce asked.

"Absolutely," Gabriel said at the same time as I said, "I hope so."

I spent the afternoon writing down reflections on my life so far and what I'd learned from my time in the camp. Seeing my milestones on paper made me realize how I had grown and become someone else.

Someone comfortable in a man's presence. Someone who had been strong enough to confront my mother, someone able to channel my emotions into my art. Someone owning my sadness and darkness as part of me instead of letting it completely consume me.

It was a small miracle what two weeks of full-time therapy, good food, plenty of sleep, peaceful nature, and the loving care of a family member had done to me.

Bruce and Gabriel had shown me that life could be more than just survival, and I was ready to go out and live it.

CHAPTER 16
The man in the Painting

Gabriel

After our last dinner at the camp, Cia was busy talking to the weird guy who had been a baby for a week. He was a child now and she was the only one he would talk to. His mom had told me a few days ago that they had already tried traditional treatments to help him with his anxiety, but after his fifth suicide attempt it had been recommended to them to call Dr. Bruce.

I had to admit the guy looked much better than when he arrived, and Cia even managed to make him smile at times.

"G, do you have a minute?" Bruce called out to me from the doorway.

"Sure." I got up and followed him down the hallway to the dining room, where Cia's paintings were placed on the dining room table.

"I thought we should wrap these for your drive tomorrow," he said.

"All right." I picked up the role of bubble wrap and carried it to the table, when he spoke again.

"You still believe he's helping her float?" I followed his gaze to the blue painting where Cia was floating on water with my hands covering her private parts.

I nodded. "Uh-huh."

"You know," he said thoughtfully. "The more I look at that picture, the more I worry for that man."

"Why?"

He looked closer. "Do you see his face? How is he breathing?"

I looked at the painting. "I don't know, it's just a symbolic painting of me bathing her."

"Well, maybe you should think about it, because if he truly is helping her float, then what's going to happen to her when he drowns?"

"What are you saying?"

He frowned and looked at me with one of his freaky X-ray glances.

"Tell me about your feelings for Cia."

"Ehh…" It wasn't the first time he had put me on the spot. Bruce and I had shared walks in the forest and talks around the bonfire about Cia, but also about my time in Afghanistan and my nightmares. I had come to the conclusion that helping others wasn't just a job to him, it was embedded in his persona. He couldn't switch it off.

"I care about her," I said.

"Do you lust for her?" he asked and I jerked back.

"No."

He held up both palms. "No judgment."

I swallowed a few times. "I don't lust for her," I lied. "But sometimes I get a little confused about my feelings for her."

"Confused how?"

I exhaled deeply. "It's all so entangled that I'm afraid I might confuse one feeling for another."

"Like what?"

"Argh, it's hard to put in words, but it's like when a bartender hands you a drink with a bit of everything and asks you: can you taste what's in it?"

"Fair enough, but try to tell me some of the emotions you can identify."

"Okay…" I said and looked at him. "Sympathy, empathy, pity, and shame would be just a few, and then there are moments when I feel something close to love."

Bruce whistled low. "Wow, a powerful cocktail like that could cause you a heavy headache."

"I know, right?"

I picked up the picture with the floating man. "I got thrown into this, but Cia is amazing and I've learned so much about myself these past two weeks."

Bruce wrapped one of the pictures and stopped midway. "You're right, she is amazing... but also very troubled."

I arched a brow. "Not compared to when I first met her."

Bruce took a step closer and placed a hand on my shoulder. "G, listen to me. Cia still has a long way to go. Please don't make the mistake of thinking that from now on she's going to be all chirpy and fine."

"I won't," I said.

"Good!" he nodded softly. "I admire what you do for her and that you've taken her under your wing, but don't enter into a sexual relationship with her unless you are really serious about it."

I tensed up. I had never told him about my physical attraction to her. *How the fuck does he know? Did he finally find the recording of us showering together?*

"You have nothing to worry about," I said. "Cia and I don't see each other like that. We're just really good friends now."

He chuckled. "Nice try, G, I may have glasses, but I'm not blind. You two can play role-plays and pretend you're family all you want, but it's not blood that you share. It's a mutual attraction."

I opened my mouth to protest, but he continued. "Just be warned that once you cross that line with her, you won't be able to go back to being just uncle and niece. It will be all or nothing with her." He patted my shoulder a few last times before he changed the subject and started talking about the Seahawks last season.

⟨ ∞ ⟩

During our three-hour long drive back to Seattle, Cia was a lot more talkative than when we drove from Seattle to the camp two weeks ago. She was dressed in the clothes we had bought her in Ocean Shores, and looked healthy and happy as she chatted excitedly about her upcoming exhibition and about the hikes we had taken the last days.

In the meantime Bruce's warning ran through my mind several times. He was right. I was the only family member she had a connection with, and no matter how much I wanted to know how it would feel like to be inside of her and hear her moan my name, I couldn't screw that up for her. Besides, I was moving to Missouri in a little over three months and wasn't looking for a long-distance relationship.

Fuck! My head was so confused. Why was I even contemplating hooking up with Cia? Blood related or not, she was still my brother's daughter and I needed to get a freaking grip on myself.

I will keep my distance, I promised myself and in that moment, I really intended to.

CHAPTER 17
Lake Union

Cia

Our first night in Gabriel's apartment I spent on the couch. In my twenty-one years of living, I had only shared a bed with one other person: Gabriel. And now that I was back to being alone, I missed his warmth and closeness.

Gabriel was out with friends while I was lying alone in the apartment, looking out on the idyllic view of Lake Union with the pretty lights from the restaurants and houseboats.

My thoughts where occupied with the people I knew and how they would react to my being Cia, compared to Black. I gave a small snicker at the thought that they might not even recognize me without my piercings and black armor. I could suit up and go find them since I had my black outfit in a bag, but surprising them with my new look might be more fun. I was pretty sure that Daniel, at least, would be shocked to see me like this.

Daniel and I used to date... or date is maybe not the right word for two people like us, but Daniel was the first to break down my wall and become my friend. He was also the first guy to ever kiss me and hold my hand.

He's older than me by fifteen years and I met him when he stayed at The Inn for a few months four years ago. Back then, I was a junior in high school and he had just retired from the army, but he was determined to get to know me and volunteered to keep an eye out for the cops when I did my street art. The thing I love about

Daniel is that he's got a great sense of humor and he takes me for who I am.

The problem with Daniel is that he's got a temper and suffers from severe PTSD. He's been kicked out of four apartments in the time I've known him because he gets in trouble with neighbors all the time. Still, he's a good guy, and I would call Daniel right now, if I had a phone.

A quick gaze at the microwave in the kitchen told me it was already a quarter past eleven. If I wanted to find Daniel, I would have to go search his usual hangouts, which weren't the nicest parts of the city. Good thing I wasn't a scaredy-cat.

⟨ ∞ ⟩

The realization that things were different creeped up on me slowly, and by the time I reached the Pike Place Market area I really missed my black armor.

When I dressed as a Goth, most people wouldn't give me much attention. Some would even cross the street. Now, wearing my white outfit and blond hair I received too much unwanted attention. Creepy guys would whistle and catcall at me. One even sniffed at me and called me his flower.

These were *my* streets, god damn it. I knew this area like my own back pocket – the best places to attract customers, escape routes if the police showed. As Black, I had walked here fearlessly. As Cia, I was constantly on alert.

Daniel wasn't in any of the three first places I searched and when I finally found him, he was down by the pier hanging out with a bunch of people that were for most parts as troubled as us.

I leaned up against a lamppost and waited for him to spot me. Several of the people in the group shot me quick looks and frowns and even Daniel glanced over a few times. None of them recognized me as their friend.

I stepped closer and stood only a few feet from them when they all turned their heads.

"Hey, lady, something we can help you with?" one of them said with a bit of hostility.

"Don't give me that tone, Boots. I'm here to see Daniel."

Boots narrowed his eyes and Daniel pushed up from the bench he'd been sitting on. "What the fuck?"

I stood still as he stepped closer to me. "Black?" he asked and took me in with an incredulous stare.

I grinned. "Hey, D... did you miss me?"

Normally Daniel would have hugged me. He was one of the few I allowed to touch me, but he looked uncertain about how to greet me. "What happened to you? Did you join a cult or something?"

My grin widened. "You could say that. I got busted for a visit to Bartell's and got taken by the cops."

He nodded. "I figured it was something like that. So is this a disguise to hide from the police?" He pointed up and down my body.

"Nahh... I've got my first court hearing in ten days, and since I stole meds the judge and my lawyer advised me to go into rehab before the hearing."

"Ohh... so that's why you look like an angel all dressed in white. Did they make you meditate for a few weeks to find your inner peace and shit like that?" he said with sympathy.

"Not exactly, but I've got good news."

Daniel and I took a walk and I told him about Gabriel and the camp. Several times he was bending over laughing so hard that he cried.

"I don't think you appreciate how traumatic it was to hear a woman dressed as a child ask me if I wanted to go play in the woods with her daddy."

Daniel had tears rolling down his face and was fighting to stop laughing enough so that he could speak. "I'm sorry, Black, but that's hysterical. Why didn't you just kick her ass or something?"

I wrinkled my nose. "I didn't want anything to do with her, or her ass."

"Tell me about the crazy therapist again – did he seriously make you wear a diaper?"

"I shouldn't have told you that…"

"Oh, come on, Black, it's me, your best friend. We tell each other everything." He was still laughing.

"Yeah, but if you tell anyone about my humiliation, I'll knock out your front teeth."

"Hey, that's just mean."

"I saw my mom," I said and that finally made him stop laughing.

He grabbed my arm and made me come to an abrupt stop. "You saw her at the camp?"

"Uh-huh. She came for a session."

"And?"

"She apologized for being a bad mom and I got to tell her how I feel about her."

"Shit… that had to be unpleasant. Did it help?"

I walked on and turned left to cut through Denny Park. "Yes, it helped. At least I'm no longer scared of her. I used to be afraid she would find me. Scared that she would suddenly confront me on the street. But now that I've seen her, I know she can't hurt me anymore and more importantly, I know she doesn't want to hurt me."

"That's awesome, right?"

"Yeah… I used to obsess about her, but now that threat is gone."

"Don't worry, you'll find new things to obsess about; that's how our minds work."

"I hope not."

He laughed. "Take it from an expert."

"How have you been?"

"Not good, but my social worker got me a new place."

"You have an apartment?"

"I'm moving in next week… it's going to be sweet being off the streets again."

"Where have you been sleeping?"

"Damian's floor mostly."

"He still got that place by the Irish pub?"

"Yep, it's a shithole, but it's better than a park bench."

"I'm happy you're getting your own place, and this time you'll keep out of trouble with the neighbors."

"Of course."

"No, I mean it. No loud music in the middle of the night, and no arguments with them."

"I only play the music to drown out the voices in my head."

"I know, but then use a headset or something. Or better yet, tell those damn voices to shut the fuck up."

"Ha," he scoffed. "As if I haven't tried that already."

"Well, try harder then. Man up, soldier, you can beat this."

He saluted me, army style. "Yes, General."

We walked on for five blocks until we could see Lake Union.

"Thank you for walking me back," I said.

"I want to meet your uncle."

"Why?"

He put his hands in his pockets and rocked back and forth on his toes and heels. "Because he sounds incredible and I want to shake his hand and thank him for being good to my girl."

"I'm not your girl, Daniel, I'm your friend."

He smiled. "Whatever you say."

"I'll introduce you, but not tonight, okay?"

"When?"

"Soon."

I rose up to hug Daniel.

"Sweet dreams," he said and kissed me on my cheek.

"You too – and D…"

"Yeah?"

"You need to take a shower, you kind of stink."

He grinned. "I took a shower this morning… it's the clothes."

"Then wash your clothes."

"Will do." He raised his hand and waved as he turned and walked back.

Gabriel

It was great being out and drinking beers with some of my good old friends. Still, three of the five guys are fathers now, so we didn't tour the city like we used to when we were in college. A little after midnight they started looking at their cellphones, talking about babies and kids waking up early.

In my tipsy state, I called them a bunch of wussies.

It took me twenty minutes to walk from the bar on Capitol Hill to the apartment, and I tiptoed through the living room to avoid waking up Cia, but when I passed the couch I stopped and stared; it was empty.

A smile spread on my lips and I entered my bedroom, but Cia wasn't in my bed either, and that's when I started to worry.

Cia

"Where the hell have you been?"

Those were the first words that met me when I got back to the apartment.

Gabriel looked like a wild boar ready to attack, with his nostrils flaring and his eyes wide open and focused in on me.

"I went out," I said and closed the door behind me. "What's wrong, did something happen to you?"

"What happened to me was that I came home and you weren't here."

I frowned in confusion. "So?"

"So I worried, and it's not like I can call you to know you're all right. What if you were hurt somewhere? I've been worried shitless because of you."

I walked closer, tilting my head and trying to understand why he would freak out like this. "It's only one o'clock... I'm not used to anyone worrying about me."

Taking a step forward, he pulled me into his arms. "Well, I'm not your mom, and I worry. You should have left a note at least."

"I'm sorry," I said, not liking his smell of beer and pushing at him to make him ease his tight grip around me.

"Where did you go?" he asked.

"To see Daniel."

"Your friend?"

"Uh-huh. I figured he was worried about me, so I wanted to tell him I was fine. He wants to meet you."

"Me? Why?"

I chuckled. "I asked him that too, and he says he wants to thank you for being good to his girl."

Gabriel tensed. "What is that supposed to mean?"

"Just that he appreciates everything that you've done for me."

"No, I mean why does he calls you 'his girl?'" Gabriel asked in a gruff voice. "Is he your boyfriend?"

I shrugged. "No, but we've been good friends for years."

"How good?" Gabriel said in a tone I didn't like.

I tried to pull back. "That's none of your business." I don't know why I said that, except that his question felt like an attack and it made me defensive.

"Did you sleep with Daniel tonight?" Gabriel asked, and there was raw accusation in his tone.

"I don't need your permission to go out and I certainly don't need to tell you anything about my sex life," I snapped back.

He released me and folded his arms in front of him. "So if I went out and fucked someone, or even brought her back here, you would be okay with that?"

My heart broke a little, but I managed to lie right to his face. "Of course. You're my uncle, not my boyfriend."

He stomped off and slammed the door to his bedroom. Whatever had just happened between us told me one thing. I needed to find a job and my own place. I couldn't be here if he ever brought a woman home and had sex with her. I would die inside.

⟨ ∞ ⟩

The next week was awkward. We shared small talk and pleasantries, but Gabriel was gone most days visiting friends and family.

Somehow it was easier that way.

I visited Darren, the gallery owner who wanted to exhibit my art, and he surprised me in so many ways. Not only was he as tall and wide as Gabriel, but he was also more feminine than any woman I've ever met, with the way he swung his hands around in an exaggerated way. When he spoke he had that peculiar articulation of the sibilants where his pronunciation of s and z sounded as if he was holding his tongue between his teeth. I suspected the man didn't really lisp but was expressing being gay in a dramatic way that was in complete alignment with his flamboyant style of clothing.

Not many would be able to pull off wearing tight leather pants and cowboy boots, supplemented with a neatly ironed blue shirt, a vest with a white and green harlequin pattern, and a pink bowtie.

It made for an interesting mix of how a cowboy, a biker, an accountant, a golf player, and a male stripper would dress. And as the cherry on top he sported a man-bun and a hipster beard. Darren Hill was a walking piece of art himself.

"I'm so happy to meet you, my little prodigy," he said. "Bruce has told me all about you."

I widened my eyes, hoping that wasn't true.

"Oh, don't worry." He swung his hand through the air. "Bruce didn't talk about *why* you were in his care, and there's nothing that goes on in that camp that can surprise me." He leaned closer, put a hand to his lips, and lowered his voice. "I've been a client myself."

Bruce had already told me that much. "Did it help you?"

"Oh God, yes," Darren said with a dramatic puff of air. "Before, I was 'Darren the Depressed,' but luckily Bruce the Almighty helped me accept who I truly am and now I'm 'Darren the Daring.'"

"Well, you certainly seem to dare being unique," I said with eyes running up and down his outfit.

"Are you saying that you don't like my sense of fashion?" The way he placed his hands on his hips made me nervous. Had I already insulted the man who was supposed to help me sell my paintings?

"I'm sorry, I didn't mean any offense," I said but Darren just broke into a laugh and patted my shoulder.

"You should've seen your face, Bonita, I'm just messing with you. As you can see I'm not chasing mainstream validation here."

"I can see that." I looked around and saw some rather disturbing and interesting paintings on the walls.

Despite my first impression of Darren as a somewhat flighty person, he turned out to be very organized and structured when it came to his business.

He brought out paperwork that needed to be signed and pointed to his outfit. "It's the shirt, vest, and bowtie part of me that keeps the business financially healthy so that the more playful part of me can have some fun." When he said "playful" he wiggled his eyebrows and patted his leather pants.

I sensed this was an area I didn't need to know about, so I just smiled up at him politely.

We got the paperwork sorted out, and since I didn't have a phone I gave him Gabriel's number.

"It's actually perfect," Darren said. "You see, I had an artist fall through, so you're filling his spot for next week."

"Okay, that sounds good."

"Ah, I'm telling you, some artists are such drama queens and impossible to work with; promise you won't be like that."

I promised

"I see great things for you, my wunderkind," he said and held my hand with both of his. "There is so much raw emotion in your paintings – they will sell fast, be sure of it."

I took a few nervous steps before I blurted out the question I wanted to know the answer to so badly.

"How much do you think the paintings will sell for?"

"Not a lot, I'm afraid." He gave a little pout. "Not because they aren't good, but it's just that you're a new name, so we can't charge more than two or three thousand per painting. But we'll get you exposed and make them hungry for more, and that's where we'll make the real money."

"And you said my cut was fifty percent?"

"Yes, fifty percent, so probably you'll make a profit of between six and eight thousand dollars on the five paintings.

To me six or eight thousand dollars sounded like a million. I had never held a hundred-dollar bill in my hand, nor had a bank account. I was used to dealing with crumpled ones and fives, so to hear Darren talk about thousands of dollars felt surreal.

I walked back to Gabriel's place in a bubble, making a mental list of art supplies I needed to buy in order to make more paintings.

To my surprise Gabriel was home when I got there and he wasn't alone.

I smelled her perfume before I saw her. It was a heavy floral fragrance that filled the small apartment and felt suffocating to me.

I walked into the living room and saw Gabriel talking to a beautiful woman with shoulder-length copper-colored hair, who looked to be his age. She had her hand on his knee and they were speaking quietly.

"Hey," I said to announce my arrival since neither of them seemed to have noticed.

"Cia," Gabriel got up and moved toward me. "I didn't expect you back so soon."

I looked at the woman, who gave me a quizzical look, and I remembered his words from last week when he asked how I would feel if he brought a woman home with him.

I had told him he could do as he pleased, but my belly didn't agree with that decision and I found it really hard to smile at her.

"Ehhm... Mel, this is Cia, my... ehhh... roommate."

She arched a brow. "As if."

"No, I'm actually his nie–" I was going to say niece, but he cut me off.

"Cia, this is my sister Melody." His eyes were communicating that she didn't know about my existence and clearly he wasn't going to tell her.

She reached her hand out. "Nice to meet you, Cia... you were saying?"

"Nothing," I said and gave a strained smile.

"Aww... that's sweet," she chuckled. "My baby brother got a new girlfriend and he's afraid of telling me."

"It's not that," he said.

"Of course it is. She even has a key to your place." Melody was about my height and dressed impeccably."

"How did you two meet?" she asked me with a sly smile.

I looked at Gabriel for help but he just took my hand and pulled me closer.

"We met a few weeks back, and I was actually thinking about introducing Cia to the family soon."

"Oh, so it's serious then?" she said, sounding pleased.

"Let's just say that we've grown close."

Melody broke into a wide smile. "I'm so happy for you, G." She gave me a nod of approval. "You should totally come and meet the wolf pack, and no matter what my brother told you, we're not so bad once you get to know us."

"I never said you were bad," Gabriel exclaimed.

"How about family brunch this Sunday at Dad's house? Wouldn't that be fun?" she suggested and to my horror Gabriel nodded.

"Sure, that could work. We'll be there."

My jaw clenched and I shot him a dirty look.

"Oh-oh, if looks could kill..." Melody chuckled and reached up and hugged Gabriel. "It looks like your girlfriend wants a word with you." Melody waved at me as she passed me and spoke over her shoulder. "I get it, meeting family can be a tough one, but my brother is worth it and we won't bite. I promise." Gabriel let Melody out and came back to talk.

"Your girlfriend?" I said with my hands firmly placed on my hips.

"Did you want me to tell her who you really are? I didn't know if you were ready for her to know, but if you are, I can run after her and get her back here."

"Maybe... I don't know. But your girlfriend, G... really?"

He clenched his jaw. "You sound like the thought is offensive to you."

"No, it's just that I've never really been anyone's girlfriend," I said and pulled off my sweater in rough movements.

"Hey, come here," he said and pulled me to the couch, where he planted me on his lap.

"Maybe this is not a bad plan. With a family brunch everyone is going to be there, and we could drop the bomb and reach everyone at the same time."

"I'm a bomb now?"

Gabriel ignored my comment. "Brent would stay away if he knew you were coming, but I could smuggle you in under his nose as my girlfriend. It could work, Cia."

"No, it wouldn't work. He would leave the minute he saw me."

"He has no clue how you look. You were a child the last time he saw you. I think he deserves to face the family's wrath when they learn what has been done to one of their own."

"You really think they would take my side?"

"Absolutely. They better take your side."

I knitted my brows. "All right then. So you introduce me as your girlfriend and then what? When do you tell them who I really am?"

He shrugged and played with a lock of my hair. "I don't know; once they're all at the table and enjoying the food, I think."

"Okay," I said slowly. "I'm terrified, but I want to do it."

He wrapped me tighter. "You won't be alone, sugar; I'll be right there beside you."

It was strange but familiar to be in his lap again, and to hear him say that he had my back made me all mushy inside.

"I'm not sure what scares me the most; meeting my whole family for the first time or being introduced as someone's girlfriend."

"Don't say that." Gabriel brushed a lock of hair behind my ear. "Whoever gets you as his girlfriend is a lucky guy, Cia," he said and stroked my hair.

I knew he was only trying to make me feel better, but it was still nice of him to say it.

"Thanks... and right back at you."

He grinned. "I don't plan on being anyone's girlfriend."

I tilted my head, "Are you sure? Because I just met Darren today, and I'm sure he would snatch you up in a heartbeat."

"Darren, the gallery owner?"

"Yes."

"Is he gay?"

"Yup, times ten."

"Well, I don't have a problem with gays as long as they don't hit on me."

"You can hardly blame a guy for hitting on you. After all, you're very attractive."

Gabriel smiled. "You think I'm attractive?"

I rolled my eyes. "I told you so the first time I met you... dreamy high school guy... remember?"

He nodded. "That's right. So if I weren't your uncle, would you have wanted to be my girlfriend?"

I didn't want to answer that question. That was just mean, as we both knew he was way out of my league.

"I don't date assholes," I said with a smile and moved away.

"Hey, you told me I was beautiful both inside and out."

"You are."

"So why am I suddenly an asshole?"

I looked back over my shoulder. "For asking such a shitty question."

"How is that a shitty question?"

"Well, you might as well have asked me if I wanted to go to the moon."

"I don't understand – how is that the same?"

I shook my head and stepped to the kitchen to get a Coke from the fridge. "Never mind, let's just drop it, okay?"

"No, Cia, talk to me. Why am I an ass for asking you to be my girlfriend... I mean... for asking you if you wanted to be my girlfriend... if I wasn't your uncle," he babbled.

Why the hell won't he just drop it? I turned around and faced him. "It's a stupid question that shouldn't be answered. What if I said yes? That would just be awkward for both of us... and if I said no, I would be kind of rude, don't you think? There's no right answer to that question, so I don't want to answer it.

"But if..."

"Stop it, G – how would you like it if I asked you the same question? You wouldn't want to tell me no and potentially hurt my feelings, would you?

"No."

"See, and it would be equally cruel of you to say yes and give me hope that someone like you would ever want someone like me."

Gabriel's eyes widened. "Someone like you? What is that supposed to mean?"

"I'm not exactly the cute college girl you would proudly take home to meet your mom."

"No, you're the cute artist who is compassionate and fun and a great friend."

"Stop it."

"No, I won't stop it," Gabriel said and got right in front of me. "I think you really need to hear this." He cupped my face but I kept my eyes on the floor.

"Look at me, Cia."

I lifted my gaze to meet his warm brown eyes.

"If you weren't family, I would have hit on you so hard that it's not even funny."

I frowned in confusion. Surely he didn't mean that.

"I'm sorry if it makes you feel uncomfortable," he said. "But you're a badass, and the way you face your fears and conquer every obstacle in front of you puts me in awe of you."

"You're not serious, are you?" I asked.

"Yes…" He smiled. "I want to be as tough as you when I grow up."

That made me laugh. "You look pretty grown-up to me, and you even got a medal for bravery."

"Don't brush me off, Cia. If you could see yourself through my eyes you would see how special you are."

I shook my head. "You need to have your eyes checked then, because I'm a mess, G."

"You might think so, but from what I've seen these last three weeks, I think you can do anything."

I didn't know what to say, but I managed to produce a what-do-you-know "Huh."

"So now that your uncle has admitted to being a pervert, tell me the answer to my question."

I arched a brow. "Would I want to be your girlfriend if you weren't my uncle?"

"Yes."

I thought of a millions smart-ass replies to get out of telling him the truth, but in the end I just nodded.

His eyes widened. "You would?"

"Yes."

He swallowed hard. "Fuck..."

"Yeah, well, it doesn't really change anything. It's all hypothetical anyway." I put down the Coke and turned my back on him, stepping over to the balcony door to look out at the stunning view. But Gabriel wasn't done with this conversation and moved up behind me. His closeness made me hold my breath.

"Cia."

"Uh-huh." I stood quietly, hugging myself, feeling out of my comfort zone, and hoping that our admissions wouldn't make things awkward between us.

"What if I told you I want you?" His voice was low and raw and I could feel his warm breath on my neck.

His closeness and the dirty images his words inspired in my mind made me close my eyes and take a deep intake of air.

"Cia." He turned me around. "Look at me."

When I opened my eyes, his gaze was boring into mine, asking questions I couldn't answer out loud.

"Tell me you want me too?" he murmured in a hoarse voice.

Swallowing hard, and focusing on my breathing was all I could do before he leaned in to kiss me, and with the touch of his lips, answers came pouring out in an instant. *Yes,* I wanted him too.

I've seen movies with people kissing greedily and sloppily and I've always found that repulsive, but the way Gabriel kissed me was nothing like that. It wasn't intrusive or aggressive but more prodding and testing, as if he understood that this was new territory for me. I grew bolder and our kisses became more passionate, but

I was still so focused on the strange sensation of his tongue in my mouth that I almost didn't notice him backing me into his bedroom.

Only when he pushed me softly down on his bed and started to undress me did it fully register where we were headed. What if Gabriel wanted to go all the way?

The room was brightly lit with sunlight shining through the large window, and a shyness crept up on me when he removed my bra.

"What's wrong?" he asked when I covered my chest.

"Nothing, it's just..." I trailed off, painfully aware that Gabriel's ex-girlfriend had been a lingerie model, and that he had always been popular with women. How could I even begin to measure up to the women from his past?

"You are beautiful, Cia." His eyes shone with sincerity and he lowered his head to kiss my belly button and unzip my pants.

"I know what you want," I burst out. "I mean, I want it too... but..." My face heated up with the mortification I felt inside. *God, I am such a loser.*

"But what?" he asked with a confused expression on his handsome face.

Unable to express my thoughts, I looked away.

Gabriel moved up to stroke my hair and kiss me again. "What is it? Are you afraid I'll do something unpleasant to you, like that Dennis guy?"

I shook my head. I hadn't even thought of Dennis before he brought him up.

"You trust me, right?" G asked softly.

"Yes."

"Then what is it?" he asked and placed a kiss on my naked shoulder.

"I don't think I'll be very good at it," I said almost inaudibly.

"What?" Gabriel asked and lifted my face with a hand under my chin. "What did you say, sweetie?"

"I don't think you'll like it."

A smile reached his gorgeous brown eyes. "You don't think I'll like being with you?"

His smile made me feel stupid; it wasn't funny at all. This was a big mistake and I wanted to get up and leave. What was I thinking? Making out with Gabriel would just make things awkward between us. A long time ago, I had attempted to make out with Daniel and it had been a complete failure, with me closing down and lying as passively as a stiff board.

"I'm not good with intimacy," I explained and pushed away from him.

"Don't do that." He reached out for me. "You're just scared, babe, but don't believe for one second that you're no good at intimacy. You're talking to the man who woke up completely entangled with you every morning for two weeks, remember?

"That was different."

"How so?"

"Because it wasn't anything sexual. I'm not a very sexual person," I suggested.

"Really?" He arched a brow. "And what are you basing that assumption on?"

"I'm not interested in sex and I just don't get turned on easily."

"Is that so?"

"Yes." It wasn't a complete lie. I was twenty-one and only two guys had ever gotten close enough to kiss me, and Gabriel was the only man to evoke real desire in me. Typical, that my thoughts of inferiority would pop up at the most inopportune moment and crush the fire that had been burning between us a few moments ago.

"I can turn you on," Gabriel claimed. "If you give me a chance."

"Trust me, you're not missing out on anything. Daniel once tried, and I sucked at it." I was trying to put my bra back on, and it gave me an excuse to avoid looking at him.

"I'm not Daniel." His hard tone made me lift my gaze. "And I don't want to hear about you being with other men when I'm standing here with a raging boner and you're pulling away from me."

"It's not you. Don't you get it? It's me!" I exclaimed forcefully. "There's something wrong with me, you should know by now how fucked-up I am."

Gabriel was deeply frustrated; it radiated from him. "Why won't you at least give me a chance to prove to you that I can make this pleasant for you?"

"I'm sorry. But I just can't."

"You mean you won't," he said and turned on his heel.

Two minutes later I heard the TV in the living room and picked up my courage to walk in and sit down next to him. *American Ninja Warriors* was on, and one after one, brave men competed for the title by pushing themselves to the limit through some insane obstacles.

"Ouch," I said with a grimace when one of the guys took a nasty fall. "How come there are no women competing?" I asked.

"There are a few, but in general women aren't strong enough."

We watched another handful of fit guys struggle, and only one of them made it all the way through.

"Finally... a woman," I said when a short woman came on the screen looking super fit. "I bet she can do it."

"No way," Gabriel snorted. "She's too short."

"Wanna bet?"

He smirked. "What do you wanna bet?"

"The loser has to cook for a week," I suggested.

"I have a better suggestion." He moved forward and gave me a challenging stare. "A massage. The price should be a massage."

"You mean like a back rub?"

He shrugged. "Make up your mind... she's about to start."

My eyes were glued to the screen as the tiny woman rolled her shoulders and prepared to start racing.

"Okay, I'm in," I said and sat on the edge of my seat holding my breath and cheering on the inside for this female Ninja Warrior who was completely focused as she jumped, climbed, and pulled herself through monstrous obstacles to prove to herself and the world that women can do this too.

"You got this," I called out loud when she moved back to maximize the runway and get enough speed to run up a steeply curving wall that was sixteen feet high.

"There's no way she can do that," Gabriel said, and unfortunately he was right.

While the audience applauded the woman for trying her best I turned to look at Gabriel, who was watching me with a smug smile on his face.

"Okay... you win. So where do you want your massage?" I asked.

I got my answer when he got up and moved into his bedroom, stripping out of his shirt on the way.

"Do you have some lotion?" I asked.

Without talking he found lotion and pointed to the bed. "Lie down."

"Why?... I lost, so I'm giving you the massage," I said.

"I never said I wanted a massage if I won."

"You said the price was a massage."

He nodded. "In my case, I prefer to give it, so for the next hour, you will allow me to massage you."

CHAPTER 18
Pleasure

Cia

"But…"

"A bet is a bet."

I didn't feel too good about this. With what had just happened between us, I was a bit on edge and unsure of what Gabriel's agenda was.

"What kind of massage are we talking about?"

Gabriel moved closer and kissed me. "The kind you only get from your boyfriend."

I stiffened, and in response he pulled me close and spoke into my ear.

"I know you're frightened, but I'm asking you to trust me. Can you do that?"

My eyes were closed and my breathing shallow. "Okay, I'll try." This was like standing on a cliff, wanting to jump into the inviting blue water beneath, but feeling scared shitless. Gabriel was that annoying friend that pushed you from behind, and I wasn't sure yet if I should hate him or thank him for it.

"It's easier if you take your clothes off," he said and went to put on some nice music.

I undressed but kept my panties on and made sure to lie on my belly.

To my surprise Gabriel started talking about the TV show while rubbing my neck, shoulders, and back. It didn't feel sexual and I started to relax more. Maybe I had misjudged the situation.

His hands were strong and the way he braided his fingers into mine and made sure to stretch my palms was extremely nice.

Gabriel seemed completely at ease as he moved around in his pants only. I think he did it on purpose to taunt me, knowing that his trim torso would affect me. Of course I could have told him that the thing that got under my skin was his aroma. After crying in his arms during therapy, his smell was familiar and reminded me of comfort and care. I loved the smell of Gabriel.

"Turn over," he said after twenty minutes of massaging me.

I slowly rolled onto my back. The lovely music, his touch, his masculine fragrance, and his calming voice had relaxed me to the point where I wasn't as guarded as before. Besides, this was completely different, as I wasn't competing with any of his ex-girlfriends like I had before. There was no way for me to suck at getting a massage, because everyone knows that there is nothing else to do except lie still and relax.

Gabriel was moving up my legs, massaging my thighs with long strokes, and I noticed that he kept getting closer and closer to my private parts. The tingling sensation I'd been feeling during the last ten minutes increased, and when he put pressure on the insides of my legs they started spreading for him.

I didn't fight it.

Not even when his strokes started centering more and more around my pelvis and down to the vee of my thighs.

"You've got the cutest belly button," he said and placed an innocent kiss on it. It made me smile.

"Thanks."

His hands moved down and spread my legs wider.

"What are you doing?" I asked, lifting my head to look at him.

"Just relax. I promise I won't hurt you."

There was a moment when my heart forgot to beat while he grasped both sides of my panties and slowly pulled them off me while stubbornly keeping eye contact. "I won the bet, remember," he reminded me. Since I couldn't argue with that, and my whole body was vibrating with a tingling sensation, I simply took a deep breath and closed my eyes again.

"If you could only see what I see..." he muttered in a raspy voice and then I felt the strangest sensation. It was like a warm breeze hitting my most sensitive spot, but what followed made me jerk. It had to be his tongue, because nothing I had ever done to myself had felt remotely like this. All my nerve endings were on fire from his strong fingers knitting into my inner thighs and his tongue licking up the center of my folds.

I moaned and arched my back; it was the most incredible body sensation I'd ever experienced – I honestly had no idea oral sex would feel like this.

Gabriel groaned and circled his tongue around my clit, which made me gasp out loud.

"Gabriel," I exclaimed in a breathy voice. It sounded like a plea, but even I didn't know if I was pleading with him to stop or continue.

My hands were grasping the bedspread and I cried out in pleasure when he kept licking and teasing. It was like he was determined to explore every inch of my pussy, and it felt amazing.

Helpless whimpers and deep moans erupted from me when his strong hands kept me in place and spread my legs wider.

"You taste like fucking candy," he groaned, and took another long lick as if I was his favorite lollipop.

"Gabriel," I repeated in a sharp cry that was my best way to communicate the overwhelming sensation I was feeling. "More," I moaned.

The vibrations from his low chuckle against my clit made muscles in my belly contract and my legs shiver. I was getting close to coming and even though I had masturbated in the past, this was completely different.

"You want more? But you said you're not interested in sex." He chuckled again.

His words didn't register with me in my orgasmic state. I was so close to the edge that I shamelessly grabbed hold of his hair and pressed his head against me, wanting him to shut up and bring me to heaven.

He did.

In my case heaven felt like jolts of electricity making my inner walls cramp, and my toes curl. It lasted less than three seconds, but it was better than any Oxy pill I'd ever taken, and as soon as it was over I pushed him away, my clit too sensitive to be touched.

Out of breath, and overwhelmed by my first orgasm with a man, I was staring up into the ceiling unable to form a coherent thought.

"I love how responsive you are to me, sugar," Gabriel said and nipped at my inner thighs.

"Best massage in the history of mankind," I sighed.

"But we're only getting started." He winked.

The best way to describe my state would be the word "bliss." Our earlier discussion was forgotten. If this was how sex felt, then I was all in.

Gabriel moved up to kiss me, and the taste of myself on him was dirty and forbidden.

"Is that how I taste?" I asked.

"Yes," he said into my mouth... "More addictive than chocolate."

I wouldn't say that... to me, it tasted strange but not unpleasant.

"And you, how do you taste?" I asked.

His lip lifted in a cheeky smile. "Why don't you find out?" He didn't wait for my response before he got rid of his pants and I was face to face with his large erection.

"I've never..." I started saying.

He weaved his fingers into my long blond hair. "You don't have to suck me, but you can taste if you want to."

Slowly I leaned forward and planted a kiss on the head of his long shaft. My hand was drawn to touch it and the skin was surprisingly soft.

Once or twice I had found porn magazines at the motel when I cleaned so I had a good idea what a blow job looked like, but some of the pictures had scared me with the way the guy pressed himself down the woman's throat, and with my eyes wide open I looked up at Gabriel. "Promise not to hurt me."

He frowned and nodded. "You don't have to if you don't want to."

But I was curious and reached out my tongue to lick along his shaft. It didn't really taste of anything. Only when I reached the top and licked off small drops of pre-cum did I know what he tasted like.

It was a mild taste... reminding me of an exotic fruit I once tasted, but couldn't remember the name of. I wondered how much of him I could fit into my mouth and experimented by sliding my mouth over him.

It was his turn to grip the bedspread and moan, and a strong surge of power shot through me. He liked it... I wasn't sucking at it... or at least he liked me sucking at it.

A small chuckle escaped me as I mused about sucking.

"What's so funny?" he asked in a strained voice.

I gave him a wink. "That you don't mind me sucking at it."

My joke escaped him... "You have no idea... seeing you with my cock in your mouth has to be most erotic sight I've ever seen. You're fucking gorgeous."

A bubbly sensation filled my chest. I could do this... in fact I *was* doing it, and there was nothing disgusting or disturbing about it. It gave me pleasure to please him like he had pleased me.

I kept sucking him, exploring his balls with my tongue and using my hands to get to know this part of his anatomy better. The fascination with sex that other people seemed to have, but I had never shared, was starting to make sense to me.

"I want so badly to be inside you." He groaned and pushed me down on my back, positioning himself between my legs and kissing me deeply. Apparently he didn't mind tasting himself either.

"Please Cia... I want you so bad..." he whispered against me. "Say yes..."

I had my hands around his neck and was nuzzling his shoulders, feeling his long hard shaft pushing up against the folds of my core. I answered him by pushing against him and whispering into his ear. "I'm all yours."

His hands weaved into my hair holding my face in place as he pulled back to look at me with an earnest expression in his beautiful almond shaped eyes. "If we do this, you know what it means, right?" he whispered.

"That you'll be my first?" I asked.

"And your last," he said.

"Why? Do you plan on killing me afterwards?" Patterns are hard to break; G and I always used humor to cope with our emotions, and this was heavy stuff.

"No," he said and kissed my nose. "I plan on making you mine forever."

I narrowed my eyes. "I think you've been too long abroad. In this country men and women can have sex without committing to a lifetime together."

He kissed me again. "Just don't say I didn't warn you."

I didn't take his words too seriously, but figured it was all part of him making me feel good about the situation. I wasn't one of those women who had saved myself for marriage. I had avoided sex for other reasons, and marriage wasn't for me anyway. Still, I appreciated his gentleman manners.

Three seconds later he had a condom on and was licking me again, this time using a finger to stimulate my insides. It felt intrusive but incredibly good, and when he expanded it to two fingers I started rocking against him in a rhythm as old as time.

"You're so tight, but I want you so badly," he said, leaning back on his heels and pulling me into his lap. From my position I could see him point the head of his cock against my opening and push forward.

"Oh fuck… this is beautiful…" he groaned as pressure built below. If one finger had felt intrusive, it was nothing compared to his plum-sized head. He had a look of concentration but kept pushing and then he stopped.

"I'm inside you now."

"I can see that…" It was only the top of his cock that was inside me; I doubted I could take all the rest of him.

"What if you don't fit?" I asked.

He was still looking down, circling my clit with his thumb.

"How far in do you have to go?" I asked.

In that moment he pushed a bit deeper and then he retracted, starting to go in and out at a slow pace.

"You like that?" he asked with hooded eyes full of lust.

"Uh-huh," I moaned.

For a little while that was all he did, and I was starting to think that this was it. He was sitting in front of me, one set of our hands merged, his other hand massaging my clitoris, and all the while he was moving in and out in slow movements that felt nice.

"Are you ready?" he asked.

"For what?"

"For me to take your virginity."

"I thought you already had," I said but he just shook his head and shifted to lie on top of me, kissing me thoroughly again.

"I'm ready," I said into his mouth, feeling his cock enter me again.

And that's when he pushed all the way in, breaking through my hymen and holding me in place when I tried to pull back in pain.

It hurt.

It really hurt, and I think it might have hurt Gabriel too because he made some strained groans and stopped moving inside me. For a moment we lay closely merged with his cock spearing me like a goddamn shish kebab.

And then he started rocking back and forth like we had done before and the pain slowly but surely grew to pleasure.

We were having sex... I was no longer a virgin, and from Gabriel's moans in my ear, I got the sense that I wasn't terrible at it.

"Fuck, you feel amazing," he almost growled and half bit, half kissed my neck. "Do you like it?"

"Yes," I assured him and met him in his slow thrusts, which were becoming harder.

"Tell me if it hurts," he warned me and pushed up on his hands, looking down to where we were joined and slowly increasing his pace to... *fast*. The whole bed started shaking as he took me with an intensity and determination I had never imagined.

"Yes... yes... God, yes," I chimed in and felt all those little jolts of electricity that had played with my body earlier return. But this time they had brought friends and the party was so much bigger... the orgasm so much more violent. "OH FUCK!" I cried out as bliss took me again and my insides cramped around him.

"Cia... I'm... cumming." Gabriel threw his head back and roared out with such awesome force that it left no doubt in me that I had just passed the "good in bed" test. I had done something right, and mentally I was standing like a champion with both hands raised in victory.

Gabriel collapsed on me and I didn't mind the colossal weight of his muscled body one bit – until I ran out of oxygen, that is.

When I pushed at him, he slid down to rest beside me, still with his arm possessively around me.

"That was fucking amazing!" he said with his eyes still closed.

I stroked his arm up and down, glancing around the bedroom with its simple furnishings of nothing more than the queen-size bed, a large closet, and two nightstands. Not even a picture on the wall gave the room any personality, but then, it was just a rental.

Still, it felt strange that nothing had changed when inside me everything had changed. If the room should reflect how I felt, I would have opened my eyes to see rainbow colors on the wall and picture frames with Gabriel and me kissing and holding hands.

I was in love. Big time!

"I wanted to do this for so long," he muttered in my ear and nuzzled his nose against me. "This is it, we're together now." He intertwined his fingers with mine. "You're mine and I'm yours."

His words healed a broken part of me. I had been alone all my life, and hearing him say that we were now a couple made tears trickle from my eyes. I had finally found my missing piece.

"When you came..." I said quietly.

"Yeah?"

"Well, you looked almost pained for a moment and the veins on your neck stood out kind of prominently. Did it hurt?"

"No, it didn't hurt. In fact, it was torturously good." Gabriel opened his eyes and we smiled at each before he sat up and pulled off his condom to tie a knot in it. "I can't wait to take you bareback without those suckers."

He got back beside me, resting his head on my chest. I let my hands play with his hair and ear, silently wondering what had just happened and what it all meant, when Gabriel turned to look at me and said the last thing I would have expected to ever hear from him.

CHAPTER 19
Future

Gabriel

From the moment Bruce warned me that getting together with Cia would be a commitment for life, and not something I could just test out and pull out of if it didn't work, my mind had been spinning.

After she scared me half to dead by not being home last Saturday night, I had tried to keep my distance.

But it was impossible.

I missed her when I wasn't with her. I thought about her nonstop, and sleeping was almost impossible, knowing she was in my living room.

Hearing her talk about Daniel had made me jealous and possessive, and it was hard to ignore that whenever Cia was around me the biggest butterflies known to mankind were flapping around in my belly.

So yeah, the signs were all there, telling me that I was madly in love with Cia. Despite a whole orchestra of internal voices telling me it was risky and crazy, and kind of perverted with the family relation too, I had to pursue the idea of a future with her.

Making love to Cia was emotionally loaded, and when I saw her virgin blood on my flesh, it reminded me of Bruce's warning not to cross that line, unless I was serious.

I was very serious.

In the aftermath of our lovemaking Cia was caressing my hair and playing with my earlobe when I turned my head and looked up at her.

"I want to marry you out in the middle of nature," I said.

She gaped at me as if I had just told her I was really an alien.

"What is it? Do you prefer a church?"

"Did you fall and hit your head or something?" she asked me.

Ignoring her comment, I propped myself up on my elbow and let my finger slide down her torso. No, I hadn't bloody fallen on my head. Marriage wasn't a new thought to me; I had always known I wanted to get married someday, and now I knew I wanted to marry her.

"I never told you why I got the Silver Cross, did I?" I asked.

"No."

"Do you want me to tell you?"

She nodded, so I began telling her.

"It happened about four weeks before I came home. The Afghan National Army got a tip from the locals that ISIS warriors were hiding in a building, and tried to clear it. Four of them were shot in the first try.

"Then they came to us requesting assistance, and I was in the team of fourteen US and Afghan soldiers that went to get the job done.

"We expected to meet a handful of men occupying the building, but we walked into a death trap. Our platoon leader, medic, and two Afghan soldiers were killed within the first half hour of battle.

Her face fell into deep frown lines as she listened without interrupting me.

"I was the next in command so I took over, and we cleared the first two levels of the building. There was only one staircase leading up to the third floor, and I told my team to stay back.

"Instead of storming up the stairs, like the ISIS fighters expected us to, I stationed four of my men to make sure no one escaped down those stairs, while the rest of us went quietly to another part of the building where I engineered a breaching device that got us through the ceiling to the third floor.

"They never saw us coming before we opened fire, and within ten minutes the building was cleared.

"How many died?" she asked.

"Almost twenty from their side and we lost five in total, but we would have lost more if we had gone up the staircase."

She caressed my arm. "You could have died."

I took her hand. "You're right, I'm twenty-nine and lucky to be alive. I'm sorry if I'm moving fast, and I understand that you're young. But I want you to know how serious I am about us and make my intentions clear."

She blinked and seemed to be thinking. "You just seemed to go from wanting nothing to everything in a blink of an eye. I remember you telling me that you preferred your women a bit less Goth."

"Yeah, and you are... a lot less Goth."

"So, what you're saying is that if I was still dressed in black, you wouldn't want to be with me?"

Okay, how do you answer that? I didn't.

"I think we should just take things slow. I can't even think about marriage at this point," she said.

"Why not?"

"I just can't." She looked away.

"Okay.... Fair enough, but at least we've established that we're a couple now."

She sat up and swung her legs over the bed. "I'm sorry for getting blood on your sheets." She looked at the red spot.

I touched the spot and chuckled. "I've never been with a virgin before." The primitive part of my brain took pride in her innocence.

"Are you disappointed that I'm inexperienced?" she asked.

"No, it just makes you more special to me. I'm proud that I got to be your first."

"Good... I'm going to shower really quickly, okay?"

"Okay."

While Cia was humming in the shower, Bruce called on my phone.

"Hey, I was hoping to catch Cia for our weekly session."

"Oh, shoot, was that now?" I said and banged my head with the palm of my hand. "She's taking a shower."

Bruce chuckled. "Then you can tell me how things are going until she's done."

It burst out of me; I told him about what had happened, my intentions, and her reaction to my proposal.

"So she said she wants us to take it slow," I ended.

"You're lucky she hasn't run the other way," Bruce said dryly.

"Excuse me. You're the one who said I should only cross that line if I was serious, so I showed her that I am."

He sighed, and I could almost see him remove his glasses and rub the bridge of his nose. "I'm sorry, I would never say this to a client, but since you're not one, I'll say it."

"Say what?"

"You're an idiot."

That shut me up.

He sighed again. "Cia is trying to find herself, and the last thing she needs is you putting extra pressure on her."

"I'm not, I'm supporting her."

"You just took someone whose love life has been nonexistent and asked her to commit to you for better or worse. And you did it five minutes after you took her virginity, which can be emotionally overwhelming in itself. On top of that, Cia has just gone through some of the most emotionally stressful weeks of her life and has more stress ahead of her.

"What you did, G, is like taking someone skydiving without warning or preparation. She must be terrified of getting hurt."

"An idiot, huh?" I was still pretty offended by that comment, although I could see he had a point.

"Take it slow or you'll lose her. It's that simple."

In that moment Cia came back into the bedroom.

"Cia is back. Do you want to talk to her?" I asked Bruce.

"Yes, please, but before you go…"

"What?"

"Congratulations."

"For being an idiot?"

"No, for getting your girl."

"Thanks," I said but I didn't feel too chirpy when I handed her the phone. "It's Bruce, I'll leave you some privacy to talk to him."

I took time in the shower and thought about what Bruce had said. Maybe he was wrong. After all, Bruce only saw the frightened child in Cia, while I saw the brave woman in her. Not everyone was crippled by a bad childhood; some grew stronger and more resilient because of it. At least I had heard him tell Cia so himself, and with all the mental closets he had helped her clean out she would be fine.

So what if she hadn't had a relationship with a man before? I had lived with her for two weeks in the cabin and she was completely at ease around me.

Maybe Cia was simply born to fly – and even if she wasn't, maybe flying in tandem with me would make her feel safe. I sure hoped so, because I wasn't prepared to let go.

CHAPTER 20
Judgment day

Cia

Three days after Gabriel and I became a couple I had to face the judge who would sentence me.

That day, Gabriel took me shopping for a nice outfit for the courtroom. Never had I looked more unlike myself. The good side was that if I ever decided to work in a law firm, I had a skirt and jacket set to wear that would make me fit right in. The bad thing was that since I had no law degree, Gabriel had just wasted a lot of money on an outfit I would never use again.

He didn't seem to be too concerned about that part, but we were both scared about the potential jail time. We turned up in municipal court with our lips pressed into fine lines of worry.

Gabriel held my hand as long as he could, and it felt nice to have his support. Michael Young, the lawyer who had been present when I was originally charged, was there to represent me.

I have no other lawyers to compare Michael with, but he seemed to be doing a good job and I trusted him when he advised me to plead guilty as a sign of taking responsibility.

Michael went on to tell the judge about my complete change since the arrest, which was supported by a letter from Bruce stating that I was now drug-free and had gone through intensive therapy with impressive results. Michael talked about my upcoming art exhibition, and how I was now living with my fiancée, a military hero with a good education and a stable financial situation. It was hard to recognize Black in anything Michael said, and for a moment I missed her. I didn't miss her depressive state, but I missed her strength and independence.

I wasn't just me anymore; I was a part of a unit now, and Gabriel had hopes, fears, and expectations too.

I was slowly growing into my new identity as Cia, but hearing Michael describe me as someone successful made me feel like a fraud.

What they saw was a young woman dressed in clothes I wasn't comfortable in, with a status as engaged that I'd never really agreed to. Yet above all my confusion with who I really was came the guilt.

Life was handing me chances, opportunities, and even love. I should be euphoric with happiness for having a bed to sleep in, a fridge with food, the prospect of making money, and a gorgeous man who supported me.

And I *was* happy... in glimpses.

I didn't worry about what to eat or where to sleep, but most of the time I was worrying about meeting the expectations that Gabriel, Darren, and my new family had. I suppose the problem with getting what you always wanted is the fear that you might lose it again.

When the judge finally gave his verdict, I held my breath and listened.

"I hereby sentence you to three hundred and sixty-four days of jail with three hundred and sixty-four days suspended. There will be a five-thousand-dollar fine with four thousand five hundred suspended and another one hundred and fifty dollars in court costs. Since you have already undergone extensive therapy and been deemed drug-free by the therapeutic center, the court will make no further demands for drug treatments other than the weekly sessions that you have with your therapist. You will be on probation, which means that if you steal or do drugs again, you will go to jail."

Once we got out of the courtroom Michael and Gabriel were shaking hands and looking satisfied while I was trying to sum up what the judge had said.

"So I won't go to jail then?" I asked Michael to be sure.

"Not unless you get in trouble with the law again. You got suspended jail time, so if you mess up, you have both a fine and jail time hanging over your head."

"She won't get in trouble with the law again," Gabriel said earnestly and put his arm around me.

"Good, well, in that case you should be fine. There's still the five-hundred-dollar fine and the one hundred and fifty dollars for the court, though."

"Can I borrow it from you until my paintings sell?" I asked Gabriel, who nodded.

We celebrated in a sushi restaurant, which was a new experience for me. I knew what sushi was, of course, but I'd never tasted it. Turns out that all the years I've wondered what it would be like to have money and go to exotic sushi restaurants was a complete waste of my time. I would take a burger any day compared to that crap.

Gabriel introduced me to different rice thingies with shrimp, salmon, cucumber, carrot, and what have you, but it all tasted salty and I didn't like any of it.

At least I would never again envy someone walking with a box of fine sushi.

We spend that Friday night and most of the following Saturday in bed, where Gabriel introduced me to a lot of things that I liked far better than sushi. Being in love and feeling desired was a strong aphrodisiac, and when he asked me to move with him to Missouri in the fall I said yes. I didn't have anything holding me in Seattle except for a few friends, and I could paint anywhere in the world.

Clashing Colors #1 BLACK

Life was good. We were happy together, and being in his arms made me almost forget that come Sunday morning, I would be facing all of my family for the first time.

CHAPTER 21
Family Brunch

Gabriel

Cia was quiet on the twenty-minute drive from the apartment to my parents' home in Medina. My stepdad, Steve, is the CEO of one of the largest tech companies here in the area and his house – or rather mansion – reflects his status and wealth.

"Don't get overwhelmed with the size of the house when we get there," I said to warn her.

She frowned. "Why? How big is it?"

"Almost eight thousand square feet, and it's beautifully located by the lake."

"Wow, how many people live there?"

"Just my mom and Steve."

She whistled low. "That's a lot of cleaning to do for your mom," she pondered out loud.

I drummed the steering wheel. "Yeah... about that. My parents have people to help them, so you'll probably see a caterer today."

"What do you mean?"

"It's just that with Steve's job they host a lot of social events, and they have someone to take care of the practicalities so my mom can focus on being a hostess."

"But I thought today was only family?"

"It is, but the last time we had a family brunch my mom didn't cook anything."

"She can't cook?"

"No, she can... but I think they just find it easier to let others do it for them."

"All right. Well, I'm not really there for the food anyway."

"I know, I just didn't want you to be surprised and stunned by the... ehh... situation."

"Why would I be stunned?"

I chose my words carefully. "I just figured that the contrast from what you've been used to would be... ehhm... substantial."

"Because I'm poor?" she said and looked out the window.

"I'm not criticizing you, babe, I just worry that for someone who until recently slept in a closet, a house bigger than The Inn might feel a bit overwhelming."

"Thanks for the warning."

"Are you nervous?" I asked her, because I was.

"That's the fourth time you've asked me that question, and you're making me more nervous every time."

"Sorry. Don't worry, it'll be fine," I assured her and took her hand.

Once we got there most of my family had already arrived. Janet, Brent's wife, was balancing a Bloody Mary and sporting a new outfit to show off the results of her latest liposuction. As always, Brent was busy talking business in the garden with his father Steve, but they both waved at me and smiled. Brent's and Janet's three children were all there. The oldest, Mia, was on the couch with her head in a book as always. I couldn't see the title but figured it was probably something in the genre of fantasy because last time I had asked her, she'd taken almost fully ten seconds to look up at me and tell me that it was her favorite genre. Her brother Nick is ten and three years younger than Mia but her complete opposite, and as soon as he saw me, he came storming with his younger brother Andy on his heels. They wanted me to come and play badminton with them in the garden –

something I would have normally been happy to do, but today I wasn't leaving Cia's side.

My sister Brittany was there with her husband Gareth. They've been together since high school but the guy is a jerk and has cheated on her at least three times and then there was the "Oops-I-fell-into-a-door" black eye that she turned up with six years ago. I don't trust him and he keeps his distance whenever he sees me.

My sister Melody hadn't arrived, but my grandparents on my mother's side were there and my mother came rushing to give us a warm welcome.

"Mom, this is Cia," I told her and was delighted when my mom broke into a warm smile and shook Cia's hand. "I've heard so much good about you."

"Likewise," Cia said politely and was nudged around the room by my mother to be introduced to everyone.

I stayed close by and smiled when my grandmother, who is partially deaf and a bit senile, thought Cia was Mia.

"I can't believe how much you've grown, child. How old are you now?" Granny said, and Cia looked confused.

"I'm twenty-one."

"Twenty-one?" Granny looked to Charlie, my grandfather. "How can that be?"

"No, Mom," my mother, Katie, said. "This is Cia, she's Gabriel's new girlfriend. Mia is still thirteen and over there." She pointed to the couch. "See, she's reading."

My granny nodded her head. "Oh, I see... I apologize," she said to Cia. "But you do look a lot like Mia, though."

Cia's eyes fell on Mia, who looked up at the mention of her name, and yes, Granny was right, there was a resemblance between the two half-sisters.

Melody came when we all sat down at the table. She gave Cia a quick hug. "I'm so glad to see you decided to give us a chance." She smiled.

It was a funny thing to sit there and observe the normal family dynamics with new eyes. I kept trying to see it from Cia's perspective - the way we lovingly teased each other, especially Melody, who for some reason has chosen to become a vegan and start a vegan specialty shop in the University district, despite the fact that she's a lawyer by profession.

She's been a vegan for five years now and gets absolutely no support from the family except from my mom, who shows good intentions.

"I ordered some special bacon for you," my mom told her and pointed to a plate in front of Melody.

Melody set down the bowl of fruit she had in her hands and picked up the small plate. "What is this?" she asked.

"Vegan bacon," my mom said reassuringly.

Melody sniffed at the bacon. "This isn't vegan... it's turkey," she said with her nose wrinkled up.

"Well, isn't that better than pigs?" my mom asked.

"It's still an animal. I can't eat anything from animals."

"Here, have some eggs at least," Mia said with sympathy.

Melody sighed and shook her head. "Mia, where do you think eggs come from?"

Steve sat in his captain's chair at the end of the table like the patriarch he was.

"Melody, how is your business going?" he said and drew everyone's attention.

"Good. Don't worry, your investment is safe. We are expanding our market share," Melody said and took a bite of a large strawberry.

"And are you dating anyone?"

"Nope, and please stop trying to set me up with any more men. The last guy called me fourteen times before he gave up."

"John is one of the richest bachelors in the country," Steve defended.

"So what? He's over fifty and has been married four times. Just stay out of my love life, Dad."

"We'll see." Steve turned his head to Brittany's husband. "And what about you, Gareth? Did you get that promotion you talked about?"

Gareth took a sip of his juice and shook his head. "No, I'm afraid not."

"We're thinking of taking a cruise to Alaska this fall." my mom interjected. It was her specialty to change the subject before Steve ruined the fun with his business talk and hard questions.

"That's nice," Melody and Brittany said in unison to support the change of subject.

"We went on a cruise to Alaska once," Granny said dryly. "I didn't like it."

"No, honey, that was Mexico. We went to Mexico and we loved it," Granddad Charlie chimed in. "Remember all the great food and how we danced in the ballroom."

My grandmother, who is close to ninety and has been married to my grandfather since she was twenty-two, gave her husband a grim stare. "I've never been to Mexico with you. Did you take someone else?"

He rolled his eyes. "Of course not. It was in nineteen-eighty-four, and I can show you the pictures when we get home."

"What are you laughing at?" Brent said to Nick, who snickered at his great-grandmother. "Did you even wash your hands before coming to the table? And don't stuff your plate like that."

"It's okay, we have plenty of food," my mom said softly. "He's only ten."

"No, it's not okay, I don't want a fat kid who is too stupid to wash his hands," Brent said coldly.

Nick's shoulders slumped down and his smile was gone. I had a flashback to Brent sitting in that same chair twenty years ago and being reprimanded for everything on this earth by his father. The fact that the only thing he had learned from taking all that abuse was how to pass it on to others made me resent him.

"I've got something exciting to share," I said and felt my heart race triple-speed when everyone turned their heads to look at me.

"It turns out that we have a family member that we never knew about."

Brent put down his knife and fork with a warning glance. But I didn't budge.

"Twenty-one years ago, before meeting Janet, Brent had a daughter, and I'm really excited about bringing her into our family today."

"I have another sister?" Nick asked excitedly. "Where is she?"

I nodded toward Cia. "Right here. Cia is your half-sister."

"What is he saying?" Granny asked Charlie.

"Gabriel says that Cia is Brent's daughter."

My grandmother squinted her eyes. "Of course Mia is Brent's daughter; we always knew that."

"No, Granny... Cia. I'm talking about my girlfriend." I pointed to Cia on my right side.

"Your girlfriend is Brent's daughter?" Granny said with confusion. "Since when?"

"Well technically since she was born, I would assume," Gareth said and seemed mildly amused.

"Is Brent okay with Gabriel dating his daughter?" Granny asked Charlie in a loud whisper. "You should talk to them about how improper incest is and warn them not to have children... inbreeding makes for weak and sick offspring."

Charlie shushed her and placed his wrinkled hand on hers.

I spoke up. "We're not blood related, Granny," I pointed out.

A big puff of air came from Brent, who shot me a death glare. "I told you not to bring her here."

Janet kept looking from Cia to Brent. "You had a child and you didn't tell me?"

My mom opened her mouth to speak but closed it again and sat back in her chair. Apparently, not even she knew how to smooth these waters.

"Well, this is just nice," Brent said sardonically, "While you're at it, *brother,* why don't you tell them about what kind of person she is and how she got arrested by the police? Oh, that's right… you didn't mention that, did you, because as always you let people use you, just like Heidi used you."

"What the hell does that have to do with anything?" I asked.

"God, you're so naïve, G. Don't you see – she's just another of your pet projects, another lost soul to fix, and while you're pouring your soft heart into healing her, she's using you, just like Heidi and all the others did. When will you ever learn? There's a reason no one else wanted her."

Mia surprised me by smiling unsurely at Cia. "That's not true. I always wanted a big sister. I would like to get to know you."

"Me too," Melody said. "I think it's great that…" She was cut off by Steve, who pounded his fist down on the table. "How do you even know she's not an impostor? Anyone can make such a claim. Was there a paternity test done?"

"No," Brent said through clenched teeth.

"Don't even go there, Brent," I protested. "You've known about Cia since the beginning and it's time for you to own up to your responsibility. You abandoned your own daughter and let her live in abuse and poverty all these years."

Brent snorted in rage but it was Steve who spoke. "My son would never do such a thing. This girl might have tricked you." He pinned Cia with his glare and spoke in an accusatory tone. "How can you be sure my son is your father?"

"Because my mom was a virgin when Brent took her at a high school dance," Cia said matter of factly.

"A virgin... ha... for all we know that's just what she told you."

"Steve, please," my mom said and held out her hand.

"No, I won't have anyone make accusations at my son, in my house, without solid proof to back it up." He raised his voice and pointed a finger at Cia. "We're a good Christian family, and as it says in the Bible, you should never throw stones when you live in a glass house. Don't think I can't sniff a gold digger when I see one."

I grabbed Cia's hand and opened my mouth to speak, but she beat me to it when she abruptly stood up.

"I don't have to listen to this shit. Now I see where Brent got his lack of courage from. You're just as big a coward as he is." She pushed her chair out. "Oh, and by the way, read your Bible one more time, because misquoting the book you say you live by makes you look ignorant."

Steve flew up from his chair and his facial color was changing from red into purple real fast. "I can assure you I know my Bible inside out – how dare you say otherwise?"

Cia snorted at him and it made me love her even more. There was no fear in her eyes when she crossed her arms. "I think you're confusing the metaphor of stones and glass houses with the story from John 8:7 when Jesus approached the men about to stone a woman to death. *He that is without sin among you, let him first cast a stone at her."*

Steve gaped like a fish on dry land and I wanted to stand up and salute her. Cia had just owned the biggest, meanest bully I knew, and that says a lot coming from someone who's been nine years in the army.

Nobody spoke. No one. Not even the kids.

Until Granny said in a clear voice. "Are there any more bagels?"

I wanted to stay and sort this out. I wanted them to accept Cia into our family, and I'm sure everyone except Brent and Steve would have, but Cia turned around and left, so I followed.

When we got into my car and took off I realized that I had known this outcome was a possibility all along. Why else would I have parked on the street instead of the driveway like I usually did? Had I unconsciously known I might need to leave in a hurry?

I looked over at Cia, who sat pale and quiet beside me.

"Hey, are you all right?" I asked.

"Can we just not talk until we get back to the apartment?" she said, and I respected that.

About the time we had crossed the bridge to the Seattle side, my phone started ringing. I ignored the first calls but when I parked the car it rang again.

"Hey, Mom," I said when I answered.

Cia looked like she didn't know whether to stay in the car or leave me to talk in privacy, so I stopped her with a hand on her arm and mimed the word "Stay."

"Mom, I'm putting you on speaker. I want Cia to hear it too."

"Oh, hey ,Cia," my mom said and gave a nervous chuckle.

"Hey."

"I'm so sorry things got out of hand. I've talked to Steve and he's calmed down. We think you should come back and we could all try and talk about this calmly."

Cia shook her head vehemently.

"Maybe another time, Mom. I think Cia needs a little time to digest what just happened. I mean, she already knew Brent is an ass, but Steve just topped that."

"Yes, I know he sometimes speaks before he thinks, but he doesn't mean it like that."

"You always protect him, Mom," I said and felt annoyed with her.

"No, I don't, and he even said in the kitchen just now that if your accusations are really true and if Brent left our granddaughter to abuse and poverty, then there'll be hell to pay."

"Oh, they are true alright, I can testify to that. I heard her mom admit to the abuse and I know for a fact that when Cia finally escaped the horrors in her mother's house she came to Brent for help, and he turned her away and left her to live on the streets when she was only fourteen."

"Oh, Jesus, I'm so sorry." My mother's voice broke. "If only we had known... She could have lived here; I would have gladly taken her in..."

"I know, Mom, I know."

"Why don't you both take the time you need and then come see us when you're ready. We would love to get to know you better, Cia."

"Thanks," Cia said and brushed a tear away with the back of her hand. "I think I would like that."

"I'll call you later, Mom," I said, hung up, and turned to Cia.

"Do you think they'll have me do a DNA test to prove I'm really Brent's daughter?"

"No, you look like Mia – they're not stupid. Anyone can see that you're his kid."

"It's the eyes, isn't it?"

"Yeah, you've got his green eyes for sure."

"I shouldn't have lectured Steve on the Bible," she said quietly.

I reached up and stroke her chin. "Are you kidding me? That was the coolest thing that has ever taken place in that house. First of all, to see anyone actually win a face-off with Steve is a historical event, but to do it using the Bible was spectacular.

"Why?"

"Because the Bible is his favorite trump card in discussions. You just moved from badass to superhero in my world."

She laughed, and it felt amazing to see her white teeth. I kissed her, long and hard, and we walked up to the apartment and made love for the sixth time.

Cia was curious and playful with me, and in return I was patient and let her explore my body.

Making love to her was much more fulfilling than with anyone else, and I think it was because I had committed myself to her. Sure, I had had sex with women who were wilder, more experienced, and even more beautiful than Cia, but I would pick her over them any day.

"I love you," I whispered and kissed her. It was the first time I spoke those words to her, and she widened her eyes.

"You do?"

"Yes."

"How do you know?"

"I just do."

"And you're not scared that Brent might be right about me just using you?"

I shook my head. "You've never asked for anything. It's always been me offering."

Her face drew into a serious expression with her brows knitting together. "What did he mean about Heidi using you?"

I sighed. "Heidi and I were together for three years and half that time I was deployed abroad, so she lived in my apartment while I paid for all expenses."

"And Brent felt that she was using you because she didn't pay rent?"

"Yeah, and because it all ended when I realized she was cashing in by renting out two of the rooms."

"How did you find out?"

"I came home unannounced to find two male models living in my apartment, and when I recovered from that shock I got the next one: finding a used condom in my bedroom trash can."

"Shit."

"Yeah... she wasn't a very nice person."

"How long ago was this?"

"About two years."

"And she was your last serious girlfriend?"

"Yes."

"Haven't you been with anyone else since?"

I nodded.

"Anything serious?" she asked.

"No."

"Anything recently?"

I scrunched my face, assuming she meant besides my night with Therese. "I already told you I was in Afghanistan for a year."

"And you want me to believe you didn't sleep with anyone for a whole year?"

"Not unless you count masturbation."

She snickered but didn't reply.

"So you'll forgive me if I'm still trying to catch up," I said and pushed her back down on the mattress.

She chuckled in my ear as I moved on top of her. "How many times do you think it'll take for you to catch up?"

I arched a brow and gave her a sly smile. "A few hundred times of good sex should do it. I'm thinking that if we do it twice a day for a year, I'll be okay."

"Twice a day?"

"We could speed up the process and do it three times a day… that way I would be a happy man by August, I think."

"And you're not happy now?" she teased.

"No, I'm miserable, can't you tell?" I said and suckled on one of her nipples with a smirk. "I'm a starving man, so feed me please."

She tilted her head and looked down at me with a speculative glance. "How many women have you had?"

I sighed. "Does it matter?"

"Have you ever been unfaithful to any of your girlfriends?"

I tried distracting her by kissing her and taking her mind off her question, but it didn't work.

"I asked you a question."

Shit. Conversations like these never went well, and I wanted to be inside her physically, not have her examine me mentally.

"Uh-huh." I muttered and lifted her leg up over my hip. Maybe if I got inside her, she would drop the subject.

She didn't. "What does uh-huh mean? Uh-huh, I've been unfaithful or uh-huh, I heard your question – which is it?"

"I want you," I muttered against her neck and reached for a condom. She answered with a slight moan, so clearly she was affected by my hands and mouth on her body.

I'm sure that if I didn't have to think of protection, and could have slipped right in, it would have worked.

But in order to put on the condom I had to pull away from her and look down. It gave her time to refocus.

"I take your silence on the matter as an admittance of guilt. You have been unfaithful to girlfriends in the past, haven't you?"

I swallowed hard and raised my gaze to meet hers.

Cia

I don't know why it mattered so much to me what Gabriel had done in the past. It wasn't like I was perfect myself. After all, being unfaithful in a relationship wasn't a criminal offence. Still, my whole life had changed dramatically since he walked into it, and now he was talking about loving me and asking me to move to Missouri with him. The whole package of Gabriel Thomas seemed perfect, and I'm old enough to know that nothing ever is perfect. So yeah, I was searching for his flaws.

His answer to my question was in his eyes. Yes, he had been unfaithful.

"Do you want to tell me about it?" I asked.

Gabriel sat on his knees in front of me with his hand on his cock where he had rolled on a condom. He shook his head and reached out to cup my breast but I pulled the cover over me and signaled that there would be no sex until he answered me.

With an annoyed exhalation of air, he looked up at the ceiling. "What do you want to know?"

"Has it happened one time or every time you've had a girlfriend?"

He rubbed his forehead. "Remember how you assumed I was popular with the girls in high school?"

"Yeah."

"Well, I was."

"And?"

"And so I shopped around a little."

"Meaning what?"

He shrugged. "Meaning I wasn't always the best boyfriend, and when something better came along I moved on."

"Ohh… okay." I pulled back a little.

Gabriel placed a hand on my knee. "Look, I'm a different person now than I was back then. It's different with you, sugar."

For the first time I couldn't stand him calling me sugar. It wouldn't take a lot to find something better than me. Heck, a quick walk down the street would be enough since most women between twenty and thirty would qualify as better than me.

I got out of the bed and started to get dressed. "Can I borrow your phone?" I asked.

He reached out for me. "Come back here… I'll never cheat on you, I promise."

"Can I borrow your phone?" I asked again in a harder tone.

"Sure," he said and looked miserable.

I picked it up and handed it to him, waiting for him to unlock it.

When I got it back I dialed Daniel's number and waited for him to pick up.

"Hello?"

"Daniel, it's me."

"Hey, Black… what's up?" He sounded happy to hear from me.

"Where are you?"

"Got the new place early… wanna come over and see my crib?"

"Yeah… what's the address?"

"Ehhh… hang on, I can text it to you."

"Okay, do that."

"Will do."

I hung up and waited for the text.

"Please tell me you aren't leaving to go hang out with another guy?" Gabriel said in an incredulous tone.

"I'm sorry, but I want to check up on Daniel."

Gabriel looked down at his naked body. His erection was gone and he pulled the condom off.

"We're in the middle of having sex and then you insist on roaming through my mental garbage until you find a piece of my past you don't agree with... to what? Get an excuse to get away from me and go be with another guy?"

"He's a friend. There's nothing sexual between us."

Gabriel got up from the bed and picked up his clothes with rough movements. "Did you even hear me when I said I loved you?"

I tensed my jaw, feeling unworthy.

"Did you? Because it sure doesn't feel like we're on the same page right now."

I put on my shoes and stood back up. "It's just been a hard day and I need to see my friend."

The pain on his face made me wince inside. I had just delivered a blow to his head.

"Are you saying Daniel is more important to you than I am?"

"No." The phone vibrated and I read the address three times, memorizing it.

"Well, it sure feels that way when you run directly from being naked with me to needing to be with him."

I was already halfway out the door.

In hindsight I wish I could have stayed and talked it through like normal people do, but normal people have role models who teach them how to cope with emotions. I only knew how to run from my pain or drown it with pills, and I desperately needed a pill right now.

"Don't go, Cia," was the last thing I heard before the door slammed behind me.

CHAPTER 22
The Psychic

Cia

It took me almost an hour to reach Daniel's apartment in West Seattle. The neighborhood was a bit sketchy, and I was glad it wasn't dark yet.

"Hey, girl, you made it," Daniel said in a loud whisper after buzzing me in. "Come in but be quiet – Violet is doing a cleansing of the place."

I stepped into the one-bedroom apartment and saw Violet, a friend of ours, walk around with something that was smoking in her hands. It had a peculiar smell.

"How long will it take?" I whispered and retreated to the kitchen, where I pulled myself up on the counter.

Daniel shrugged and opened his fridge, where sodas and beers were lined up. He handed me a Coca-Cola and popped a beer open for himself before he leaned against the kitchen counter and watched the show of Violet doing her thing.

Violet is in her mid-twenties and one of the quirkiest people I know. She's a psychic or at least she says she is, and apparently it's made her the black sheep in her family. Sometimes she can be completely sane and almost normal, until she starts talking about spirit guides, angels, crystals, healing stones, and what have you.

It's not that I don't believe her, but I also can't say that I do, so seeing her walk around mumbling blessings and burning that grassy thing looked comical to me.

Luckily it only took a few more minutes and then she was done.

"Oh hey, Black," she said. "I didn't see you there."

"Hey, Violet... how are you."

"Good." She walked closer and reached out for my Coke. "You changed."

I didn't even think, I just handed her my can. You see, when you've been homeless and poor for years you learn to share things, and it's ingrained in me that we take care of each other. Not that Violet is homeless, but still.

"Yeah, I'm trying out a new look," I replied.

Violet took a sip and nodded with approval. "I like it." And then she turned to Daniel. "It's okay now, I helped him pass on and he crossed over. The sage was just to cleanse out the negativity that lingers. Keep the windows open for a few more hours."

My glance at Daniel was quizzical, silently asking; what the hell is she babbling about?

"The previous owner killed himself last month, and the reason I got the apartment is because the woman who moved in after him said the place is haunted. She left in the middle of the night completely freaked out," Daniel explained.

I looked to Violet. "Is the place really haunted?"

"Not any longer. The guy was just confused and lost, but I talked to him and he's in the light now." She looked dead serious. "He won't bother you." Her last comment was directed at Daniel.

I couldn't help it; I had to ask her. "Did he tell you his name?"

She turned her head and gave me a glance that felt as if she was looking into my mind.

"You think I'm making it up?"

Noise from screaming kids reached us through the open windows and I turned my head to see a playground close by. Inside the apartment everything was quiet until Violet repeated her question.

"Admit it, you think I'm a fraud," Violet said calmly.

"I didn't say that."

She arched a brow. "Your energy said it for you."

"I'm sorry... it's just all a bit strange."

"Not to me. I've never known anything different, but I understand. I'm used to skeptics."

"So did he tell you his name and how he died?"

"No, and I didn't ask."

"Why not?"

"Because he wore his Costco work uniform with a name tag on it that said Kyle, and the big bloody mess on the side of his head told me he shot himself."

"I didn't know that," Daniel muttered.

"Come with me," Violet walked resolutely toward the bathroom and pointed. When we both stood beside her she said, "See that tile with the lighter lines around it?"

"Yeah."

"That's where the bullet hit after going through his head. They replaced that tile."

Daniel wrinkled his nose. "Are you sure he's gone?"

"Of course. I even cleared out the old grumpy man who was here too."

"Good thing you're not superstitious, right?" I told Daniel, who looked slightly pale.

Violet rolled her eyes. "Don't tell me a big tough guy like you is afraid of spirits."

"No, of course not." He plumped down on his couch and looked around the room as if to make sure there really weren't any intruders in his new home.

I figured it was time to change the subject so I told Violet of my art exhibition.

"That's so cool, Black," she said. "Can I come to the opening?"

"Of course. It's tomorrow night at seven."

"We'll be there." She looked at Daniel. "Right?"

He nodded. "Absolutely."

I tilted my head. "Violet, do you still have your car?"

"Yes, I still have Arion."

I chuckled, not commenting on the fact that Violet had named her car. "I promised I would drop my paintings off at the gallery today. Do you think you can give me a lift?"

"Sure." She pulled out her cell phone, and somehow the contrast of the newest IPhone with her old-fashioned looks amused me. I don't think I've ever seen Violet in anything but long dresses, preferably dark green and flowery. Today she was wearing brown ankle-high leather boots with a two-inch heel, a simple long green velvet skirt, and a white blouse with lace around her neck. With the way her long brown hair was arranged in a bun on top of her head and a few tendrils falling down, she could have stepped right through a time warp from the eighteen hundreds.

"Sure, I can give you a ride, but we need to go soon, because I have a reading at six-thirty and I'm never late for my clients."

I bit my inner lip, conflicted that we would have to go so soon, since it felt as if I'd only just arrived and I wanted to spend time with Daniel.

"How about you, do you need help with anything?" I asked him with eyes glancing around the apartment. From what I could tell he was pretty much settled in. I only spotted a few boxes, but then of course, he doesn't have a lot of furniture to begin with.

"Don't worry about me, I'm fine, and I'll see you again tomorrow. How are you and Mr. G doing?"

"Fine," I lied and diverted my eyes to the door. "I'll tell you some other time," I said and was already at the door. Daniel is an excellent interrogator, and if he sensed I was upset about something he would try to make me talk, which I wasn't ready to do just yet.

"Hey, wait up." Daniel stepped closer and kissed me on my cheek. "Thanks for checking in on me."

"No problem, and remember to be nice to your neighbors."

He agreed and gave Violet a hug and a kiss on the cheek too. "Thanks for clearing my place," he told her.

"No worries – that's what friends are for, right?"

"Right," Daniel agreed with a smile.

"Do you want me to swing by tomorrow on my way to Black's exhibition? I don't mind giving you a ride."

Daniel accepted the offer and Violet and I left to find her car. This was my third time driving with Viola and every time I'm floored at the unlikelihood of this car still being on the streets. I'm no expert on cars so I can't tell you the model or year of Violet's, but it's a station wagon with wood paneling that must be way older than my twenty-one years.

"Can you open the glove compartment?" she said when we got in. "Good, there's a box… do you see it?"

"Uh-huh," I said and pulled out a box from Tiffany's and handed it to her.

"Thanks," she said and opened the box, revealing five different stones, in different sizes and shapes, that she picked up and rubbed in her hands, bowing her head in what looked like a silent prayer. Thirty seconds later she returned the stones to the box and handed it back to me with a soft smile. "Energetic hygiene is very important when you deal with entities. I always make sure I don't bring work home, so to speak."

"All right," was the only thing I could think of to say.

"So where are we picking up your paintings?"

"At my… ehh… boyfriend's place. He lives by Union Lake."

Violet whistled and started the engine. "So that explains your new looks."

"Yeah. He wasn't a big fan of the Goth look."

Violet didn't comment on that but kept up a casual conversation until we got to the apartment.

"What's wrong?" she asked when she parked. "You just had a major energy shift."

"Oh… it's just that we had a fight before I left."

She looked up at the building. "Do you want me to stay here or go with you?"

"Well, there are five paintings, so I could use your help carrying them."

"Then let's go."

My heart was hammering like a sledgehammer when I stood outside the door, and for a moment I was unsure whether to walk in or ring the bell. I chose the latter, suddenly not sure I was welcome.

When Gabriel opened the door he pinned me with a pissed-off expression. "Glad to see you're back," he said but his body language said otherwise.

"This is Violet," I said and pointed to her. Violet reached out her hand and stepped closer to him. I wish I was that brave, but I could see he was mad at me and I didn't know what to do about it.

"I'm just giving Black a ride to the gallery with her paintings," Violet said in her soft melodic voice and didn't break eye contact with Gabriel.

I didn't like it. Yeah, my friend was a weirdo and part witch of a sort, but she was more feminine than I could ever be, and the way her beautiful brown eyes looked up at him gave me the chills. What if he preferred her to me?

Gabriel finally broke the intense stare between them and took a step back to let us in.

"You know where the paintings are, Cia," he said. "Melody is here… she wanted to see you."

That made me stop in my tracks. His sister Melody had been here before and I had seen her at the brunch too. It seemed that every time she came around she got the worst version of me – and today was not a good day either, with the tension between Gabriel and me.

"Hey, Melody," I said when I stepped into the living room and saw her.

"Hey, Cia." Her eyes trailed to Violet. "Oh, that's nice, are you an actor?"

Violet tilted her head. "What do you mean?"

Melody smiled and waved her hand at Violet's clothes. "Because of the costume... are you doing some sort of historical play?"

Violet looked down at herself and then to Melody again. "No, this is how I dress."

Melody's eyebrows shot up to her hairline. "Oh, really? Well, it's... ehh... lovely."

"Violet is my friend and we're just here to pick up my paintings for my art exhibition tomorrow," I interjected, hoping to move away from the awkwardness.

"You have an exhibition tomorrow?"

I nodded my head.

"Are we invited?" Melody asked. "I love art, and I would love to come and see it."

"Sure, everyone can come. It's an open event," I said.

Melody broke into a wide smile. "Great, then I'll spread the word."

"It's at the Urban Gallery on Pike Street," Violet added.

"Can I talk with you for a minute?" Gabriel asked me.

"Yeah, sure," I said, trying to hide how nervous he made me.

"Then I'll start carrying the paintings down to my car." Violet said. "Where are they."

Gabriel and I brought out the five paintings, which had been standing against the wall in his bedroom.

"Let me give you a hand," Melody said and while the two women carried down two of my paintings, Gabriel signaled for me to join him in the bedroom.

"What the hell happened?" he asked with his hands on his hips.

"I don't know."

"How do you think it makes me feel when you leave me like that?"

I looked down.

"Are you afraid I'm going to cheat on you?" he asked.

Yes... the thought terrifies me, I wanted to say, but only gave him a shrug.

"Cia, look at me, god damn it, I'm talking to you."

I raised my eyes to meet his and saw immense frustration. "Talk to me," he pleaded. "Please don't shut me out."

"It just freaked me out to hear you say that you move on when something better comes along," I finally managed to say.

"But that was the old me. I'm not like that anymore. You got to learn how to stay and talk about things... you can't just run off when it gets hard."

We heard footsteps in the living room and I pulled away from him but he grabbed my hand. "Why didn't you ask *me* for a ride?"

"I have other friends, you know."

He took a deep intake of air and released it in a breathy sigh. "I never said you didn't. Will you come home afterwards?"

"Yeah, I'll see you later."

Violet and Melody had already picked up two more paintings and left again, so I took the last painting and headed to the elevator.

It didn't take long before the door opened and Melody stepped out, Violet was still in the elevator and smiled. "We've got to hurry, I'm parked in a no parking zone."

"Okay," I said and gave Gabriel a last glance before I stepped inside the lift with Violet. He raised his hand as the door slid closed, and the absence of him made me wish I had given him a quick kiss before I left.

Violet and I loaded the last painting and got in the car again.

"All right, Arion, take us securely to Pike Street, please," Violet told her car and stroked the steering wheel. I sat next to her and wondered what kind of mental illness talking to cars fell under.

"Gosh, your boyfriend is hot."

I clenched my jaws. "Yeah, he's handsome."

"I can understand why you worry he'll cheat on you."

I whipped my head around. "Why would you assume I worry about that?"

She gave me a side-glance smile and tapped her index finger against her temple. "Psychic, remember."

"Well, if you're that good, then why don't you tell me if he's going to be unfaithful to me?"

She got an earnest expression on her face. "People think there is only one future ahead of them but it's like a trail system all leading to the same place. What you'll experience on your journey all depends on what choices you make.

"I could tell you he'll cheat on you, in which case you would break up with him and not even give him a chance.

"I could tell you he doesn't cheat on you, which is true if you and he find a way to communicate better. But untrue if you don't, as he'll be so lonely that another woman might tempt him in a moment of weakness.

"I can't give you any guarantees, Cia, no one can, but I can tell you that he's one of the good guys."

"Why do you call me Cia?"

"Because the first time I heard him say it, I knew that was your real name. That's what your soul wants you to be called."

Oh Christ... what do you even answer to craziness like that?

It shouldn't have surprised me that Darren and Violet were an instant love match. When she walked into his

Clashing Colors #1 BLACK

gallery and spoke about the loveliness of the energies in place, he was all in. Turns out that Darren believes in this stuff, and before long he had arranged for her to do readings at the evening's art exhibition.

"I'll make sure to set up a table in the corner for you."

"Wonderful, I'll bring my own tablecloth and tarot cards."

I rubbed my face and groaned, afraid to tell him that I didn't really think that fortune telling had anything to do with my exhibition. It was his gallery, and I didn't want to make demands like some sort of diva.

Violet hummed with internal sunshine as she dropped me off at Gabriel's place forty minutes later. I, on the other hand, walked up to have a grown up conversation, feeling nervous and defensive.

To my surprise Gabriel wasn't there. There was a note saying:

> *Hey Cia,*
> *Melody and I are going to grab something to eat.*
> *I'll see you later and the box is for you.*
> *G*

I picked up the package wrapped in tin foil and found a phone inside and another note saying, *I already set up the phone. Your pin is 9999, your phone number is on the other sticky note, and my number is already in it. Please text me when you're back.*

It was a thoughtful gift that would make my life much easier, but he had already given me so much. Surprisingly, one of my first thoughts was that I would only keep it as long as we were together, meaning I didn't believe we would stay together. Someone like me wouldn't be enough for someone like him long-term, especially since he had already admitted it was his pattern to swap when something better came along. It was pointless to fool myself into thinking otherwise.

I sent Gabriel a text, thanking him for the gift and telling him that I was back in the apartment.

He answered right away. "Good, I'll see you in a bit."

It was past six and I was hungry, so I grabbed a snack and played around with my new phone.

When Gabriel walked in an hour later he came to sit beside me.

"Do you want to talk?" he asked.

I did, but I didn't know how to. It wasn't like he could apologize for being honest... I wanted him to be honest with me, the problem was that the truth was hard to handle.

"Do you want to talk to Bruce?" he asked.

I actually did. Despite how insane Bruce's methods were, he had a way to make me understand myself better.

"Yeah... but I don't have a session with him until Wednesday," I said.

"I'm sure he'll talk to you if you reach out," Gabriel speculated.

"Maybe. Or maybe we could just finish what we started," I suggested, hoping that if we could be physical, we could somehow get past this.

"You want to have sex?" he asked with obvious surprise.

I gave a small nod.

"Wow... I didn't expect that."

"You don't want to?" I asked nervously.

"Yeah... but something weird is going on between us and I was thinking we should talk it through. I'm still mad at you for leaving me without explaining why."

I wanted to reach out and touch him but some immense force inside me held back – afraid of a potential rejection.

"Cia, tell me how you feel about me," Gabriel said and moved closer, looking intently into my eyes.

I cleared my throat. This noon he had told me he loved me and I wasn't stupid. I knew he was hoping to hear the same from me.

"You are the first person to love me," I said in a small voice.

He didn't speak but took my hand and waited for me to continue.

"I've never loved anyone or used those words with anyone. They feel alien to me. Like something that has to do with other people, but not me."

"But I do love you," Gabriel repeated and it made me look away. There were so many things I wanted to say and questions I wanted to ask. Like "Why do you love me?" But I had no voice and sat quietly with tears flowing down my face.

"Oh, sugar," Gabriel said and pulled me into his lap. And then he kissed me, hot and hungry, and I kissed him back, expressing everything I couldn't say in words.

His hands were almost shaking when he undressed me and his eyes were burning with fire. He wanted me. His entire being was hungry for me. I didn't need a psychic to tell me that.

I wanted him too and zipped down his pants, letting my hand slide inside. He was hard as a rock, and when I struggled to get his jeans and briefs off him he lifted me up into his arms and carried me into the bedroom, where he let me down on the bed. I sat hypnotized and watched him undress and stand completely naked in front of me.

This gorgeous man had declared his love for me. For some unknown reason he was blinded and saw something in me that no one else saw, not even me.

He was beautiful, strong, kind, funny, and generous, and being with him was like winning the freaking lottery. But everyone knows that when poor people win the lottery they do stupid things and always end up losing all the money again. It would be the same with me. I would end up losing Gabriel, and I couldn't bear the thought.

Gabriel moved up on the bed and crawled over to kiss me. I clung to him and kissed him back feeling like this might be the last time I got to hold him.

He got a condom and while he took me missionary style, he kept whispering that he wanted me and that he loved me. My eyes were closed the whole time but I couldn't hide the tears that were falling down my temples.

I love you too and I want you too… for always. It was right there in my mind, but the words wouldn't come.

When he came, I squeezed him tight with my legs around his hips. A part of me wished that there was no condom and that he would bind me to him with a child. Maybe then he would stay with me, but as quick as the thought entered my mind, just as quickly it made me nauseated. It was just another reminder that I alone would never be enough to keep his interest.

Gabriel and I didn't talk much that night. Things were better after the sex – at least we were comfortable touching each other – but I knew we hadn't solved anything and that under the surface there were still hurt and unresolved emotions, that would most likely come back to bite us in the ass. Turns out, I was right.

CHAPTER 23
The Art Show

Gabriel

I had been out hiking with a friend most of the day and was eager to see Cia. I wish I knew what she was thinking. I had declared my love to her, but she hadn't said it back. Still, this was Cia, and a mental flashback to my first meeting with the angry Goth girl she had once been reminded me how far she had come.

I parked my car, and as I got out and locked the door I looked down at my outfit, making sure I looked fine in my dark jeans and nicely pressed cotton shirt. It was the right kind of casual smart. I rolled up my sleeves before crossing the street to the gallery where she had told me to meet her. Just from looking through the glass façade I could tell a lot of people had already arrived, and when I entered with a smile on my face, I was met by a man who handed me a brochure.

"Hello, and welcome, handsome," he said.

"Hello." I did a double take at the peacock in front of me, not sure if his outfit was meant to be a part of the exhibition or if it was how he normally dressed. If it was a costume, I seriously had no idea what he was supposed to be in that mismatch of colors and textiles with animal print. *Tarzan meets Highlander meets Native American... maybe?*

The colorful man swung his hands out and spoke with a lisp. "I'm Darren. Tonight we have five extraordinary paintings from a local gal who is a new rising star on the art scene. Nothing is for sale, as all the paintings have already been sold, but if you like them you can come see me to get on a list for her next exhibition."

"Did you say everything has been sold?"

"Yes," he said with pride. "When there's a true talent, buyers snap it right up."

Fuck! I had wanted to buy the blue painting of her and me. Why hadn't I just made a reservation for it? *Because I never thought it would be sold within the first ten minutes of the show.*

"G." A voice broke through and made me look ahead at Melody, who was waving her hands at me. I made my way to my two sisters, my mom, and Steve, who all stood with wine glasses in the back of the room.

"Have you seen Cia?" I asked and they shook their heads.

"No, but Gareth is having his fortune read." Melody snickered and nodded her head at the opposite corner, where Cia's friend sat at a table with a sign saying "Psychic readings."

I cringed a little, trying to remember the girl's name. I had met her yesterday and she had seemed the sweetest girl, but this... this was a disappointment. Was this the kind of nutcase Cia associated with?

"Do you think she's for real?" Melody asked me. "I mean you should have seen her car yesterday; she's definitely a character."

"Maybe she's an actor with the clothes and that..." I waved my hand discreetly. "Everything she's doing is all for entertainment."

Steve gave me a grim look but didn't comment on the freak show in the gallery. Artistic people are allowed some leeway, but Darren seemed to attract people as eccentric as himself. Like the guy in a kilt or the tiny old lady in too much make-up and a large fur coat. For god's sake, it was June.

Now, to be fair, there were some normal-looking people too. Two men about my age stood and discussed one of Cia's paintings, and then there was another man who was leaning in with narrowed eyes to study the painting of Cia as a child balancing the cotton candy.

"Hey, Black," he called over his shoulder. "Is this supposed to be you?"

I almost choked on a sip of wine when Cia walked over to him and he placed his arm around her.

Cia was Black. I mean literally. She was dressed as the Goth girl I had picked up at the police station – even the fake piercings were back – and my eyes flew to her hair. I couldn't see if she had colored her hair black again because she was wearing a black beanie that covered all of it.

Every nerve in my body tensed up and I wanted to scream. I had done everything in my power to get her out of the black depressive place in her life and she chose to go back. *What the fuck?* To me, her outfit was a representation of her past. A statement that I had failed and she was rejecting me.

My mom was saying something, but I had tunnel vision and could only see Black as I stomped over and grabbed her elbow in a hard movement. "Cia," I said roughly and made her turn to face me.

Her friend, whom I assumed to be the mysterious Daniel, stepped forward in a protective manner.

"What the hell is this?" I asked in something between a hiss and a whisper.

Her black eyeliner and purple lipstick offended me. I wanted to take her to the bathroom and make her wash it off, but unfortunately I was no longer in charge of her and if Cia wanted to be Black, there wasn't a damn thing I could do about it.

"Hey, G," she said with uncertainty but didn't make excuses for her appearance.

"Are you for real?" I asked and felt like punching something. The four words expressed so many questions, but she never answered.

"What do you mean is she for real? Black was real before you came along and tried to change her into something she's not. Love her or leave her," Daniel said with an attitude that I didn't appreciate. *Did he put her up to this?*

The thirty or so people in the gallery all had their eyes turned to us, and both Darren and Violet came to stand beside Black.

Seeing her in her Goth clothes, surrounded by her friends, made it sink in how different we were. Cia was a creation of my imagination – the perfect girl I wanted her to be – but Black was someone else. Someone who was more comfortable with freaks like Darren and crazy people like Violet than she would ever be with my kind.

"I'm sorry," I said and felt it deep in my core. I truly was sorry. Sorry that I had done this to her. Sorry that I had tried to mold her into something she clearly didn't want to be. But most of all sorry that the woman I had wanted to marry and share my future with didn't really exist. With a last glance into her moist eyes I walked out the door, and only then did I realize that I still had a glass of wine in my hand. Without even thinking I smashed it to the ground and growled in agony.

Cia

"I can't believe you sold all your paintings," Daniel said and put his legs up on a chair. I was still in awe of the eight thousand dollars in my hands.

Only Violet, Daniel, and I were left when Darren closed the door and locked it before he came to join us in the back of the room.

"Is it normal for people to pay cash?" Violet asked Darren.

He shrugged. "Sometimes... but not usually. I don't care as long as they pay."

"Here," Violet handed him a glass of wine.

"You know how some people say that size doesn't matter?" Darren asked Violet.

"Size?" she repeated with a flustered expression on her face.

"Yeah, it's not true. Size does matter."

I looked over, confused over how the conversation had taken such a turn.

Darren arched a brow. "I'm telling you, size matters a great deal. No one wants a small glass of wine. Fill it up."

With a slight headshake and a smile, Violet filled his glass completely.

"Thank you, my dear," he said. "I will say that except for the matrimonial drama, I thought it was a perfect night." Darren crossed his legs and leaned back his head, taking a big swig of his red wine.

Violet turned to me. "How are you feeling?"

I had been two inches from crying all night, but had managed to put on a brave face the entire time.

"I always knew this would happen..." I said in a low voice and crossed my arms protectively. "He never loved the real me."

Darren made a dramatic sigh. "You know, darling, it has taken me a long time to become this fabulous, and I had a few stops in Normalville trying to fit in before I found my tribe in Come-as-You-are-Ville. You really should see it as a blessing. It's better to see him for what he is than to waste your time and maybe have children before you find out down the road."

"That's right," Daniel agreed. "And just for the record, we all like you no matter how you dress."

Darren took another sip. "Since I'm the oldest in this group and most likely the smartest" – he grinned – "I'll give you a piece of world-class advice."

"I don't know if you're the smartest, but you're definitely the most conceited," Violet said with a chuckle, but Darren just put his hand to her mouth and shushed her.

"No, honestly, this is supreme-quality advice and you are all extremely fortunate that I'm willing to share it with you.

"All right." I furrowed my forehead in concentration. "Then let's hear it."

Darren leaned forward, and a scent of his strong perfume hit my senses.

Like a true showman, he made sure he had our full attention before he spoke in a solemn tone of voice. "You should only fall in love with a person who enjoys your madness. Not an idiot who forces you to be normal."

There was a moment of absolute silence.

"That's it!" Darren said and leaned back again.

I replayed his words in my mind. *You should only fall in love with a person who enjoys your madness. Not an idiot who forces you to be normal.*

"Gabriel isn't an idiot," I said in a sharp tone.

"Maybe not, but he's a fool if he thinks he can change you."

"He did change me... well, maybe not him alone, but Bruce and Gabriel did change me."

Violet tilted her head and there was a small smile in the upper corner of her lips. "Change you how?"

"I grew stronger... more confident... and I didn't need..." I trailed off and looked down at all the black clothes.

"That's right, you don't need him," Daniel said. "You got us."

Without thinking I reached my hand up to pull the black beanie off my head and let down my blond hair.

But Darren wasn't going to dwell anymore on my major life crisis and the revelations that were going through my head. He was already moving on to the next subject.

"By the way, Miss Violet, who was the man in the charcoal gray shirt that you kept looking at all night?" Darren asked. "Don't think I don't see what goes on in my shop."

Violet played with her long hair, which was hanging loose tonight. "Oh, that's just Jake. He was here with my older brother Christian."

"You like him!" Darren said. Not as a question but a statement.

Her smile was enough to confirm Darren's observation. "I've had a crush on Jake since fifth grade, but he doesn't see me that way." There was a chipper smile on her face that didn't hide the sadness below. "Jake is three years older than me and he always just saw me as Christian's annoying younger sister."

"But a three-year age difference means nothing when you're both in your twenties," I objected.

"No, I guess not, but back when we were kids it did, and maybe that's why I'm still invisible to him."

"Are you sure he isn't just shy or something?" I asked.

She laughed. "Yes, I'm sure. Jake tolerates me because I'm Christian's sister, but he thinks I'm a candidate for an asylum, I think."

"You don't know that."

"No, strangely enough I can't read him very well. He's not a very emotional guy, and while I pick up all sorts of things from other people, Jake has always been a bit of a mystery to me. But" – she threw her hands in the air – "it doesn't take supernatural abilities to figure out that when someone avoids being alone with you or never asks you any questions, it's not a sign of affection."

"He's a jerk," Daniel said. "I would be ecstatic if you would be my girl. I don't care how crazy you are, you are kind, intelligent, and beautiful."

"Oh my, aren't we a little support group tonight," Darren said dryly. "It's time for you to move on, Cherry Pie, it's obviously not meant to be."

"I know," replied Violet. "I just always hoped that someday he would look up and see me, but it's like I'm air to him."

"What does he do?" I asked.

Violet brushed some nonexistent crumbs off her dress with a sad smile on her face. "Jake is a scientist and very rigid about everything having to be based on evidence. You could say that he's my complete opposite since I'm all about intuition and spiritual energy."

"Sometimes opposites attract," I said to make her feel better.

"True, and sometimes opposites clash, but in our case I just seem to be tidally locked to him, like the moon rotating around the earth, but never getting closer.

She reached out and squeezed my hand. "Thank you for trying to cheer me up, though."

"Enough of your soppy love stories," Darren said and sat down his glass. "Too bad it's only Tuesday or we could go and get hammered at some bar and get you two ladies laid." He put his hands behind his head and leaned back with his elbows pointing out. "I have the equipment to do it of course, but I'm afraid I would have to be extremely drunk to find you attractive enough to offer my services, since I'm more into..." He eyes trailed to Daniel. "Well, handsome men obviously."

Both Daniel's palms flew up. "Sorry, champ, but I'm straighter than straight."

Darren made a long heavy sigh and his arms fell down in his lap. "Well, isn't that just great... then I'll join the sad chorus of those two lonely ladies over there." He waved a hand in the direction of Violet and me. "That leaves only you, Daniel, do you at least have a love life worth sharing?" he asked Daniel, who coughed.

"I don't know about that, but I sure as hell don't mind offering my services to Black and Violet like the good friend I am." He winked. "I could distract you both tonight if you're up for it."

I arched a brow and didn't even want to comment on that absurd idea. Me, Daniel, and Violet in a threesome... yeah, right, when pigs fly.

There was only one man I wanted to touch me, and from the way Gabriel had looked at me with anger and disgust, I was certain he would never want me again. Suddenly the dam burst and all the suppressed emotions came full force, making my lungs feel three sizes too small. I got up, desperately needing some fresh air.

As I struggled to unlock the front door and get out of the shop I heard Daniel behind me. "What's wrong... I didn't mean to upset you... I was only kidding... I'm sorry, Black."

"Just give her a minute, Daniel," Violet said in the distance but I couldn't stop and turn to look at them... I had managed to subdue reality for hours and now it had come back with a vengeance, ripping me up from the inside.

I walked aimlessly, keeping my feet moving as if they could somehow take me away from the pain.

But of course that's not how pain works. No amount of miles can separate you from your own heartache.

I can't say how long it took me, but even though I walked in a bubble of sorrow, my heart steered me toward the man I loved and I ended up standing in front of Gabriel's building, looking up at the apartment.

The lights were still on.

A brave woman would have gone up to talk things through, but I would rather face a night on the streets than knock on his door looking like this.

The expression of disgust and disappointment on Gabriel's face earlier today made me wince inside.

He might say that he loved me, but it wasn't true. Not really.

With my shoulders slumped forward I pulled up the phone I'd gotten from him and made a last call before I dumped his phone, and half of the money I had made tonight, in his mailbox. I couldn't bear the thought that he might feel like I used him for his money. Four thousand dollars wouldn't cover rent, food, and everything he had paid for the therapy, but hopefully he would know it was all I could pay at the moment and understand that I never meant to exploit his kindness.

With a last glance up at his window I whispered a last goodbye and disappeared into the night.

CHAPTER 24
Loss

Gabriel

Cia didn't come home that night and she didn't return any of my texts messages asking where she was. Part of me figured she was just upset with me and needed a little time to recover from my harsh reaction to her outfit before she was ready to talk to me.

But Cia didn't want to talk with me again. I realized that much when I emptied the mailbox the next day and found her phone and four thousand dollars.

Everything we had gone through together – the emotional ups and downs that had bonded us over the last month – weren't enough after all.

I was heartbroken and blamed myself for having pushed her too far, too fast. Maybe Bruce was right when he called me an idiot and maybe Brent had been right when he said I was naïve and chose women I could fix.

For days I walked around in a vacuum trying to understand how we had gone from lovers to strangers in a flash.

Everything reminded me of Cia, and like a freaking pendulum I would swing daily from being angry with her for leaving me without any closure to being sad that I had lost the love of my life.

No other woman had made me feel like Cia did. Every girlfriend I had ever been with had wanted something from me and ended up sucking me dry, emotionally, financially, or both.

Cia was different! She didn't have much but never asked for anything, and the way she used to look at me made me feel like fucking Super Mario. Like the time she told me I was beautiful both inside and out. I think I grew a foot from that compliment alone.

I'm far from perfect of course, but the way Cia looked up to me, admired me, respected me, and expressed how she thought herself lucky to be with me made me feel better about myself than I ever have before.

In reality it was always the other way around.

I was lucky to be with her.

So what if she didn't have a fine college degree, a fat bank account, or a face and body like a supermodel?

Cia was the most talented painter I knew, she was smart enough to challenge complicated ideas and concepts, and brave enough to stand up to someone as intimidating as me, Bruce, or Steve. And on top of all that, she was humble and had a great sense of humor.

I had learned more from Cia in a month than I had from anyone else during the last decade, and I fucking missed her.

Sleeping in the empty apartment without her was close to impossible. I worried all night long that Cia was somewhere out on the streets. I prayed that she would be safe and that she had enough money. At the same time, I worried that she would spend the money from the art show on Oxy pills and end up in jail.

After five days I couldn't take it any longer and decided to track her down.

Cia

"G called again... he wants you to call him."

I didn't raise my head to look at Violet since I knew her eyes would be scanning mine for answers. "I know," I said and took another spoonful of the soup. "He also told Daniel, Darren, and Bruce to tell me."

"Are you just going to ignore him?" Violet said, and there was a critical undertone.

"Yup."

"He's not a bad guy, you know," she tried to object, but we had already been over this many times and I didn't want to go there or I would just start to cry again.

"Your brother stopped by while you were shopping," I said to change the subject.

"Christian?" she asked.

"Do you have other brothers?"

She tore off a piece of bread and started spreading butter on it. "Yes, my oldest brother Fred, but he wouldn't stop by."

"Is he with the part of your family who wants to burn you on the stake for being a witch?" I teased, but Violet didn't laugh; instead she raised her shoulders in a small shrug.

"Fred lives in Ohio," she said softly and then held up the butter knife as if she just remembered something. "Do you know if Christian looked at the water faucet in the bathroom?" she asked.

"Uh-huh." I nodded and swallowed another spoonful of Violet's delicious tomato soup. "He fixed it so it doesn't drip anymore."

"Sweet... I'll have to thank him for that."

"Christian seems nice," I said.

"Yeah, he is." Violet looked thoughtful. "He's overcompensating for the rest of the family, though... I've told him he doesn't have to but he feels worse about the situation than I do."

"About them shunning you?"

"I wouldn't say that. They still invite me to family dinners and such, but it's the constant pressure that gets to me."

"What do you mean?"

"My family is just deeply disappointed with my choices in life and they don't understand that it's a deeper calling for me. My mother keeps asking me what she did wrong."

I chuckled. "What did she do wrong?"

Violet smiled. "You've been living with me for almost two weeks now and you still think I'm a fraud?"

"Hey," I held up both hands. "I need to see to believe... so if you can ask your ghostly friends to move a few things around right now, then I'll declare myself a believer."

Violet bowed her head and took another spoonful before she spoke. "I used to beg them to move things to prove I wasn't crazy."

"Did they?"

"Sure... but never at the right moment or the right place." She put her spoon down and leaned back in her chair. "I can remember one time when my dad gave me a spanking for lying and I begged the spirits to do something that would convince him I was telling the truth about them being there."

"And nothing happened?" I asked.

"Not while he spanked me, but the next day his car had a flat tire, and he walked into a door and it slammed in his head."

"Sounds like a coincidence."

"That's what he said when I told him it was the spirits, and then he grounded me for telling more lies."

I looked down and considered how to put my words. "Violet... did you ever consider that maybe there are no spirits?"

She crossed her arms. "You mean, did I ever consider that I'm just a mental basket case who hallucinates?"

"Well, did you?" I said softly.

"Of course."

"Did you try to talk to someone about it? Like a doctor or a psychologist?"

She snorted. "Trust me, my parents pushed lots of health professionals on me."

"And it didn't help, I assume."

Violet got up from the table and carried her bowl to the kitchen sink, where she placed it with a loud clunk. "No, it didn't help, because I'm not sick, Cia. I think of it this way: some people are colorblind… they have to trust other people's description of color. I have a different kind of sight and can see things that most people can't, but just because you can't see it doesn't mean it's not there."

"Okay, then let me ask you this. Doesn't it freak you out?"

"It used to freak me out, but I've learned to control it and now I can close off if I'm not in the mood to deal with the paranormal and if someone is unpleasant I ask them to leave."

"But what about the houses that are haunted? Doesn't that scare you?"

Violet came back to the table and sat down. "I try not to get scared. Most often it's just a confused spirit who's causing the disturbance, and when it's something malicious I get protective of the living and use my powers to throw them out."

I got chills from talking about it but curiosity made me ask my next question. "Can you see your own future?"

Sadness crept over her face. "I used to think I could, but…" she trailed off. "I've always had this clear vision of me and Jake, married and living together in a house with our two daughters."

"Jake is your brother's friend, right?"

"Right… but as you know, we're not together."

"But in that case isn't your vision just a dream or a childish fantasy like we all have? I mean, I used to imagine my dad would come and rescue me from my mom, and had very clear images in my head about how that would go down."

"Maybe," Violet said.

"Then how do you know that *all* your visions aren't just your imagination?"

"I trust my abilities, and most often the visions come true."

"Except when they don't," I challenged.

She tilted her head and smiled. "Let's hope for you that they do come true, because I had a good vision about your future."

Gabriel was the first thing that popped into my mind, but I didn't ask if he was involved in her vision. "What did you see?" I asked.

"I see money around you. I can't tell if it comes from your art or if you win the lottery, but very soon you'll be rich."

I took a sip of my water and suppressed a laugh. "I like that vision. It's what I dream of." *When I'm not dreaming about Gabriel.*

"If you want I could give you a reading," Violet offered.

"No thanks, I'm good." I told her politely and when she raised a brow I continued. "No, seriously, I'm in a good place right now; my art is selling, I have a couch to live on thanks to you, and I haven't touched any pills since before I got arrested."

"And Gabriel?" she asked quietly.

"I don't want to talk about him."

And so we didn't.

CHAPTER 25
Alki Beach

Gabriel

Eight weeks later.

Alki Beach was crowded and there was no place to park. With a quick look at the clock I cursed low. I was already late and the girl I was meeting had texted me four times.

I took another round and thanked my lucky stars when, finally, a car blinked to signal they were leaving.

After parking my car, I walked at a fast pace to meet up with Caroline, a young nurse that my friend Nate had set me up with.

For ten weeks I had moaned about Cia disappearing on me without as much as a goodbye, and I was still angry at her for not even giving me a chance to talk things through. To say I hated how we had ended our relationship would be an understatement.

After I had called Daniel, Darren, Violet, and Bruce, who all promised to tell her I wanted to speak to her, I still heard nothing, and in the end I gave up.

If she didn't want me, there wasn't much more I could do about it except lick my wounds and try to move on.

Caroline met me outside the French restaurant. She looked beautiful, with long honey-blond hair and a blinding smile. Nat had already spoken highly about her, and at least her looks didn't disappoint.

"Hey, I'm G. You must be Caroline," I said politely and leaned in to give her a small hug.

She smelled nice.

"God, you're tall," she said with a nervous laugh and leaned her head back to meet my eyes. I'm really not freakishly tall, only six foot two, but Caroline was petite.

"Do you want to eat now or take a walk on the beach first?" I asked her

Two minutes later we were walking along Alki Beach and talking about Nat, who was the only friend we had in common.

"Did he tell you I'm moving in three weeks?" I asked her.

"Yeah, he did. That's why I agreed to meet you."

"Right, he told me you weren't into anything serious."

"No, I'm not."

"He didn't tell me why, though."

Caroline shrugged. "I had a very controlling boyfriend for seven years and missed out on a lot. Now I just want to spread my wings and not be tied down by anyone."

"That makes sense," I said.

"Oh, look." Caroline pointed ahead to a small marketplace with pavilions and some musicians singing and dancing. "Let's check it out," she said eagerly and lit up with a childish delight that I liked. "I love places like this.... look, we can have our future read." She grabbed my elbow, nudging me along to a small pavilion.

I recognized Violet instantly and I could tell that the minute she looked up and saw me, she knew who I was too. Her eyes slid to Caroline and back to me.

"Would you like a couples reading?" she asked.

I shook my head and felt annoyed. "No thanks."

"Can you do a reading just for me?" Caroline asked excitedly.

"Of course."

I kept a bit of distance thinking that Caroline might want answers to some private questions, so while Violet

Clashing Colors #1 BLACK

took the gullible girl's money, I walked around the marketplace and waited for her.

It wasn't a big place but the group of people gathered in front of a pavilion was the reason I didn't see Cia at first. She was sitting on a chair, drawing a portrait of a boy around seven, and her eyes kept going between him and the paper in front of her. I couldn't see the portrait, but I could see her.

How could I have thought she wasn't the most beautiful woman I had ever been with? She looked stunning with her long golden hair tucked behind her ears and very discreet make-up. Her clothes were feminine and simple – a black summer dress with spaghetti straps, that revealed her summer tan.

I stood hypnotized for minutes, just taking in the beauty of Cia, wondering why I hadn't seen this all along. I had considered her pretty, but never the most beautiful of my girlfriends. Something had changed and I couldn't tell if it was my eyesight or her looks, I just knew that she was exquisite and that my whole body was buzzing with excitement.

After another ten minutes of drawing, she was done and handed the portrait to the parents. I was quick to step closer, wanting to be first in line to have my portrait made and get her to talk to me.

Cia took the money and thanked the father of the boy before she turned. The shock on her face when she saw me made me hold my breath.

"Hey," I said and waited for her to speak.

She took a step back.

"Can I have my portrait painted?" I asked.

She looked around at the people in the crowd that seem to be scattering now that she wasn't drawing.

"I'm sorry, but I'm on a break now," she said and turned her back to me.

My hands acted by themselves and pulled her around to face me. "How have you been?"

"Fine," she said but I didn't have to be a psychic to know she was lying.

All the anger I had felt towards her seemed to evaporate in the summer sun.

"I miss you," I said and looked deeply into her eyes. It was the truth.

A ghost of pain flashed over her face before she tensed up and looked to my right. I turned my face to see what she saw and found Caroline and Violet watching us.

"Are you ready to go, G?" Caroline asked.

Violet gave me a grim stare but said nothing.

I whipped my head around to explain to Cia that Caroline and I weren't a thing but her face had turned into a hard façade again.

"Can we talk?" I asked.

"What do you want to talk about?" she said and turned to a Chinese couple who were looking at her portraits. "Would you like to have a portrait done? It's fifty for one person and eighty for a couple."

The couple exchanged a few words before they nodded and pointed to both of them.

"Just take a seat over here." Cia pointed to two chairs and moved to pick up her pencil.

"Hey, I wanted a portrait painted – you said you were taking a break," I complained.

"G, are you coming or not?" Caroline asked behind me and in that moment Cia looked up at me.

"I think your girlfriend is getting impatient."

"She's not my girlfriend," I protested.

"I'm not his girlfriend... it's just a casual thing," Caroline said in what I assumed was intended as a helpful comment.

Cia looked at me and then back at Caroline. "That's a shame, because you look just like his *type*."

I huffed out air with annoyance, wishing I could have just ten minutes alone with her.

"Can I have your number at least?" I asked in a last attempt, but she pretended not to hear me.

"Cia, can't you at least look at me?"

She turned her head and raw emotions shone from her eyes. "Please just leave me alone," she said in a brittle voice that hit me hard.

I backed away, not wanting to cause her more harm.

Needless to say, I didn't have dinner with Caroline. Instead I apologized to her and explained the situation. I had to try and make Cia talk to me and get some closure. Caroline took it well and gave me a hug before she walked away.

I went back to the marketplace and saw that Cia was still working on her portrait of the Chinese couple. Violet, however, was in between clients.

"Can I talk to you?" I asked her.

She pointed to the chair. "It's thirty dollars for a ten-minute reading."

"I don't want a reading, but I'll give you a hundred dollars if you give me Cia's phone number."

"Tsk." She smacked her tongue.

"Okay, two hundred dollars if you help me get ten minutes alone with her."

"Sit," Violet ordered and I did.

"Why do you want her number?" she asked.

"Because I want to talk to her... I want answers."

"What kind of answers."

"Like where does she live? I've been at the motel and she doesn't sleep there. I just want to know she's okay. She's still my niece, you know."

She shook her head with a small grin.

"It's not funny. Do you know where she lives?"

"Yes."

"Will you tell me?"

"No. Do you have other questions?"

"Yes," I said annoyed that she wouldn't tell me. "I still don't understand why she would dress as a Goth that night. Was it a statement of some kind? I mean she dresses normally now."

Violet looked thoughtful. "Give me your hands," she said and I complied.

"You are a soldier, yes?"

I nodded.

"If a woman told you she loves a man in uniform, would you be flattered?"

I wrinkled my forehead. "I don't know."

"Let say you fell in love with this woman and she asked you to wear your uniform all the time; would you?"

I continued to frown, but didn't answer.

"Now let's say you've been wearing your handsome uniform for your girlfriend for weeks and she tells you that she loves you."

"Yeah?"

"How would you know if she loves you or just gets excited by your uniform?"

"That's easy. I would take it off," I said quickly.

Violet didn't speak for a while; she just looked at me expectantly.

"What?" I asked blankly.

"Ask yourself: did something happen between you two that would make Cia feel a need to test if you loved her or her uniform?"

I closed my eyes with a sudden clarity. I had told her I loved her and she had pulled this stunt on me. It had been a fucking test and I had failed big-time.

"Fuck." I groaned and rubbed my face with both hands. "I screwed up."

"Yes, you did," Violet said and let go of my hands. "I've known Cia for a few years," she said quietly, "and I was really happy to see her come out of her shell and curious to meet the man who would make her want to. When I saw her in the gallery that night as Black, my thought was that she was under pressure and needed the armor that outfit provides."

"She was scared." I pondered out loud.

Violet nodded. "Cia had a lot on the line that night. What if her paintings didn't sell?"

"What if my family attacked her again?" I added.

"What if someone criticized her art, which was very personal to her?"

I crossed my arms and lowered my head, thinking a hundred miles an hour. For ten weeks I had been digging around in those questions without finding answers, and this crazy person had just given me those answers as if they were there for everyone to see.

Seeing her today had made one thing clear to me. I wasn't over her and I needed to talk to her.

"How do I get her to give me a second chance?" I asked

"I think you'll need patience," Violet answered.

"I'm moving in three weeks. I can't be patient, I need to fix this now," I said, tapping my right foot with nervous energy.

"In that case, you might be out of luck."

I felt chills down my spine. "Why? Is she seeing someone else?"

Violet was quiet too damn long. "Is she?" I repeated with a slightly raised voice.

"Those are things I can't tell you."

"So much for you being a psychic," I said with a combination of sarcasm and desperation. "Why don't you use your special powers and tell me how to win her back?"

She watched me closely for a few seconds before she spoke in a low voice. "I could tell you if I wanted to, but…"

I cut her off. "I'll give you three hundred dollars, if you tell me."

Violet tilted her head with a small smile. "Show me the money."

"I don't carry cash, but I promise I'll get you the money."

"I'm afraid I don't give credit. Get me the money and I'll tell you how to win her back. But I warn you: you might not like what I have to say."

I was back with the money ten minutes later and handed Violet three hundred dollars.

"So tell me what I need to know to get Cia back."

Violet picked up the money and put it in her bag before she spoke.

"The first step is to apologize."

"I can do that," I said decisively just as a group of women with high pitched voices and loud grins passed the tent. Violet waited for the women to pass before she continued.

"The second step is to convince her you can give her what she needs."

"Okay."

"The third step is to empower her to take another chance on you."

I summed up the steps. "Apologize, convince, empower... got it, but how do I do that?"

"Well, first of all, you need to know what she needs. Do you?" She drummed her fingers on a stack of tarot cards.

I thought of our time together at the camp and all the things I knew about her childhood. "She needs someone to love her unconditionally," I said.

Violet nodded. "Don't we all?"

I got up from my chair full of restless energy. "But how do I get her to believe I'm that person after fucking up so badly?" I asked with frustration.

"That's where patience comes in, but since you're in a hurry, you might have to speed things up a little."

"How...? I can't even get her to listen to me."

Violet rolled her eyes and gave a long deep sigh. "I'm sorry, but aren't you a military engineer of some sort?"

"Yeah."

"Aren't you supposed to be inventive and get rid of obstacles?"

I leaned back. "That's hardly the same thing."

Her light brown eyes narrowed. "So you want me to believe that you can go to war and come home with some sort of medal, but you're not strategic, brave, or determined enough to get Cia alone for an hour?"

I tensed my jaw. "Military tactics don't really work with civilians. I can't just capture her and interrogate her to make her tell me how she feels and get her to listen to me."

Violet got up to stand in front of me. She was a head smaller but felt like she was towering over me with an immense force. "You can't or you won't?"

"You are crazier than I thought, if you're seriously suggesting I kidnap Cia. That would make me a criminal."

She gave me a wry smile. "Ahh, and what a pair of criminals you would be."

I gaped at her when she clapped her hands. "I'm afraid this is all I have to offer you, because we're closing up for today."

At first I didn't catch the hint in her voice, but then it dawned on me – that if Cia was off for the day too, she might have time to talk to me. I wasn't even going to consider kidnapping her; that was just insane.

I hurried to Cia's pavilion, where she was packing up her things. "Do you need help?" I offered but she just lifted her head and then quickly looked down again.

"No thanks."

"I could use some help," Violet called out behind me. "Would you mind carrying this table to my car?"

My eyes shot to Cia once again. I would much rather be helping her and getting close to her.

"All right," I said and took the table from Violet, who surprised me by holding out her car keys.

"It's the classic station wagon with a bumper sticker that says *They told me I'm crazy, but my unicorn says I'm just fine.*"

I took the keys she held out for me and started walking in the direction she had pointed to. How the hell was I going to get Cia to talk with me?

The answer came when I saw Violet's car…

CHAPTER 26
Desperate Times

Cia

The moment I saw Gabriel I felt like I had been punched in my stomach. Why hadn't he grown a humongous beard or gotten a beer belly or something? Why did he have to look as darn handsome as he ever did and why did he have to look at me like he had just found a long-lost treasure?

I was rude. I realized that, but what choice did I have? It would have been so easy to fall for the illusion that we could have it all. But I wouldn't. Not this time. I was finally getting back on my feet, and with the money I was making on selling paintings through Darren and my street art, I was able to support myself. Of course it helped that I lived with Violet, who didn't charge much rent for her couch.

Although I've known Violet for about three years we hadn't been close until now. As Black I was never close to anyone, Daniel being the exception. But as Cia, I'm softer and more open to letting others in. In small doses.

Violet is freaky, though. She'll say things that I have no clue how she knows. Some days she almost has me convinced that her psychic abilities are real, but then I kick myself for being so naïve.

I haven't forgotten about the spooky cleansing she did in Daniel's apartment. Daniel is convinced she's the real thing, but the more I think about it, the more it seems likely that she could have known the name of the man living there, what he did for a living, and even how he committed suicide. I mean, Daniel must have given her his address and that would have given her time to look it up... if she has access to the right IT systems.

But who am I to judge how she makes her money? I've hustled people in the past and stolen things, so if some gullible schmuck wants to pay Violet to read their future, talk to some dead relative, have a house clearing, or tell them the name of their spirit guides, then peace to them.

All I know is that Violet is the kindest and most generous person I know. She always does her best to make me feel better when I'm having a bad day. And I've had a lot of bad days after I lost Gabriel.

Some say it's better to have loved and lost, but I say it's better to live in ignorant bliss. The pain of having your illusions crushed will break you.

I think I would have broken too, if not for Violet.

But I'm still here... working, living, existing, and hoping that, someday, Gabriel won't be the first thing I think about in the morning and the last before I go to bed.

I was annoyed that Violet allowed him to help her carry her things to the car and I insisted on carrying my own. You can't both ask a man for his help and at the same time tell him to leave you alone, and I certainly didn't want to send him any mixed signals. I had trusted him once and he had blown it. As far as I was concerned we were better off walking our separate ways.

When we finally got all our gear packed into Arion I got into the passenger seat without as much as looking at Gabriel, who stood on the sidewalk. I kept my eyes straight ahead and was fully focused on not showing how affected I was by his presence.

"Thanks for the help," Violet called out to him and got behind the wheel.

"Let's go! Hurry up and get this old thing moving." I muttered, harsher than I intended.

Violet gave me a reproachful glance and stroked the steering wheel. "I'm sorry, Arion, Cia didn't mean to offend you. We would appreciate if you could get us safely home."

She turned the key in the ignition and it cranked but didn't fire up. Violet turned the key again and it was the same thing.

"See, I've told you not to talk poorly about Arion."

That's when I lost it. "Will you stop talking about this car as if it's alive? This is an old crappy car, not some Greek stallion with magical powers. Normal people don't name their cars and they certainly don't speak to them."

Violet narrowed her eyes. "I'm sorry if you were under the impression that I'm normal."

Of course Gabriel chose that exact moment to tap on the window. "Is everything all right?" he asked.

I covered my face with both my hands, feeling the need to scream.

"He won't start," Violet said and got out of the car talking to Gabriel about what could be wrong. I stubbornly stayed in the car until Gabriel got in to try and start Arion. That made me get out.

"It's probably the battery. Have you had issues with it before?" Gabriel asked.

"No, Arion never gives me trouble."

"Don't worry, I have a portable jump-starter in my car."

"Great, can you go and get it?" Violet asked him.

Gabriel looked at me. "Sure, if Cia walks with me so we can talk. It's only a few blocks from here."

Violet looked at me with a pleading glance.

"Just call a tow truck company," I said, not wanting to be pushed into a conversation that I knew would bring up emotions I was trying hard to suppress.

Violet did call a tow truck company. She called several in fact, but all of them had hours of waiting time, and in the end I was so desperate to get home that I agreed to walk with him to his car.

"Thank you," Violet called after me as I walked stiffly next to the man who had been my first love.

"Why didn't you ever call me?" he asked.

"There wasn't much to talk about," I answered shortly.

"Did you ever consider that some closure would have been healthy for both of us?"

I shrugged... *God damn it, where is his car?*

"Everyone has been asking about you."

I knew he was referring to his family... but that was the double curse of my situation. I hadn't lost just him, but the chance to be a part of my family too. Even if they would accept me into their fold, I wouldn't go... because he would be there.

It hurt too much.

"Where do you live?" Gabriel asked and I told him it was none of his concern.

"Do you have enough money?"

"Yes."

"Are you still off the drugs?"

That made me whip my head around and pin him with a dirty look. "You make it sound like I was a hardcore drug addict."

"I'm sorry, I just worry about you."

"Don't, I'm fine." *If heartbroken can be called fine.*

When we finally got to his car, he asked me to get in. "The battery is heavy, I don't want to carry it, so we'll take my car back," he explained.

I shook my head. "That's okay. You drive, I'll just walk back."

He crossed his arms. "Are you really so disgusted with me that you can't sit in a car with me for two minutes?"

"No." Didn't he understand that my coldness had nothing to do with disgust and everything to do with self-preservation?

He took a step to get in front of me. "Cia."

I looked down, unwilling to meet his glance.

"I'm sorry, Cia. I'm so sorry that I hurt you."

My eyes glanced up to meet his, finding only sincerity in his expression.

"Please accept my apology," he said, low.

Some say that words are cheap, but for someone like me apologies don't come by very often. My mom was about the only person who had ever apologized for all the shit she put me through, and that apology came much too late.

To hear Gabriel apologize was huge in my world and I was genuinely touched by it. I think that's why I got into his car and agreed that we could drive to Violet together.

Of course that's not what happened at all.

We drove off and because the streets were so narrow he went slow. I didn't say anything, still trying to process his apology.

"Can I give you a lift home after we jump-start Violet's car?" he asked. "I would like to talk with you."

I was a tiny bit tempted to say yes because the truth is I still loved him, but there was the one thousand four hundred and ninety-five times these past weeks where I had promised myself I would never allow anyone to hurt me like he had. And this was exactly why I didn't want to go with him in the first place. It would be no different from the first time Daniel gave me the Oxy pill. It feels innocent but gives a taste of more, and soon you're hooked. If I allowed Gabriel to give me a ride home, it would be another forty minutes in his company, and I knew from experience how addictive he could be to me.

"Thanks, but no thanks, I'm going with Violet."

He didn't say anything but kept driving.

Two blocks later I spoke up. "Hey, you're going in the wrong direction." I turned my head in the direction we were supposed to go.

"No, I'm not," was his short answer.

"Violet is waiting for us."

"Then call her up and tell her you're going with me."

I got angry with him. "I'm not going with you. Stop the car."

"No."

"I tried to open my door, but as soon as my hand touched the door handle I heard the locking mechanism and it made me turn my head around. "Unlock this door, *right now*," I demanded.

"No," he said and kept on driving.

"G, I swear that if you don't pull over and let me go right now I'll call the police."

He tensed up but didn't stop or even look at me. I figured he knew I was bluffing, and he was right; I wasn't interested in coming into contact with the police.

"I'm not going to harm you; I just want to talk," he said, clamping onto the steering wheel so tightly that his knuckles were white.

"By freaking kidnapping me?"

He didn't reply to that.

"I'll never speak to you again."

"Cia, you haven't spoken to me in ten weeks. I already told you that I'm not going to hurt you and that I just want to talk."

I crossed my arms and pressed my lips into a thin line, signaling that it would be a one-sided conversation.

As I sat next to him contemplating what would make him do something as absurd as this, my phone rang.

"Is it Violet?" he asked but I ignored him and answered the phone.

"You won't believe what G is doing."

"What's wrong?" Violet asked, concerned.

"He asked if he could give me a lift home and when I said no he decided to take me anyway. I'm in his car and I can't get out."

"Ohh." Violet didn't sound as shocked as I would have expected.

"Put her on speaker," Gabriel insisted.

"I heard him, it's okay," Violet told me so I pressed speaker.

"Hey, Violet," Gabriel said out loud. "I'm sorry about the set-up but I took your advice, and now I'm going to drive around until she listens to me."

"What advice? What the hell are you talking about?" I asked in a raised voice. "Violet, what did you tell him?"

She sighed loudly. "I just told him to talk things through with you and when he said you wouldn't listen, I suggested he should be more inventive to make it happen."

I gaped, unable to fathom that she would say something so stupid.

"Listen," Gabriel spoke. "If you look under the driver's seat there's a small fuse that I took out of your engine. It's really simple to put back in – just go get it and I'll guide you on the phone."

For the next few minutes Gabriel patiently guided Violet and made sure her car was running.

"Will you take Cia to my house when you're done talking?" Violet asked.

He gave me a sideways glance. "Is that where you live?"

I wasn't talking to him… or her, so I said nothing.

"I'll take her wherever she wishes to go, when we're done talking."

"All right, I'll see you later, Cia," Violet said and hung up.

There was silence in the car as we drove across the bridge. Even though I kept my face turned away, refusing to look at him, I still noticed that we were going east.

"We could drive all night, or you could talk to me and be home in an hour," he said in a placating tone.

"I don't negotiate with terrorists," I said grumpily.

He chuckled. "I don't think you understand the definition of a terrorist."

When I didn't speak he continued. "A terrorist is someone who uses violence in the pursuit of political causes. My reasons are different so you can hardly call me a terrorist."

"It's still wrong to hold someone against their will," I sputtered.

"You're right. But it's just as wrong to leave someone heartbroken and refuse to talk things through."

"Heartbroken," I snorted. "You looked all right to me when you showed up with your new girlfriend. Where is she, by the way – did you tie her up and dump her in the trunk?"

"I told you, she's not my girlfriend; she was just a girl Nate set me up with because he was tired of hearing me moan about you."

It gnawed at me that he had been with her, especially since she was much prettier than me.

"Cia, what you and I shared was special, don't you think?"

"I used to," I admitted and looked straight ahead watching the houses, the cars, the trees - well anything but Gabriel really.

"You mean before I screwed up and made a scene at your art show?"

I didn't respond since the answer was obvious.

"I'm sorry about that..." he said, low. "I think seeing you in that costume just felt like a rejection of me."

"Oh, come on, *you* felt rejected? I wasn't the one wrinkling my nose at you or humiliating you in front of people by showing my disgust."

"I already admitted I screwed up," he said and cleared his throat while I turned to face him with a grim expression on my face.

"You know we wouldn't even be having this conversation if I was still dressed as a Goth. You only want Cia and couldn't care less about Black."

"That's not true. I bailed you out of jail and went with you to the camp when you were still Black."

I knitted my brows and gave an imitation of his deep voice. "I prefer my women a little less Goth."

He tensed up but kept his eyes on the road.

"You only want the pretty part of me. Not the angry, troubled part... but guess what, soldier, I'm done trying to be the perfect version of myself around you or anyone. I'm fucking flawed and imperfect, and the fact that you judge me tells nothing about me but *everything* about you."

Darren had spoken those words to me and I had clung to them for weeks. I couldn't be with someone who couldn't accept me for who I was.

For the next fifteen minutes we didn't speak. Gabriel took Exit Thirteen and made his way up the mountain, and he didn't stop until we arrived at a forest.

"Come," he said and got out of the car.

"Can't you just take me home?" I asked, but he had already closed his door before I finished my sentence.

Ten seconds later he opened my door and offered me a hand. I ignored it and got out by myself.

"Have you ever been here?" he asked.

I looked around. "Where exactly is here?"

"Cougar Mountain Regional Wildland Park," he said calmly. "They used to do mining here – I'll show you."

"So what are we now...? On some kind of historical sightseeing tour that I never asked for?"

He reached his hand out to me but I ignored it and marched on.

"So if me judging you tells everything about me... then what does you judging me tell about you?" he asked behind me.

I had to repeat his words in my head before I understood what he had actually said.

"I never judged you," I scoffed.

"Really? So you are allowed to be flawed and imperfect, but I'm not?"

"What are you talking about?" I asked annoyed.

"I already apologized for screwing up, but you won't forgive me or give me a second chance... so I'm concluding that there wasn't room for me to make mistakes in our relationship. You want me to accept your flaws but expect perfection from me, is that it?"

"Of course not," I said, offended. "All my friends are different and kind of crazy... I don't judge and I don't need perfection."

He arched a brow. "Is that what you're telling yourself?"

I moved on, annoyed with his insinuating that I was asking more than I could give.

When I came to a split trail I stopped. "Left or right?"

"Left."

"I don't know what your problem is. How do you expect me to be with a guy who finds me repulsive?" I asked.

"I don't find you repulsive," he said. "I never did."

I turned around so fast that he almost bumped into me. "So are you saying that if I was dressed as a Goth you would still be attracted to me?"

"No. I don't like that look, it does nothing for me."

"Aha... See, I rest my case."

We stood there on a narrow trail with the forest all around us and glanced deeply into each other's eyes, stubbornness burning brightly.

"I won't lie to you, Cia. I'm a guy and we're visual. I like it when you dress in feminine clothes and I don't like it when you dress like an angry boy."

"That's what I said. You only want the pretty version of me."

"That's not true. I've seen you in awful clothes at the camp and still felt attracted to you."

"But you can't accept me as Black."

"Seeing you like that makes me feel like a failure."

"Why?"

"Because that darkness represents your past... and I wanted to be your future." Words hung in the air... Gabriel's eyes grew moist and he swallowed, making his Adam's apple move several times. "I wanted to marry you and give you the life you deserve," he whispered.

I could hear my heart beat and feel water rise in my eyes. I should look away, but I couldn't.

"I trusted you, and you broke that trust," I whispered.

"How? I never lied to you. You always knew I didn't like that look on you. I still don't. You can trust that."

"But you hurt me."

"I was angry and upset. I would have apologized sooner if you would have only talked to me, Cia, but you cut me off, as if what we had didn't mean much. Like *I* didn't mean anything to you at all." A tear started running down his cheek and he dried it away with annoyance. "Do you have any idea how much that hurt?

"I asked you to marry me, I told you I loved you... and one single mistake made you give up on me."

"You meant everything to me," I protested and blinked away tears too.

"Apparently not, or you would have fought for what we had."

"But..." I was confused and affected by the sadness on his face.

"So I'm a flawed man who doesn't always think before I speak. And maybe it's an imperfection that I prefer you in feminine clothes compared to black military boots and pants. But how can you blame me for judging you when clearly you judge me just as harshly?"

I wanted to argue that he was wrong... that I didn't judge him... but I couldn't.

The contradiction in my head was that I wanted him to be open-minded and take me as I was... Black or Cia. But that I wouldn't accept his narrow-minded behavior suddenly stood out as hypocrisy.

"I'm sorry," I muttered. "I cut you off when I should have talked to you about what happened."

"Well, talk to me now... I need to understand what made you dress that way."

I lifted my shoulders in a small shrug. "I don't know. It was an impulsive act. Maybe I thought I looked more like an eccentric artist in that outfit, but I certainly didn't do it to hurt you or push you away from me."

"Didn't you stop to think about the signals you were sending me?" he wanted to know.

"No." I lowered my head, ashamed that I hadn't considered how he would interpret my clothes as a personal failure.

Gabriel reached out and took my hand. "Cia," he said and I lifted my gaze to meet his. "Did you ever love me?"

Someone was squeezing my chest and making it hard for me to breathe and those damn tears came dripping out of my eyes without permission.

"Did you?" he repeated.

It took everything to push out the word. "Yes."

"You loved me?" He broke into a sad smile.

"Yes," I confirmed and we both stood there like a pair of sissy-pants sniffling up our tears when he leaned in and hugged me.

He was holding me in a tight hug and I placed my arms around his waist and hugged him back. *God, I've missed him so much.*

When he spoke it was softly muffled against my hair. "I still love you and I always will."

That made me hide my face against his chest and give in to my tears. I'd felt so hurt and rejected by him, and now that I was beginning to see both sides of the story, I was overwhelmed with the stupidity of my stubbornness.

He pulled back to look at me. "I know you think I only love you when you act and look a certain way, but it's not true. My love for you is unconditional…"

"How can you say that and at the same time say you don't like me as Black?" I asked in a brittle voice.

He kissed me on my hair. "Don't confuse my sexual desire with my love. I'll always love you, even when you have a cold and your eyes are puffy and your nose is running, but I probably won't feel sexually attracted to you in that moment though."

I wrinkled my nose. "Of course not."

"It's the same with the Goth costume. I love you but seeing you in that black gear is a turn-off."

"But if I chose to go back to wearing black, would you still love me?"

"I would, but our relationship would suffer, because I would feel rejected by you."

"Why?"

"I already explained that to you. So who do you want to be… Cia or Black?"

I looked down at myself. I hadn't dressed as Black since that night, nor had I wanted to.

"Maybe the two aren't opposites in my mind. I'm wearing a black dress now," I said. "You got a problem with that?"

He slid his hand down my arm. "No, it's very feminine and you look beautiful."

"Good, because I won't let anyone dictate how I dress," I told him.

"Hey, you can dress any way you want. You'll just get a different reaction from me."

"Because you're imperfect," I said dryly.

"If you call being male imperfect, then yeah…"

"Are you saying all males are visual?"

A smile lurked at the corner of Gabriel's mouth. "I'm sure it's just a male thing. Because as we all know, women never try to make their men wear certain things or complain about men in sandals and white socks."

I tilted my head. "Very funny… I see your point: so we're all visual to some extent."

"Yup… and I honestly don't care if you dress in sweat pants and a ponytail… in fact I like your natural beauty… but when you hide it behind that black armor it makes my dick shrink."

"Thanks a lot."

"Hey, just keeping it real," he said and picked a leaf from a branch close to us.

"Did you sleep with the blonde?" I asked out of the blue.

"No." Gabriel pointed back over his shoulder. "Do you want me to open the trunk so you can ask her yourself?

I stuck my tongue out. "I still think it was wrong of you to kidnap me."

He raised both palms. "Hey, desperate times call for desperate measures. I had to do something, and besides – you should see it as a sign of my devotion to you that I'm willing to become a criminal to prove my love to you."

I didn't think before I caressed his face. "Is that what this was about? You proving your love to me?"

"Yes, Cia... this is me telling you that I still want to share my future with you." He took my hand and kissed it. "If you'll spend your time with someone as flawed, and judgmental, and imperfect as me."

Gabriel had asked me to marry him before and I had never really committed to him. My hands were shaking, my chest was heaving, and I was seeing spots in front of my eyes. But none of it could distract me from the intensity in Gabriel's eyes that spoke of unconditional love for me – something that I had always wanted. Life was reaching out an olive branch to me; all I had to do was reach out and accept it.

CHAPTER 27
But

Gabriel

I hadn't planned to propose to Cia today. I hadn't even known I would run into her after ten weeks apart, but standing here in the green forest with all emotions raw and real, the moment just felt right.

She was looking down at me as I kneeled in front of her, tears running down her pretty face.

"Will you marry me, Cia?"

She swallowed air and took a deep breath.

"I mean it, sugar," I said, hoping this would be enough to convince her that I really loved her unconditionally. "I want to share my life with you."

Cia didn't say yes or no. Instead she sank to her knees in front of me, still holding my hand. "You are amazing," she said and looked down.

The fact that she wasn't looking me in my eyes was a bad sign and made me sink back on my heels waiting for the "but."

"I love you too," she whispered and gave me a small smile.

I blinked... dreading the "but" that was sure to follow.

"But..." she said and I sighed in defeat. *Fuck!*

"You're moving too fast. I'm still pissed at you for kidnapping me and rejecting me that night at the gallery. I can't just go from being angry at you to saying yes to marrying you. It doesn't work that way."

"But..."

She leaned in and kissed me softly. "I'm sorry."

"Me too," I muttered and for a while we sat in the grass without speaking.

"Do you still want to go and see the mining thing?" she asked quietly.

"Maybe another time," I said with a heavy feeling inside.

We got up from the ground and made our way back to the car in silence. My head was spinning with questions that I wanted to ask, but she had been specific about not going too fast.

I tried to cheer myself up by focusing on the fact that at least we were talking again, but in reality the ride to Violet's house was very quiet.

"This is it," Cia said and pointed to a small cottage-style house in shades of red.

"Wow... I didn't expect her house to be so..." I trailed off when I saw Violet's old station wagon and a large sign on the front lawn saying Psychic Medium. Yep, this was Violet's domain all right.

"Nice?" Cia suggested.

"Right... I didn't expect it to be so nice. I'm just surprised that a fraud like Violet would be able to afford something so well maintained and idyllic-looking."

"You know she comes from money, right?"

"No... what do you mean?"

Cia spoke in a calm voice. "Well, her family isn't as rich as yours or anything, but she grew up on the east side with private school and that sort of thing. Of course, now she hardly sees them anymore."

"Why not?"

Cia sighed. "I think you know why. They don't like the whole psychic medium thing and want her to get a normal job. She's got a college degree and everything."

"You're kidding, right?" I said.

"Nope, true story."

"But why the hell would someone with a college degree sit in a market square and read people's fortunes?"

"To make money. She has a mortgage to pay."

"But couldn't she make more money using her college degree?"

"Maybe, but she made enough for the down payment of this house and she's determined to never ask her family for anything." Cia sighed. "Violet is... unique."

"You mean weird."

She shrugged. "Definitely weird, but I like her."

I nodded. "For what it's worth, I'm impressed that she's living life on her own terms. I mean I don't understand why she would choose this line of work, but at least she's living out her dream."

"Yeah... I agree," Cia said and fiddled with her hands.

"So what now?" I asked Cia and turned off the engine.

Cia unbuckled her seat belt and turned her body to me. "I don't know. What do you suggest?"

"I think you know what I want."

"What?"

"I want you to go in and pack your things and come home with me," I said and even while saying the words I was mentally slamming my forehead. *What part of take it slow is so hard for me to understand?*

Cia looked up at the house and then back to me.

"I think I need to process this all. How about I call you tomorrow? Bruce and I are talking tonight."

"You still do weekly sessions?"

"No, we only talk every two weeks now."

"Good."

There was a moment of awkward silence between us. "Can I see you tomorrow?" I asked.

"I'll call you," she answered noncommittally.

"Okay... just remember what I said."

"You said a lot of things," she said, in an attempt to lift the mood, I suppose.

"About loving you and... you know."

There was a quick frown on her forehead so I didn't repeat my proposal.

"I'll think about it," she promised and then she got out of the car with a small smile and waved at me. "I'll see you around."

I only drove three blocks before I parked and pulled out my cell phone to call Bruce, who luckily picked up on the third ring.

"G... how are you doing?" he asked in a cheerful tone.

"I need your help," I said quickly.

He was quiet for a few seconds. Then: "I already told Cia that you want to talk to her. There's nothing more I can do. It's her choice."

"No, that's not what I need help with. I already talked to her. That part is fine."

"Oh, you talked to her?"

"Yes and I apologized to her," I explained.

"All right, how did she take that?"

"Good. I think we managed to talk things through."

"Wonderful."

"Yes, but then I proposed to her."

"Again?" He sighed.

"Yes."

"And what did she say this time?"

"She said I'm moving too fast."

Bruce chuckled. "Well, no one can accuse you of commitment issues. That's for sure."

"How do I make her say yes to me?" I asked.

"How would I know? And why are you in such a hurry anyway?" he asked.

I rubbed my forehead. "Because I love her and I want her to understand that... I want her to commit to me and stop running every time there's a bump on the road." I didn't tell him that a bloody psychic had told me to apologize, convince, and empower her.

"And you think she doesn't know that you love her?"

"She's upset that I don't like Black and she feels like I only love Cia."

"Okay… so just to clarify… she didn't say no to your proposal, she just said not right now?"

I nodded although he couldn't see it. "Something like that."

"But that's good news, right?"

"Yes. But how do I get her to understand that even though I prefer her as Cia, I still love Black too?"

"Did you tell her?"

"Yes, but I don't think she believes me."

"That's because there's a difference between understanding something on a cognitive level versus accepting it to be true in your body and your heart."

"I'm listening."

"It's like walking on hot coals. You can see that other people get away with it and the instructor tells you to trust him and that you'll be fine, but your body is conditioned to associate burning coal with pain and suffering, so it becomes a battle between your mind and your body.

"Okay."

"In this case you're like the instructor telling Cia to trust you and that she'll be fine, but she probably needs to walk on the hot coals herself and experience not getting hurt before she believes it fully.

"So what are you suggesting exactly?"

"I think she needs to experience your love, more than hear it."

"All right, but how?"

"Well, you know me, I believe in hands-on interventions. If she feels you don't love Black then the obvious way to convince her would be to make love to her as Black."

I scratched my chin. "You want me to make love to her while she's Black?"

"No, I don't want you to do anything. But if you're asking me how to make her overcome the rejection she's been feeling these past weeks, then that is my best advice. It will definitely be a powerful intervention."

I groaned. "You know, after ten weeks of missing her I would have thought that the mere idea of sex with her would be enough to make me say yes to anything…"

"So what's the problem?" Bruce asked.

"It's just that Black is my troubled niece while Cia is the woman I'm in love with."

"Aha."

"What do you mean, 'aha'?"

"I mean, that's interesting, but listen – I actually have another session I need to get to, so the question is: can you make love to Black and show her that you accept her?"

"That depends… Can I undress her and make love to her naked?" I asked.

"I would say yes, as long as she's Black when you start."

"But will she still have all the piercings and the black make-up on?"

"Yes, of course, and before you ask me if you can take her from behind so you don't see her face, the answer is no. If you want to succeed in making Cia feel completely loved by you, you'll need to make love to her and kiss her while you're having sex."

"Oh, man…" I ran my hands through my hair.

Bruce sounded calm. "Can you do that?"

"It's going to feel like bloody incest, but if that's what it takes to make her understand that I'm the right man for her, I'll do it."

"It might work, but of course I can't guarantee it."

"But how do I get her to dress as Black?"

"You don't; it will happen before you know it."

"How?"

"Sorry, G, but I really have to go now. I wish you the best of luck and cross my fingers that you and Cia will work through this."

"Okay, thanks, Bruce."

For a few minutes I sat with my head leaned back and my eyes closed. I had immense respect for Bruce but this had to be one of his most insane ideas ever.

Cia

Talking to Bruce was nice, and when I told him how I had run into Gabriel he was very interested in all the details.

"So he asked you to marry him?"

"Yes, but of course I told him it was too soon."

"Right."

"I mean, I'm still angry at him, but he wants us to pick up right where we left off."

"And you don't want to do that?"

"How can I when I still remember his look of revulsion from that night and how much it hurt?"

"I understand."

"He says that he loves me unconditionally, but it's not true – he loves Cia but the part of me that is Black is a turn-off for him. He even said that part of me made his dick shrink."

"Did he now?" Bruce said quietly. "I think you need to test that."

"Test that how?" I asked, not following him.

"I suggest that you dress as Black, and ask him to make love to you."

I gasped. "No way. He would never do that."

"Then tell him that it matters to you."

"Didn't you hear how I just told you the Goth look makes his dick shrink?"

"I heard you. It was just an idea to find out once and for all how deep his love is."

"Thanks, but he'll only reject me again and then I'll be hurt again. It won't work."

"No, it won't work unless you try it, that's for sure."

"Bruce…" I said in that tone that really meant: Scale down your craziness, will you?

Our conversation continued another twenty minutes and when I hung up, his suggestion stayed in my thoughts. I couldn't dress up as Black and go visit Gabriel, could I?

On the other hand, it would be just me and him, so even if he did reject me, at least this time there wouldn't be an audience. I would be able to leave with closure knowing that he wasn't worth crying over.

I didn't intend on dressing up as Black after that, but if he truly did love me, he would behave nicely, hug me, and accept me no matter how I looked. I didn't need him to make love to me; I would settle for a big long hug.

Violet popped her head into the living room. "Is the coast clear?"

"Yeah, come in."

"So you're done talking to the crazy doctor?"

"Yes… but I'm still mad at you for setting me up like that."

Violet sat on the armrest of the couch. "I can live with that if it helps you move on, either with or without him."

"He asked me to marry him again."

"Wow…" She whistled. "That's something."

"I know."

"Can I be your bridesmaid?" she asked. "I've never been a bridesmaid."

"I haven't said yes."

She chuckled. "Yet."

"I don't think I will."

She smiled knowingly.

"Why do you look at me like that? I won't marry him; you know?"

"You just said that you didn't *think* you'd do it and now you changed it to you *won't*... seems you're still making up your mind."

"Don't be stupid. This is Gabriel; you all agreed I should find someone who could accept me for who I am."

Violet tilted her head. "But do you know who you are?"

"I'm Cia."

"Does he love Cia?"

"Yes, but he doesn't love Black – or he says he does, but I don't think he does."

"I'm a little confused. You say you want him to love who you are – which is Cia – who you say he loves."

"Yes. But he can't just love the person I am now without accepting my past, which is Black."

"Accepting or loving?" Violet asked.

I didn't answer.

"Why do you care how he feels about Black, if you're not her anymore?"

"Because even though I don't dress as Black, she's still a big part of me."

"Ohhh, okay... I get it." Violet nodded and headed toward the kitchen. "Do you want pasta? And by the way, I need to do another cleansing of the house. I think I dragged home a small demon or something. Have you noticed how things keep moving around in here and the lights flicker?"

"You need to do that tonight?" I asked, already annoyed. I just wanted to watch a movie and chill.

"You can help me if you want or you can take my car and go somewhere. Daniel isn't home, though."

Shoot, my first thought had been to go hang out with Daniel. "Where is he?"

"He's going on a date tonight."

That's right. He had told me about it yesterday.

"Don't worry… it shouldn't take more than a couple of hours to do the ritual," Violet said, as if that would make me feel better. Suddenly going to see Gabriel sounded like a great idea.

CHAPTER 28
Loving Black

Gabriel

My phone vibrated with a text message.
"Are you home? Can I come by?"
"Who is this?" I wrote, hoping it was Cia.
"C," she replied and I smiled and saved her number in my phone.
"Mi casa es su casa," I wrote and thirty minutes later there was a knock on the door.

I wasn't surprised when I opened to find Cia dressed as Black on my doorstep. There was a big difference between this Black and the one I met the first time; the expression in her eyes was much softer and full of uncertainty... Her outfit might have been Black's but there was no doubt in my mind that this was Cia.

"Hey," I said and opened the door to let her in. "Good to see you again so soon."

Cia didn't say "Hi," she just walked inside.

"Violet was doing a cleansing, so I didn't want to stay at home."

I closed the door and followed her into the living room, where she went straight to the large window overlooking the lake.

"As far as I'm concerned, this is your home."

Cia looked back at me with dramatic black eyeliner around her eyes and purple lipstick on her mouth. "You don't mind that I'm dressed this way?"

"I told you. You can dress however you like; I'll love you no matter what." It was the truth.

"You don't feel rejected by me and all that?" she asked with some slight confusion on her face and went over to take a seat on the couch.

"That depends," I said and moved closer.

"Depends on what?"

I winked. "If you're here to reject me or love me."

Cia bit her lip and met my eyes. "I'm not here to reject you," she muttered low.

"Good…" A roar of excitement rose all the way from my toes to my head. She was probably here to talk to me and take things slow… but my whole body was screaming that this was my chance to convince her that I loved her completely. Like a chess player seeing an opening, I made my move.

"I missed you," I said and sat down on the coffee table in front of her.

"I missed you too…" she admitted.

I leaned in and kissed her softly when she whispered: "I told you to take it slow."

I smiled. "I heard you, and I intend to take it slow…" I lowered my head and gently nibbled at the lower lip she had just been biting. "I'm going to slowly make love to you until you beg me to stop, and I intend to take my time and enjoy every minute of it."

Her eyes followed my every move as I removed her shirt and bra, kissing my way from her shoulder all the way down to her wrist before pushing her gently back so I could tug her pants off. I couldn't help a small smile when I saw her bright purple panties that were a stark contrast to all the black clothing I had already peeled off her.

"You're so beautiful," I whispered.

She was as ticklish as she had been ten weeks ago, and the way she squirmed and laughed made the whole room seem brighter.

"Stop, I don't like it when you tickle me," she chuckled and pushed at my torso. I pulled back and stood up in front of her, undressing without ever breaking eye contact with her. The desire in her eyes only enhanced my already significant lust for her. Stepping out of my boxers I stroked my cock up and down, spreading the pre-cum.

"I can't wait to be inside you," I muttered and got down on my knees in front of the couch, bringing her closer to me with a firm grip around her thighs.

"Come here." I lowered my head to taste her and heard her gasp for air. She tasted as sweet as I remembered, and sniffing in her pheromones made my dick jerk with anticipation.

"I want to feel you inside me," Cia said in a breathy voice full of need.

From licking her folds and teasing her clit, I kissed and licked my way up to her jaw, biting her earlobes just enough to hurt a little. "You'll feel me inside you, again and again. I don't care how you fucking dress, I want you."

I only heard her moan in response, so I tightened my grip around her hips, digging my fingers deeper into her skin. "We're not playing around, Cia, this is fucking it. Do you understand?"

When she still didn't answer me, I cupped her face with one hand and looked into her eyes with determination. "Do you understand?"

She pushed my hand away and pulled me in for a kiss.

"Inside me... now."

There was some kind of strange tug of war going on between us. I wanted her to surrender to me and in my state of primal lust, "taking it slow" was not an option.

"You want to feel me inside you?" I said and with a smug smile I positioned myself against her entrance, letting my hard erection slide up and down, spreading moisture from the head of my flesh over her delicious pinkness. Slowly I circled her clit, offering just enough pressure to make her lean her head back and open her mouth in a deep breathy moan.

"You like that?"

"Yes."

"It could be yours every day, if you say yes."

Her eyes were glazed over and she reached for me, wrapping her legs around me.

With everything inside me trembling with excitement, I pushed against her, watching her open up for me.

"Wait," she said. "Don't forget the condom."

I didn't respond. I wanted so badly to feel her bareback, just a little. "Have there been other guys?" I asked her in an earnest tone.

She shook her head. "And you?"

"No one," I said and rejoiced in the relief on her face. "I promise I won't come inside you, but I'm going to take you like this... just a little?" I don't know why it was suddenly so important to me, except that I wanted nothing between us.

"But what if...?" she whispered with a ragged breathing, telling me that my heart wasn't the only one beating faster than fast.

I didn't give her time to think too much about it, but slid inside her, feeling her delicious snugness all around me. "God, you feel amazing." I groaned and closed my eyes for a second, taking in the rightness of being inside Cia before I started pumping at a steady pace.

Cia and I had always used condoms but this felt a thousand times better. Her warmth, her tight inner walls giving way to me, her soft skin with the fragrance that would make me recognize her in the dark. Cia was mine, and this was how it should be.

"I want this with you every day." I moaned and pushed deeper.

She moved against me, meeting my every thrust while leaning her head back with a breathy, "Ohh."

"That's right, babe, you and me forever," I groaned.

Cia opened her eyes and reached up to touch my face.

"Gabriel, I love you," she said and it made me pause and bend over her to kiss her deeply. "Why are you using my full name?"

"I love your name... I want to call you Gabriel."

"You can, on one condition... you have to move in with me," I said with a mischievous smile.

She smiled back at me and caressed my shoulders. "You are so strong." She sounded full of admiration but I knew she was trying to avoid the question.

"Hey, woman." I grinned and pulled all the way out only to thrust in hard, showing her that I wouldn't be ignored. "You heard me. Tell me you'll move in with me or I'll do it again," I threatened with a grin.

She grinned back at me and wiggled her butt. "I'm not scared of you taking me hard."

"I think you're trying to distract me, but it won't work. I want you too much."

"Even like this?" Cia asked.

I pulled all the way out again and took her in. Yes, she was wearing dramatic black makeup and those damn fake piercings, but it made no difference, I still wanted her.

"What part of me wanting you is unclear to you?" I asked and thrust balls-deep into her again.

"But I'm Black," she said sardonically, as if to test me.

I arched a brow. "And you're my brother's daughter, but I still don't care. I want you."

There was a radical change in the way she looked at me. "You sure about that?" she challenged.

"Yes, really, I want you. All of you."

She closed her eyes for a second and when she opened them again there was pure hunger and lust shining from her.

"You want me?" she asked in a low seductive voice and surprised me with her strength, when she pushed me back and guided me down on the floor.

"You want all of me?" she asked again.

I wanted to say yes, but she drowned my answer with a violent kiss and planted herself on top of me. "Look at me," she demanded.

I did.

"Tell me again that you love me... all of me," she said in a gruff voice and slid down over my hard cock.

"I love you."

"All of me."

"All of you."

The fire in her eyes was intense when she started moving. "You want to take me?"

"Yes."

"Fill me."

"Fuck, yes."

"You want to make me yours?"

"Uh-huh." She was riding me faster and harder, and it was getting impossible for me to answer her when my balls were screaming for release.

"You want me to move in with you and be your girlfriend." Her voice was breathy.

"My... wife..." I moaned with my eyes soaking her up. "I want you to be my wife."

She placed her hands on my chest, riding me with long circular movements that felt like fucking nirvana. "If I say yes..." She lowered herself and whispered into my ear. "Will you promise me something?"

"Anything!" I groaned and closed my hands in her long soft hair.

Her hands were digging into my shoulders and her eyes were radiating with intensity. "Promise to never leave me."

I didn't answer her as I was focusing so hard on not coming that I hardly heard her request. "Sugar," I groaned and tried to lift her off me. "I can't hold it any longer, I'm so close."

She used her strength to stay in place. "Promise me," she said and bit my shoulder.

"I promise," I growled and forced her off me – long spurts of cum landing on my belly.

Both Cia and I were breathing fast and shallow when our eyes met. "I warned you that I was close," I said.

"I know... I heard you."

"Then why didn't you move?"

"I couldn't, it felt too good."

I looked at the semen on my belly and chest. "I think I spurted inside you."

Cia didn't look too concerned and propped herself up on an elbow, looking at me while I got up from the floor to find some tissues.

"You really want to do this?" she asked.

I walked back and pulled her off the floor, nudging her into my bedroom while drying off my belly.

"What?" I asked distractedly and stopped in front of the bed.

"Be a couple, move into together... don't you think we need to know each other better?" she asked and lay down on the bed.

I dropped the tissues in the trash and crawled up to spoon her.

"I already told you. Being at war changes your perspective. I know that what we have is special... I don't need to wait four years to be sure. This is the real thing, Cia... why can't you see that?"

"Maybe because I have nothing to compare it to," she pointed out. "And I'm scared."

"Of what?"

"Of you changing your mind."

I kissed her cheek. "You've got to take a chance on me, just like I've got to take a chance on you. There are no guarantees."

Cia turned her head. "Gabriel..."

"Yes."

"As your friend, I think I should warn you not to marry someone as messed-up as me. You can get someone much better than me, you know." Her eyes were wide, moist, and sincere.

I pushed a strand of hair away from her face and looked deeply into her green eyes. "I appreciate your warning, my friend, but may I offer you a bit of advice too?"

"What?"

"Don't push back against me like that unless you're ready for round two."

"But we just..." she said when I kissed her and stole her words.

"Ohh... but we have ten weeks to make up for and I told you I would make love to you all night, didn't I?"

She giggled in response.

"Were you serious?"

"I'm always serious when it comes to you," I said.

We made love three more times that night, each time bonding us closer; and when we finally drifted off, I slept like a rock with Cia in my arms.

Cia

The room was stuffy when I woke up. No doubt it was a warm day, because the sun was already making the room unbearable hot.

"Gabriel," I whispered and patted his arm, trying to get out of his tight grip.

He pulled me closer in his sleep and it made me laugh. "Hey... wake up. I have to use the bathroom."

He was cute in the morning with his puffy eyes and all his stretching and yawning, which gave me enough time to hurry out of the bed to open a window and welcome the breeze into the room. "Come back to bed," Gabriel murmured with his eyes hooded.

"I will," I said and moved around the room to find my clothes.

"Don't get dressed... I'm not done with you," he muttered into his pillow.

I shook my head with a smile and headed to use the bathroom.

When I got out, Gabriel was sitting up and looking out the window.

"Hey," he said when he saw me and then he laughed.

"Don't laugh," I said, knowing exactly why he was amused. "It's your fault I'm walking like a freaking cowboy; I'm so sore all over."

"I'm sorry," he said but the grin on his face said otherwise. "But I can't deny it makes me happy to see my woman thoroughly fucked and pleased."

I blushed a little as I sat down on the bed. Last night had been incredible and worth the soreness a thousand times over, but now my head was close to exploding with the big question on my mind.

"What is it, sweetie?" he asked with a concerned expression. "What's wrong?"

"Were you really serious, Gabriel?"

"About what?" he asked and started playing with my fingers.

"You want me to move in with you?"

"Uh-huh."

"Like for real?"

"Yes," he confirmed.

"Okay, I'll do it."

He lifted his head and looked at me with slightly raised eyebrows. "You will?"

"Yes. If you don't mind living with a partly crazy person, then I'll move in with you," I said.

He chuckled and kissed me with satisfaction. "At least you're not as crazy as your friend Violet," he teased. "I can't see her ever getting a man."

"Really? I thought you looked quite taken with her the first time you met her," I said with a poorly disguised pout.

"No, I'm not saying she isn't attractive… there's definitely something about Violet that is intriguing… until she opens her mouth and starts talking about crazy psychic stuff," he argued.

"Again with the judging, Gabriel," I objected, feeling a bit like a hypocrite, because although I'd never verbalized it, I had definitely thought the same things. "Violet is the kindest person I know. I truly hope there is someone out there who will love her uniqueness."

He planted a kiss on my nose. "Like I love yours?" he said and I rewarded him with a sly smile.

"That remains to be seen."

"Could we marry before we move to Missouri?" Gabriel asked.

"I thought we were just talking about moving in together," I said and pulled back a little.

He shrugged. "Whatever you want."

I had the feeling he was playing me like an instrument. Pushing me a little and then pulling back. With every push I grew bolder.

We spent the day together and went to Violet's house to pick up my things that afternoon.

"Did you get rid of the demon?" I asked her.

"Demon?" She looked puzzled.

"Yeah, the cleansing you were doing here yesterday.," I reminded her and it made her tilt her head and smile at me.

"There was no demon; I just wanted to give you a reason to go to Gabriel's house."

I gaped at her. "Why?"

"Because you needed one."

"So what did you do last night?"

"I watched a movie and did my nails," she said with a shrug.

I couldn't be angry with her. When Gabriel came and told me he'd packed all my things in his car, she leaned in to hug me. "You sneaky little witch," I muttered with a smile.

"You honor me," she grinned. "I'll see you soon, my friend."

Gabriel and I brought take-out food back to his apartment, wanting nothing else than to be alone in our love bubble.

"Why do you want to marry me?" I asked when we lay in another post-sex daze.

"Because I love you and I feel at ease when I'm with you. Maybe it'll also prevent you from running away the next time we get into a fight. I want you to commit to me and acknowledge that it's you and me from now on."

"You and me," I repeated.

"That's right, babe."

"What do you think your mom will say?" I asked.

He looked at me. "I think she'll be all over our wedding."

I turned my head and gave him a quizzical glance. "Can't we just elope?"

"We could," he said slowly. "But my mother would never forgive me. Look, it doesn't have to be anything big, just a small ceremony for friends and family in my parents' garden. If we give my mom that, she'll be eternally grateful."

"Okay... sounds reasonable. But nothing fancy, all right?"

"Who are you going to invite?" he asked me.

"Just three of my friends."

"Violet and Daniel," he guessed.

I nodded. "Yeah, and Darren... he's actually a really cool guy."

"All right. Would it be strange if I want to invite Bruce too?" Gabriel asked.

I smiled at him and shook my head. "I would like that."

Gabriel broke into a huge smile. "Did you just agree to marry me?"

I blinked and returned his intense stare. "Maybe."

"No." He sat up, suddenly serious. "There's no maybe. I know you're young but either we do it or we don't."

I swallowed hard. "Okay."

"So are we really doing this?" he asked me with excitement, "Getting married, I mean?"

I couldn't say anything, but I nodded. Gabriel had walked into the pitch-blackness that had been my life and pulled me into the light. If he needed a ring on my finger to feel secure in our relationship, then I would happily give it to him, although with no positive role models to look to, marriage in itself meant little to me.

CHAPTER 29
Family

Gabriel

"It'll be fine. They are all excited to meet you again," I assured her, feeling nervous deep to my core.

"Is Brent going to be there?" Cia asked.

"I don't know for sure."

As I drove up to the large house, I once again parked on the street, just in case.

"You look beautiful," I told Cia and took her hand. Her long blond hair was flaring in the light breeze and her black dress fit her perfectly, making her look both feminine and elegant.

She gave me a smile that didn't reach her eyes; clearly she was as nervous as I was.

The doorbell was loud, and when my mother opened the door ten seconds later she spread her arms to welcome us.

"Cia and Gabriel, come in... come in."

I kept Cia's hand in mine and stepped into the house I had grown up in, and once again we walked into the living room to find most of the family already gathered.

"Hey," I said and took the glass of champagne Steve handed to me.

"Do you drink champagne?" he asked Cia in a friendly fashion.

"Uhm... yes."

"Good – this is an excellent champagne that won several awards at the world championship in 2013," Steve explained. "I find that I prefer champagne produced with chardonnay grapes. How about you?"

Cia took a sip. "I always preferred apple cider because it's sweeter and much cheaper."

Steve wrinkled his forehead. "Cider, you say?"

"Yes... the one from Martinell's is really good and it kinda looks like a champagne bottle... you know?"

I suppressed a chuckle. No one but Cia could humble Steve.

"I'll remember that," he said with a lurking smile before my mom came to move us along.

"Come say hi to Granny. She just had a cold, but she's feeling much better now."

My grandparents were sitting in a small couch and I was a little shocked to see how poorly my grandmother looked. According to my mom, Granny's dementia and hearing were only getting worse. "You remember Cia, right?" my mother asked them both, and Charlie reached out his hand. "Ah yes, I remember you. Welcome back," he said politely and shook hands with Cia.

Cia reached her hand to Granny, who looked at her with squinting eyes. "I've seen you before," she told Cia almost accusingly.

"Yes, I was here for a brunch some months ago."

But Granny ignored her comment and pointed her finger in Cia's face. "You are that woman who stole my stamps."

"Your stamps?"

"Yes." She turned to Charlie. "Remember when I couldn't find my stamps and I knew the maid had taken them?"

"I'm not a maid," Cia said quickly. "And I didn't take your stamps."

"You didn't?" Granny asked suspiciously.

"No, I didn't."

Granny looked at me. "Gabriel."

"Yes, Granny."

"Since when are you dating the maid?"

"I'm not dating the maid. Cia is an artist."

"An artist?"

"Yes, she paints portraits."

"I could paint yours if you want," Cia offered but Granny waved her hands dismissively.

"Why would I want a portrait of me. It's offensive enough that I have to see my reflection when I wash my face." Again she turned to Charlie. "Remember how pretty I was when I was younger?"

"I do... you were the prettiest girl I ever saw."

"Aww... Daddy, that's so sweet," my mom said beside me.

"It's true..." Granny said. "There was no one prettier than me, and look at me now. I look like an old hag."

Charlie chuckled.

"What's so funny?" Granny asked in a grumpy tone. "You're even older and uglier than me and I have to look at you all the time."

It was hard not to laugh, and luckily Charlie had a good sense of humor.

"We are just a pair of old goats," he said and took her hand.

"What did you say?" Granny held a hand to her ear.

"Nothing," my mom interjected. "Mom. Come on, let's get you some more champagne."

When we moved away, my mom turned to us. "I'm afraid Brent, Janet, and the kids won't come today. I invited them all, of course, but when Brent heard that you two were coming, he declined."

Cia actually looked relieved, but I felt anger in the pit of my stomach. The man was a moron for rejecting Cia, especially now that we, his family, all knew about her anyway.

"His loss," my mom said with a sad smile to Cia. "I thought we could have a barbeque in the garden." She swung her hands toward the French doors.

"I love burgers and hot dogs," Cia whispered to me.

"Don't count on getting any," I whispered back. "It's not that kind of barbeque."

As I had predicted, my mother's idea of a barbeque meant French cuisine prepared on a grill.

We had delicious fish with asparagus and white sauce as an appetizer, followed by a tender chicken marinated in French herbs, with small potatoes and vegetables on small spears, accompanied by a delicious red wine sauce.

The desert was crème brûlée, Steve's favorite.

All the while through eating the three courses, everyone asked Cia questions about her past, her art, and her plans for the future.

"I'm going with Gabriel to Missouri."

"Oh, that's nice," my sister Melody said. "I'll come and visit you."

I smiled at her. "You're all welcome to visit us and actually, Mom and Steve, we have a favor to ask before we move."

Steve sat up straighter. "What do you need, son?"

"I've asked Cia to marry me, and we thought we could have a small ceremony and reception here in your garden."

There was absolute silence around the table for seconds before my mom clasped her hands together. "But of course."

Steve looked a bit shaken, but he managed to congratulate us both and raise his glass. "Let's all raise our glasses to Gabriel and Cia and their bright future," he said in a formal voice.

"What are we drinking to?" Granny asked.

"Cia and Gabriel are getting married," Melody told her.

Granny raised her glass. "But weren't you already with Brent's daughter or did I misunderstand that?"

"Cia *is* Brent's daughter," my mom explained patiently.

Granny downed her glass of champagne. "Everyone knows you shouldn't marry family... but you're all celebrating." She shook her head.

"We're not blood related, Granny," I told her again.

"That's good, my child. That's good," she said but I could tell she had given up and wasn't paying attention.

"When is the date?" Steve asked.

"We are flexible as long as it's before we move."

Melody and Brittany leaned closer and starting firing questions at Cia and me. Had we thought about what food we wanted, what colors, what kind of ceremony, how many people to invite? The wedding was getting them really excited.

"I would have preferred to just get married at the city hall with a hot dog and a walk along the pier afterwards," Cia said and received looks of horror from my mom and my sisters.

Steve chuckled. "And to think I accused you of being a gold digger."

There was a look between Steve and Cia, and if she had known him better she would have realized that he respected her.

"But if you don't have any fixed ideas, we'll be more than happy to help organize it all," Melody offered. "I doubt I'll ever get to plan my own wedding, so I would be more than honored to help plan yours.

Cia smiled. "Would you? That's so nice of you."

Melody lit up in a beaming smile, while Steve signaled for me to come with him. As we walked away from the table I could hear the women talk about where to buy a wedding dress and what flowers to get... Cia might not want a dream wedding, but she wanted family, and right now she was the center of attention with a bright smile on her face.

"This comes as a surprise," Steve said.

"Yeah... but it feels right to me."

"She's only twenty-one," he said with a raised brow.

"So?"

"That's young."

"I know, but Cia isn't like others, she's older than her age."

Steve nodded slowly. "She is. Normally I would argue that you needed her to sign a prenuptial agreement, but in this case I won't. Soon, she'll have more money than you."

I frowned. "Who, Cia? No, she's doesn't have much."

"I think I should tell you that I transferred Brent's inherence to his children. Including Cia."

"What do you mean?"

"Well, each year I pay a significant amount to all my children. From now on, Brent's portion will be split among his children.

"You never paid me anything," I said, confused.

"Because you're not my biological son. I believe your mom has been generous toward you, though."

"Yes." My mom had always helped me out, even when I told her I could take care of myself.

"Brent's million will be split in four, meaning that each year Cia will get a quarter of a million."

I gaped. "You gave Brent a million dollars a year?"

"Yes, it's better that way. What is it worth leaving millions behind when I die? I'd rather spread my riches while I'm alive."

"But a million?" And to think I had felt bad about my mom filling my fridge or buying me my first car. A freaking million a year... for how many years?

"We'll need to get the paperwork done of course, but my lawyers will set it up. I trust you can help Cia feel good about the whole thing."

"What do you mean?" I asked.

"She might not want to accept the money."

I looked over to see her and it made me smile. She looked so happy sitting at the table and talking about our wedding.

"And of course, your mom and I will be happy to sponsor the wedding."

"Thank you... really, we just want a small ceremony."

Steve chuckled. "I'll remind your mother when she goes overboard... but you are her only son, so I can't make any guarantees."

Cia

If I thought being homeless and penniless was stressful it was only because I'd never tried pulling off a wedding in two weeks.

Never did I imagine how much was involved. The benefit of it all was that I got to spend a lot of time with my family. Melody, Brittany, and Katie were taking me under their wing and pampering me. I know that from their perspective the wedding was tiny in scale, but to me it was grand.

There were times when I had to put my foot down and say no. Like the time Katie insisted I should spend the night before the wedding at their house because it was bad luck to see the groom before the wedding.

First of all, I'm not superstitious.

Second of all I would have seen him if we had just gone to the city hall like I originally suggested.

Third... well, I don't think I need more reasons to decide where I sleep.

Gabriel said I could do as I pleased. He would never refuse me access to his bed, and a night with me was always welcome in his world.

Still, in the end Violet asked to have a girl's night, and I figured it wasn't such a bad idea to stay at her house the night before the wedding. Violet is a good cook; she made her homemade lasagna and freshly baked bread that is to die for. When she offered a tarot reading I politely declined, and instead we ended up talking all night about life.

Violet is funny that way. She believes in all sorts of different things that will make you see ordinary things in a new perspective. Some of it is far out, like part of the human race descending from other planets, but other things sound pretty believable, and now she even has me wondering if the human race is older than archeologists claim.

Either way, talking with Violet is different than talking with anyone else, and she challenges my view of the world and myself. She got quiet when I tried to find out more about her past, and like she so often does when she wants to avoid a subject, she distracted me with a pop quiz on songs from our past.

I never did have many friends to begin with and Violet was my first and only girlfriend, which meant that my night at Violet's house was the closest thing I'd get to a bachelorette party. Gabriel had been out last weekend with a whole bunch of his pals, but this was fine with me because a loyal and fearless friend like Violet counts for ten normal friends, in my opinion.

The next day Violet took me to Steve and Katie's place, where I was met by a stylist who did my hair, nails, and makeup. Christ, I never knew how many hours go into a makeover like that.

My dress was simple but gorgeous and I had picked it out myself. Of course Katie had suggested making a rush order with a well-known designer who could custom-make a dress just for me, but I had preferred to walk into a normal bridal store with a large selection and make my choice.

It might not be the right brand or the right style for this season... or whatever... but I couldn't care less. I felt beautiful in this dress; it was beyond my wildest dreams to get married in a dress like this, with a guy like Gabriel, in a beautiful garden overlooking the lake.

"You look so pretty," Violet said and took a look at me as I stood in front of the mirror in a room on the second floor.

I smiled at her. "So do you, and you get to be a bridesmaid."

She beamed and was just about to speak when there was a knock on the door.

"Come in," I called out and was surprised to see Mia pop her head in. Her cheeks were red and she was slightly out of breath.

"Mia," I said with surprise. "What are you doing here?"

She stepped into the room and closed the door.

"My dad says we're not going to your wedding, but you're my sister."

"Half-sister," I corrected.

She nodded with an earnest expression. "I know he's been a jerk to you, even my mom says so, and he's a jerk to me sometimes too. I don't know why."

"Did you come here alone?" I asked.

Mia looked from me to Violet and back again. "I snuck out and took my bike to get here. It's only three miles, but the hill is pretty steep so I had to walk my bike up, or I would have been here sooner."

I smiled at her, impressed with her courage. "I'm glad you decided to come."

She shifted her balance and pulled off her backpack. "I packed the prettiest dress I have," she said and opened the back to pull out a pale pink dress.

"It's lovely," Violet said and tilted her head, "But you know you'll be grounded for sneaking off, right?"

Mia bit her lip. "Yeah, I know… but it doesn't matter, I want to be here. Besides I spend most of my time with my nose in a book anyway, and being grounded gives me plenty of time for that. It's really not half as bad as it sounds."

"Would you like to be my bridesmaid?" I asked her, and the girl lit up like a firework.

"I was hoping you would ask me that."

"Of course. I would be honored."

"Just give me a second to get dressed." Mia was working fast to get out of her jeans and into the dress. I smiled when I saw her stick her tongue out in concentration, because I do the same thing.

"Oh, no…" she froze and gave me a horrified expression. "I forgot to pack my ballerinas. I only have these shoes." We all looked down at her turquoise Converse shoes that had stains on them.

"They are perfect," I said and gave her a hug. "You are perfect, Mia…"

"You think so?" she said and tried to brush the wrinkles out of her dress.

Another knock on the door was followed by Katie's voice. "It's time, Cia, are you ready?"

I stepped to the window and looked out to see the setup on the lawn. The white rows of chairs were all filled with guests, and the red carpet led up to where the priest and Gabriel stood in front of the white wedding gazebo. My god, he looked amazing in his formal uniform with his medal on his chest.

"Are you ready?" Violet said and gave a nervous smile.

"Why are *you* nervous?" I asked her and started walking out of the room.

"I'm picking up on your emotions – I can't help it," she said and followed right behind me with Mia.

"So if I calm myself down, I'll calm you down?" I asked.

"Yes, but don't worry about me. Today is all about you."

Steve stood by the end of the stairs and looked at me with awe. "You blow me away," he said and offered his arm to me. A week ago he had asked me if he could lead me down the aisle and I told him yes with a large knot in my throat. Steve was, after all, my grandfather – and the fact that I hadn't seen Brent, my father, since the big clash at the brunch three months ago was actually a relief. Gabriel had always spoken about Steve as a bully and maybe he was... he did, however, treat me with care and courtesy and looked proud when he led me out into the garden.

"If I get nervous, promise to hold on to me and don't let me run away," I joked. "I really want to marry Gabriel."

He tightened his hold on my arm. "And you will, my girl," he promised with a gleam in his eyes.

As the music started playing Violet took Mia's hand and with a last smile of reassurance they went down the aisle together to take their positions.

Steve inclined his head to me and then we started walking. I heard murmurs and people taking pictures but my eyes were fixed on Gabriel, who stood tall and straight, glancing right back at me. When I got closer I saw that his eyes were moist and that his lips were slightly quivering. It made me squeeze my bridal bouquet harder, trying not to cry myself.

Steve had a satisfied smile on his lips when he handed me over to Gabriel, who leaned in to hug me.

"God, I can't even describe in words how radiant you look or how much I love you," he whispered before releasing me from the hug. Meeting his large brown eyes, with that almond shape that I love so much, I saw promises of devotion and loyalty mirroring the emotions in my heart. I blinked, hoping that my mascara would be as waterproof as the stylist had promised.

I have no clue what the priest spoke about. I couldn't focus on his words because all I could see was the man in front of me, so insanely out of my league and yet here to commit to me for the rest of his life.

We exchanged rings, we said *I do* at the right time, and then the priest announced us man and wife... Mr. and Mrs. Thomas.

"You may kiss your bride," the priest said with a smile, and Gabriel didn't hesitate but pulled me into a deep kiss that had everyone in the wedding party breaking out in joyous cheers.

"My wife." He beamed down at me and stroked my cheek. "It's official."

"I know," I said and leaned up to kiss him again. "You're mine now. Every part of your deliciously tattooed body belongs to me."

Humor sparkled in his eyes. "You better believe it, because your sweet ass belongs to me too."

The reception was centered on the large terrace; Katie had outdone herself with beautiful food and expensive wine for everyone.

I found Daniel and Violet standing by a high table enjoying themselves. Daniel squinted his eyes because of the sun and smiled. "It's hard to get used to seeing you like this... but I have to say that you look real pretty in white."

"She looks gorgeous," Gabriel said from behind.

I introduced him to Daniel, who'd never really had a proper chance to meet Gabriel. Violet, of course, he knew, and they smiled at each other.

"I see my advice worked," she said.

"Yup, the best-spent three hundred dollars of my life," Gabriel said and winked at me.

"What did you pay Violet three hundred dollars for?" I asked.

"To give me advice on how to win you back."

I grinned. "So you actually believe in her abilities."

"Not as a psychic... just as a friend who knows you well." He turned to Violet. "No offense."

She shrugged with a soft smile. "None taken."

I spotted Darren and waved him over. To my delight he was with Bruce, which made sense since Bruce was the one who originally introduced me to Darren.

"Come here, my little angel," Darren said and kissed me on my cheeks. "Such a beautiful wedding."

Bruce nodded and shook our hands. "Very beautiful indeed."

I had never seen Bruce outside of camp and he looked so small next to Darren – who had dressed extra formal for the occasion, which in Darren's case meant that he was wearing tight yellow pants, brown leather shoes, a green vest, and a blue topcoat in velvet with a yellow bowtie. Funny enough, he did look elegant, in a sort of stylish-nobleman-from-eighteen-hundred-and-something way.

I knew Gabriel would comment on Darren's attire when we were alone, but to his credit he kept his judgmental comments in check and stayed polite.

Daniel on the other hand shook Darren's hand and made a low chuckle. "Where's the hat?"

"What hat?" Darren asked.

"Aren't you trying to look like the mad hatter from Alice in Wonderland?" Daniel snickered.

Darren looked down at himself and pulled at his vest. "It took me a long time to put this splendid outfit together and I really feel I nailed it, wouldn't you agree?"

Violet and I agreed enthusiastically. "You look very good," I said and meant it.

Violet leaned closer. "And you know, Darren, with an outfit like that you never have to worry about that awkward moment when you realize someone else is wearing the exact same thing."

Bruce gave a discreet laugh and covered his mouth. "That's a good point," Darren said and squared his shoulders. "I was a little afraid of outshining the star of the show, but your dress is to die for." He ran his eyes down my dress. "I mean, a little more fluff and a few more details in the back would have made it even more astonishing, but you carry the dullness so beautifully," he said with that rude humor of his.

"Thank you, Darren." I gave him a large smile. "You're too kind."

"I was just admiring your gifts," Bruce commented and pointed to the house. "Who bought the paintings for you?"

"What paintings?" I asked and looked up.

"Your paintings," Bruce said, puzzled. "Didn't you see the gift table yet?"

I felt my heart miss a beat and pulled up the skirts of my dress. "Excuse me," I said and headed for the house. Both Bruce and Gabriel followed and stood right behind me when I faced a large table in the living room where the presents were placed in all shapes and sizes. But right there against the table stood all five of the paintings that I had made in the camp – the ones I had sold at my first art show at Darren's gallery.

My hand flew to my mouth as I saw my own mental journey portrayed in the paintings. There was the depressive girl sitting in the black and yellow jumpsuit with her dark hair covering her face and her arm protectively shielding her from the swarm of bees about to attack from above.

"Who are they from?" Gabriel asked out loud and started looking for a card.

I squatted down in front of the painting of me lying in water with Gabriel's hands holding me up and covering my private parts. It symbolized the way he had carefully bathed me and carried me around.

"I don't see a card," Gabriel said, while still looking around for it.

I moved on and gently touched the painting of me in a tutu skirt balancing a cotton candy and remembered how awful I had felt about wearing that damn pink outfit and how Gabriel had made it bearable by joking with me and calling me Candy and Sugar. He still did.

"This is the best gift ever," I said in a brittle voice and turned my head to the painting of me shedding the blackness to reveal my Superwoman suit underneath.

"I know..." Gabriel looked at me. "I wanted to buy the blue painting at the gallery, but it had already been sold when I got there."

"Darren said it was a collector," I remembered. "I can't believe they're all here." These were the most personal paintings I had ever created, and it had pained me to sell them.

I looked up at Bruce. "Was it you?"

He chuckled. "I wish it was me, but I don't have that kind of money. I'm afraid I only brought you a vase." He pointed to a square gift to the left.

I got up and took a step toward Bruce. "You've given us something much more precious than anything on this table. If not for you and your interventions I don't think we would be celebrating our wedding today."

Bruce swallowed before he looked away and took off his glasses, polishing them on his sleeve. "Yes, I'm glad to see that last intervention helped you," he said softly. "I'm glad you decided to dress up as Black one last time."

Gabriel smiled. "Yeah, it worked. When you first suggested it I thought I wouldn't be able to do it, but it turned out that once I looked into Cia's eyes, her hair and make-up made no difference."

I looked from Gabriel to Bruce and back again. "Wait a minute... what are you not telling me?"

Gabriel took my hand. "It's just that I called Bruce for some advice on how to convince you of my love and he suggested making love to you as Black."

I returned my glance to Bruce. "You're like a damn puppet master, aren't you?" I wasn't mad at him; after all, his intentions had been good and the results were in our best interest.

"I still don't think your methods are legal," I said and elbowed him.

He responded with a secretive smile.

"Oh, there you are," Katie called out from the French doors... "It's time for the groom's speech. Come join us out here."

Gabriel took my hand and we went out to our guests. With a glass of champagne in hand, he began his speech to me.

"Dear Cia, some people may think that we are rushing into this marriage. They couldn't be more wrong.

"I spend almost thirty years getting ready to recognize you when I found you. At first I didn't see clearly that you were the one I was destined to share my life with, and I blame the fact that you were in disguise and hiding behind a veil of blackness, but once I got a peek behind your cover I fell fast and hard, knowing in my heart that it's an extraordinary thing to find a person you can be completely at ease with. To me, you are that person.

"Some are maybe wondering how we can ignore the fact that you're my stepbrother's daughter, and you and I both know: it took us some time too."

He smiled. "I can't tell you how relieved I am that you agreed to marry me, because I can honestly say that there is no one I would rather live my life with. I love you, Mrs. Thomas, and I'm proud to call you my wife."

Tears broke out from my eyes at the same time as applause broke out from the small crowd standing in front of us.

"Do you have anything you want to add?" Gabriel asked.

I was drying tears away and shook my hand. "Just that I love you," I managed to say.

"What did she say?" Granny said loudly from her seat next to the wedding cake.

"She said she loved him," Charlie told her in a loud voice.

Granny threw her hands up in the air. "Of course she loves him. Why else would she marry him? Ask them when they are cutting the cake," she said in that loud clear voice that cut through the crowd and made everyone smile and burst into laughter.

"We'll cut the cake now, Granny," Gabriel assured her. "And you can have the biggest piece."

"Good, because this will probably be my last wedding cake ever."

"Don't say that, Mom," Katie shushed her.

"Why not... I'm adult, and you know what that means."

"Yes, Mom, you tell me often enough."

"That's right, because I always say that the best part about being an adult is that you don't have to ask anyone's permission." Granny looked around at all the people standing with their best clothes and champagne flutes.

"Except for that guy over there." Granny pointed her walking stick to Darren, who stood in the middle.

"He clearly needs help with dressing. He looks like a clown and he's fat too."

Chuckles broke out all around, and Katie shot Darren an apologetic look. "I'm so sorry, I think you look very stylish."

Darren didn't even flinch. He walked closer to Granny with an amused expression on his face.

"You really think I look fat?" he said and she squinted her eyes at him.

"I actually just lost five pounds," he said and brushed off some invisible crumbs from his sleeve. "In case you're wondering how, it was simply because I got circumcised."

"Impossible," she exclaimed.

"Not at all, do you wanna see?"

Granny widened her eyes when Darren pretended to unzip his pants. A lot of people were laughing and some just held their breath.

"Does he want me to see his penis?" Granny asked Charlie, who nodded.

"Yes, he said he lost five pounds of skin when he got circumcised."

"I heard that." Granny looked up at Darren, who stood in front of her with a calm expression on his face. "Five pounds?" she repeated in awe and then her eyes lowered to his crotch as if she was ready to see the wonder.

"He's joking," my mom said and tried to get between Granny and Darren.

Granny pushed her away. "I haven't seen a penis in twenty years... if he's showing I want to see."

A roar of laughter broke out all around.

"I would show you," Darren said with a smile and backed away, "but I never brag at weddings."

"All right then!" Gabriel clapped his hands. "Who wants a piece of cake?"

We did the mandatory thing about feeding each other cake before everyone else got a piece. The cake was a gift from Melody and tasted deliciously of vanilla and strawberry."

"Uhhm, this is sooo good," I told her and she lit up.

"I'm so glad you like it. It's all vegan."

"It's super delicious." Gabriel gave her a thumbs-up. "By the way, are you the one who bought us Cia's paintings?

She shook her head. "No, I gave you a gift card to my store."

"Thank you so much – I love your store."

Gabriel and I had been by last week; it was a really cool place with high-quality, organic food and a great atmosphere.

"Mom got you at least one of the paintings," Melody said. "I'm sure of it because I saw her hand her credit card to your friend that night at the gallery."

Gabriel and I both looked at Katie, who was still calming Granny down and trying to convince her that Darren had been joking and that no man had five pounds of foreskin.

"Mom," Gabriel and I made our way to her. "Are the paintings from you and Steve?" he asked.

She lit up in a smile. "Just from me. Steve has another gift for you." She looked up. "Steve, come here for a minute. Why don't you tell them about your gift?"

Steve came over and looked almost mild when he patted Gabriel's shoulder. "No wedding without a honeymoon, this is for you."

He pulled out an envelope that Gabriel opened. "Wow... jeez," Gabriel stood baffled for a few seconds. "I don't know what to say, Steve, that will make for a lot of honeymoons."

I resolutely gave both Katie and Steve a big hug. "Those are the best gifts you could have given us. I can't thank you enough."

Steve actually kissed me on my forehead and Katie gave me such a genuine warm smile that it wasn't hard to see why Gabriel had turned out to be such an amazing person himself.

"I thought you might like the paintings," Katie said. "My idea was to give you one painting for each of your birthdays but with the marriage I figured it was better to give them to you as a complete set."

Gabriel and I both hugged her again.

"Don't I get a hug?" Granny said grumpily. "I bought you a present too, you know."

Gabriel leaned down to hug her and I followed him. She smelled of old lady, a bit sweaty and with a too-sweet perfume.

"What did you give us, Granny?" Gabriel asked her.

She looked up at Charlie. "What did we get them?"

"A rocking chair," Charlie said.

"Why would you buy them a rocking chair?" she complained.

"Because you told me to. Remember you said it will be good for Cia when she nurses the little ones."

"What little ones?" Granny looked down at my belly. "Are you with child already?"

"No, I don't think so."

"A rocking chair," she snorted at Charlie. "What a stupid gift."

"I love rocking chairs," I hurried to say and saw Charlie light up a bit. "That's a very thoughtful gift. Thank you!"

Granny held a hand to her hearing aid. "What did she say?"

Charlie leaned in and talked loudly into Granny's ear. "Cia said thank you. She loves rocking chairs."

Granny nodded. "Of course she does. That's why I told you to get her one. I know about things like this."

We moved on and I looked at Gabriel when we were out of earshot. "You know I love you, right?"

"Yeah."

"But if you grow to be as mean to me as Granny is to Charlie, you better prepare to suffer."

"Ditto," he said and winked at me. "I'll put itching powder in your bed if you ever talk that way to me."

"I'll put Super Glue on your dentures so you can't get them out." I retorted.

"I'll put laxative in your tea and laugh when you run like this to the bathroom." Gabriel imitated an old person hurrying in slow motion with a bellyache.

"It would be more like this." I did the same imitation but this time making farting sounds, and we laughed hard.

Gabriel was still laughing when he pulled me into his arms. "I hope we'll laugh together for the rest of our lives, and I want you to know that I intend to love you and cherish every minute with you."

I closed my eyes when he kissed me, knowing in my heart that I was the luckiest woman in the world.

This concludes Clashing Colors #1 - BLACK

Thank you so much for reading Cia's and Gabriel's story.
If you liked it, please, please, please take a second to leave a review on Amazon. Your word has power and helps other readers take a chance on this book, which makes it possible for me to write books full time for your entertainment.

Want more?
In the next book we'll follow Violet, whom you've come to know as Cia's friend in this book.

Clashing Colors #1 BLACK

Aren't opposites supposed to attract?

Ever since I fell in love with Jake as a teen, I've thought of him and me as opposites that would one day complement each other.
Unfortunately, adulthood has only increased our differences and to Jake, and people around us, we're more like clashing colors that should avoid mixing.

Jake is a scientist who only believes in things that can be proven with hard data while I'm a psychic medium who works with spirits and tarot cards.
I know he thinks people like me are frauds, but I've been given a chance to prove him wrong. The lab where Jake works is dealing with paranormal phenomena and his boss has hired me to investigate it.
If I can produce evidence strong enough for the biggest skeptic to take me seriously, maybe Jake will finally see me as more than his best friend's younger sister.

Violet is the second book in Elin Peer's contemporary romance series Clashing Colors. Science and faith face off in this story full of lovable and witty characters, displaying a firework of humor, sizzling romance, and the supernatural.

If you like stories that offer much more than just a romance, and you don't mind a paranormal twist, then Violet will have you laughing out loud and reflecting on your own spiritual beliefs.

Order this wonderful book on Amazon today!

Have you read all of my books yet?

Clashing Colors:
These five contemporary romance stories dive into the theme of opposites attract.
From romantic comedy to dramatic scenes offering food for thought; these books will make you both laugh and cry.

The Slave Series:
Five intense "enemy to lovers" books portraying strong women who won't be defined as victims.
Expect some dark scenes and steamy sex.

Men of the North:
One prequel and ten romantic sci-fi stories that take place 400 years in the future where women rule the world.
These stories are unlike anything you've ever read and have made several bestselling lists on Amazon.
It's a tug of war between the crude alpha men on one side of the border and the altruistic women on the other side.
Can they find a way to integrate?

Cultivated
Set in the USA and the gorgeous Ireland, these six contemporary romance books take on the question of mind control.
They're suspenseful, fast-paced, and full of humor.
As always, they carry Elin's unique style of writing, which readers refer to as 'self-help that reads like fiction.

For a full overview of my books and to be alerted for new book releases, discounts, and give-aways, please sign up to my list at
www.elinpeer.com

About the Author

With a background in life coaching, Elin is easy to talk to and her fans rave about her unique writing style that has subtle elements of coaching mixed into fictional love stories with happy endings.

Elin is curious by nature. She likes to explore and can tell you about riding elephants through the Asian jungle, watching the sunset in the Sahara Desert from the back of a camel, sailing down the Nile in Egypt, kayaking in Alaska, river rafting in Indonesia, and flying over Greenland in a helicopter.

After traveling the world and living in different countries, Elin is currently residing outside Seattle in the US with her husband, daughters, and her black Labrador, Lucky, who follows her everywhere.

Want to connect with Elin? Great – she loves to hear from her readers.

Find her on Facebook: facebook.com/AuthorElinPeer
Or look her up on Goodreads, Amazon, Bookbub or simply go to elinpeer.com

CPSIA information can be obtained
at www.ICGtesting.com
Printed in the USA
LVHW050720050520
654997LV00015B/3307